Stars Maintain T

By

M G da Mota

Copyright

STARS MAINTAIN THEIR GLOW
First published in Great Britain
by Flowing Prose / M G da Mota, 2023

All rights reserved. You may not copy, store, distribute, transmit, reproduce or otherwise make available this publication (or any part of it) in any form, or by any means (electronic, digital, optical, mechanical, photocopying, recording or otherwise), without the prior written permission of the author. Any person who does any unauthorised act in relation to this publication may be liable to criminal prosecution and civil claims for damages.

The right of M G da Mota to be identified as author of this work has been asserted by her in accordance with sections 77 and 78, Designs and Patents Act, 1988.

Copyright © M G da Mota 2023

Cover Image of the Milky Way © Malcolm Bull
(https://www.flickr.com/photos/malcolmbull)

Cover Design by Sandra Lopez of Xciting Designs:
www.xcitingdesigns.com

A CIP catalogue record for this book is available from the British Library.

M G da Mota's Website: https://www.flowingprose.com

ISBN: 9798393991258

COPYRIGHT

DEDICATION

VALERIA'S JOURNAL, 2022 – THE BEGINNING

PART 1 – GERALD

CHAPTER 1 – LISBON
CHAPTER 2 – ESPIRITO SANTO'S HOME
CHAPTER 3 – THE DUKE'S DAUGHTER
CHAPTER 4 – DINNER
CHAPTER 5 – MARIA EDUARDA
CHAPTER 6 – GERALD
CHAPTER 7 – THREE DAYS LATER
CHAPTER 8 – BITTERSWEET AFTERNOON TEA
CHAPTER 9 – CONSPIRACY AND RETRIBUTION
CHAPTER 10 – SINTRA
CHAPTER 11 – THE LANGUAGE OF LOVE
CHAPTER 12 – TIME GOES BY
CHAPTER 13 – THE THEFT
CHAPTER 14 – ALENTEJO
CHAPTER 15 – ENDING

PART 2 – HERTIE

VALERIA'S JOURNAL, FEBRUARY 2020
CHAPTER 1 – THE RECURRING DREAM
CHAPTER 2 – TAKEN
CHAPTER 3 – EARLY NIGHT IN THE PEAK DISTRICT
CHAPTER 4 – HUNGER
CHAPTER 5 – CHRISTMAS 1944
CHAPTER 6 – ESCAPE
CHAPTER 7 – THE JOURNEY
CHAPTER 8 – AUNT ELSA'S FARM
CHAPTER 9 – PEACE
CHAPTER 10 – THE STEPFATHER
CHAPTER 11 – LATE NIGHT IN THE PEAK DISTRICT

CHAPTER 12 – UNDER THE BERLIN SKY
CHAPTER 13 – UNFINISHED STORY IN THE PEAK DISTRICT
CHAPTER 14 – GERALD'S CONFESSION

PART 3 – CONNECTING DOTS

CHAPTER 1 – XAVER
CHAPTER 2 – OMA'S TALE
CHAPTER 3 – THE WOMAN WITH THE RADIANT SMILE
CHAPTER 4 – NEXT STEPS
VALERIA'S JOURNAL, APRIL 2020
CHAPTER 5 – DACHAU
VALERIA'S JOURNAL, APRIL 2020
CHAPTER 6 – THE MANUSCRIPT
CHAPTER 7 – THE DETECTIVE
VALERIA'S JOURNAL, MAY 2020
CHAPTER 8 – RESULTS

PART 4 – THE VISIT

CHAPTER 1 – DRIVING THROUGH ALENTEJO
CHAPTER 2 – ARRIVAL
CHAPTER 3 – PHOTOGRAPHS
CHAPTER 4 – TRANQUIL REVELATIONS
CHAPTER 5 – STARS MAINTAIN THEIR GLOW
VALERIA'S JOURNAL, 2021-2022 – THE ENDING

AUTHOR'S NOTES AND BIBLIOGRAPHY

Dedication

In memoriam:

My father (1925-2023) – for what he taught me and for being the greatest Dad anyone could wish for
Gerda (1938-2016) – for her friendship, her generous, kind self and the story she didn't write
Brian (1953-2020) – for the stars
Jane (1958-2021) – for the ballet

STARS MAINTAIN THEIR GLOW

FlowingProse / M G da Mota

Valeria's Journal, 2022 – The Beginning

My name is Valeria Silva-Strachan. People tell me it sounds exotic. But this story is not about me. It is about two extraordinary women and the man who connected them. But, as I am part of it, an introduction of sorts is required.

My father, Patrick Strachan, is Scottish and my mother, Maria Helena de Arantes Silva, is Portuguese. I was born in 1988, the youngest of my parents' four children and the only girl. My three brothers are almost identical triplets, meaning close family perceive small differences but most people don't. They are seven years older than me. For a long time my parents couldn't bear the idea of trying for a girl, fearing another set of triplets. Understandable. Luckily, when they eventually decided to have a go, the desired girl came along on her own, meaning me.

I am a writer and historian – my second career choice – and in parallel also a musician. I wanted to become an opera singer. I studied and pursued that goal until I was nineteen. Then I caught pneumonia and was hospitalised. While recovering I unfortunately came down with an infection in my vocal cords. My singing voice vanished forever but I couldn't completely give up music. I love it too much. So I play the piano. On occasion I perform as an accompanist to singers who were once my colleagues but it is not a regular professional occupation. I often attend concerts, the opera, and the ballet but, unable to sing, I didn't wish for an alternative career in music. At least not full time.

My brothers and I grew up bilingual in Portuguese and English. While in Italy to study music I learned Italian and it was easy for me to later study at the University of Sussex German and French as first choice languages. I turned to history and writing, simultaneously completing two degrees – one in History and the other in Foreign Languages and Literature.

Now I write music and book reviews as a freelancer, conduct interviews with various artists, occasionally take on pupils for piano lessons and, as mentioned, accompany singers at their recitals.

My mother, Maria Helena, is the youngest daughter of my grandfather's marriage to Rosa Delgado, a Lisbon socialite and his third wife. My grandfather, Ludovico de Arantes Silva (and a dozen other names I usually forget), Duke of Beja, was a personal friend of Portuguese dictator Salazar. They were born in the same year though under very different circumstances. My grandfather was born into wealth and social position; Salazar was a few months older and had rather modest beginnings.

Ludovico was also a good friend of the country's most important banker, Ricardo Espirito Santo, and of many other grandees of the first half of the 20th century in Portugal. He lived a long life. Born in July 1889 he was a witness to many changes in his country and the world. He died in May 1989, two months short of his 100th birthday. In spite of the fact that the monarchy ended in Portugal in 1910 and the country became a republic, Ludovico continued to use his title of duke, as it brought him and his family social advantages. Possessor of enormous wealth – a house in Lisbon, a mansion in Sintra, a coffee plantation in Cape Verde, a tea plantation in the Azores and a large estate in Alentejo – he was a staunch supporter of Salazar and the Estado Novo[1], a devout Catholic and a bon-vivant. My grandfather and his family lived a privileged life until the revolution of 25th April 1974 that ended forty-eight years of fascist dictatorship.

Ludovico didn't like to be identified as a fascist, though Salazar's ideology and policies were in line with fascism. He would say it was a very simplistic view of the world. There were many factors that needed consideration which, in his opinion, was exactly what Salazar did. The difference possibly being that Salazar did not instigate the cult of personality, as Hitler and Mussolini did. According to my mother, her father wasn't a bad person, had later been horrified at what Hitler and his supporters had done and was always loyal and kind to his family, friends, and country. I never met Ludovico. He died when I was a seven-month-old baby. My brothers vaguely remember him as they were eight when he died and had on occasions visited him in

---

[1] Portugal's fascist dictator Antonio de Oliveira Salazar called his policies and ruling of the country the New State or Estado Novo in Portuguese

Portugal with our parents. I remember my grandmother, Rosa, as I was eleven when she died in 1999 at the age of 86.

I have always had trouble understanding how my grandfather could have been loyal and kind to his family and simultaneously behave in such a rotten way to his eldest daughter Maria Eduarda – the one nobody talks about. My mother knows almost nothing about her half-sister and has never met her. Two men had an idea of what might have happened to Maria Eduarda, as they were the instigators in a manner of speaking. One of them was her own father, Ludovico, the Duke of Beja, my granddad; the other the man who changed her life.

What I am about to write is the tale of Maria Eduarda, as told to me, and the memoirs of my friend Hertha Lohmeyer – Hertie, as family and friends affectionately called her. By one of those life's serendipitous moments these two stories crossed, touched and eventually turned into one.

Hertie is the origin of what I'll lay bare in this book. She and I were close in spite of the fifty-two-year gap that separated our ages. She died in 2018, shortly after her 82nd birthday. One night she told me about her life. Fearful of forgetting details she digitally recorded everything she could remember. She left me the recordings and asked me to make a book out of them in whichever format I chose though her preference was for a novel. Hertie had always wanted to write her memoirs, never felt she had the ability but believed I did.

I could have started working on the book much earlier but Hertie didn't want anything revealed while she lived.

This year, 2022, sees the fourth anniversary of her death. The Covid-19 pandemic started in late December 2019 in China and spread all over Europe and the World in the early part of 2020. No-one thought it would last this long. We now have vaccines that didn't exist in the beginning but for how much longer it's going to rage is anyone's guess. I thought about Hertie today, as the task she gave me is nearing its end. Remembering what a kind-hearted, warm, dear person she was I knew it was time to start shaping the stories into the book she wanted when the pandemic began. The long months of lockdown in 2020 and

then in 2021 were ideal. I lost no more time.
And so the story begins…

Part 1 – Gerald

(Portugal, 1940-1942)

"By day Lisbon has a naïve theatrical quality that enchants and captivates, but by night is a fairy-tale city, descending over lighted terraces to the sea, like a woman in festive garments going down to meet her dark lover."

Erich Maria Remarque (1898-1970), "Die Nacht von Lissabon", Kiepenheuer & Witsch, Köln, 1961 – taken from the English Translation "The Night in Lisbon" by Ralph Manheim, originally published by Harcourt, Brace & World Inc., 1964

Chapter 1 – Lisbon

Gerald Neale arrived at the Portuguese capital in late June 1940 and was dazzled by the light, the luminous blue of the sky and the warmth of the sun. Young, irreverent, adventurous, and devastatingly handsome Gerald was a bit of a maverick. His father, Frank Neale, had been a cultural attaché to the British embassy in Lisbon for many years. Gerald and his two-year older brother Jonathan were born in Portugal but after their mother's death, a few months after Gerald's birth, they moved back to England where their father went to work for the government and never remarried.

Frank and his boys took with them a Portuguese nanny, a young woman with no family who had been raised in a convent but who didn't feel a call to become a nun. Maria Filomena, her name, was happy to leave her country. She looked after the two boys until they were old enough to go to a prestigious public school in the Sussex Downs. After the boys went away to school, Mena, as they called her, married an English pub owner and moved with her husband to the town of Horsham, south of London in West Sussex, continuing to be in touch with the family. Both Jonathan and Gerald looked at her more like a mother than a nanny, as neither of them could remember their birth mother. With Mena, Gerald learned Portuguese and grew up bilingual. From his father he inherited the passion for old books and rare first editions. Frank owned a valuable, enviable collection of famous authors' first editions, spanning centuries and different countries. Jonathan's interests were in machinery and engines. He didn't care much for art, literature or other humanities subjects. So, Frank had told his younger son the collection of first editions would one day be his. Gerald was over the moon and from an early age began searching for first editions himself, having acquired three and gained his father's praise. He and his brother didn't really get along. Jonathan was serious, quiet, sensitive and dedicated to his work after obtaining an honours degree in Engineering. Gerald couldn't be more different. Exuberant, extrovert, talked and laughed loud, sometimes flamboyant, vindictive on occasions when someone angered him, and completely crazy about women, switching girlfriends with the same speed as one changes socks. Jonathan didn't understand his brother's attitude to life or his behaviour towards women, finding him irresponsible and troublesome. He married while still at university and his wife became pregnant at the beginning of the war. At the other end of the scale Gerald couldn't cope with his brother, finding him irritating, humourless and with no sense of fun. After Jonathan's marriage the brothers only met at Christmas or other family occasions.

Gerald had a knack for languages, easily learning Spanish and French in his teenage years. It was his deep knowledge of the Portuguese language and his ability to speak it accent-free that got him the job in Lisbon during the war. Always a lover of adventure and excitement, he told his father he intended to apply to MI6 once finishing his degree. He wanted to be of assistance to his country on the one hand and to lead an exciting life on the other. The outbreak of WWII in 1939 answered all his wishes. He finished his history degree at the age of 20, successfully applied to MI6, completed his training the following year and was sent to Portugal in 1940, aged only 22, officially to serve as private secretary to the British ambassador in Lisbon; unofficially as a spy to gather intelligence on the Portuguese bankers and officials doing business with the Germans, as well as sabotaging German trade in Portugal as much as possible.

Before the war Lisbon was a dilapidated city. Its once splendid buildings were decaying through decades of poor maintenance. Plaster fell off walls, beautiful typically Portuguese blue decorative tiles showed cracks, broken windows left unrepaired showed paint peeling from their frames where the wood was left to rot. Shutters and glass panes were more often than not covered in dust. Clothes and bed linen were hung to dry from rusty railings of balconies once boasting elegant, pretty ironwork. Some buildings with flats had rather attractive façades which concealed poorly maintained common entrances that smelled of damp and mould.

But with the advent of war and Portugal's neutrality the

city changed completely.

During the years of World War II Lisbon became a vibrant, colourful city at the centre of world attention. It was the only European city where both the Allies and the Axis powers openly operated. Lisbon's story was set within the context of a country frantically trying to hold on to its wartime neutrality. It was strenuous, arduous work for its prime minister, fascist dictator António de Oliveira Salazar, creator of the so-called Estado Novo. Portugal became increasingly caught in the middle of the economic and naval wars between the Allies and the Nazis. No shot was fired or bomb dropped in Portugal but it was a tale of intrigue, betrayal, opportunism, and double dealing. All of which took place in the Cidade da Luz (City of Light) and along its unspoiled, picturesque Atlantic coastline.

The designation City of Light came mostly not from the dazzling sunshine and daytime luminosity but from Lisbon's night life. During the war years it was the only European city shining brightly after dark. Vivid white lights from the streetlamps, intensely colourful neon signs on top of buildings advertising the most varied goods, lights from nightclubs, cafés, hotels, restaurants and gambling houses ebullient with refugees, spies from both sides of the war, Portuguese prostitutes and opportunists, as well as the opposition to Salazar's iron regime which sought to take advantage of the situation and use it to topple the dictator.

Allied and German agents operated openly in Lisbon, actively monitoring each other's every move. Allied spies logged German shipping movements in and around Lisbon's busy port. And the Germans did the same regarding the Allies. Both sides spread propaganda and attempted to disrupt the supply of vital goods to each other. As British and German agents watched one another, their movements were shadowed and recorded in return by the Portuguese secret police, the Polícia de Vigilância e Defesa do Estado (PVDE).

The gambling houses in the city itself were more or less sordid, sleazy, and disreputable, associated with pimps and prostitutes. But on the stunning Lisbon Atlantic coast there was a glamorous casino located in the attractive resort of Estoril – the last grand casino in war time Europe.

Gerald had intensively and extensively read about the situation in Lisbon. He was well informed. For a young man who sought excitement and adventure, Lisbon during the war years was the perfect placement. He relished the lively atmosphere of the city, breathed in its shifty air, and loved its aura of decadence. The olive-skinned, dark-haired Portuguese beauties attracted him enormously. A touch of the exotic for a young man eager to taste and fully enjoy the pleasures and the buzz that a life of risky, unexpected undertakings could offer him. After only two weeks in the Portuguese capital Gerald Neale moved at the embassy or among the Portuguese grandees of the time with the assurance of someone born in their midst, feeling equally at home among the prostitutes or the sailors that filled cheap night clubs along the Lisbon docks.

Gerald flew into Lisbon in a BOAC[2] operated flight from Whitchurch, near Bristol. The flights operated three times a week both ways between the two cities, as Lisbon was also the end of the line for escaped Allied prisoners of war who arrived in the city to be flown back to England. Allied and Axis agents worked at the airport continuously, bribing local customs officials to gain access to the cargo and passenger lists of their respective opponents in the war. Both BOAC and Lufthansa operated flights out of the city's airport. Their aircraft were parked almost next to one another on the tarmac. The daily scene at Lisbon's airport was a bit like being in the movie Casablanca but twentyfold, according to eye-witnesses at the time. During the hours of darkness Lisbon Airport is highly susceptible to mist from the river, especially during autumn and winter, which at the time added to its atmospheric mystery.

The British ambassador's personal driver was waiting for Gerald at the airport to take him to the Hotel Aviz, a glamorous luxury hotel where he was to stay to begin with. He enjoyed the drive, identifying squares, streets, avenues and landmarks from

---

[2] British Overseas Airways Corporation

the city map he had memorised. After checking in he returned to the car and the driver took him to the embassy.

The ambassador, Sir Ronald Campbell, received Gerald in person in his private working office, adjacent to his living quarters. As Gerald walked in, Sir Ronald stood up to greet him with the words, 'welcome to Lisbon, Mr Neale.'

'Thank you, sir,' Gerald replied shaking the ambassador's hand. A firm handshake. Gerald liked it. In his mind it showed a strong character. He added, 'I'm looking forward to working with you, sir. Your reputation precedes you.'

The ambassador nodded but said nothing. Sitting down at his desk he indicated Gerald should take a seat on the chair opposite.

'I won't beat around the bush, Mr Neale,' the ambassador began, 'I know and respect your father who had a distinguished career in this country and continues to do so in England. I hope you will honour his name.'

'Of course, sir.'

'You come highly recommended in spite of your extreme youth. I know you obtained an honour's degree at Oxford University and you completed your MI6 training with top grades. I congratulate you. However, I must admit that if it weren't for your deep knowledge of the Portuguese language, as well as Spanish, which may prove useful, I might have disagreed with your nomination. As you're aware your official title is that of my private secretary and as such you'll gain access to the Portuguese prime minister, Salazar, as well as to many of the most important personalities of the country. I know as well as you that your work is of a different nature. It is a secret mission and it, including your true future activities in Portugal, must remain confidential between the two of us, our MI6 and military representatives in this country but it will not...I repeat, will not under any circumstances leave this office. Am I clear so far?'

'Yes, sir. I'm aware of the mission and what you have mentioned is exactly what I expected and how I've been instructed.'

'Good. I'm glad to hear it. So, let us proceed. You will

have to work closely with Howard Bristow here at the embassy. Mr Bristow is in charge of the British and Allied anti-German propaganda officially and unofficially. His job bears certain similarities to yours. He hardly speaks Portuguese so you'll be useful to him. His knowledge and contacts will be useful to you. I expect you both to collaborate. He's a young man, thirty-one, but with five years' experience of the diplomatic service.'

'A question, sir, if I may,' Gerald interrupted.

'You may.'

'Is Mr Bristow informed of the full extent of my work?'

'Partially. He's aware that, besides your duties as my private secretary, you're expected to infiltrate…or, rather, to socialise closely with Portuguese society at all levels, due to your deep knowledge of the language, and to inform me of anything that may seem important. That's all. You report only to me, the MI6 director here at the embassy and to London but I expect you and Mr Bristow to work well together. I'll introduce you later to him and other embassy officials. Any other questions so far?'

'No, sir. I completely understand.'

'Good. Let's continue, shall we? What do you know about Portugal's current position and the head of government? I've been told you were well-informed.'

'Yes, sir. I believe I am. I know Salazar's the prime minister of Portugal and he also holds the foreign affairs' office. He's a hard-working man and more or less rules the country single handed, meaning he is a dictator like Mussolini or Hitler—'

'Wrong,' Sir Ronald interrupted.

'How so?'

'He is a dictator, yes, but he's not like Mussolini and even less like Hitler. Never underestimate Salazar. He's a master of diplomacy, an outstanding economist; highly intelligent and shrewd. Very disciplined he follows a rigorous work routine. Doesn't smoke and drinks very moderately. In winter he uses no heating, preferring to sit at his desk working wrapped up in a blanket. Since the beginning of the war our government believed that Salazar could easily be brought onto our side. The Germans believed the same. The truth is that so far Salazar has proved too clever for any plot to bring him to one side or the other. He keeps the interests of the country in sight, doesn't encourage the cult of himself as a personality – unlike Hitler and Mussolini – and firmly believes that Portugal must remain neutral to survive the war. You must be clear about all this.'

'I am, Sir Ronald. I have thoroughly informed myself about Salazar. Among other things I know he fears an invasion of Portugal by Spain or Germany, or both, if Spain actively joins the Germans in this war. Spain has so far remained neutral but there are rumours they may be drawing up a plan to invade Portugal with Germany's help. I also know that the Portuguese, authorised by Salazar himself, are doing business with the Germans, especially selling them wolfram – or tungsten, whichever one calls it – from their mines in the north-east of the country. I understand the British government isn't happy about this but hasn't been able to stop it. Salazar claims he must do business with the Germans or risk an invasion, which would be catastrophic for his country. So he ensures his neutrality by doing business with Germany and giving certain concessions to the Allies.'

'Very well, Mr Neale,' Sir Ronald smiled, 'your information is accurate. And how would you describe your mission here – the unofficial one naturally?'

'I am to establish good, friendly and trustworthy relationships with the Portuguese grandees, especially bankers and in particular Ricardo Espirito Santo – Salazar's personal friend and one of the most important bankers and influential men in the country. I'm to create regular reports about their activities, as well as a blacklist of names. I am to send these regularly and directly to SOE[3] in London, keeping a copy for yourself and the SOE director here. In turn SOE will give all information I may gather to the British government. As I'm fluent in Portuguese I'm expected to acquire information that remains inaccessible to other diplomats with less language skills. Due to my language

---

[3] SOE – Special Operations Executive or MI6 as more commonly known.

knowledge I am to establish contacts with the common Portuguese citizens and bribe as many as possible, employing them in sabotaging German business.'

Gerald noticed the pleased grin, the twinkle in Sir Ronald's eyes and felt gratified for all the hours of hard work and never-ending reading of boring documents. It paid off. He could now flaunt his knowledge and inspire Sir Ronald with confidence that he'd be able to carry out his job effectively.

'Excellent, Mr Neale,' Sir Ronald said with a nod, 'then to work. As you may already be aware, we're expecting His Royal Highness Edward, the Duke of Windsor and his wife, the Duchess in Lisbon in the next few days. Today is the 27th of June. The royals are expected on July the 3rd at the latest. Salazar has already decided and requested that Ricardo Espirito Santo hosts the Duke and Duchess at his home in Cascais.'

'Espirito Santo? Is that wise?'

Sir Ronald shrugged. 'You must put it into the context of the current Portuguese foreign policy,' he said.

'I know, neutrality, but—'

'Hear me out,' the ambassador interrupted. 'Salazar doesn't wish to jeopardise his neutral policies. From his perspective he can't be seen to favour the United Kingdom above Germany but at the same time he will not do anything that may antagonise us or the Germans. So, it is necessary to house the Duke and Duchess in a setting favourable for Britain and with the utmost care. From our perspective this means preventing any clandestine action from the Germans; ensuring Edward's contacts aren't publicised; keeping their stay discreet – Salazar's press censors will take care of that – and finally to support the couple's departure from Portugal to a destination London is yet to assign. So, I ask you, given all these points, who better to host the Duke than Ricardo Espirito Santo?'

'I see. Indeed. No-one better than a strong-positioned man who's well seen by the Germans, Salazar's confidant, equally at ease and on good terms with the British.'

'Exactly.'

'Forgive me, Sir Ronald, for my boldness but in London

in my briefings with the MEW[4] I was told Espirito Santo's a friend of the Germans though bizarrely the Foreign Office doesn't believe so.'

'No, and I agree with the Foreign Office. I've known Espirito Santo since my arrival back in March and we're on relatively friendly terms. I think he's above all a businessman who makes money wherever he can. He's not pro-German any more than he is pro-British. His policy, as to a certain extent is Salazar's, is to be on good terms with everybody. I think it's fair to call him a good Portuguese.'

'Well, I haven't met the man yet of course but I read about him and I tend more to yours and the Foreign Office's views; however, I suppose we shouldn't be complacent.'

Suddenly Sir Ronald laughed and then, with an amused smirk, said, 'I'll eat my hat if Ricardo is pro-German.'

'Your confidence is reassuring, sir, but—'

'Don't be alarmed. We won't be complacent but I'm pretty certain we haven't anything to fear from Espirito Santo.'

'Very well.'

'So, let's continue. For the next two days you are expected to acclimatise and familiarise yourself with the city, as a brief holiday of sorts. Enjoy the Aviz and your free time. After that, you'll move to the embassy rooms being prepared for you at present. Your first assignment will be to begin translating Portuguese secret documents – some from Salazar himself – that were obtained for us.'

'Who obtained them?'

'A Portuguese woman, a janitor who cleans offices in the government buildings and who was bribed by one of our agents. You'll also need to determine whether the information is real or fake. We can't be certain because Salazar is extremely careful and doesn't trust many people.'

Gerald nodded.

'Your second assignment,' the ambassador continued, 'will be to go with me and other embassy officials to a dinner at

---

[4] Ministry of Economic Warfare.

Ricardo Espirito Santo's home in Cascais, which he's throwing in honour of His Royal Highness, the Duke of Windsor. It'll be a discreet social event on Saturday, 6 July, so in ten days. Until then, you have your tasks and should also take your initiative to begin establishing a solid network, as required by your mission.'

With these words Gerald understood he was being dismissed. Thanking the ambassador he walked to the door.

'Mr Neale,' Sir Ronald stopped him.

He turned. 'Yes, sir?'

'Saturday next week, the dinner, it's naturally black-tie.'

'Naturally, sir,' he paused, then added, 'may I just ask you something, Sir Ronald?'

'Of course.'

'I understand my stay at the Hotel Aviz is limited to two days. So, just making sure, you expect me to move in here after that, correct?'

'Yes. This coming Saturday, 29 June, in the afternoon you must be established in your quarters here. After you check out of the Aviz, bring your things to the embassy and ask for Mr Jackson, the butler. He'll take you to your rooms, which by then will be ready for you. Is that all?'

'Yes, sir. Thank you.'

Closing the door to the ambassador's private office he saw a man, early to mid-thirties, waiting in the corridor. Glancing at Gerald he stood up and knocked on the ambassador's door.

'Come in,' Gerald heard Sir Ronald say.

Approaching the staircase he suddenly heard someone calling out his name. Gerald turned. It was the man who had entered the office after he'd left.

'Yes. How may I be of service?' he asked.

'Sir Ronald calls you back to his office, Mr Neale, if you please.'

Gerald turned around and walked back in. Sir Ronald smiled and said, 'Mr Neale. Capital. We caught you in time. Close the door, will you?'

The ambassador stood up, indicating Gerald and the other man to move to the sitting corner of his office while making introductions.

'Mr Neale, this is Howard Bristow, head of British propaganda. Mr Bristow, this is Gerald Neale, my newly arrived private secretary.'

They shook hands as the ambassador sat down. Howard Bristow was an athletic, not unattractive man, square jaw, square shoulders, brown hair, blue eyes, one inch shorter than Gerald, with a strong handshake. He appeared taciturn. Gerald gained the impression Bristow was a man of few words who wouldn't waste time in frivolous conversation.

They followed the ambassador's sign and sat down in front of him, the other side of a low table. Once all comfortably installed Sir Ronald rang a bell and, as the butler came in, he ordered tea for three. Shortly after the butler returned with fine porcelain cups, saucers, spoons, a pot of steaming tea, a sugar bowl and a small jug of milk on a silver tray. He served the tea with the ease of someone who has done it for most of his adult life.

'Thank you, Mr Jackson,' Sir Ronald said as the butler finished.

'You're welcome, sir,' the butler replied with a nod and left the room. Sipping from his tea the ambassador said, 'since Mr Bristow had just come in, I thought better to call you back, Mr Neale, and introduce you.'

Both men nodded.

'Mr Bristow,' the ambassador continued, 'will you please inform Mr Neale what you know about the city and Ricardo Espirito Santo? Thank you.'

Bristow extracted a map from his briefcase. Carefully unfolding it he placed it on the table in front of Gerald, then began, 'this is a detailed plan of Lisbon and its Atlantic coast. We're here,' he pointed at an area to the west of the city centre by the name of Lapa, 'it's a noble, smart neighbourhood. Most embassies are located around here, including the German embassy.' Taking a red pencil out of his jacket pocket Bristow marked a spot on the map with an X he added, 'the German embassy,' he looked up and Gerald nodded.

Drawing various circles on the map, Bristow proceeded, 'these are all places of interest for you...for us, generally,' he moved his finger along what looked like a long, wide avenue in the heart of the city, 'this is the Avenida da Liberdade, the most glamorous of the city's avenues, long and wide, lined with cafés, two theatres and four cinemas. There—'

'I think I've seen it,' Gerald cut in, 'a pretty sort of boulevard lined with trees. Isn't it where my hotel, the Aviz, is located?'

'Indeed. Along the avenue, or close to it, there are some luxury hotels. Yours is one, the Tivoli is another. Here,' he pointed to a circle.

'Why's the Tivoli marked?' Gerald asked.

'Because it has a large bar, connected by a corridor to the dining-room. It's popular with residents and non-residents...with everyone really, meaning German spies, our agents, refugees and locals. Its windows are low and so one can sit and watch the comings and goings on the Avenida da Liberdade, which can be...shall we say, instructive at times.'

Smiling Gerald sipped from his tea and said, 'I understand.'

'This square here,' Bristow placed his finger in the middle of the largest red circle, 'is the Rossio. There are many cafés around the square, a few bars and the Hotel Metrópole where many of the Germans working in Lisbon – mostly not embassy staff – are staying. The Rossio and its cafés are a good place to meet refugees, undercover agents but also locals who are often easy to bribe. You can walk from the Rossio up the Avenida da Liberdade all the way to Parque Eduardo VII, the most important park in the city. The Rossio is also relatively close to the docks by the river; Cais do Sodré, the main part, is only about a twenty-minute walk away. The docks are important too. Night clubs, prostitutes, sailors, etc. hang around there at night and one can sometimes obtain interesting information.'

Gerald nodded while looking at a set of smaller circles in a neat row along Lisbon's Atlantic coast. He pointed at them.

'And these places?' he asked.

'They're in Estoril, the luxury resort at Lisbon's door, a gate to the Atlantic. The largest circle is the Casino do Estoril, glamorous and attractive not just for the obvious reasons but important to us. All the Portuguese grandees, rich refugees, foreign royals, government officials from all over Europe, bankers, influential socialites, you name it, frequent the casino regularly. Most crucially, significant business is made, information exchanged, false documents bought and sold between games of blackjack and roulette,' he paused to drink some tea, then resumed, hovering his fingers above an area close to the casino, 'these three little circles are Hotel Palácio, Hotel Inglaterra – very popular with us and our allies – and the Hotel Atlântico, the favourite watering hole of the Germans.'

'Interesting,' Gerald exclaimed, 'are these divisions real or unspoken rules?'

'Unspoken.' It was Sir Ronald who answered, 'it doesn't mean that one can't find the enemy having breakfast or dinner at the next table.'

'I see. What about that circle a bit further away, right by the sea?'

Bristow followed Gerald's finger with his eyes, smiled and said, 'that's the slightly remote area of Cascais. The circle marks Ricardo Espirito Santo's home. The most important, most influential Portuguese banker and the host to be of His Royal Highness the Duke of Windsor and the Duchess.'

Glancing at Sir Ronald, Gerald asked, 'is that where we're going Saturday evening, next week?'

'Correct,' the ambassador replied with a nod, 'I will attend, naturally with my family, the two of you and a few other officials. Since the dinner is in honour of the Duke and Duchess, the British must be well represented.'

'Of course.'

'Mr Bristow,' Sir Ronald said, 'tell Mr Neale what we know about Ricardo Espirito Santo.'

Howard obliged. 'Ricardo Ribeiro do Espirito Santo e Silva – his full name,' he began, 'is forty-two and the president of BES – Banco Espirito Santo – his family's bank. He's also an economist, a patron of the arts and, in his younger years, a world-class athlete. We suspect he prefers the Germans to the Allies.'

'You suspect,' the ambassador intervened.

'Right, sir. I suspect.'

'Based on what?' Gerald asked.

'He regularly dines with the German ambassador, Baron Oswald von Hoyningen-Huene, and plays a central role in the trade between Portugal and Germany,' Bristow replied.

'Yes, but he's in line with Portugal's neutrality policy. I honestly saw no evidence that Espirito Santo is pro-German. I agree with Sir Ronald.'

Bristow grimaced and said, 'I know Sir Ronald's thoughts. May I ask on what you're basing yours?'

'Well, to begin with, Espirito Santo married a Jewish girl, Maria Pinto de Morais Sarmento Cohen, in 1918. He does trade with the Germans but equally with the Allies. You say he regularly dines with the German ambassador but he does the same with you, Sir Ronald, does he not?' Gerald glanced at the British ambassador who nodded, 'furthermore he agreed to host the Duke and Duchess in his own home—'

'Because Salazar ordered him to,' Bristow cut in.

'No doubt. But there are also rumours he's helped many Jewish refugees and that he's financially aiding a prominent Jewish family, meaning the Rothschilds. Would he do all that if he were a Nazi sympathiser?'

It was Sir Ronald who spoke.

'I agree, as I've said before and just told you earlier, Mr Neale. Again, I'm glad to see you're very well informed. But a word of caution. As Mr Bristow mentioned, Espirito Santo is hosting the Duke and Duchess because Salazar ordered him to. The prime minister considered and I think correctly so, these royals are a very sensitive matter and therefore couldn't and shouldn't be exposed in any of the city's hotels, which Salazar has deemed unsuitable. It's natural he asked his most trustworthy friend to host them himself. Espirito Santo is Salazar's eyes and ears regarding the country's grandees and it's therefore a little worrying that he'll have continuous daily access to the Duke who isn't pleased with the war or with the way the British government has treated him and his wife, especially after he abdicated the throne in 1936. You'll meet Ricardo Espirito Santo a week on Saturday, Mr Neale, and you'll see for yourself what a charming, elegant, intelligent and well-educated man he is. You mustn't be seduced by his or any of that circle's affable, attractive and charismatic personalities. At this point in time in the war, we need to treat the Portuguese with care but we can't in any circumstance underestimate any of them.'

'I understand, sir.' Gerald acknowledged.

Shortly after he and Howard Bristow left the ambassador's private office together. Bristow stopped him in the corridor and said, 'shall we have dinner tonight, Neale? We can carry on our conversation and maybe I can introduce you to some of my contacts within the Portuguese and the refugees, as well as…' he paused and coughed to clear his throat, appearing slightly awkward, 'as well as some interesting female company.'

Gerald grinned. 'Oh yes, please,' he said, 'I've seen some of the local beauties on the streets on my way here and at the Aviz. I'm impressed and can't wait to have a roll in the hay with one of them,' slapping his companion's shoulder and smirking he added, 'thank you, Bristow. I think you and I understand each other and are off to a good start.'

Chapter 2 – Espirito Santo's Home

Two days after his arrival in Lisbon Gerald moved to his rooms at the embassy and spent his first week working light. Mostly enjoying himself. On the Saturday morning of Espirito Santo's dinner in honour of the Duke and Duchess of Windsor, he woke early with yet another hangover. The night before, as almost every night since his arrival, Gerald and Bristow had dined together at the Hotel Tivoli, hooking up with two rather attractive girls of obvious dubious reputation. After a succession of drinks at the hotel bar, they visited another bar in Rossio and from there went to the docks.

As he opened his eyes, Gerald didn't immediately realise where he was but then remembered to have ended in a room at the Aviz. Female company for unmarried officials wasn't allowed at the embassy. He retained little memory of the previous night, vaguely remembering being introduced to a multitude of men and very few women – some Portuguese, some British and some foreign refugees, as almost every night when out with Bristow. Invariably, the next morning he didn't recall their names, where they came from or why they were in the city. Massaging his aching forehead it was obvious he must control the amount of alcohol ingested daily or risk failing his mission. He needed to pay attention and keep a cool head. Being sober was paramount to succeed in his job. More than anything he wanted acknowledgement of his skills. And for that he must triumph in his work.

Stretching and yawning he picked up his wristwatch and glanced at the time. Eight fifteen. Too early to rise, after the night before, but he must get ready for a nine-thirty breakfast appointment at the embassy. Sir Ronald wanted to discuss a few topics concerning the evening's dinner at the home of Ricardo Espirito Santo, the famous banker. Gerald was eager to meet him and Salazar in person after what he had learned about them. Exhaling he rolled onto his back and was surprised to see a woman in his bed. Of course. His reason for ending up in a room at the Aviz. Christ. He'd nearly forgotten. His state of drunkenness having been very high. Pulling back the covers he admired the girl's beauty. The soft olive skin, the black hair spread over the pillow. Laying on her belly she was deeply asleep. Gerald sensed his desire grow but decided there was no time for another round. He needed some aspirin and to then leave. It wouldn't do to arrive late. With a sigh of lust he smacked the girl's naked bottom and said in Portuguese, 'wake up, sleeping beauty. Need you to go. I've work to do.'

The girl woke with a start, visibly confused as to her whereabouts. She mumbled something he didn't understand but then rolled out of bed and quickly enough put on her clothes, scattered all over the floor. Stopping in front of him she silently stretched her hand. Gerald understood, opened the side table drawer, extracted a bundle of Portuguese notes and handed them over. She counted them, smiling, visibly happy, then picking up her shoes and handbag left the room without a word.

Gerald laughed amused, exclaiming aloud to himself, 'good girl. Knows the rules and is used to this. That's just how I like them. Silence's a virtue in a woman.'

Rolling out of bed he swallowed an aspirin, dressed, picked up his hat, quickly paid his bill and ran out of the hotel to get a taxi. It took him a while to hail one but with the promise of a few extra escudos[5] the taxi driver delivered him to the embassy in record time. Gerald entered the building with thirty minutes to spare, which enabled him to go to his rooms, shower and change into clean clothes, arriving punctually at the meeting.

Breakfast lasted almost until lunch time. Gerald had difficulty concentrating and was forced to take a second aspirin halfway through the working session. He exhaled with relief when it finally ended. Having agreed with Bristow to be ready in the embassy's front garden at 8 p.m. sharp Gerald went back to his rooms with the intention of napping before preparing for the dinner. Finding himself restless he tossed about in bed until deciding it was better to do something rather than sleeping. He was excited about the evening's assignment. Quite simple but

---

[5] The escudo was the Portuguese currency at the time.

thrilling: Keep an open ear to anything said in Portuguese, insinuate himself with some of the better-placed families using his position and his charm. Part of it depended on the ambassador introducing him as his new trustworthy and brilliant private secretary, implying he might become the next deputy once the current one retired and returned to Britain. According to Bristow and Sir Ronald such an innuendo would open doors and a shower of invitations.

Gerald found it difficult to contain his excitement. Staying in his rooms wasn't an option. He felt like a caged animal. A hike? More precisely a long stroll would do the trick. He walked from the embassy for thirty minutes until reaching the Avenida da Liberdade, then strode it up and down repeatedly. It was interesting to watch the engraxadores, the young men who polished male customers' shoes on corners or adjacent to cafés while the clients read the newspaper. During his first inspection of the city centre, Gerald had immediately noticed most Portuguese café goers were men. The majority of the women were foreign, mostly refugees. From all the information digested before travelling to Lisbon he expected to hear a wide variety of tongues being spoken in bars, cafés and hotels but it was still surprising to listen to a muddle of European languages from English and French to German, Polish and even Russian. Because of his fluency in Portuguese he could clearly recognise it when someone used it but a person who didn't speak it might be forgiven to think they were in some international hotspot rather than the capital city of Portugal.

Gerald reached the Rossio square and directed his footsteps to the Chave d'Ouro – the largest Rossio café, also containing a spacious billiard room. He knew from the stories his Portuguese nanny used to tell him that a woman who would go alone to a café or a bar was frowned upon as being a bit of a slut but things were clearly gradually changing. The until recently male dominated Portuguese café society was now more cosmopolitan and one could see families and couples at different tables. Gerald could readily tell apart the locals from the refugees, agents or escaped prisoners of war, mostly due to his mastery of the language. He had noticed a few times that most foreign refugees tended to speak in hushed tones so their conversations couldn't easily be overheard. Having asked Bristow whether he'd noticed it too, he received the reply that there was a good reason for this behaviour. The much-feared Portuguese secret police, the PVDE, were responsible for watching the foreigners during their stay in Lisbon, providing regular updates directly to Salazar.

Gerald entered the famous Chave d'Ouro, picked up a newspaper and ordered a coffee. He admired the shelves filled with appetising cakes and sweets, unthinkable anywhere else in war torn Europe where rationing had become the norm. For a minute he hesitated whether to order one of those delicious pastéis de nata[6] or a fradinho[7] but then decided too much sugar wasn't a good idea. The waiter brought his coffee and a glass of water, placed them on the table and asked in broken English and a grumpy tone whether he would like anything else. Gerald realised his platinum blonde almost white hair and blue eyes easily identified him as a foreigner. He smiled and replied in perfect Portuguese, 'I'll want a second cup once I've finished this one.'

The waiter opened his eyes wide, visibly surprised. His mood changed. He bowed his head and displaying a thin smile said in his native tongue, 'forgive me, sir. I didn't realise you were Portuguese and mistook you for a foreigner. I'll bring you a second coffee as soon as you've finished the present one.'

'Thank you,' Gerald acknowledged, a hint of amusement in his voice. He didn't correct the man.

Picking up the little cup he swallowed the coffee in two quick sips. He enjoyed the ultra-strong, short, very small black coffee served in Portugal, named bica[8]. The word literally meant spout and he had no idea why the coffee had such a name. He

---

[6] These pastries are known in England as Portuguese custard tartlets but the name doesn't do them justice, as custard is the tiniest percentage of their ingredients.
[7] A pastry made of beans, almonds and sugar. Unusual and delicious.
[8] A *bica* is an espresso coffee.

loved it and the immediate rush of energy it provided, badly needed at the moment. He could still taste the residues of his night out drinking and fooling around with a local cheap beauty.

The waiter from before solicitously came with the second cup of coffee. Gerald paid, giving him a good tip. He drank it in one go, then exhaled satisfied, beginning to feel his usual self again. The injection of caffeine the little bicas supplied could resurrect a corpse. He laughed silently at his own joke, then glancing at his wristwatch, stood up and walked slowly back to the embassy. It was very hot. Gerald wasn't used to such temperatures, guessing the thermometer must be around forty centigrade or higher. His long stroll not the best of ideas but it had calmed him down, achieving its purpose. Back in his rooms he showered for the second time that day, taking great care with his appearance. Clean-shaven, with a discreet eau de cologne and impeccably dressed in his dinner jacket he adjusted the bow tie and the cummerbund in front of the mirror.

'You look good, you old rascal,' he said aloud to his image, 'no man will doubt your class and women will find you irresistible.'

Gerald collected his wallet and keys and left his rooms, heading for the embassy front garden. He reached it fifteen minutes before the time agreed with Bristow and made himself comfortable on a garden chair to wait for his ride.

A black car with diplomatic number plates stopped in front of the embassy's main gate at 8 p.m. sharp. The driver left the engine running and Bristow stepped out, motioning to Gerald but Gerald was already heading towards him. Bristow appeared uncomfortable in his dinner jacket, continuously running a finger along the inside of his shirt collar. The car pulled out and within a matter of minutes rolled alongside the water on Lisbon's attractive Marginal – the road that followed the river, leading from the city to its Atlantic coast. The two men remained silent. Bristow leaned his head back and closed his eyes, saying he'd taken aspirin but still had a bit of a headache and wanted to rest for the circa forty-five minute drive to Cascais. Gerald nodded, settling down to quietly watch the landscape passing him by.

He admired the river and its banks. Lisbon was on the north bank and the municipality of Almada on the south. The Tagus – or Tejo as the Portuguese called it – was a wide river that flowed into an estuary before reaching the ocean. It gleamed in the sinking colours of the sunset, painting the sky and the water in shades of orange and red. Beautiful. There was no bridge connecting the two banks of the river so the water was always busy with the cacilheiros – the Portuguese ferries – crossing from one side to the other, carrying people and cars. Gerald knew more about the city and the country than the average English agent who landed in Lisbon. Partly because he had read everything he could grab before travelling but also because of the many questions he'd asked Mena, always patient and kind to answer.

The car left the city and soon entered the pretty parish of Belém, a suburb of Lisbon, with two of the most beautiful, most remarkable Portuguese monuments – the Torre, or tower, of Belém and the Mosteiro dos Jerónimos. Both had been built in the 16th century in the elegant late Portuguese gothic style, called Manueline, with its unique ocean and mariner motifs. Both the tower and the monastery rose against the clear sky, the dusk colours playing with the intricate, gracefully laced stonework. Gerald knew the white stone used was a type of hard limestone that existed in the region around Lisbon. He made a mental note to return to Belém on a day off and visit the two buildings. He also wanted to see the former harbour of Praia do Restelo where ships used to be able to anchor safely and shelter from the winds when entering the river. He remembered well an episode from the Portuguese epic poem The Lusiads – Os Lusíadas – by Portugal's most brilliant and celebrated poet Luis de Camões. Most people in England had never heard of him or his work but, being fluent in the language and naturally curious about everything remotely connected with his mission, Gerald had read many books on the country's history as well as writings by its most outstanding authors. At first he was simply impressed with the numbers regarding The Lusiads – an epic poem on an epic scale, formed of ten chants – or cantos as the Portuguese called the main divisions in an epic poem, which were like chapters in a manner of speaking – and a total of 1,102 stanzas, each with eight verses, so-called in octave rhyme. He made up his mind to read it then and was stunned by the beauty of the language and knowledge of the poet, deciding he wanted to find out more about him and his life. Not easy in England. He hoped to achieve this personal goal during his stay in Lisbon.

The car was now rolling along the ocean. They passed splendid white sand beaches, charming bays, magnificent bluffs and attractive houses. When they reached Estoril the buildings became glamorous, some grand. Gerald saw the famous Casino, intending to visit it very soon, not just for recreation but as part of his mission. If one could combine business with pleasure then why not? Simply perfect.

After Estoril the coast became rugged. Soaring cliffs and twisted promontories perilously and precariously hung over the sea below where the waves incessantly battered their bases, wearing them away. The ocean appeared untamed, wilder, with white-crested fierce swells breaking out on the sand or against the rocks.

They arrived at Ricardo Espirito Santo's home at quarter past nine that evening. The red sphere of the sun slowly sank in the ocean, creating a path of fire on the water. Darkness had not yet fully descended to engulf their immediate world. A faint orange glow in the sky allowed Gerald to see his surroundings albeit not very clearly.

Espirito Santo's weekend house was located in a place called Boca do Inferno, at the end of Cascais when one arrived from Lisbon. Cascais was a small, quiet fishing village on Lisbon's Atlantic coast. Boca do Inferno literally meant hell's mouth – a name that Bristow told him derived from the fierce, dangerous sea at that particular stretch of coast. Marked by sheer vertical walls of rock, full of slippery, razor sharp edges and treacherous vents, the cliffs were continuously battered. During storms it was particularly scary. The ocean roared, the waves climbed up the vents with raucous, turbulent sounds, reaching the road more often than not and washing out anything in their path.

Gerald faced the sea. It was relatively calm today but he

noticed that spray and white foam almost reached the edge of the road that ran along the cliffs; to his left heading towards the centre of Cascais and to his right towards the open, wild dunes of Quinta da Marinha, eventually ending at Cabo da Roca, the most westerly cape in mainland Europe, as Bristow had explained.

Boca do Inferno was remote, quiet, appearing almost untamed and primitive until one turned one's back to the ocean. A few large, visibly upscale houses faced the sea, all conveniently one hundred metres apart, surrounded by high walls and hedges for complete privacy.

The road was unlit and, as darkness tightened, only the lights from the houses allowed them to see where they headed. There were a few cars already parked along the road and two more arrived as Gerald and Bristow made their way inside, which was brightly lit and with porters in tails directing the guests. They arrived at a spacious reception room with a parquet floor, large silver framed mirrors and two elegant crystal chandeliers. There were two fireplaces at opposite sides of the room with pretty, unusual porcelain figures on their mantelpieces. Small tables covered in red cloths were placed against the walls facing the large windows from where in daylight one should be able to admire the ocean. The curtains were drawn but the windows open, allowing a gentle refreshing breeze from the sea to make the room more comfortable. Matching chairs upholstered in red velvet were scattered around the room for guests to sit if they so wished. There were interesting paintings on the walls, showing scenes that appeared to be from rural Portugal, Lisbon and a couple of views of Cascais and Boca do Inferno. Gerald knew Ricardo Espirito Santo was a patron of the arts and promoted Portuguese artists so the pictures made sense.

The butler announced the British government officials Mr Gerald Neale and Mr Howard Bristow. They glimpsed the British ambassador in conversation with the Duke of Windsor and a tall, elegant man. Sir Ronald signed Gerald to come forward and placing a fatherly hand on his shoulder said, 'your Royal Highness, Ricardo, may I please introduce to you both my new private secretary? A young, promising talent with a bright future ahead of him, Gerald Neale. Gerald, His Royal Highness the Duke of Windsor and my friend Mr Ricardo Espirito Santo.'

Gerald bowed to the Duke who acknowledged his presence with a smile and a couple of words of courtesy and politeness. Ricardo Espirito Santo shook his hand graciously and appeared genuinely pleased to meet him. His voice was warm and engaging. He at once involved Gerald in the conversation, making him feel welcome and comfortable. Gerald grasped Espirito Santo's legendary charm. The man was handsome, elegant, gracious, friendly and appeared genuine at all times. His conversation, in impeccable English, was intelligent and he always seemed absolutely interested on whatever people around him were saying as if the rest of the world did not exist. He had a special way about him, like an inner light that made Gerald instantly feel as if he'd known the man all his life. He couldn't help but like him.

A waiter carrying a silver tray with glasses of champagne approached them after Espirito Santo had clicked his fingers in the man's direction. Gerald took one and after a moment of polite conversation excused himself. As he walked away he heard Espirito Santo say, 'an engaging, charming young man, your new private secretary, Sir Ronald.'

'Indeed,' the ambassador replied, 'highly intelligent, speaks various languages and is actually tipped to become the next deputy when the current one retires.'

'Interesting,' the banker replied, 'I must introduce him to some of my…'

Gerald didn't hear the end of the sentence but couldn't hide a satisfied grin. Moving in the higher circles of Portuguese society appeared to be secured. As for the lower or more vulgar sphere of the Lisbon social groups, he was already part of them through his week of lively coexistence with his colleague Bristow.

Chapter 3 – The Duke's Daughter

Gerald searched for Bristow and together they did a turn around the reception room, quietly watching the people already present. Bristow introduced him to various British government officials and embassy employees. In passing Gerald saw the Duchess of Windsor and thought she seemed a little bored though making an effort at cheerful conversation. They stopped a few times more on their round for Bristow to acquaint him with a couple of Portuguese ministers and other representatives of the Portuguese government. Turning to his friend Gerald asked, 'is Salazar here?'

'No. He rarely appears at such social occasions but by tomorrow he'll know everything that happened and was discussed during cocktails and dinner, either from Espirito Santo himself or from one of the secret police agents in disguise.'

'Really? Are there any?' Gerald asked, glancing around the room as if expecting to see a sign on the lapel of one of the male guests, marking them as members of the secret police.

'Of course. I've recognised two as part of the group of waiters currently serving champagne.'

'Fascinating. I assume Salazar likes to keep an eye everywhere.'

'Oh, yes. He's in absolute control, uniting his post as prime minister with that of minister for foreign affairs.'

'I read about it.'

'Salazar's a tough nut to crack and rather difficult to read.'

They stopped at the side of the room, close to the entrance, leaning on a pillar in front of the large windows where they could enjoy the breeze coming from the ocean. The red velvet curtains were drawn, as it was completely dark outside, but let in the air. The place they chose as their hangout was a good vantage point. They could scrutinise the arriving guests unnoticed. Discreetly, Bristow pointed out the important ones.

'The elegant woman in the black dress, who just came in, walking now in the direction of Sir Ronald, is the hostess, Maria

Cohen, Espirito Santo's wife.'

'Jewish, right?'

'Correct. That man,' he indicated a red-faced, middle-aged, slightly rotund man who had stopped at the door with a woman on his arm, 'is one of the richest Portuguese wine makers from the region south of Lisbon. The lady's his wife.'

'He does look like he enjoys wine,' Gerald commented.

Bristow smirked. With his head he then indicated a man mid to late thirties, medium height, thin, dark hair already receding at the temples and a nervous twitch when he walked, 'that's one of the Port wine barons from up north. He's in Lisbon at the moment on his own. Left wife and family in Porto. Rumours have it that he's in financial dire straits and came to ask Espirito Santo for help.'

'Interesting.'

'Well, Espirito Santo's known to readily help the ones in need and not just his friends. He's also a patron of artists and the arts and crafts of Portugal, as well as a benefactor of orphanages and playgrounds for children. You may have noticed some of the valuable and attractive pieces of furniture, paintings and other objects on display. Or the jewellery worn by his wife, which is delicate, traditional Portuguese filigree.'

'I did notice. Anyway, from what you're saying the man's good inside out. Almost a saint.'

'Hmm. Too good to be true if you ask me.'

'Perhaps you're wrong. He seems genuine enough to me.'

'Maybe.'

Bristow extracted a cigarette case from the inner pocket of his dinner jacket, opened it and offered one to Gerald.

'Thank you. I forgot mine back at the embassy,' he said.

Bristow nodded, took a cigarette for himself and then lit both. Gerald continued to watch the guests still arriving. He inhaled the smoke deeply at the same time as his eyes rested on a trio of people at the door, just being announced to the hostess who had returned with her husband to stand by the butler. Gerald choked.

'What's the matter, man?' Bristow asked, 'not used to

smoking?'

'No, I mean yes, it's not the smoke. Who is that?' He indicated the three people at the door, shaking hands with Ricardo Espirito Santo and depositing two kisses on his wife's cheeks.

'Oh, that's the Duke of Beja, Espirito Santo's and Salazar's personal friend. A very rich man. He owns a large coffee plantation on the island of Fogo in Cabo Verde – the islands off the west coast of Africa that are a Portuguese colony. He's also the proprietor of a tea plantation in the island of São Miguel in the Azores, a vast estate in Alentejo with a farm and extensive lands where he organises hunting in the autumn, plus a lovely house not far from our embassy and a delightful mansion on beautiful grounds in Sintra, a charming little town where rich Lisboetas[9] enjoy spending the summer.'

Although Gerald wasn't referring to the Duke when asking his question, he observed the middle-aged stately man attentively. Tall, elegant with a typical aristocratic bearing, a full head of wavy salt and pepper hair, impeccably cut. His dinner jacket sat perfectly on his shoulders. He was clean shaven and his vivid brown eyes seemed to take in the whole room along with everyone inside it.

'The woman to the Duke's right is his wife, Ro—'

'A bit young for him, isn't she?' Gerald interjected, 'I mean he must be at least fifty or thereabouts. She can't be more than thirty.'

'She's twenty-six. He's fifty-one. Her name's Rosa Delgado, a Portuguese socialite and heiress. She's his third wife.'

Gerald raised an eyebrow. 'Third?'

'Yes. He's twice a widower. His first wife—'

'And who's the delightful creature on his left?' Gerald interrupted yet again. 'A vision of sin in a royal blue satin dress.'

'Ah,' Bristow grinned, 'that's the Duke's eldest daughter, Maria Eduarda, the only child from his first marriage,' he paused then added, 'and I dare say the one who made you choke earlier.'

---

[9] The native people of Lisbon are called "Lisboetas" in Portuguese.

'She. Is. Gorgeous.' Gerald punctuated each word in wonder, ignoring Bristow's comment. 'Exotic. I think…the most beautiful woman I've ever seen.'

'Take your sight and hands off her. She's out of your league, old boy, and the Duke watches over her like a hawk.'

'Still, tell me what you know about her.'

'Well, besides her beauty, which is obvious, she's well educated, cultivated, speaks several languages and people say she's highly intelligent. It's known that she often helps her father with the managing of their vast estates and with writing complicated, sensitive letters to politicians and businessmen. It's also rumoured she wants to attend university but I don't know whether that's true. Somehow I find difficult to believe her father would allow it. He intends her to marry well and by that I mean to a suitably rich, well-positioned man who moves in the highest social circles. You don't fit the bill.'

'Really?'

'Really. Don't even think about it.'

'What did you say her name was?'

'Maria Eduarda.'

'Lovely name. It's musical.'

'Forget it, Casanova. She's not for you.'

'Tell me about the Duke and his first two wives. What happened to this exquisite creature's mother?'

'At the time it was a bit of a scandal. Ludovico – that's the Duke's Christian name – was a bon-vivant, actually a bit of a libertine, according to gossip. He went around with lots of different women, spending his father's money in trips abroad, hunting in Alentejo, gambling at casinos, lavish parties, dinners, etc. Then the old Duke died when Ludovico had just turned thirty and was still unmarried. There are no other siblings and so he inherited the title and all the immense fortune. At the time their coffee plantation in the Island of Fogo in Cape Verde was struggling, as most of it was very old-fashioned. Ludovico decided to sail there and sort it out. He stayed for several months and while there met Gabriela, an Afro-Portuguese beauty, native of the islands, daughter of his coffee plantation steward and a

Portuguese woman. He fell in love with her and asked her to marry him. She accepted.'

'So, that's why the adorable Maria Eduarda looks so unusually exotic.'

'Yes. Her mother, though half Portuguese, half Cape Verdean, was a typical beauty of the islands. Elegant, graceful, with green eyes. Cape Verde's natives are often attractive in an unusual way. They tend to be tall, slim, and remarkable for blacks they sometimes have light coloured eyes – blue or green.'

'Well, Maria Eduarda certainly fits the bill. Dark velvet skin with grass-green eyes. She positively glows.'

'She does, but I've told you to keep your fingers off her. Anyway, resuming the story, Ludovico returned to Portugal already married to Maria Eduarda's mother. It was a scandal.'

'Because she was black?'

'No, because she was merely the steward's daughter, an employee, and Ludovico was the new Duke of Beja and immensely rich. As I said, he's an only child and so his mother, the dowager duchess, couldn't forgive him. She retired to their Alentejo estate where she died ten years later without having seen her son again or meeting her granddaughter.'

'My goodness. Harsh.'

Bristow shrugged. 'I suppose. Maria Eduarda was born in 1920.'

'So, she's twenty now.'

'Not quite. She'll be in September. Poor girl never met her mother. She died giving birth to her.'

'A sad story.'

Bristow nodded in agreement. 'Ludovico has had his fair share of tragedy. He was devastated when Gabriela died. Apparently he loved her deeply and, for a long time, didn't want to meet other women or frequent his usual social circles, hiding away in his Sintra mansion with the little girl and his staff. Eventually he began recovering from his loss and in 1929, at forty, met and married the youngest daughter of a financier from the north – a woman called Maria Isabel who was only twenty-four. With her, in 1930, he had a son who tragically died of polio at the age of only six. In 1933 there was another baby but sadly still-born. For a while there were no other children but in 1936, shortly after the boy's death, Isabel got pregnant again and gave birth to another girl, Ana Maria who's not yet five, which's why she isn't here. But the tragedy didn't end with the death of the boy. In 1937, Isabel became ill with cancer. She died a year later in the summer of 1938.'

'Christ! I take it the current wife is recent?'

'Yes. They only got married two months ago, late April.'

'Presumably the Duke wants more children?'

'I don't know. Rosa Delgado is certainly young enough. I imagine children will come when they've been married for longer.'

'How do you know all this, Bristow?'

'I make it my business to know things.'

Gerald couldn't take his eyes off Maria Eduarda. She had a neck like a swan, wore diamond and sapphire earrings with matching stones, shaped like little flowers, on her cleverly pulled up hair, beautifully contrasting with its black colour. Her skin had a bronze gleam. It made her positively sparkle in the lights of the room, outshining her jewels. The blue satin of her dress shimmered, enhancing the overall impression that she radiated light. She glided past him and as she did, perhaps sensing his admiring gaze, glanced his way, briefly blinking. He felt the intense grass-green of her eyes and noticed the long, dark eyelashes touching her cheeks like a fine caress. She was dazzling, exquisitely beautiful, moving with the elegance and grace of a ballet dancer. Gerald felt like a fish hooked by an angler's rod and unable to escape. He sensed he wanted to possess such a treasure. Maria Eduarda. What a lovely name. Something occurred to him.

'Bristow,' he said, 'what's with all these Marias? All the women and girls in the Duke of Beja's family seem to have Maria as part of their Christian names.'

His friend grinned. 'It's the fashion in Portugal. It has to do with religion. Portugal in general and the Duke in particular profess Catholicism. Maria is the name of the Virgin, Jesus's mother, so it's the prevailing taste that all girls should be named Maria something or something Maria. Some of the men also have the name Maria but as a second Christian name. For example, Ludovico's boy who died of polio, was called Manuel Maria.'

'I see. Interesting even if a little weird.'

Bristow shrugged then elbowed him on the side.

'Hey! That hurts,' Gerald protested.

'Stop staring at her.'

'Who?'

'Maria Eduarda. You haven't stopped looking at her since she arrived. People will notice. She's not for you.'

'I've got to meet her,' Gerald declared, ignoring Bristow's words of warning, 'come. Introduce me.'

'No. Besides even if I wanted to, I can't. I'm not on those terms with the Duke.'

'Who could introduce me then?'

'Sir Ronald or our host but—'

'Brilliant,' Gerald cut in with a friendly slap on Bristow's shoulder. Without another word he walked towards the British ambassador who was still talking to the Duke of Windsor. The Duchess had joined them. He noticed the Duke of Beja was heading that way with his wife and his charming, lovable daughter.

Gerald caught Sir Ronald's eye. Continuing to speak the ambassador made him a sign to approach. Over the moon he had to stop himself from running.

'I'd like to introduce my new personal secretary, Gerald Neale, to you, Your Grace.'

Gerald bowed to the Duchess and she acknowledged him with a graceful nod. From his peripheral vision Gerald noticed the Duke of Beja arriving at their side with his wife and daughter. He respectfully greeted the Windsors and then the ambassador. Sir Ronald placed a friendly hand on Gerald's shoulder and addressing the Duke of Beja said, 'Ludovico, my dear friend, may I please introduce my new private secretary, Gerald Neale. Gerald, this is His Grace, the Duke of Beja, Her Grace Rosa Delgado, his wife, and Lady Maria Eduarda, his daughter.'

Obliged to follow etiquette, he had to greet the Duke and his wife first. The Duke's handshake was firm. Gerald bowed his head, barely kissing the duchess's hand. Finally he turned to Maria Eduarda, resting his lips on her gloved fingers a nanosecond too long. They all chatted amiably for a while, making polite conversation. Gerald had difficulty taking his gaze from Maria Eduarda's almost spellbinding eyes. Later that night, alone in his bed, unable to sleep and conjuring the image of her exquisite face he wouldn't remember anything said during those moments.

A couple of minutes later the butler announced loud and clear that dinner was served. Ricardo Espirito Santo approached with his wife on his arm to escort the guests of honour to the dining room. His wife led the way with the Duke of Windsor, Ricardo behind her with the Duchess, followed by the British ambassador and his wife. To Gerald's complete delight the Duke of Beja addressed him, 'Mr Neale, would you be so kind as to escort my daughter to the dining-room please?'

'Nothing would give me more pleasure, Your Grace,' Gerald replied.

Maria Eduarda opened her lips in a lovely, dimpled smile. It lit up her face, unknowingly sending a dart straight into Gerald's heart. Gently she placed her gloved hand on his arm, barely touching it. Gerald's chest swelled. In passing he caught Bristow's eye who grinned and shook his head, possibly wondering how he'd managed to be introduced to Maria Eduarda so quickly.

Chapter 4 – Dinner

The butler directed the guests to their places. It was a large dining-room with a white and grey marble floor. Obviously not the family's but the official dining-room for formal dinners such as the present. There were large windows facing the front of the house and the drawn curtains were red velvet too. The room was a little stuffy. Gerald noticed Espirito Santo making a sign to the waiters who disappeared behind the curtains to open the windows. Five round tables were covered in immaculately starched white tablecloths, glittering crystal glasses, blue and white Vista Alegre[10] fine china, silver cutlery and a centre piece with fresh red roses. The hosts led the way to the table in the centre of the room, which sat eight people; the other four arranged in an even circle around it sat six people each. Ricardo Espirito Santo pulled the chair for the Duchess of Windsor, then to his own wife. The British ambassador and the Duke of Beja did the same for their ladies. The three men waited until the Duke of Windsor had taken his place next to the Duchess. Ricardo Espirito Santo then sat down and the other two followed him.

Gerald led Maria Eduarda to the table indicated by the butler. He quickly scanned the name place cards and having found hers pulled the chair to help her sit. He was ecstatic to realise his seat was next to her on her right-hand side. Taking his place he began frantically thinking what topic of conversation to tackle in order to get to know her better. She was a vision and he wanted to enjoy her company to the full. He remembered Bristow's words that she was intelligent, well educated, cultivated, and spoke several languages. He couldn't adopt his regular lines that he used to charm and flatter the women he desired and wanted to pick up. Maria Eduarda had class, style, elegance and stood head and shoulders above the girls he normally chatted up. Talking about the weather would probably bore her; besides his former nanny had told him people in Portugal didn't generally talk about the weather, not like the

---

[10] Portugal's oldest and most prestigious factory of fine porcelain.

British, possibly because more often than not the weather was good. He remembered the drive earlier with Bristow in the embassy's car. The monuments in Belém had made him think of Camões and The Lusiads epic poem. As a waiter came with a cold tomato soup, called gaspacho alentejano, suitable for the summer heat, and another served the wine and water, Gerald leaned towards her and asked in Portuguese, 'do you enjoy poetry, Lady Maria Eduarda?'

'I do,' she replied graciously, then added, 'I didn't realise you spoke Portuguese, Mr Neale. We can speak in English if you prefer.'

Her voice was soft, slightly husky. He thought of velvet. Then shaking his head he replied to her offer courteously, 'no. I love your language and I'm very happy to speak it.'

She nodded, then asked him, 'do you enjoy poetry, Mr Neale?'

'Oh yes, very much,' he paused, considering what to say next that would capture her attention, then added, 'on the drive from Lisbon over here, earlier today, we passed Belém…do you know it?'

'Yes, I know the area well.'

'As I saw the Jerónimos Monastery and the Tower of Belém, I suddenly remembered that the Praia do Restelo is there too. Ships used to anchor and depart from there and I recalled an episode in The Lusiads that is set th—'

With glittering eyes she interrupted him, 'the episode with the old man from Belém – O Velho do Restelo.'

'You know it?'

'Of course, it's in Chant IV and begins in Stanza 94. It's when Vasco da Gama's ships are about to sail and the crews are waving everyone goodbye. An elder, a venerable old man, raises his voice and expresses his opposition to the trip to get to India by sea. His speech can be interpreted as the survival of the feudal, agrarian mentality, as opposed to expansionism and navigation – then the modern views of the bourgeoisie and the monarchy. What the old man says is the strict expression of conservatism. It's fascinating because the poem is an epic to exalt the great navigations of the Portuguese, yet Camões also gives voice to those who opposed the programme of expansion. O Velho do Restelo represents the opposition, meaning the past versus the present and the old versus the new. The old man calls to those who decide to go on the overseas adventures because he believes they will regret it. According to him, they depart on these voyages out of greed or longing for glory, wanting to prove their audacity or courage. The old man symbolises the concern of those who foresaw a dark future for Portugal.'

'Impressive. You've obviously read and studied The Lusiads.'

'Naturally. I'm Portuguese, have a love of poetry in general and Luis de Camões in particular. It's no surprise I've studied the poet and his work. What I think is impressive, Mr Neale, is that you, a young Englishman, appear to have read The Lusiads too and presumably in the original Portuguese.'

He could almost have jumped for joy. Poetry and Camões seemed to have struck a chord. Delighted Gerald said, 'as I told you I love the language and so I tried to read as many Portuguese authors and poets in the original as I could before coming to Portugal.'

'Is it because of your knowledge of Portuguese that you obtained the job as Sir Ronald's private secretary?'

'To a certain extent but I have other skills.'

'Undoubtedly,' she smiled.

'What's your favourite part of The Lusiads?'

'All of it, I think. I love it but if I should choose one then perhaps, the episode of Pedro and Inês[11].'

'Ah, aquela que depois de ser morta foi Rainha,' he quietly recited, 'the one that after death became Queen.'

'Yes. I think those verses particularly beautiful.'

'Romantic too. Are you a romantic, Lady Maria Eduarda?'

'A little. No more than anyone else.'

She looked up. The grass-green eyes sparkled. He'd never

---

[11] See author's notes and bibliography for the story.

been so close to a girl like that. One day he must own so much beauty for himself alone.

'We have a precious edition of The Lusiads,' she was saying, 'perhaps if you ever come to Sintra with Sir Ronald, my father can show it to you.'

'Precious?'

'Yes. It's a first edition of the poem.'

'You mean from 1572?' Gerald was incredulous.

'Indeed, Mr Neale, and the real one, meaning where, on the first page with the title and name of the poet, the pelican – part of the decoration – is turned to the left from the point of view of the reader.'

'I don't quite understand, Lady Maria Eduarda. Do you mean to say that there's a different first edition?'

'Yes and no. It isn't really a first edition. But there is one other edition that appeared in the same year, 1572, where the pelican I mentioned is turned to the right from the reader's perspective. For many years there was controversy but there is no doubt anymore. Where the pelican looks left is the most perfect so it must be the edition overseen by the poet. The other was apparently done without his revision or permission. At present there are only five or six copies of that first edition – the pelican turned to the left – that we know of. My father owns one. It's been in the family for centuries.'

'Its value must be incalculable.'

'Possibly. I don't think Papa has ever had it valued. He also owns four pages of what is said to be part of Camões's original manuscript for The Lusiads, meaning pages of the manuscript he saved when the ship he travelled in sank and he was forced to swim to shore with only one arm, holding the other high above the water to save the manuscript.'

'Is that true?'

She shrugged and grinned, 'no one knows for sure. But you must admit it's a rather good story.'

'I agree. What about the pages your father owns?'

'Oh, no idea if they're real. Papa hasn't tried to find out. I'm not sure why. I certainly would. If our pages were proven to be authentic then we could also prove Camões saved the manuscript in the way I just described or very similar.'

'Perhaps. And...'

Gerald couldn't continue, as waiters came to take the soup bowls and bring the salads that would accompany the fish dish. White wine was poured into the glasses. As the waiters walked away Maria Eduarda asked him, 'tell me, Mr Neale, have you read anything else by Camões, the sonnets for example? I find them beautiful.'

'I've read a few,' he paused then added with a cheeky grin, 'I even know one by heart. The one describing love. To me the best definition there is of love. Would you like to hear it, my Lady?'

Without waiting for her reply Gerald began reciting the sonnet with his eyes fixed on her. Maria Eduarda lowered her gaze, appearing slightly uncomfortable. Perhaps he'd been too bold too early. He finished the poem in a hurry then said, 'I'm sorry. It's silly of me to just recite the whole sonnet.'

'It's all right,' she said graciously, then added, 'perhaps we should change the subject. So tell me, Mr Neale, where did you learn to speak Portuguese so well? You speak it accent free and, to be honest, I have never met an Englishman before who was even interested in learning the language.'

Flashing a smile he answered, 'I grew up bilingual. My father was a cultural attaché to the embassy in Lisbon for a few years. Then after my mother died, my brother was two and I still a baby, we went back to England but we took with us a Portuguese nanny – Maria Filomena or Mena, as we call her. A wonderful lady. She was more of a mother to us than a nanny; brought us up, my brother and I, and always spoke Portuguese with us.'

'I see. Interesting.'

'What languages do you speak, Lady Maria Eduarda?'

'French, English, German and Spanish.'

He was impressed. 'Fluently?'

She nodded with an innocent expression of visible pride.

'Fascinating. What other skills do you have, my Lady?'

'Nothing special,' she replied, lightly heaving her shoulders.

'I beg to differ. I've heard you're accomplished.'

'Maybe. I don't know, at least not in the real sense that people in general refer to when speaking about a woman's accomplishments. I love music. I play the piano and continue to study the instrument, music theory and singing. I adore reading, learning, studying. But I'm not very good with things that are supposed to be ladies' occupations – embroidery, crochet…that sort of thing. I don't like it much but I like languages and I prefer to read originals rather than translations. I also very much enjoy maths, physics and history.'

'Unusual subjects for a lady,' he commented.

'Perhaps. But I'm a modern woman, Mr Neale. I don't see why a woman can't be interested in subjects that are traditionally the realm of the male sex. I intend to go to university and study astronomy. For that I need maths and physics.'

Gerald stared, taken aback by her statement. She ate a bit from the salad, sipped some wine and just then the waiters brought the fish. They ate for a while in silence. Gerald wondered how he could impress Maria Eduarda. How to seduce her and make her his. Would she be interested in politics? He doubted but he might as well probe her for information. After all, his assignment was not only to find as much as possible about Ricardo Espirito Santo but also about Ludovico, Duke of Beja – both Salazar's personal friends and confidents. He decided to change the topic of conversation drastically.

'I'd hoped to meet Salazar here today,' he dropped, 'but he's not around. Do you know him, Lady Maria Eduarda?'

Having finished the fish and salad she delicately placed the cutlery on the plate before answering.

'Salazar seldom attends big social occasions,' she said, 'if this dinner were in honour of your prime minister or your king, he would have come.'

'So, you know him well.'

'No, not well. Ricardo, our host, and my father are his friends. I've met him a couple of times, mostly when he visited us in Sintra for the weekend. Two, three times at most. As you may imagine, his conversation wasn't with me but with my father. If he spoke to me at all it was during lunch or dinner and to make polite chat. Nothing more.'

'What do you think of him?'

Maria Eduarda remained quiet for a stretching moment. The waiters lifted the fish and salad dishes, brought sliced roasted meat, potatoes and vegetables, and served the red wine. She waited until they had moved on and Gerald didn't press her.

'Your government and your ambassador, Mr Neale, probably know a lot more about Salazar than I do myself.'

'I'd like to hear your personal opinion though,' he insisted.

She raised her eyebrows, blinking a couple of times, possibly surprised but after a moment of hesitation said, 'I think Salazar's a very astute politician and a rather intelligent man.'

Gerald nodded. No news there. 'Do you agree with his policies?' He asked, attempting to provoke her but Maria Eduarda remained calm and collected.

'I agree that his policy of neutrality for Portugal during this horrible war…is the right one.'

'Even if the Allies are trying to stop a mad man in Germany who has taken half of Europe and, we believe, has ordered atrocities and crimes?'

'Portugal's a very small, poor, slightly backward country, Mr Neale. We entered the Great War of 1914-18, which proved disastrous in every imaginable way. The only hope of a balanced economy and social stability is for Portugal to remain neutral.'

'So you think it's right Salazar is selling wolfram to the Germans – which ultimately prolongs the war – and receiving gold as payment when he must know that most of this gold was stolen by the Germans from Jews and other people they prosecute? And you also think it right that Salazar encourages people like our host and your father to do business both with the Germans and the Allies?'

'Mr Neale, there are many things Salazar does that I don't agree with.'

Gerald was about to interject but she stopped him with an imperious gesture of her hand.

'What I was going to say,' she resumed, 'is this: If a country intends to remain neutral then to do so it must carry on business with both sides otherwise there's no neutrality because it will support one side in favour of the other. It may not be right from your point of view but it's the best for Portugal.'

'Are you a Nazi sympathiser then?'

'No. Absolutely not,' her answer was indignant and sincere. Gerald believed her.

'What about your father and Espirito Santo?'

'I don't believe so. I think they're neutral, like the country.'

'And Salazar?'

'I've no idea. I don't presume to know his opinions or sympathies, Mr Neale,' she paused, then added, 'why are you shaking your head in obvious disapproval?'

'I just don't think it's possible to be one hundred percent neutral. They must feel more for one side than the other.'

'Perhaps. I don't know. But, anyway, Salazar only believes in himself and what he thinks is right for the country. As for my father and Ricardo, they certainly agree with Salazar in terms of neutrality. They may not agree with everything Salazar does or stands for but they wouldn't confide in me. My father isn't a Nazi sympathiser. His businesses follow what any good Portuguese must do and that's to be neutral. Ricardo isn't a Nazi sympathiser either. He's a good, kind man. A friend to my father, my own godfather and really like an uncle to us – me and my little sister. Like my father he follows the policy of neutrality and agrees with it; therefore does business with both sides. You may or may not know but Ricardo's wife, Maria, is Jewish and he's been personally, financially and actively helping many Jewish refugees, running away from France, Belgium and Germany. Do you think a Nazi would do that?'

'No, actually I don't but the Allies in general and the British in particular are angry with Salazar and his position. They think that Portugal, as Britain's oldest ally, should enter the war on our side or, at least, openly support us even though keeping its neutrality.'

'It may be so from your perspective. When has Britain ever behaved as our oldest ally unless it was for its own advantage?'

'We came to your aid during the Napoleonic Wars especially when Spain allied themselves with France and carried out the first invasion of Portugal, then later—'

'Yes, Mr Neale,' she interrupted him, visibly irritated, 'however, during that first invasion Britain didn't stop anything or help much. The Portuguese royal family still left for Brazil and the country was abandoned to its bad luck. Under the guise of protection Britain didn't interfere against the Treaty of Fontainebleau, signed between France and Spain, which divided Portugal into three principalities. Napoleon wanted to arrest the Portuguese royal family and force the prince regent of the time to abdicate. Then put a Bonaparte on the throne and create an alliance with Britain under which the British would be allowed to take possession of the Portuguese colonies.'

'Perhaps you're right, Lady Maria Eduarda, but in this war it's really important—'

'Important to whom?' she immediately interjected.

'Well, obviously—'

'To Britain of course. Not to Portugal. A neutral Portugal is the only way of saving the country from a repetition of the disaster that resulted from our participation in the Great War of 1914-18. Besides, why should Salazar trust the British government? The policy of appeasement towards Germany led by your prime minister, Neville Chamberlain, could have had bad consequences to us and Britain couldn't have cared less. Mr Chamberlain—'

'We've a different prime minister now,' he cut in, 'Winston Churchill is—'

But she didn't allow him to continue and interrupting him resumed, 'Mr Chamberlain, attempting to stop Hitler's aggression, offered parts of the Portuguese colonies in Africa to Germany *without* the consent of Lisbon.' She had deliberately stressed the word *without* and Gerald couldn't help but be stunned by her knowledge and her palpable outrage for Britain's dubious attitude. He wasn't sure how to oppose her view and defend his country. Before he could speak she resumed, 'it's more than enough to drive one up the wall. So why should we support you?'

Gerald remained silent for a moment, finally deciding it was best to leave the topic of the old alliance between Portugal and Britain. Her words were true. He couldn't deny the facts. Inhaling and exhaling deeply he then said, changing the subject slightly, 'but don't you think Salazar must worry that, should the Allies win, he'll have to return most of the gold received from Germany in payment for wolfram? The country will be punished with economic sanctions by the Allies.'

'I don't know what goes on in his mind, Mr Neale. I don't know him well, as I've already told you. However, I'm aware of Salazar's fears, quite rightly I may add, that Germany, aided willingly by Spain, will invade Portugal if we don't comply with the wolfram sales. So, not only is it important Portugal remains neutral, but it is also paramount that Spain does the same. The last thing we want is to lose our lovely little country to the Spanish with the help of the Germans. We've learned something from the succession crisis in the 16th century and then the twenty-year restauration war, after regaining independence from Spain in 1640...' she stopped talking for a moment, visibly trying to pull herself together and to calm down. After a short while she continued in a cooler tone, 'I don't agree with Salazar's policy of total control, censorship, secret police and lack of freedom. He's a dictator, a fascist if you will. I've no idea whether he's a Nazi but he definitely puts the country or what he thinks is best for the country first.' She went quiet as if gathering her thoughts. With a slightly wicked smile she added, 'besides, where the Allies are concerned Salazar has a trump card up his sleeve.'

'Oh. And what would that be?'

'The Azores.'

Gerald's jaw nearly dropped. How did she know so much? It was true the British were very keen to use the Azores as a military air base. Geographically speaking and even more so than Portugal mainland at the end of Europe, the Portuguese islands of the Azores were strategically placed in the middle of the Atlantic. Therefore important for the war effort and perhaps for whatever might happen if the Allies won the war.

'You're very well informed for a...' he stopped, slightly embarrassed.

'For a woman? Is that what you were going to say, Mr Neale?'

'Yes,' he confessed awkwardly, 'I must apologise, Lady Maria Eduarda.'

'No need. Most people have that type of reaction. It may be true of many women, Mr Neale, but I've got a brain, love to read and like being informed.'

She seemed amused. There was that mischievous smile again, making her look even more desirable if that was at all possible. He dried the perspiration off his forehead with his handkerchief. Suddenly, the room felt very hot.

'I...really...well, I must admit I'm impressed,' he told her with genuine admiration.

She ate a bit of meat and potato, then had a sip of wine. Lifting her long eyelashes she held his gaze and said, 'don't be. Information on any important or interesting subject shouldn't be the prerogative of the male sex.'

'You're right of course. I didn't mean to offend you.'

Placing her cutlery on the plate she replied gracefully, 'you didn't. I merely explained my thoughts. I respect yours. They're common among your sex independent from nationality, political views or religious beliefs.'

To Gerald's relief he didn't have to answer her comment. Espirito Santo stood up at that precise moment, asking his guests to make a toast in honour of the Duke and Duchess of Windsor. Obliged to follow his gesture and raise their glasses everyone said in unison, in what seemed like a well-rehearsed chorus, 'to the Duke and Duchess of Windsor.'

Chapter 5 – Maria Eduarda

Riding in the back of the limousine with her father and stepmother Maria Eduarda pretended to doze to avoid conversation, mentally reviewing the evening.

The dinner at the Boca do Inferno weekend home of Ricardo and Maria had ended well after midnight. Once coffee and petits-fours were served and finished, Ricardo stood up and took the men to a separate room where there was Port and cigars. Maria led the ladies to the music room where a magnificent grand piano stood in a corner.

Maria Eduarda guessed what would come. It wasn't long before Ricardo's wife asked her to play. She gladly obliged. It allowed her to be free of everyone and everything for an hour or so, present in the room but almost removed, quietly playing her favourite instrument and immersed in the music. Later, when the men returned from their Port and cigars, several bridge tables formed. The hosts and the Duke and Duchess of Windsor played at one table; the British ambassador and his wife, as well as her own father and stepmother at another. The other guests built groups and partnerships around the remaining tables.

Disliking card games Maria Eduarda quietly retired to a balcony to listen to the sound of the sea and admire the sky above it. The road where Ricardo's weekend home was located had no lights and what illumination escaped from the handful of houses was minimal. It meant the heavens were more spectacular than in Sintra. The vastness of the ocean allowing for the immense arch of the sky to showcase in all its glory. She lifted her eyes to the black-blue velvet heavens above. The immensity of the universe never ceased to amaze her. Like a child she followed the embroidered shapes of light with her finger. Wouldn't it be wonderful to walk away from the house, stroll along the dark ocean road leading to Cabo da Roca, and absorb herself in the limitless, soundless firmament, dotted with stars? The outward arm of the Milky Way was clearly visible. Its soft light playfully scintillating on the white crested waves below.

Maria Eduarda cherished the area where Ricardo's home

was located. She loved the darkness at night, the silence only broken by the crashing waves. It was still wild and remote. There weren't many such places left so close to a big city. She wondered whether it would last. She thought about Ricardo and Maria. She liked them very much, often feeling more comfortable with them than her father, especially now that he was smitten with his new wife. Her stepmother Rosa, only half a dozen years older than herself, was difficult to relate to. Odd to address her as step-mama but her father and Rosa both insisted that she must. Maria Eduarda would prefer to simply call her by her name. At that instant she sensed a movement. It distracted her thoughts. A person came to stand beside her. The young Englishman, her companion at dinner. He disturbed her peace but it didn't mean it was unwelcoming.

Her mind returned to the present inside the limousine. Her father's chauffeur drove slowly from Boca do Inferno back to the city. Eduarda enjoyed the drive, feeling comfortable in the darkness of the car, occasionally looking out its windows and admiring Lisbon by night. After dark the city appeared different. Peaceful. Bright but without the glare of the summer sun or the heat that rippled the air, distorting everything in the distance.

It was pleasant to be driven through Lisbon. Main roads and wealthy quarters were quiet. The city seemed deserted, ghost-like. It was different by the docks, the Rossio or the Avenida da Liberdade. Overcrowded night-clubs and bars burst with the current, mostly temporary, colourful population of refugees, prostitutes, sailors and foreign agents paying a king's ransom for a useless piece of information. Locals sold them "top secret, genuine" British or German intelligence, as the case might be, depending on where the operative came from.

Maria Eduarda and her family arrived late at their Lisbon house in the upper-class area of Lapa. A church clock struck four in the morning. She wished her father and stepmother good night, immediately retiring to her room, not due to fatigue but because she wanted to be alone. To remember. To reflect. To try to understand the young Englishman. Gerald Neale, his name was. Stubbornly the image of his handsome face refused to vanish from her head. The careless tuft of blonde hair, almost white, falling lightly on his forehead, the bright blue eyes, the sensual mouth and the cheeky-boy smile. He was tall, fit and elegant. Must practise different sports, she thought. He filled the dinner jacket as if born to wear it. She didn't know many men who looked so good in evening wear but then she didn't know many men as handsome as this Mr Neale.

Maria Eduarda opened her bedroom window and looked out over the roofs of Lisbon, wishing she were in Sintra. The heavens above the village and its surroundings were very dark, enabling her to clearly see and identify the constellations almost as at Boca do Inferno. She missed Sintra and their house, its beautiful grounds, the garden and the woods. The horses. Her morning rides. Her father's dogs and her little sister's cats. The buzz of the city wasn't her thing. Although the drive from Boca do Inferno went mostly through quiet places, once they had arrived in Lisbon's city centre the silence was gone though deep in thought inside the car she had hardly registered a sound. The smart area of Lapa was quieter than the heart of the city but with the window ajar all noises rushed through the air to her ears. She detected the rattle of the trolley-trams and the screech of tyres from the many taxis criss-crossing the city at night. During the day their house offered superb views of the river, supported unfortunately by the continuous grinding of metal from the cranes, or the screaming sirens and ships' horns rising from the busy docks at the bottom of the hill. Now, in the middle of the night, there was a hubbub of different noises. Dogs barking. Cats fighting. Roosters crowing. In Sintra the silence was complete. The darkness immersive. Here she couldn't even see the stars properly. Too much brightness from the white streetlights and the multi-coloured neon advertising signs.

Maria Eduarda exhaled in slight frustration but did not withdraw from the window. Her mind wandered back to the handsome, young Englishman. Denying he'd caused an impression would be a lie. He spoke perfect, accent-free Portuguese. The first time she'd met an Englishman able to speak her language with such a degree of proficiency. But it was his interest in Portugal's culture and poetry in general and Camões in particular that had captivated her. Whenever she remembered him reciting Camões' sonnet of love, his eyes telling her things she didn't dare think, goosebumps rose, making her shiver. It had embarrassed and thrilled her in equal measure. Nonetheless something about him slightly irritated her. Was Gerald Neale a spy? His questions about Ricardo and Portuguese politics, especially his implicit criticism, had infuriated her. Who was he to judge? What right did he have to criticise Portugal when Britain had often behaved in a less than honourable manner?

On the other hand, she wasn't indifferent to his good looks but what did his flirtation mean? A tactic to achieve an end? He had clearly attempted to gain information from her once he realised her knowledge of politics and history. Eduarda often sat with her father and Ricardo when they were talking business. She frequently helped Papa with letter writing or to crush numbers, knowing more than most of the family or some of the employees. Papa didn't enjoy doing any of it and preferred her eloquent writing style to his own. But, and although Papa and Ricardo allowed her to participate in their conversations, sometimes even requesting her opinion, they would send her out of the room as soon as there was a confidential topic to discuss. So, unknown to Mr Neale, she wouldn't be of any use to him if he were searching for secret information.

He was extremely attractive, engaging and a good conversationalist but could she trust him? His attentiveness, his open admiration and boldness appealed to her but Maria Eduarda was used to men's attentions and aware of a queue of admirers, hoping she'd pick one of them as her husband. Her father shared the same hope but she had no interest in marriage. At least not yet. Like her mother, Gabriela, Eduarda was conscious of her beauty but took it naturally. She'd been born that way. Wasn't ashamed of it and didn't care whether people were jealous or envious. She strongly resembled her mother whom she knew only from black and white photographs, and grandmama Leopoldina's tales. She owned the same high cheek bones, the same grass-green eyes, the same full lips, the same graceful walk and elegance as her mother.

Sadness briefly shadowed her face. Sometimes she couldn't help but feel guilty. Mama had died giving birth to her. She missed her grandmother. If she were here they could talk. She also wished Isabel were still alive. Her previous stepmother had been a calm, tolerant woman, inviting confidence. Maria Eduarda had always felt at ease talking to her about anything, even intimate matters. Speaking with Isabel had been a natural action but Rosa, his father's present wife, was too young. Eduarda felt awkward and couldn't see her as a mother figure. She sensed Rosa's similar feelings toward herself. It was different with Ana Maria, her little sister. Easier to relate to a four-year old child than to a young woman when one was only six years older than the stepdaughter.

Maria Eduarda's thoughts returned to Gerald Neale, recalling their conversation at dinner and especially his words later, after he had joined her on the balcony. Stepping out and drawing the curtain behind him he had said, 'I thought you'd gone home, Lady Maria Eduarda.'

'No. I wish I had but no such luck. Papa won't go until the party's ended. But I've done my bit. Played the piano as requested. I don't enjoy card games so came out here to wait until my father and Rosa are ready to return home.'

'I heard you play.'

'You did?' she exclaimed, genuinely startled.

He nodded. 'You play beautifully.'

'Kind of you to say so. But how could you hear me if you were in the smoking room with the other men?'

'Oh but I wasn't. I kept my cigar for later,' he tapped his jacket pocket, 'took my Port and stood quietly by the door to the music salon. I saw and listened to your performance. You're outstanding. Have you ever thought about pursuing a career in music as a pianist?'

'Oh, really, Mr Neale, you flatter me. I play well, yes, but I know my skill is not good enough for that.'

'Don't be so modest.'

'I'm not. I'm just being honest.'

After a moment of silence, he asked her, 'why're you really out here all alone?'

She gazed up and pointed at the sky. 'That.'

'The stars?'

'In general. I love watching the skies, identifying the constellations, admiring the beauty of the Milky Way when it's visible from March to September. The summer is a good time to admire it when the nights are clear and dark, as is the case here today. Have you ever seen anything as beautiful as the Milky Way stretching across the night sky, its soft light twinkling and dancing in the waves to the calming music of the ocean?'

He seemed entranced at her words and touched her arm above the glove. She felt his fingers on her skin, sending a shiver down her spine, forcing her to give one short step to the side, putting more air between them.

'That's wonderful.'

'What? The sky?'

'Well, yes, but I meant what you just said.'

She had smiled but kept silent. It was better not to encourage him. He remained by her side, quietly watching the night. It was lovely and tepid. The stars invited confidence and romance. She remembered thinking perhaps it was prudent to go back inside but before she could suggest it he asked her, 'did you really mean what you said at dinner?'

'About what?'

'Studying astronomy.'

'Absolutely. I'm having trouble convincing my father but I'll get there and once I'm twenty-one I'll be of age and he can't stop me.'

'Why doesn't he want you to study?'

'My father's a religious old-fashioned man. He wants me to marry well and doesn't understand my desire for knowledge and learning. If I were a man it would be fine but, as a woman, he has other ideas for me.'

'Wanting you to marry well is nothing unusual for a father to wish for his daughter.'

'I never said it was.'

He had put his hands on her shoulders. She felt the heat of his palms through the silky material of her dress.

'Don't you wish to get married?' He asked her.

'I didn't say that either. Probably one day, maybe...yes. If I find a man worth it, I'll think of marriage...but not now. I'm young and I want to make my dreams come true.'

'And astronomy is one of them.'

'Precisely.'

He had then grabbed her hand, pulled off her glove, turned her palm up and placed a long kiss on it, gazing into her eyes, making her tremble. His lips burnt her skin. Attraction sailed through her body. Maria Eduarda was flustered, not knowing how to react. She tried to withdraw her hand but he held it firmly and whispered, 'you're an exquisitely beautiful and fascinating woman, Lady Maria Eduarda.'

At that moment she had decided to stop him before he tried to kiss her.

'We must go back in,' she said, averting her eyes from his.

He had remained quiet and simply nodded, following her into the room. Standing by one of the bridge tables, as if following the game, he had continued to look at her with an admiring gaze but Maria Eduarda thought his eyes betrayed more. Playful lust perhaps. A definite desire to at least hold and kiss her...and more, much more than that.

Yes, she told herself quietly, watching over the roofs of Lisbon, Gerald Neale was attracted to her and had openly flirted. She knew what he wanted. Although a virgin Maria Eduarda wasn't an ingenue. From the moment she became a woman, her maternal grandmother opened her eyes to the world of men, teaching her to be careful.

Grandmother Leopoldina was an unusual, determined, courageous woman and Eduarda loved, admired and looked up to her as an example of the person she wanted to become. Leopoldina had been a governess to the girls of the Count of Tomar, a personal friend of Maria Eduarda's paternal grandfather, Lionel Maria, then Duke of Beja and whom she'd never met. After a visit to his coffee plantation in the Island of Fogo, he brought with him to Portugal the talented son of one of his Cape Verdean employees, to give the young man a proper education and prepare him to be his next steward. Lionel was firmly convinced that the plantation would run smoother if he had a native in charge rather than sending someone from Portugal mainland.

Daniel do Livramento, Maria Eduarda's maternal grandfather, had been a handsome man. He and Leopoldina fell in love. Once his education was complete he returned to Cabo Verde to take over the job as steward. Deeply in love, Leopoldina followed him shortly after. She travelled alone on a ship to a place she'd never been to meet the man she was in love with. For a woman at the time it was highly unconventional behaviour. Leopoldina and Daniel married soon after her arrival. She was well accepted by her husband's family but her own parents in Portugal were disappointed with her choice. Departing for one of the Portuguese colonies to marry a native and leaving all her family behind was unheard of. But Leopoldina wasn't moved by social conventions or people's opinions.

Daniel and Leopoldina led a happy marriage. Sadly, out of the four children they had together only Gabriela had survived to adulthood. They were proud when she married Ludovico and became the next duchess, only to be devastated when three years later, she died in childbirth. Grandmama Leopoldina became a widow when Eduarda was two years old. For a time she moved back to Portugal, living in Ludovico's home and looking after her granddaughter. Missing the place where she had known happiness Leopoldina had returned to Cabo Verde four years earlier when Maria Eduarda was fifteen, having had plenty of time to instil her granddaughter with strong views and a love of nature, music and learning.

Maria Eduarda had been brought up believing in herself. Her grandmother taught her to naturally accept her uncommon beauty in a world of mostly white people. Her head was filled with tales of the islands of Cabo Verde and the wondrous sky above Ilha do Fogo where the plantation was located. Once

Grandmama returned to Cape Verde Eduarda visited a few times, accompanied by her governess but now, with the war, it was more difficult. Her consolation being the letters they wrote each other. Eduarda had learned from her grandmother to be careful where the opposite sex was concerned and to not have her head easily turned.

'Now you've had your first period, darling,' Leopoldina had told her when she was thirteen, 'and have become a woman you must beware of men, especially white men.'

'But Papa is white and so are you,' she remembered saying, bewildered at her grandmother's words.

'Well, I'm a woman and your father is different. He was truly and deeply in love with your mother and didn't hesitate to marry her, much to the dowager duchess's disgust. When my Gabriela died, Ludovico was devastated. It was difficult for him to bring up a girl on his own so I came. But anyway, my darling, like your mother, you are a beauty, an exotic beauty. Men in general will want to seduce you and white men in particular because of your exoticism. Most men only want one thing, which is to take a girl to bed. They worry about nothing but their enjoyment. That's why you must take great care. If a man seduces you and turns your head enough for you to accept him and go all the way, you may get pregnant. And then what? Your life will be destroyed but he can just walk away and carry on.'

'Surely not all men are like that, Grandmama?'

'No, my love, of course not. Your father and your grandfather. Naturally, many other men are decent too. These are words of caution because you'll have men swarming all around you like flies over a jar of honey. I want you to be careful, discerning and not allow yourself to be taken easily.'

A faint line opened up her lips. Eduarda remembered hugging her grandmother, promising to take great care and be suspicious of any man's intentions first before believing their words. With these thoughts revolving in her mind she knew better than to trust Gerald Neale's attentions and flirtation at Ricardo's dinner.

Chapter 6 – Gerald

He watched the first colours of dawn spreading across the sky, glimpsing them through the open window of his bedroom at the embassy. Tossing and turning all night, unable to get a wink of sleep his head was filled with images of Maria Eduarda's face.

'I must have her. What am I to do?'

Gerald startled himself. He had unintentionally spoken the question out loud. Placing his pillow behind his back he pulled himself up and sat leaning against the bed's headboard. He reached for cigarettes and matchbox on the side table and lit one. The smoke spiralled leisurely towards the ceiling. It was just after six in the morning but in spite of the open window the room was hot. He lay on the bed wearing only underpants, unable to endure the bedlinen on his body. The thermometer would almost certainly leap above forty degrees centigrade today. At least it was Sunday and he didn't need to work.

Eyes shut he invoked memories of the previous evening's moments with Maria Eduarda. He remembered their conversation at dinner and especially later, on the balcony, admiring the starlit sky and its reflection on the ocean surface below. How could he impress a girl like that? And he truly wanted to impress her. To seduce her. He craved those lips, the long neck. Wanted to dive into those eyes. But how? She wasn't an average girl. She was a well-educated lady, the eldest daughter of a duke, himself a personal friend of the two most influential men in Portugal. Opening his eyes Gerald expelled the cigarette's smoke through his nose and unwittingly he recalled Bristow's words, 'take your sight and hands off her. She's out of your league, old boy.'

Bristow was right. Maria Eduarda was way above his league but he couldn't stop thinking about her. One evening and he was hooked. He wanted to enjoy that divine creature. But how? He would have to marry her. A girl like that could only be taken through marriage. Exactly what he didn't fancy.

With a degree of irritation Gerald crushed the cigarette in the ashtray. What would a girl like Maria Eduarda expect from him after last evening's extensive conversation and his kiss on her hand? Surely nothing. She was probably deeply asleep in her comfortable bed – a peaceful, innocent, dreamless sleep. He didn't even fit in her thoughts. Nonetheless, goosebumps had mottled her skin when his fingers touched her arm above her elbow, deliberately searching for the naked skin beyond the edge of her long gloves. But perhaps she had been cold. Nonsense. The night was warm. Later he sensed the light tremor when he had removed her glove and kissed her hand in the intimate darkness of the balcony. Or was it his imagination? His wishful thinking that she hadn't been indifferent to his charms?

Bristow had told him the Duke of Beja's Lisbon house wasn't far from the British embassy. Perhaps he could find it and walk in front of it until he saw her. No. That was stupid. He could write her a letter and state he'd like to see her again. Invite her for dinner or something but a girl like Maria Eduarda would politely say no. Perhaps he could send her flowers, thanking her for the wonderful conversation and companionship last night. Would she expect such an action? He felt certain she wouldn't. But it was better not to turn up at her door. The flowers should be delivered with his card, written by hand. For that he needed the address. How to obtain it without raising suspicion? Not from Bristow for sure. He would just tell him again to leave Maria Eduarda alone. Gerald thought about Mr Jackson. He could ask him. The embassy's butler seemed to know everything and everyone within a ten-mile radius.

Gerald jumped out of bed to fling himself into action only to stop dead. It was pretty early on a Sunday morning. Even if he could catch up with Mr Jackson it'd be impossible to find an open florist to deliver his flowers. It would have to be tomorrow. Monday. The city would be back to normal. Catching a glimpse of himself in the mirror he didn't like his image. Perhaps a bath was a good idea and then out, walk towards the river or catch a train to the beaches in Estoril. He could swim in the sea. An attractive notion in this heat. What about a hop to the casino? No, not during the day. Another time. Next Saturday, if no other plans, or any other evening during the week. After all it was part of his job to monitor foreign agents, German spies and refugees at the glamorous casino. Stretching and yawning Gerald walked to the bathroom and turned on the cold and hot water taps.

Concentrating on her music at the piano Maria Eduarda didn't hear the soft knock on the door until the person's third attempt.
'Come in.'
The housekeeper, Lucinda, opened the door with a wide smile, carrying a big bunch of flowers. She moved around with the confidence of someone growing old with the house, searching for a glass or crystal container. After finding a suitable vase she walked to the piano and presenting Maria Eduarda with the flowers said with a wink and a slightly cheeky grin, 'whose heart did you break, my dear, on Saturday evening at Mr Espirito Santo's house?'
Maria Eduarda shook her head and parted her lips amused. Lucinda had been her father's housekeeper for as long as she could remember, had carried her as a baby, given her the bottle, fed her, encouraged and guided her first wobbly steps as a toddler, and put her to sleep, telling her stories. No-one else in the domestic staff would dare to address anyone in the family with such familiarity but Lucinda was an exception. She was nearly fifty-seven but showed no signs of slowing down. Always energetic and electrically overcharged, as Maria Eduarda liked to say, Lucinda was an integral part of the Duke's household. Nothing ran without her saying so and even Pereira, the head butler, wouldn't dare take action about anything without consulting Lucinda first.
'These flowers have just been delivered for you, my dear,' Lucinda told her and, lifting her eyebrows, added with a mischievous smile, 'there's a card.'
Maria Eduarda accepted the bouquet of beautiful red, white and pink roses. More than a dozen. She extracted the little card from the envelope attached to the flowers and read it. Her heart leaped a beat. She swallowed her embarrassment.
'Who's it from, my love?' Lucinda asked, standing in front of her with the vase.
'Just a kind Englishman I met at Ricardo's dinner. He's

the new private secretary of the British ambassador and happened to sit next to me.'

'Aha. An English gentleman. You broke his heart, just as I thought.'

'Don't be silly, Lucinda,' Eduarda said with a laugh, 'he's just being kind and attentive, thanking me for a stimulating, pleasant conversation.'

'Well, well, well. Stimulating, pleasant conversation…of course.'

'What are you implying?'

'Nothing, my dear. Where would you like me to place the flowers? Your bedroom?'

'No. Just leave them here, perhaps on the mantelpiece.'

Lucinda nodded and left the room, returning shortly after with the vase full of water in which she expertly arranged the roses.

'There you go, my love. Now just carry on with your playing,' Lucinda said over her shoulder while walking out of the room.

She left, closing the door behind her. Maria Eduarda opened the little card to read it a second time.

Good morning my lady of the wondrous green eyes, thank you for your interesting conversation at Espirito Santo's dinner. I hope you will enjoy my roses as much as I enjoyed your company. Respectfully, Gerald Neale

It was a nice gesture, the flowers. But what did he want to achieve? Were the roses the first step in a well delineated plan to approach her? To seduce her? And if he succeeded, then what? Would he propose? And did she want it?

Maria Eduarda decided it was appropriate and better for her peace of mind to give him the cold shoulder. For the time being. She could revisit her decision later. If needed. A sensible move, avoiding potential embarrassment or awkwardness. In a week they would move to Sintra for most of the summer and she wouldn't see Mr Neale for some time. Exhaling, Eduarda dropped the card in the wastepaper basket next to the piano and resumed playing. She was practising Schubert's Impromptus, involving a lot of hard work and her full concentration.

Chapter 7 – Three Days Later

Gerald stopped at the bottom of the hill and wiped his face with a handkerchief before initiating the climb. Not quite ten in the morning and the heat already unbearable. For the last few days the thermometer had consistently reached well above forty degrees Celsius during the day. Gerald had taken off his jacket a while ago, carrying it on his arm. Now he removed his tie and unbuttoned the top of his shirt. His body wasn't used to this kind of temperature and had difficulty coping. He felt exhausted from the unrelenting hot weather and for other reasons. A night at the casino, shadowing in vain the exchange between a German agent and two minor Portuguese government officials added to it. Nothing had emerged that the British secret service didn't already know. Gerald had taken a train from Estoril back to Rossio and headed to the docks to meet with an informant. A pointless exercise. The said informant was as useless as a chocolate teapot. The man had talked for hours, but after analysing the information Gerald was left with nothing. He was now returning home, feeling frustrated and grumpy. A walk might clear his head and put him in a better mood, or so he thought before starting out. It had seemed like a good idea down by the docks. On the riverbank it didn't feel so hot. Cursing the moment he'd decided to walk all the way Gerald wiped his face for the second time. He'd kill for a glass of cold water.

Looking up he roughly measured the distance and time it would take him to reach his quarters at the British embassy. Another ten minutes if he walked briskly, longer if at a moderate pace – the best option in the heat. He thought about the welcoming coolness inside the embassy and dreamed of a glass of iced lemonade in the shade of the garden trees. His tongue almost dropped out of his mouth with longing. Exhaling deeply he resumed walking. Just then, in the distance, he noticed a woman coming slowly down the hill on the same side of the street as himself. She was at least two, maybe three hundred yards away but he recognised her immediately.

Maria Eduarda glided, looking fresh and carefree,

carrying a small handbag and a large black folder. She was glancing around at trees, gardens and the pretty house façades and didn't notice him until he was nearly upon her.

'Good morning, Lady Maria Eduarda,' he greeted.

She started at the sound of his voice. He watched her quietly, detecting the surprise in her eyes. She wore a light, short-sleeved, white dress with tiny, printed blue and red daisies. Flat white sandals, no socks, no stockings, no gloves, no make-up but still she looked beautiful. Her unruly black curls and twirls fell down to her shoulders, pulled up on one side with a white hairclip. Tiny pearl earrings enhanced her lovely face. She seemed well prepared for the heat, unlike himself, and wasn't even breaking a sweat.

'Mr Neale,' she exclaimed, visibly astonished to see him, 'good morning. What are you doing here?'

'I could ask you the same.'

'Well, I live here. The house at the top of the hill.'

'And the British embassy is just there,' he pointed.

'Oh, of course. I didn't remember that.'

She smiled, appearing a little embarrassed. Those perky little dimples formed each side of her mouth. He wanted to kiss them.

'Did you receive my roses last Monday?' he enquired instead, wondering whether she had. No thank you note came his way, as good social etiquette dictated, but perhaps she had no idea where to send it.

'Yes, Mr Neale, I did. Thank you,' she paused, appearing to hesitate but then added, 'forgive me for not having already thanked you but I was busy and it slipped my mind. In any case, it was very thoughtful of you to send me flowers. Totally unnecessary of course but kind and courteous nonetheless.'

'I'm glad you liked them. May I ask where you're heading burdened like that?' He indicated the large black folder with his head.

'You may and I'm going to my music lesson. My teacher lives only a few minutes away.'

Impulsively he blurted, 'would you have a coffee with me

at the Chave d'Ouro in Rossio after your lesson?'

She seemed to hesitate, then replied, 'the lesson lasts until half past eleven. Afterward I have some errands to run and need to be home by one o'clock for lunch with my family.'

'I could help you with your errands.'

'No need, thank you. I'm only visiting an old friend and…well, getting some books.'

'From the library?'

'What is this, Mr Neale? The Holy Inquisition?' She looked serious but her tone was amused.

'I'm sorry,' he said, 'it's just…well, I find you interesting. I enjoyed our conversation last Saturday at Mr Espirito Santo's home. And the truth is…' he paused, wondering whether to continue.

She stared at him inquisitively, then prodded him gently, 'the truth is?'

'The truth is I'd like to know you better.'

'I'm flattered. But I'm afraid it's impossible right now. I just told you why.'

'What about later? This afternoon for example. We could have afternoon tea together.'

'Alone with you?'

'Why not? Are you afraid of me? I'm a gentleman, Lady Maria Eduarda.'

She seemed to be debating with herself, visibly hesitating whether to accept his invitation. He expected a clear no but then grinning playfully she said, 'all right then. I'll meet you for afternoon tea at five o'clock but not at the Chave d'Ouro. I don't particularly like it. Too busy and noisy.'

'Anywhere you want. I don't mind.'

'Very well. At the Versailles Patisserie. It's quieter, very pleasant and with wonderful cakes.'

'Where is this patisserie?'

'In the New Avenues, not far from Avenida da Liberdade. Ask around there. Anyone'll be able to give you directions.'

'I will. Thank you. I look forward to it,' he tried to grab and kiss her hand but she removed it and throwing him a dazzling smile quickly disappeared down the hill.

Gerald felt suddenly re-energised, forgetting the heat, the frustration and fatigue. He ran the remaining yards up to the embassy and once inside, climbed the stairs, two steps at a time, to his rooms to have a rest, shower, eat something light and prepare to meet that divine creature later in the afternoon.

He was coming out of the bathroom, a towel around his waist when the internal phone in his bedroom began ringing. Gerald picked it up.

'Ah, Mr Neale, glad you're in.'

The ambassador. Blast. Gerald hoped his afternoon tea with Maria Eduarda wouldn't be spoiled.

'Sir Ronald. How may I be of assistance?'

'I'm summoning up an emergency lunch in my private office in an hour, twelve thirty sharp. I want you there.'

'What's it about, sir? If I may ask.'

'You may. Come to the lunch, be punctual and you'll find out.'

With these words the ambassador hung up on him. Gerald stared at the receiver for a moment as if expecting Sir Ronald's head to suddenly emerge from it. Placing it down he searched for a fresh shirt and tie, put his trousers on but decided to carry the jacket over his arm. He sat on the couch by the open window, trying to read until it was time to go to the ambassador's lunch. Concentration was difficult. Maria Eduarda's face, eyes dancing amused, kept materialising in front of him. He read the same page for the third time. Sighing Gerald dropped the book on the floor. What was the matter with him? He mustn't fall in love with this girl. But he wanted her so. Desired her. Maria Eduarda wasn't a loose girl of dubious reputation. She was a society young lady. Surely a virgin. Marriage material. He could marry her. Nothing to stop him if he wanted to. He was of age. But would Dad accept a black daughter-in-law however exquisite, intelligent and well-educated she might be? Gerald wasn't sure. And did he want to marry so soon just because he lusted after this girl?

Glancing at his wristwatch Gerald realised it was time. He must go if he wanted to be punctual, find out the reason for the meeting and partake from what would probably be a pleasant lunch. Maria Eduarda's image had to be pushed aside for the time being. Duty called. At twelve thirty sharp he arrived at the ambassador's private office. The door was open but Gerald knocked briefly, then walked in.

'Good afternoon, Mr Neale,' the ambassador greeted him, 'take a seat.'

Gerald greeted back, nodding at Bristow. The round table in a corner of the office was covered with a white cloth, plates, glasses, cutlery and napkins, two tall jugs of icy water, a plate of ham sandwiches, another of cheese sandwiches, a large bowl of tomato salad, a plate with sliced fruit cake and another with peaches. Gerald eyed the fruit, his mouth watering, annoyed he needed to wait. There were two empty chairs. He sat next to Bristow in front of Sir Ronald who said, 'we're just waiting for Commander Wheatley and Rear Admiral Thorp...ah, and here they are.'

Two men came in, shutting the door behind them. Gerald knew them. Clifford Wheatley was the top agent and director of MI6 at the embassy. In practice his real boss. He was fifty-five, short, bald, with permanently bloodshot eyes, drooping cheeks and a little overweight, suffering continuously with the heat. Gerald wondered not for the first time why he stayed in Portugal. The man had been offered other positions but insisted on remaining in Lisbon. As for the second man, Edwin Thorp, Royal Navy Rear Admiral, he couldn't be more different. Thorp was forty-nine but looked much younger. The top navy officer at the embassy he was tall, almost the same height as Gerald, lean and athletic. Brown hair, growing silver, perfectly cut. A marking presence. Both men nodded as a form of greeting and took their places at the table. Sir Ronald indicated they should all help themselves to water and food before officially beginning the so-called emergency meeting lunch.

'Gentlemen,' the ambassador began, 'I will get straight to the point. Two things. First I received notice from the Ministry of Economic Warfare that they have started to draw up a blacklist of names trading with Germany in the neutral nations. They intend to keep this list quiet for now but growing so that, after the war, action can be taken against individuals and countries accordingly.'

'Assuming we win the war,' Gerald interjected.

'You don't believe we will?' Thorp asked him, visibly scandalised.

'I hope we will,' Gerald replied, then added with some irony, 'but we've been at war with Germany since 3 September last year – ten months – and so far Herr Hitler seems to have the upper hand.'

'Your opinion isn't very patriotic, Mr Neale,' Thorp said.

Shrugging Gerald stated, 'it's the truth.'

Thorp opened his mouth to possibly oppose him but Sir Ronald was quicker. 'No-one is questioning anybody's patriotism or opinions. The MEW has asked all embassies in neutral countries for MI6 co-operation in the compilation of the list. Your department, Clifford.'

Wheatley took a mouthful of ham sandwich, then gulped his water and cleaned his face with a handkerchief before speaking. He was perspiring profusely. There were large sweat stains on his shirt under the armpits. Out of breath, as if he'd been running, Wheatley said, 'I see no problem with that. I'll look into it myself and would like Mr Neale's assistance, as well as your input, Thorp.'

'Of course,' both men replied in unison.

Visibly satisfied, the ambassador nodded and then said, 'the second matter we need to urgently discuss – perhaps more pressing and important than this so-called blacklist – is the Duke and Duchess of Windsor.'

Thorp rolled his eyes. 'What have they been up to now?'

'Nothing much. Yesterday, His Royal Highness played golf in Estoril with Espirito Santo and the Duke of Beja while the duchess had tea with the wives.'

'So? Nothing new,' Wheatley commented.

'You're right,' Sir Ronald agreed, 'the thing is, apparently Edward expressed his great interest in visiting Sintra while he's in Portugal. As the Duke of Beja has a property there, he immediately invited Edward and Wallis to spend a couple of days in two weeks' time, starting Thursday or Friday to Monday, with himself and his family, extending the invitation to Espirito Santo and his wife and formally sending me an invitation this morning too.'

'We can't allow the Windsors to just go to Sintra and spend a few days cut off from us and the city in a remote place and with only those two keeping them company. Notwithstanding you've also been invited, Sir Ronald, it does have the potential to become an issue,' Wheatley exclaimed.

Thorp agreed, appearing worried.

'You're both probably right,' Sir Ronald said, 'but Edward hasn't asked us for permission. You know how he is when he gets something into his head. He immediately agreed and confirmed he and the Duchess would be delighted to accept the invitation.'

'Could we try and convince him otherwise?' Thorp asked.

'We could but he won't agree,' Sir Ronald replied.

'What can we do?' It was Wheatley's turn to speak.

The ambassador shrugged. 'Nothing, I think. To be honest, I don't believe there's any danger of anyone trying to approach Edward and turn him to support Germany so he can act on their behalf for a quick end to the war with Britain.'

'Espirito Santo has been mentioned a few times by the MEW and I'm certain he'll eventually figure in their blacklist,' Wheatley said.

'I'm not worried about Espirito Santo,' Sir Ronald stated, 'I've said before, I'll eat my hat if he's a Nazi sympathiser. He isn't. I'm certain. I'm not so sure about Ludovico, the Duke of Beja. He's circumspect and doesn't openly share his views.'

'What will Salazar say to the visit? He was never very happy about having the Windsors in Lisbon,' Thorp pointed out.

'He's agreed apparently,' Sir Ronald said, 'Ludovico spoke with him immediately and Salazar authorised the invitation in good faith.'

'Oh, that's just—' Thorp began but the ambassador stopped him.

'It's been decided and in the process of being organised. There's nothing we can do about it.'

'So what do you propose, Sir Ronald? I presume you'll be going?' Wheatley asked.

'Yes, I can hardly refuse. What I propose is to take Mr Neale with me.'

Gerald looked up and could hardly contain his excitement. Maria Eduarda. Surely she would be there. And the first edition of Os Lusíadas that she'd mentioned her father owned. He was very keen to see it. Beaming, Gerald replied, 'of course, sir. Count me in for anything you need.'

Sir Ronald smiled, appearing amused at his enthusiasm. 'Very good, Mr Neale. I've already told Ludovico that I'd need to take my private secretary as I couldn't possibly spend three or four days of leisure without despatching any work. He agreed at once and tomorrow at the latest you should have his written invitation. If you don't receive it, let me know.'

'Yes, sir.'

'And what do you anticipate Neale can achieve?' Thorp asked sardonically, obviously not convinced of Gerald's abilities.

It was Wheatley who answered. 'His knowledge of Portuguese is almost as good as a native's. He'll be able to discreetly listen to any conversations or plans that the Duke of Beja and Espirito Santo may conduct in a more private environment.'

'Precisely my thoughts,' the ambassador confirmed, then turning to Bristow, who hadn't said a word so far, he added, 'Mr Bristow, Salazar has the press in his grip and there's strong censorship, as you know. However, the Windsors' visit to Sintra needs to be kept quiet from the Germans so they don't start having ideas. I want you to help Espirito Santo arrange it. I've already told him and he agreed. You're expected at his bank in the city centre on Monday morning at ten o'clock. Be punctual. Ricardo will follow your advice. In the meantime I suggest you meet with Rear Admiral Thorp and Commander Wheatley here for details of what is expected of you.'

'Of course, sir,' Bristow acknowledged.

With this, the ambassador finished the meeting and they ended their lunch in relative silence, complaining about the extreme heat. Gerald had difficulty concentrating. He kept thinking about his impending afternoon tea with Maria Eduarda and simply couldn't believe his luck about the Sintra weekend.

As they left the room one hour later, he heard Thorp say, 'Sir Ronald, would you have a minute? I'd like a private word, please,' then turning to Wheatley he added, 'please stay, Clifford. In a way it concerns you too.'

Gerald wondered what Thorp wanted to discuss. His heart missed a bit with a sudden realisation. Thorp didn't like him. He'd made it clear during lunch and a couple of times before in a more indirect manner. Was he going to complain about him to Sir Ronald and Wheatley? Gerald glanced around and slowed down his pace, falling behind Bristow who turned.

'Are you coming?'

'Have to visit the john first, old boy. Then need to get some papers from the library and later I've got a date.'

'Oh, okay. I'll see you this evening or tomorrow morning then.'

'Yes, see you.'

Bristow disappeared down the corridor and Gerald heard his footsteps on the marble staircase gradually fading away. He turned, pretending to enter the nearby toilet, then glanced around to ensure no-one was watching. Silently, on tiptoes, he approached the door to Sir Ronald's private office. It was ajar. Pressing himself against the wall he strained to better listen to what they were saying. No need. He could hear perfectly.

'Why?' Thorp was just exclaiming, sounding surprised. 'Well, sir, I'd have thought it's obvious. He's too young – a boy still. Wants adventure, excitement and hasn't got much in his head except women, fun and enjoyment.'

His hunch was correct. Thorp could only be complaining about him. Gerald felt hot under the collar. How dare that idiot grumble about him to the ambassador and his direct boss?

Sir Ronald was now speaking, 'I understand your concern, Rear Admiral Thorp. To be honest, I wasn't inclined to accept his nomination either because he's only twenty-two, inexperienced at pretty much anything, except possibly girls,' he paused, then added, 'but he came highly recommended. It's said he's a quick, outside the box thinker, creative and pro-active as well as reacting fast to unusual situations. Besides, he speaks Portuguese like a native and he comes from a distinguished family of diplomats. His father served many years at this embassy here in Lisbon, as well as in Italy and his grandfather was ambassador to Spain and France.'

'I know all that, sir, but I'm not convinced of his discretion.'

Thorp again.

'I fear for him this is all a game that he'll play for his own enjoyment. I've also heard too many…shall we say unacceptable rumours of female stories.'

'They may be just rumours.'

'There's no smoke without a fire.'

'You may be right, Rear Admiral Thorp,' Sir Ronald said, 'but we have no-one else who speaks Portuguese like he does. He's a valuable asset to find out information; to detect collaboration between the Portuguese and the Germans. Remember that in general many German high officials who work here and the German ambassador in particular speak Portuguese fluently. It's an advantage they have over us.'

'I know von Hoyningen-Huene is a very able, clever man who speaks the language and knows Portuguese culture and history. I also know he actively encourages all the German agents or government officials who come to Portugal to learn the language. To be honest I don't think it's essential. After all, we're on the right side.'

'Which isn't always enough,' Sir Ronald pointed out.

'Besides,' Thorp continued, 'although Neale's knowledge of Portuguese is excellent – and I do grant him that – he's too conspicuous.'

'What do you mean?' This from Wheatley, speaking for the first time.

'I mean,' Thorp replied, 'how can he infiltrate any

Portuguese groups with his looks? He stands out with that platinum blonde hair and the blue eyes, the height, the athletic build. He looks nothing like a Portuguese man though he may speak like one.'

Sir Ronald again. Gerald thought he sounded slightly amused.

'Hmm. I grant you that Mr Neale looks like an Adolf Hitler poster boy for the so-called superior Arian race. It's a shame he doesn't speak German. Then we might be able to place him under cover at the German embassy or even in Berlin, close to the Führer. As it happens we have to make do with him. What do you think about him, Clifford? Any concerns?'

'None at the moment. I've heard the rumours but so far the boy has done everything he was asked,' Wheatley replied, 'however, it's true that he's a bit of a cad regarding women but he's young. It's normal he wants to enjoy himself with the fair sex.'

'I know from trustworthy sources that he's been spending many nights with prostitutes local and foreign,' Thorp stated, sounding irritable.

'Probably true,' Wheatley said, 'but as I pointed out he's young and I'd rather he goes around with harlots than get involved with some society girl. And as long as he does his job I don't see a point in admonishing him.'

There was a period of silence. Then Sir Ronald one more time.

'I agree with Clifford, Rear Admiral Thorp. And I can't send the boy back to England anyway. His nomination came directly from the prime minister. So, that's that. I'm sorry but I fear you've got to try and work with him to the best of your ability. However,' he paused and, after what seemed like a calculated silence, added, 'it won't hurt that both of you and naturally myself keep an eye on him and his behaviour.'

Thorp and Wheatley murmured something Gerald didn't understand but presumed it was their reluctant agreement, at least where Thorp was concerned.

'Very well. That should close the matter for now. Thank

you, gentlemen,' Sir Ronald concluded.

Fearing he might be discovered, Gerald hurried to the nearby toilet and hid until he heard the door to the ambassador's private office closing and the two men's footsteps disappearing down the corridor. Enraged, he cursed. Bloody stupid Thorp. He must get him off his back. He had no right to interfere in his life or complain about his behaviour. The gloves were off. He would find a way to keep Rear Admiral Thorp in line.

Chapter 8 – Bittersweet Afternoon Tea

Immersing himself in discreet enquiries about Rear Admiral Thorp Gerald left the embassy late. Hailing a taxi at the bottom of the hill he told the driver to take him to the Versailles patisserie. Arriving fifteen minutes after the agreed time he saw Maria Eduarda at a table by the window as soon as he stepped out of the car but she wasn't alone. Standing next to her was a stately woman, dark hair with streaks of grey, neatly cut and expertly waved. He noticed attentive brown eyes behind a pair of stylish spectacles. Dressed in a cotton navy blue skirt with tiny white printed flowers and a white blouse she held a white handbag but wore no gloves or hat. For a moment Gerald thought it might be a relative, perhaps an aunt but then remembered Bristow saying Ludovico was an only child. He wondered whether to go in at once or wait for the woman to leave. They appeared to be saying goodbye and kissed each other's cheeks. Then the woman walked out the door and waved before running to catch one of the many Lisbon trolley-trams that rattled slowly around the city.

Maria Eduarda had seen him and gestured him in. He stood briefly in front of her before sitting down and apologised, 'I'm so, so sorry, Lady Maria Eduarda. I got caught up with work. Please accept my sincerest apologies.'

She shrugged, replying graciously, 'it's fine. Apology accepted.'

Gerald glanced around. The Versailles patisserie was an elegant, pleasant, very pretty place. Echoing the French palace that gave it its name, it showcased lovely chandeliers from plastered ceilings with elaborate decorated fringes in white. Attractive watercolours with views of Paris and Lisbon embellished the pastel yellow walls. Cakes displayed in neat rows on the vitrines and tables with alternating white and claret cloths, elegantly contrasting with the dark wood of the chairs, completed the harmonious, attractive environment.

'Have you ordered?' he asked her.
'No. I've only just arrived myself.'
'Really? But I saw you with that lady—'

'Oh, yes. I mean, no, she was here when I arrived. We just had a quick chat. She was in a bit of a hurry.'

'I see. Who is she? I thought she might be your aunt but as far as I know your father has no siblings.'

'No. She's…' she paused, appearing to hesitate but then said, 'well, she's my mentor and a friend.'

'Your mentor?'

'Yes. Don't sound so surprised. Why shouldn't I have a mentor?'

'No reason. But a mentor for what? Music?'

'No, not music. Berta's a professor of physics at the University of Lisbon. She'll help me get in when I'm of age.'

Gerald let out a long whistle. He was impressed. There couldn't be, in fact he knew, there weren't many women holding such positions. Maria Eduarda stared at him for a moment then asked, 'are you going to take a seat? I can't stay long.'

'Of course I'm going to take a seat.' He pulled the chair in front of her and sat down, then said, 'why not?'

She seemed puzzled. 'Why not, what?'

'Why can't you stay long?'

'Papa likes me home by six thirty in the summer.'

'And in winter?'

'Earlier.'

'So what would you like? I'm of course inviting you.'

She shook her head. 'No. I can pay for myself and I insist on doing so, otherwise I'll leave at once.'

His jaw dropped. Gerald had never encountered a woman before who didn't expect him to pay. And he had invited her. Hesitating what to do for a moment, he opened his mouth to oppose her but somehow quickly grasped she was serious and would leave if he pressed it.

'Very well,' he agreed, 'if it means so much to you.'

'It does.'

'May I at least order for you?'

'Yes.'

The smile and the cute, little dimples again. He wanted so much to kiss them. Travel her body with his mouth. Have her.

'Get a grip, Gerald,' he admonished himself silently, 'or you'll scare her away.' Aloud he said, 'and what would you like?'

'A freshly squeezed orange juice, a coffee and a pastel de nata.'

He made a sign to the waiter and placed their order, requesting for himself the same as Maria Eduarda. Her hands were on the table, her left on top of what looked like an old magazine and a very little book. She had long, elegant fingers. Pianist's fingers. He'd love to feel those hands on his skin. Gerald scolded himself again for his less than pure thoughts. Coughing to clear his throat and pointing at the magazine and the book he asked her, 'what are those?'

'Ah, yes. These are for you, Mr Neale.'

'For me?' He was touched.

She nodded. 'I remembered our conversation about Camões. You said you like poetry very much. So, I thought to bring you something that you probably don't know.'

'Try me,' he said pleased.

'Have you ever heard of Fernando Pessoa?'

'No, I don't believe I have.'

She seemed happy he had no idea who this Pessoa might be and Gerald was rewarded with a ravishing smile.

'Fernando Pessoa is a contemporary poet though sadly he died in 1935. Not yet well known but I'm sure he will be. I like his work. It's different…unusual. I thought you'd enjoy reading the poem published in this magazine in 1926, entitled O menino de sua mãe.'

'Mother's Little Boy – never heard of it.'

'It's beautiful and very sad, about a young soldier who dies in a war while at home his mother and the maid are still praying for his safe return. I thought it appropriate for the times we're living in. It says everything about the horror…and, to my mind, the stupidity of war. There are never any winners.'

'I'm not certain you can say that—'

'It's what I think and I'm entitled to my opinion.'

'Of course. Didn't mean to offend you.'

That smile again.

'You haven't. But that's beside the point. I simply believe you'll like the poem,' she picked up the little book, 'this is also by Pessoa, published just one year before his death in 1934. It's a collection of forty-four poems about Portugal's glorious past...perhaps a little in the style of Camões and to a certain extent Pessoa's homage to him.'

She pushed the book and the magazine across the table so he could see them better.

'Mensagem,' he read aloud the title of the little book. 'Message. Well, thank you, Lady Maria Eduarda. I'm sure I'll enjoy them very much. I'll let you know.'

She had eaten her pastel de nata, gulped her coffee and was quickly drinking the fresh orange juice.

'I'm sorry but I have to go,' she said, 'or Papa will be upset. You can write to me about the Pessoa's poems if you feel li—'

'Why don't we meet here again in a few days,' he cut in, 'we can talk over another coffee and pastel de nata.'

'I'm afraid it's impossible, Mr Neale,' she replied, standing up, 'tomorrow we're leaving for Sintra for the summer and won't be back until the end of August but you can write to me at the Lisbon address. The mail will be forwarded to Sintra every second day.'

He stood up and managed to grab her arm before she could leave. She wasn't wearing gloves. Gently and with great care, as if handling a piece of fragile crystal, he turned her hand around, palm up, caressed it with his fingers, then bent down and kissed it. His lips lingered on her skin. He felt her shake slightly and glanced up into her eyes before ending the kiss. In haste she removed her hand.

'Goodbye, Mr Neale,' she said before running out.

He noticed she'd left money on the table to pay her expense. His eyes followed the back of her head, mentally willing her to glance over her shoulder, give him a last smile. But she didn't and soon disappeared from view. With a sigh Gerald dropped on the chair and finished the pastry, then the juice. Somehow, without Maria Eduarda's presence, they had lost their flavour.

Running non-stop from the patisserie to the nearby Avenida da Liberdade Maria Eduarda managed to hail a taxi and sat in the back seat, recovering her breath. Those hot lips on her hand. The way he gazed at her. Her body shook from head to toe. Butterflies fluttered in her stomach. Would she be able to resist him? She wanted to. Must. Studying music, the piano and astronomy – her greatest dream – must take priority. Those were the things she had to concentrate on. At nineteen she believed herself too young to marry but knew her father had other ideas. Approximately fifteen months until she was of age. Then, and whether Papa wanted or not, she would go to university and study to become an astronomer. Putting her father off marrying her for less than a year and a half wouldn't be too difficult.

    The car stopped in front of the house. The driver walked round the vehicle to open the door for her. Maria Eduarda stepped out, paid and thanked him, then opening the garden gate ran to the front steps. She searched her handbag but couldn't find her keys, probably had left them in her bedroom. No option but to ring the bell. One of the valets opened the door. She thanked him and headed for the stairs but her father's harsh voice, calling from his study, froze her.

    'Maria Eduarda, is that you?'

    'Yes, Papa.' She rolled her eyes, wondering what he wanted. He sounded angry.

    'Get in here,' he shouted unceremoniously.

    'Good evening, Papa,' she greeted while walking in.

    He was at his desk and looked up but didn't return the greeting, instead ordering, 'shut the door, will you?'

    'Of course.'

    Standing in front of him she waited, knowing better than to sit down before he specifically told her to.

    'Take a seat,' he pointed at the chair opposite him, the other side of the desk.

    Maria Eduarda obeyed. Hands on her lap, holding his gaze. What had she done to upset him? Papa was visibly irritated about something. There was a prolonged silence while he finished writing what seemed like a letter, signed it and pressed a sheet of blotting paper against it. Looking up he then asked her, 'what were you doing at the Versailles patisserie alone with a man?'

Peeved she exhaled. So that was it. Someone saw her and blabbed. But she hadn't done anything wrong. Controlling her irritation Maria Eduarda spoke in a gentle but firm tone, 'I went there to have afternoon tea with a friend at about five o'clock. Is it a problem?'

'Normally, no. But this friend's a man and you weren't chaperoned.'

'Oh Papa. I know how to conduct myself. I'm not a child anymore. Who does still take a chaperone in Lisbon nowadays? Perhaps in the province but not in the city.'

'I don't care what others do. You're my daughter and I expect you to behave with the maximum propriety.'

'But I did. I do. It was all very innocent. I just took him—'

'Who is he, anyway?'

'You met him at Ricardo's dinner last Saturday. He works at the British embassy and is Sir Ronald Campbell's new private secretary.'

'And what does he want with you?'

'Nothing,' she said with a shrug, 'he sat next to me at Ricardo's dinner and made mostly polite conversation. You may have noticed he speaks our language very well. He likes poetry and has read several Portuguese authors and poets. So we talked about it. Earlier today when I was going to my music lesson, I met him by chance, we chatted for a bit and I said I had some interesting work by Fernando Pessoa – a poet Mr Neale didn't know – so I suggested we could have tea at the Versailles and I'd take a book and a magazine for him. That's all, Papa.' Not strictly true of course but her father had no way of knowing. Close enough though.

'Hmm. If that is all…I hope so. Rosa told me you both looked almost entranced with each other, he especially. She said he was looking at you with loving eyes.'

Rosa. Naturally. Her new stepmother was by all accounts a silly woman.

'No, Papa. Rosa's mistaken. We were talking about poetry – a fascinating, engaging subject. That's all. And how can Rosa have noticed the way he was looking at me? Was she inside the patisserie?'

'No. She saw you from the street as she walked past. I don't think she recognised Mr Neale. At least, she didn't mention it was him.'

'Don't worry, Papa, please. I know how to behave. Mr Neale's a gentleman. He's intelligent and can discuss interesting matters. God knows there's hardly anyone my age I can have a smart conversation with.'

Her father stared at her for several long seconds. Eventually his lips parted in a tender smile and he said, 'all right, my dear. I believe you...and trust you. Friendship with this young man is fine but...' he lifted a finger, 'be careful. I don't want evil rumours about you to start spreading and ruining your reputation.'

'I know, Papa. Don't worry.'

Smiling broadly she stood up, walked around the desk and kissed his cheek.

'All right, all right, off you go, my girl,' he smiled indulgently, 'just be good.'

'Yes, Papa.'

Exhaling relieved, as she left the studio, Maria Eduarda closed the door behind her and wondered whether to confront her stepmother but then decided against it. Better to pretend nothing had happened. And nothing had. Apart from Mr Neale's hot kiss on her hand. The memory sent shivers down her spine. Chastising herself she murmured, 'you're a foolish girl, Maria Eduarda. Forget him and his hand kisses. Remember Grandmama Leopoldina's warnings.'

Rationally she decided there was no issue and all would soon be forgotten. Tomorrow she, her family and most of the household would leave for Sintra, returning only at the end of

August. Mr Neale would fail to remember her after a week or two. And her time in Sintra was always so full she would hardly spare him a thought.

Relaxing she decided to call it all a flight of fancy and concentrate on what really mattered. Broaden her mind with books, study, learn and prepare herself for admission to university for the career she desired. Men. Marriage. All that could wait. With this in mind she ran up the stairs to her room to have a quick look at the new astronomy book and the map of the sky she'd borrowed from her mentor, Professor Berta de Almeida, the only female physicist and astronomer at the University of Lisbon.

Eduarda knew her father didn't want her to meet Berta regularly. He thought the professor a bad influence. Perhaps from his perspective she was. Berta's modern ideas were not to his liking. She believed women were as capable as men, should be allowed to study, pursue a career and be independent. Maria Eduarda agreed but this way of thinking was perceived as threatening by most men, her father included.

Berta was the younger sister of Clarisse de Almeida, the woman who had turned Gabriela do Livramento, Maria Eduarda's mother, into a fine lady, as the title of duchess demanded. And so the three women had become friends. Clarisse had died a year ago, tragically run over by a car. And of course Maria Eduarda's mother had died nearly twenty years ago giving birth to her. Perhaps irrationally she sometimes felt guilty about her mother's death but Berta made her understand it wasn't her fault. Sadly, women often died giving birth. After Gabriela's death, Ludovico had permitted both sisters to spend time with his little girl, thinking the presence of two educated young women would be good. When he married for the second time, the sisters' visits happened less often especially Clarisse who had also got married and didn't have much time. Berta continued to visit and take Maria Eduarda for day outings. As soon as the little girl could write, they began exchanging letters and Ludovico didn't object, always remembering the close friendship between the sisters and Gabriela the wife he had adored. But later he began grasping Berta's subversive ideas of women being equal to men. Where would society end if such things were changed? he'd asked.

So, much to Maria Eduarda's anger, her father prohibited them from meeting except on special occasions – like a birthday or Christmas. It didn't work. Maria Eduarda continued to meet and correspond regularly with Berta. The only difference being she kept it secret from everyone. Walking daily to her music lesson she often met Berta afterwards especially during the university's holiday periods. Eduarda looked up to her. A shining example, an inspiring woman. The kind of woman she aspired to be.

Berta always encouraged her to pursue advanced music studies because Ludovico accepted a young lady must know music and Maria Eduarda was more talented than most. But Berta complemented her education with science because Eduarda had fallen in love with the subject and its logical, methodical, tested approach to life. With Berta's help, Eduarda felt certain she would succeed.

Picking up Berta's latest borrowed book and map of the sky she sat on the bed, legs crossed, quickly becoming engrossed in both, wishing she were already in Sintra. Observing the heavens from her bedroom window at night she hoped to identify the constellations with the help of Berta's new map.

Immersed in her reading Maria Eduarda was startled by the gong announcing dinner. And she wasn't even dressed. Abandoning the book on the bed she jumped off and quickly changed into smarter clothes before running down the stairs. Papa liked punctuality.

Chapter 9 – Conspiracy and Retribution

No cooling breeze in the city centre. One had the feeling the white stones of the famous Portuguese calçada that covered sidewalks radiated the heat accumulated during the day. Perhaps they did. The night brought some relief but it was difficult to sleep even with windows wide open. And Lisbon was noisy. Dogs barking. Cats fighting. An undefined cacophony of voices and cars in overcrowded streets, occasionally interrupted by sirens, screams and shouts. Not to mention the continuous jolting of the trolley-trams on the rails and the blasted roosters, never seen but hiding in backyards, crowing most of the night all over the city.

Gerald stepped out of the Tivoli hotel in the middle of the night into the heat and the noise. A little tipsy and flushed from fiery sex, alcohol and a job well done he loosened his tie, taking his jacket off and throwing it over his shoulder. Exhaling he cursed the Portuguese summer. Such high temperatures were not so common. Thermometers generally didn't exceed thirty-two to thirty-five degrees – more than enough in his opinion – in Lisbon during June, July and August with the occasional couple of days hitting or exceeding forty. But this year the country was enduring the hottest summer on record. Gerald never thought he'd miss rain but he did now, longing for the often wet, cool days of the English summer months.

He glanced at his wristwatch. Four twenty in the morning. Exhausting eighteen hours but productive. The words summed up his night. It was the third time he'd followed Thorp unnoticed. No more doubts. He knew where the man was going whenever he had a free night. Knew Thorp's inclinations. Knew how to get him off his back.

'I've got you, you insignificant little bastard,' he said aloud, raising an imaginary glass in a toast to himself.

This night Gerald had refrained from entering the establishment that Thorp so much enjoyed frequenting in an old, dodgy area of the city called Bairro Alto. He didn't need to. Knew fully well what happened inside. From there he could have easily walked to the Tivoli for his date. Too hot for the effort though and instead he took a taxi to the hotel on the Avenida da Liberdade.

Red-blonde, long-legged Helga, his latest conquest, was waiting for him there. She was a very attractive German woman, working as a secretary to Baron Hoyningen-Huene, the German ambassador in Lisbon. Gerald had first spotted her at the Tivoli bar just over a week ago. It was the evening of the day he'd met Maria Eduarda at the Versailles patisserie. Helga had large breasts and a shapely figure, accentuated by the tight silver dress she was then wearing. He asked the bartender whether she was a regular.

'Yes,' the man answered, 'I know she works at the German embassy, speaks Portuguese…not brilliantly but well enough and tends to keep herself to herself though once or twice she has taken a man to her room.'

'She lives here?'

'No but she keeps…or the embassy does, I don't know, but yes, she's got a room here but may also have one at the embassy or somewhere else. Occasionally she spends the night here but not daily. Possibly when she has a date,' the bartender grinned.

'Is it always the same man?' Gerald asked.

'No. A different one each time.'

'She's a looker.'

'Indeed she is, sir,' the waiter displayed an all-knowing grin and added, 'good luck.'

'Thank you,' Gerald returned the grin and gave the man a good tip.

He decided to approach Helga and pass himself as Portuguese. Chatting her up was easy. He'd bought her a drink, complimented her. They got talking and, on the same night, ended up in a room at the hotel. Since then they met nearly every night. Helga was a good lover. She knew how to please a man and enjoyed sexual games. She was also a bit of a chatterbox and, convinced he was just a handsome, unusual-looking Portuguese man, working in a bank, she blabbed about what she saw and heard at the embassy, including the Berlin dispatches for the ambassador. Gerald pretended not to care but carefully registered every detail in his mind, typing it after returning home.

For no apparent reason, he remembered Maria Eduarda. It seemed to happen often these days. What would she be doing in Sintra at this time? Probably sleeping peacefully.

Maria Eduarda. Her sweet name and enchanting face were never far away from his mind. Like a bolt from the blue the realisation hit him that each time he had sex with Helga it was Maria Eduarda he imagined lying naked under him. It felt like a punch below the belt. Gerald was taken aback and wondered not for the first time whether he was obsessing about the Duke of Beja's gorgeous daughter or falling in love with her. In only two days, Friday the 26th of July in the early morning, he was to leave for Sintra with the ambassador and his family. Barely able to contain his excitement he anticipated a full weekend in the company of that divine creature. There should be opportunities to seduce her. He just had to set up a plan. Perhaps a quiet conversation admiring the first edition of Os Lusíadas or a peaceful walk in the woods around the mansion. Bristow had told him that the grounds around the house were beautiful and romantic. The woods had many ancient trees. Gerald wondered how he could take her to the next level. At least a kiss. He must kiss her and see her naked. Yes, see her naked in his arms was what he really, really wanted. His desire grew suddenly and he forced himself to think about work to cool down. Sintra wouldn't all be pleasure. He had to work too. Bearing in mind the information he'd managed to obtain from Helga there would be a considerable amount of spying and listening to private conversations involved.

He stopped on the edge of the pavement, searching for a taxi. Walking all the way to Lapa where the embassy was located seemed like an impossible task. Catching one of those loud contraptions on rails that pestered the city night and day was an even less attractive option. He glimpsed a taxi approaching on the wrong side of the avenue but didn't care. Jumping onto the road he ran across the dividing middle-section, with all the trees and street cafés, to the other side, waving his arms up in the air. He was lucky. The driver saw him and halted with a screech of rubber on the tarmac. A minute later, lulled by the gentle rolling of the car, he fell asleep on the back seat, only waking up when the taxi stopped in front of the British embassy. Gerald paid, waved goodbye to the driver and rang the bell for the night porter who let him in after he identified himself. He ran up the stairs to his rooms. Shook his shoes off, brushed his teeth, threw trousers, socks, jacket, shirt and tie on the floor and, wearing only his underpants, dropped on the bed with the intention of hitting the sack. What about the new information from Helga? He couldn't sleep before preparing a report for Clifford Wheatley, the MI6 director. It was important. He mustn't forget any detail.

Resigned, weary eyed and yawning Gerald walked to the bathroom and washed his face with cold water, reviving himself a little. He sat at the typewriter and rapidly typed a report, then placed the two sheets of paper into a brown manilla envelope, sealing it. Barefoot and half-naked he quickly walked to Wheatley's office, marked the envelope urgent and confidential with red ink and left it on Wheatley's desk. Then stumbled back to his room, feeling drained and crashing on the bed. A sudden death must feel similar, he thought just before his eyelids closed and he fell into a heavy, dreamless sleep.

Thunder. So strong it shook the walls. His head wanted to explode. The noise was deafening. His temples throbbed in pain. Gerald opened his eyes wide. It wasn't a storm. He was in his bed and the sun flooded in through the windows he'd left ajar. Must have been a nightmare. But there it was again. Sitting up he realised it was someone banging on his door.

'A moment,' he shouted.

He glanced at his watch. Quarter past eleven. Damn. He'd forgotten to set up his alarm clock. The loud knocking came again.

'Coming! Coming!' Flinging his dressing gown over his shoulders he unlocked and yanked open the door to be met with the sight of his boss. Clifford Wheatley stood there perspiring profusely with the eternal white handkerchief mopping his forehead with one hand and holding some paper in the other. Brandishing the paper in the air he unceremoniously burst into the room and dropped to sit on the edge of the bed.

'For a moment I thought something must be wrong with you,' he said.

'I'm a heavy sleeper. What's the matter? Is there a fire or something?'

'If there was, you'd be dead. No, my boy, no fire. But there will be if you don't get ready immediately.'

'What is it?'

'Your report. You left it on my desk last night. We need to meet with the ambassador at once. He must be told.'

Gerald nodded, understanding. Wheatley had read his report and was up in arms about the information it contained.

'Okay,' he said, 'give me half an hour and I'll join you in the ambassador's private office…I presume?'

'Yes. See—'

Wheatley stopped whatever he was going to say and stared, 'you look like crap. A long night, hey? Well, take an aspirin and make yourself presentable,' he stood up and walked out but turned at the door, 'and make it fast.'

Gerald didn't reply. Shutting the door he went into the bathroom, showered and shaved in a hurry, then chose his creamy linen suit and a fresh white shirt. Twenty minutes later he was knocking at the door of the ambassador's private office. He heard men talking. Wheatley was already there.

'Come in,' Sir Ronald's voice ordered.

Gerald walked in and noticed first the large coffee pot, then the jug of freshly squeezed orange juice and the plate of cheese sandwiches. He needed all of it. Coffee to wake up. Orange juice to still his thirst – his mouth felt like cork – and a sandwich for his hunger. His stomach rumbled so loud he feared the other men might have heard it. Then he noticed Thorp, sitting next to the ambassador. Oh well, he just had to put up with him at least in official meetings. The man was the Royal Navy's representative in Lisbon after all and had the right to be there.

'Good morning, gentlemen,' Gerald greeted them.

'More like good afternoon,' Thorp snarled in a scathing tone.

Gerald refrained from giving a biting reply. He'd have his time soon enough and put the man in his place. Instead he smiled and addressing the ambassador asked, 'may I help myself to coffee and a sandwich, sir? I haven't had breakfast yet.'

Sir Ronald nodded. 'Of course. This is for all of us. Please, gentlemen, dig in.'

Gerald felt better once he had a few sips from his coffee. Wonderful beverage. He bit into his sandwich enthusiastically, then swallowed some orange juice and more coffee.

'So,' Sir Ronald was saying, 'the three of us have read your report, Mr Neale. This is worrying news if indeed true. Who's your source?'

He mumbled an answer with his mouth full, only to realise no-one understood a word.

'Relax, Mr Neale,' Sir Ronald said, 'wash down your food first.'

Gerald nodded and a couple of seconds later was able to speak clearly. 'Helga Haffner, Hoyningen-Huene's secretary.'

'And she just gave you confidential information?' Thorp asked acerbically, 'why? Due to your irresistible charm?'

'In a manner of speaking,' Gerald replied with a hint of irony without glancing at him, then continued, 'Helga and I have been dating. She doesn't know I work here or that I'm British. She thinks I'm Portuguese and a bank employee,' he paused and glancing sideways at Thorp added, dripping sarcasm, 'my language skills appear to come in handy after all.'

Thorp ignored him but Wheatley said, 'well played, my boy, well played.'

Gerald resumed, 'she chats and chats and in the heat…I mean the climax…well, when we make love she blabs lots of stuff to me. I think sometimes she doesn't even realise it.'

'In Portuguese?' Sir Ronald asked.

'German mostly but with a…with a…well, a certain persuasion she starts talking in Portuguese. She speaks it quite well.'

'Unsurprising. We know Hoyningen-Huene encourages all his staff to learn the language,' Sir Ronald said.

'You think the information you get from her is reliable, given that...' Wheatley paused, visibly embarrassed, then said, 'given that she's occupied with other things.' His throat and his cheeks got very red.

'I think it's reliable, yes,' Gerald replied, 'she's the German ambassador's secretary; if she isn't a dependable source, then who is?'

'You're right,' Sir Ronald agreed, 'besides, I received a confidential letter from the MEW in London, telling me they too suspect the Germans are thinking of kidnapping the Duke of Windsor and convincing him to act on their behalf against England to stop the war.'

'And Edward's going to Sintra at the weekend. What do we do?' Thorp said, almost panicking.

'Nothing. We carry on as planned. Mr Neale here will have his ears wide open to any private conversations between Ricardo and Ludovico and between any of them and Edward. Personally, I don't think anything will happen.'

'How so?' Thorp asked.

'For one thing Hoyningen-Huene is a very able man and I believe he wouldn't support such a silly plan. As for Edward, he's angry with Churchill and the Royal Family, yes, and prone to act out of spite, as they haven't given Wallis the right of becoming Her Royal Highness. It's true he believes the war will be disastrous for Britain but I don't think he'd turn to the other side. Besides, he's already told me, though privately and hasn't made it official, that he'll accept Churchill's offer. Edward is intending to travel to the Bahamas to assume the post of governor. He and Wallis will leave Lisbon soon.'

'So, we don't need to worry?' Wheatley asked.

'Probably not but I'll keep my ears open in Sintra and rely on Mr Neale's skills.' He turned to Gerald and added, 'good job, Mr Neale, good job with Hoyningen-Huene's secretary.'

With that the ambassador declared the meeting finished. As they walked out Gerald turned to Thorp and lighting a cigarette said, 'do you have a minute, Rear Admiral Thorp? I need a brief word. It won't take a moment.'

Wheatley walked ahead, telling Gerald he expected him in his office in ten or fifteen minutes to discuss the strategy for Sintra.

'Of course.' Turning to Thorp who hadn't replied, he repeated, 'you have a minute?'

'Sure. What's it about?'

Gerald sucked on the cigarette then exhaled the smoke slowly, watching its blue spirals climb gradually towards the ceiling before speaking. Finally he said, 'I know what you're up to on your free nights.'

Thorp's face muscles tightened but he commented calmly, 'no idea what you're talking about.'

'Yes, you do. I followed you a few times to that hidden night-club in a quiet alley of Bairro Alto – O Cantinho – The Little Corner, they call it. Cosy.'

He watched Thorp's face. It went red first, then white. The man looked so pale that for a moment Gerald thought he might have a heart attack. But, controlling his obvious humiliation and possible rage he simply asked, 'what do you want, Neale?'

'So, you don't try to deny it. Interesting.'

'Stop your games. If you followed me, you know it's a club for a special type of gentleman.'

'You can say that again. Special…hmm…one way of putting it. I'd say immoral, abnormal, perverse even.'

'I don't care what you say,' Thorp muttered between gritted teeth, 'what do you want?'

'Well, if your taste is more directed at men than women, it's your problem,' he shrugged, 'nothing to do with me what you get up to during your free time.'

'Spare me your comments. What do you want?'

Gerald looked him up and down with a slightly malicious smirk, then said, 'I want you off my back. I know how to do my job and I don't need your help or your opinions. I report to Wheatley, to the ambassador and to London. You've nothing to do with it. I'll work with you whenever the need arises but don't ever go behind my back again, complaining to Sir Ronald. I don't like it. I won't tolerate it. Are we clear?'

'Crystal,' Thorp answered, visibly riled but controlling his anger.

'Good. Have a nice day, Rear Admiral Thorp.'

Thorp didn't reply. Turning on his heels he walked away fast, disappearing up the stairs to the second floor.

Smiling, inwardly pleased with himself, Gerald finished his cigarette, then headed to Wheatley's office to discuss the strategy for the Duke of Windsor's visit to the Duke of Beja's Sintra home.

Chapter 10 – Sintra

Friday morning. Eight forty-five and the thermometer had already climbed above thirty-seven degrees. Gerald had a quick look around his rooms to ensure he wasn't forgetting anything. Dressed in a short-sleeved shirt and linen trousers he fetched his small valise containing his clothes and personal hygiene articles for the weekend in Sintra. Grabbing his jacket and briefcase he walked down to the garages at the back of the embassy. He was to drive one of the embassy's utilitarian cars and follow the chauffeured Rolls carrying the ambassador and his wife. They were to join Espirito Santo and his party en route. Ricardo Espirito Santo employed a chauffeur but, following Bristow's advice, was driving himself with his wife and the Windsors. Bristow and Wheatley had travelled the day before to ensure the Duke of Beja's mansion and its grounds complied with the required security and safety of the royal couple.

Gerald knew that Bristow and Wheatley would be staying in the gate cottage at the entrance to the grounds. To his delight, along with the distinguished guests, he would have a room in the mansion. Possibly more opportunities to be with Maria Eduarda and admire all the artistic treasures in the house.

Sir Ronald's car rolled out of the embassy garage and Gerald trailed behind it. Through the city their progress was slow until they reached the Marginal, the road heading along the river to the Lisbon Atlantic Coast. In Cascais, by Boca do Inferno, Espirito Santo and his party would join them and from there they would head north-west to the village of Sintra.

The sky was luminous blue. The blazing sun, scorching the earth and its inhabitants, created heat waves in the air, making people and objects appear as mirages in the desert. The ocean was green-blue with white crested swells moving majestically to the beaches. Gerald had never seen such a beautiful sea. Shame to have to drive. He'd much rather sit back and admire the stunning landscape.

It took them just over an hour to reach Cascais where they stopped briefly for refreshments provided by Espirito Santo's wife, before hitting the road again. Espirito Santo's car led the way. It was 11.20 a.m. when they arrived at the Duke of Beja's estate in Sintra. Plenty of time to unpack, freshen up and have a light lunch. Bristow and Wheatley had stepped into a car when the convoy slowly passed the cottage gate, following them to the house. Ludovico was at the entrance with his wife, Rosa, welcoming the guests. The butler and a few footmen waited to lead the visitors to their rooms and carry their luggage. Gerald couldn't help but feel some disappointment. Maria Eduarda was nowhere to be seen. He wanted to ask about her but dared not, fearing the Duke would think him ill mannered. He needn't have worried. To his delight Ricardo asked, 'where's my lovely goddaughter, Ludovico? I'm looking forward to seeing her. She hasn't stayed in Lisbon, has she?'

'No, of course not,' Ludovico replied with an indulgent smile, 'Maria Eduarda's out and about somewhere on her favourite horse but she'll be back for lunch.'

Horse riding. An activity Gerald also enjoyed though he'd hardly practised it in the last two years. Perhaps he might have a chance to be alone with her after all. Beaming inwardly, after greeting the Duke of Beja and his wife, he tracked up the stairs to his bedroom behind one of the footmen. The room, located at the end of the corridor on the first level, wasn't one of the largest but of a comfortable size. He surmised the upper floor above him must be the servants' quarters.

The footman placed his luggage on the floor next to the bed and said, 'I hope everything's to your liking, sir,' he indicated a door on the wall to Gerald's right, 'that's the bathroom. Should you wish for more towels or anything else, please ring the bell next to the bed.'

'You mean pull that red rope?' He indicated it with his head.

'Yes, sir. Will you be needing anything presently?'

'No, thank you.'

After the footman left Gerald looked around, appreciative of the comfort. Like in a hotel, he thought cheerfully. The room was spacious enough, with a dark oak double bed, a trunk of the same wood at its foot and matching side tables. A dressing table to the left of one of the windows and a desk to the right. A chaise longue between the two windows where one could comfortably sit and look outside. Three chairs placed against the walls and a large wardrobe in the same dark wood with three doors, a mirror on the middle one. The windows were wide open but no breeze blew in. The net curtains didn't move.

Gerald hoisted his valise onto the trunk to begin unpacking. The sound of clopping hooves distracted him. Craning his neck out one of the windows he watched Maria Eduarda dismount her horse and a little girl with blonde-brown curls run out towards her shouting, 'Edi, Edi, uncle Ricardo and auntie Maria are here and a lot of other people.'

Maria Eduarda lifted the little girl in her arms and smiling indulgently said, 'give me a kiss first, my little gold kitten, then you can tell me all about it.'

Gerald presumed the child must be Ana Maria, Eduarda's little sister. He watched her put her small arms around Eduarda's neck and kiss her cheek loudly. Eduarda placed her back on the ground and said, 'want to come with me to the stables and help me take care of Zuca?'

'Yes, yes, yes,' the little girl jumped around her big sister, clapping her hands.

The horse was chestnut, muscular, with flexible movements. Gerald wondered whether it could be a Lusitano, a famous Portuguese horse breed. He could go to the stables and ask, thus surprising Maria Eduarda while she tended the animal. Impulsively he left his unpacking and jacket abandoned on the bed and ran out of the room, tracing his steps back to the front door. Passing a maid coming up the stairs, carrying a silver tray with a jug of lemonade and tall glasses, he asked how to get to the stables.

'If you go out the front door, sir, then turn to your right around the house, you'll see them further down near the grass field before you reach the woods.'

'Thank you.'

Running, not wanting to miss her, Gerald arrived

breathless. He was in time. Maria Eduarda, her little sister and a stable boy were unsaddling the horse.

'Lady Maria Eduarda, hello, how lovely to see you,' he said, after catching his breath.

She turned, visibly surprised but her smile was welcoming.

'Mr Neale! What are you doing here?'

'I came with the ambassador. Didn't you know?'

'No. Papa told me about our royal guests, the ambassador and his wife and of course Ricardo and Maria but he didn't mention you.'

'Sir Ronald needs me for some work that can't wait until Monday.'

'I see, well welcome to Parque das Papoilas and—'

'Poppies Park?' He interjected, 'I don't understand.'

She laughed a crystal clear sound, like fresh water. 'It's the name of the estate. Don't ask me why because there's hardly a poppy in sight. Anyway, may I introduce my little sister Ana Maria? Anita, this is Mr Gerald Neale who works at the British embassy.'

The little girl went all shy and hid behind her sister but stretched her wee hand. He took it, bowed and said, 'it's a pleasure to meet you, Lady Ana Maria.'

She giggled, obviously finding the formal addressing of her small person rather funny.

Gerald touched the horse and turning to Maria Eduarda asked, 'is this a Lusitano?'

She appeared pleased he knew about the Portuguese horse breed. 'Yes,' she replied, 'it's a PSL – puro sangue Lusitano – or as you'd say in England a pure blood Lusitano.' She patted the horse's flank.

'It's a beautiful animal,' he commented.'

'True. Do you know anything about the Lusitanos, Mr Neale?'

'Not really...apart from the fact that they exist.'

The dimpled smile again. She said, 'well, let me enlighten you.'

'Please.'

'The Portuguese Lusitano's a horse breed, closely related to the Spanish Andalusian. Both are sometimes referred to as Iberian horses. The fame of the horses from Lusitania, now Portugal, goes back to the Roman Age. At the time they attributed these animals' outstanding speed to the influence of the west wind,' she paused, amused, then taking the saddle off the horse gave it to the groom and continued, 'when the Moors invaded Iberia in 711 they brought Berber horses from the north of Africa and crossed them with the native horses, developing a new breed, very good for war, dressage and bull fighting. They're very resilient, can have any block colour but white or black aren't so common; generally they're grey, brown or chestnut – like this one,' she patted the horse again, 'they've solid muscles and intelligent, willing natures. Very agile, with graceful, elegant movements.'

'What's his name?' Gerald asked, looking at the horse that was gently nibbling on a carrot Maria Eduarda held.

'Zuca, as he's five years old.'

'What does his age have to do with the name?'

'It's a tradition. Lusitanos are named alphabetically by year. Lusitanos born now, in 1940, will have a name starting with E. When we get to the end of the alphabet we go back to the beginning. So, if it's E this year, five years ago it was Z. Therefore he was named Zuca. By the way, there are no names starting with K, W or Y because those letters don't exist in the Portuguese alphabet.'

He grinned. She was a fount of knowledge. A beautiful, walking encyclopaedia.

'What is it? Why're you smiling?' she asked.

'Nothing. I'm sorry. Just remembered a silly joke by a friend of mine back in England. Anyway, I think I should return to my room, unpack and freshen up before lunch.'

'Good idea. Anita,' she said, looking at her little sister, 'we must do the same,' then turning to the groom she added, 'thank you, Manuel. I won't ride him again today.'

The young man nodded and, as the horse stuck its nose

into a large bucket of water, he began brushing its coat.

Gerald walked with the sisters back to the house. Eduarda stopped briefly and asked him, 'do you ride, Mr Neale?'

'As a matter of fact, yes, I do.'

'And do you enjoy it?'

'Very much.'

'Well then, if you'd like to see the grounds properly, you can ride with me tomorrow but you'll need to get up very early.'

'How early?'

'Five a.m. and be ready by five thirty.'

'It's fine. I'd love to ride out with you and see the property,' he touched her hand in an attempt to take it to his lips but she moved away and turning to her little sister said, 'come on, pet, I'll race you to the house.'

Gerald stood back watching them. His chest contracted. Had he fallen in love with her? He didn't know. But his physical desire for her was so strong it hurt. His body ached for her. He breathed in and out a few times, trying to control his powerful attraction.

Ludovico, his family and his guests had a light, cold lunch of salad and seafood taken on the northern terrace of the house, shady and fresher at that time of the day. After the coffee the Duchess of Windsor announced she was going to have a rest. Ludovico invited his guests for a tour of the house to inspect his artistic treasures. His wife exchanged a brief word with Maria, Espirito Santo's wife, then said they would stay on the terrace as it was cool and quiet. The nanny came and led little Ana Maria upstairs. Maria Eduarda and Sir Ronald's wife joined the men.

Gerald paid little attention to the precious porcelain pieces or the valuable paintings. His eyes kept wandering to Maria Eduarda who walked with her father for most of the time. But he became fully alert when they entered the library and the Duke of Beja showed his most prized possessions. The first edition of The Lusiads by Portugal's greatest poet, Luis de Camões, and an antique manuscript. The Duke explained the manuscript was incomplete, pointing at a locked vitrine where they could see a glass coffer containing the remaining pages. As for the priceless book, it was held in a specially built glass and wood display case. Locked. Ludovico showed them the key, which he carried at all times, stating, 'I'll open it for a couple of minutes so you can better admire it.'

The guests formed a circle around the glass case. Maria Eduarda stepped back to allow them enough space. Gerald's heart raced. The book was a beauty.

'How much is it worth, Your Grace?' he asked Ludovico.

'Its value is incalculable, Mr Neale. This is one of the few surviving first editions of The Lusiads from 1572. There are only six still in existence.'

Glancing at Maria Eduarda he said, 'your daughter mentioned to me once that you have one of the true first editions.'

Ludovico raised an eyebrow.

'She said,' Gerald continued, 'the real first edition bears a pelican looking to the left from the reader's perspective.'

The Duke nodded, then lifting the book from the case carefully opened it on the first page. Pointing at a figure at the top he said, 'here. You see?'

Gerald and the others looked closely.

'Magnificent,' Gerald murmured. He paused, wondering whether the question on his mind would be considered inappropriate but decided he didn't care, 'Your Grace, how much would you ask for it?'

Visibly startled Ludovico questioned him, 'why do you ask, Mr Neale?'

'Well, my father and I collect first editions. He started his collection a long time ago, years before my brother and I were born. He now owns a considerable number of first editions – they fill a room about half the size of this library,' he gestured around the room with his arm, 'some of his items are interesting; some valuable but mostly from the 19th century, with a couple of books from the 18th and a good number from the 20th century though with the war there's little chance of obtaining anything new. Father owns mostly English and American first editions but has several French and a most treasured German first edition of The Buddenbrooks by the Nobel Prize laureate Thomas Mann. But in spite of having been a cultural attaché at the British embassy in Lisbon for many years my father owns no Portuguese first editions and certainly nothing like this,' Gerald indicated the exemplar of The Lusiads in front of him with his head, 'certainly not this old – 1572. Unbelievable. I'm sure he would love to purchase this copy...and so would I. I'll inherit his collection one day. My brother has no interest in it but, like my father, I'm passionate about it.'

'Your enthusiasm does you credit, Mr Neale,' Ludovico replied graciously, 'and I've no doubt that you or your father would love to own this book but I'm afraid it's not for sale. However, I can put you in touch with a book antiquarian friend of mine. He'll be able to find you a Portuguese first edition, just not of The Lusiads. The existing six are either privately owned or held in the National Library of Portugal.'

With these words the Duke of Beja returned the book to the case, locked it and turned his attention to the vitrine with the coffer containing the antique manuscript. Opening the cabinet he picked up the glass coffer and allowed them to look but not touch the pages. 'These, as far as the legend goes, are the remains of The Lusiads original manuscript. According to the story that reached us through the centuries, Camões was travelling in a ship that sank off the coast of Cambodia. He was a good swimmer and managed to swim to the nearest beach with only one arm, holding the other with the manuscript high up above his head.'

'And is it true?' The Duke of Windsor asked.

Ludovico shrugged. 'I don't know, Your Royal Highness. But it's a good story.'

'You never tried to find out, Your Grace?' Gerald asked.

'No. I don't see how I could ever be certain it's the real thing. Anyway, we know it's very old. Together with the first edition of the book it's been in the family for centuries. One of my ancestors, then not yet Duke of Beja but Marquis of Montalvo, was offered a copy of the first edition by the poet himself and later bought it as well but one of them has disappeared. There are also no records whatsoever about these manuscript pages. It's possible the Marquis purchased them from the poet. Camões was always in need of money.'

'It'd be interesting to find out,' Gerald commented.

'Indeed. Perhaps one day I'll hand it to an expert for authentication,' Ludovico said, then turning to the Duke of Windsor added, 'Your Royal Highness, I own a little painting by the celebrated French artist of the 18th century, Madame Élisabeth Vigée-Lebrun. Would you like to see it?'

'Very much so,' Edward replied.

All but Gerald followed Ludovico out of the library. Gerald couldn't tear himself away. The book was exquisite. Unique. What his father and he would give to own such a treasure. Perhaps he should accept the Duke's offer of getting in touch with his friend, the book antiquarian. But even if another first edition were available for sale, would he have enough money to acquire it? Possibly not, but he could always offer his future inheritance as collateral. As the saying went, 'where there's a will, there's a way'.

He was distracted by a lovely melody, appearing to come from the south terrace outside the library. Stepping out through the open glass doors Gerald listened carefully. It was coming from a room at the other end of the terrace. Moving to the open doors he glanced inside and saw Maria Eduarda at the piano playing attentively. He hadn't realised she'd left the others going to look at the Vigée-Lebrun painting.

She was completely immersed in the music and he watched her in silence, admiring her profile, her long, elegant fingers floating across the keyboard.

After several minutes he coughed to attract her attention and said, 'you really are a superb player, Lady Maria Eduarda.'

Her hands stopped abruptly on the piano keys, causing a harsh dissonance. Turning she glanced over her shoulder and he could plainly see she wasn't happy.

'I'm sorry,' Gerald said, 'I didn't mean to startle you.'

'But you did, Mr Neale. What can I do for you?'

Many wonderful things, I'm sure, he thought. Aloud he said, 'I didn't realise you'd left our little touring group.'

'I've obviously seen my father's treasures often and as Sir

Ronald's wife went to join Maria and my stepmother, I thought I'd employ my time practising.'

'I see. Well apart from the first edition I can't say I remember most of the other things.'

She smiled. 'I can't believe your questions to my father.'

'About having the manuscript authenticated?'

'No. Whether he'd sell the first edition and how much he wanted for it.'

Gerald shrugged. 'Why? The question was genuine. My father and I would give a lot to own such a precious item.'

'I've no doubt but Papa will never sell it. He told you. It's been in the family for centuries. He would as soon part with one or more of his estates.'

'Really?'

'Yes. Really. It's always passed on to the eldest child in each generation. It's tradition.'

'So that'll be you...the book will be yours eventually.'

'Should be.'

'But you're a woman.'

She frowned. 'So? You don't think I'm capable of looking after it?'

'No...I mean... that's not what I meant. Your father has just married for the third time. Your stepmother is a young woman. They'll have children. If there's a boy, surely he'll inherit everything before you.'

'Not the book. As I said, it's a family tradition.'

She turned to face the piano but Gerald ignored the hint.

'I loved what you were playing earlier. What was it?'

'Chopin.'

'I'd like to listen. Please continue.'

Shaking her head she said, 'I don't like practising when someone's watching.'

He could tell she meant it. So, bowing respectfully he agreed, 'very well. I'll go then.'

'Thank you.'

He went to his room with the intention of doing some work but couldn't concentrate, ending up on the bed, hands crossed under his head, day-dreaming. What he'd give to caress Maria Eduarda, kiss her, admire her naked. He could hardly wait to go riding with her in the morning. With luck it'd only be the two of them. Perhaps then, a chance would present itself and he'd be able to take her in his arms.

He scarcely slept a wink for fear of being late. She might ride without him. At 4.30 a.m. he was out of bed and ready to go. The sun had not yet risen. He dithered. Where were they to meet? Should he go to the stables? Or wait in the hall? Stupidly he'd forgotten to ask . The stables of course. The horses were there. It guaranteed he wouldn't miss her. Once there he stood by the door and waited. Waited. Waited. Waited. And waited.

He glanced at his wristwatch. Twenty past five. Where was she? Perhaps she wasn't coming. Or had forgotten her invitation. Maybe she was unwell. Jumpy and restless he paced in front of the stables, wondering whether to go back to the house and knock on her bedroom door. When he heard footsteps and her voice his relief was palpable. He looked up. She was approaching, with that quality she possessed that made her seem to float, to glide elegantly as if she didn't belong to the same earthbound world as other people. Her eyes danced in amusement as she spotted him, her dimples indenting her cheeks. He felt very hot.

'Here you are, Mr Neale. Bom dia.'

'Good morning, Lady Maria Eduarda. You look…' he swallowed to clear the lump in his throat, 'luminous. Hope you don't mind me saying so.'

Inclining her head back gracefully she chuckled brightly. God. How he wanted to grab her, kiss her dimples, her mouth. Every inch of her body. Get a grip, Gerald, he told himself silently, not for the first time.

'I don't mind,' she was saying, 'thank you for the compliment. Not sure I deserve it though,' she looked down at her outfit, 'I'm just in simple riding gear.'

'You look lovely to me,' he whispered.

'Have you been waiting long?' she asked him, visibly wanting to change the subject.

'No, well, yes but it's fine. My fault, really. Got here too early.'

'I knocked on your door,' she said lightly, 'but there was no answer. Thought you'd forgotten and were still asleep.'

He shook his head vehemently. 'How could I forget an invitation from yourself?'

'Well then, let's go in and get you a horse,' she was opening the stable doors as the same groom from the day before came running.

'Good morning, Lady Maria Eduarda, I'm sorry I'm late,' he said, attempting to comb his dishevelled hair with his fingers.

'Good morning, Manuel. You didn't have to come so early. I told you yesterday we could look after ourselves.'

'I know, My Lady, but if your father found out I'd be in trouble.'

'All right then. Thank you, Manuel. I appreciate it. Anyway, since you're here which horse would you recommend for Mr Neale?'

'That depends,' Manuel said. Turning to Gerald he asked, 'are you a very experienced rider, sir?'

'I wouldn't think so. I can ride and my father has a small country estate in England. When there I always ride but that's four, five times a year. I haven't been on a horse for nearly two years now.'

'In that case I'd say we give you an older horse. Experienced. Quiet. Easy going. Won't mind someone he doesn't know. I was thinking about Moreno, My Lady.'

'Good choice, Manuel,' turning to Gerald she added, 'Moreno's also a Lusitano but sixteen and a half years old. You'll be fine with him and I promise I'll contain Zuca so we go slower. He's very excitable.'

Gerald nodded. He didn't care. His gaze, his whole self were lost in her contemplation. His senses craved her. His body pined for hers. He wanted her. But how to get intimate with such a girl?

When Manuel returned he was leading a large, dark brown horse with black tail and mane. The animal appeared calm, placid, especially next to Zuca. The chestnut Lusitano seemed anxious to jump into action. Gerald held the reins and patted Moreno absent-mindedly, his brain fixated on devising a plan to have Maria Eduarda.

Surreptitiously she watched him. She liked his bright blue eyes, the boyish smile and the way his platinum blonde hair flopped onto his forehead. He was handsome. No denying she liked his good looks. He was also attentive. Kind. Charming. And obviously attracted to her but could she trust him? Did she want more than friendship? More than a harmless flirtation? Maria Eduarda didn't know. She'd never been in love and although not completely innocent or naïve, thanks to Grandmama Leopoldina's warnings, she was a virgin in every sense of the word. Not even a kiss, though many of the young men she danced with in society balls had tried.

She mounted Zuca and waited for Gerald to be ready on Moreno. Manuel handed her a saddle bag. Looking at Gerald who seemed slightly uncomfortable she pointed at the bag and said, 'our breakfast. There are sandwiches, coffee and fresh orange juice. I thought we'd have a light picnic, as we'll probably be too late for breakfast with the others by the time we get back.'

Gerald nodded without looking up. Maria Eduarda wondered whether he was afraid of the horse. He seemed to be taking a long time.

'You don't need to worry, Mr Neale,' she said kindly, 'Moreno's a calm animal. He won't throw you.'

'I hope not.'

He finally mounted, still appearing as if he didn't quite understand what he needed to do. But Moreno was an experienced horse and stood patiently until sensing the man on his back was ready.

It amused Maria Eduarda but she thought better than to comment. It might hurt his pride. Instead she said, 'ready?'

Gerald nodded.

'Good, then let's go. We'll start slowly until you're used to Moreno. Then perhaps a little gallop will be in order but not at full speed.'

He lined his horse next to hers and the animals strode sedately out of the stable yard and into the woods. At first Maria Eduarda contained Zuca and they moved leisurely but gradually she allowed the horse to break into a trot, glancing over her shoulder to ensure Gerald wasn't left behind. She needn't worry. Moreno was a reliable horse and instinctively suited his pace to Zuca's.

She took her favourite route through the woods, shouting names of trees and pointing out some of her most cherished places. After a while the path left the dense woods, thick with bushes and ancient tall trees, and emerged into a pine forest. Lighter. Intensely fragrant. After lingering for a moment Maria Eduarda turned and galloped across a couple of meadows and a stream, dry now due to the intense summer heat, until they reached what she called the rock garden. A hilltop with a few granite rocks scattered about. It was nearly seven thirty and the sun beginning to warm. She suggested a stop and Gerald agreed. Dismounting, Maria Eduarda led her horse to the shade of nearby trees and unhitched the saddle bags as Gerald followed her.

Handing him a packet of sandwiches wrapped in parchment paper she lifted two thermos flasks and asked, 'coffee or juice?'

'Coffee first, please' he replied.

She took out paper cups and filled two with coffee and another two with the fresh orange juice. They ate and drank in silence until she broke it by saying, 'you should admire the view, Mr Neale. It's quite something from here.'

'I am admiring the view,' he said, his blue gaze fixed on her.

Maria Eduarda pretended she didn't understand his meaning. Looking away and pointing at a bright yellow and red building perched on top of a steep crag in the distance she said, 'that's the Palace of Pena. Have you heard of it?'

'No. It's flashy. Colourful.'

'Yes. It was built in the 19th century by Prince Ferdinand of Saxe-Coburg and Gotha-Koháry, the Catholic branch of the better known House of Saxe-Coburg and Gotha.'

'A relation of Prince Albert, Queen Victoria's husband?'

'As a matter of fact, yes. They were cousins. Fernando, his name in Portuguese, married Queen Maria II of Portugal. He was influenced by the romantic castles of his native Germany and decided to create one here too. There used to be the ruin of a very old monastery at the top of the cliff where the palace is now. Fernando purchased it and the vast lands around it, having the palace built and paid for from his own money. It's a national monument at present. One can visit at certain times of the year.'

'Interesting. So tell me, all these vast lands we've been riding through belong to your father?'

'Yes. The estate's extensive but still only half the size of the one in Alentejo. Sintra is fresher and more pleasant than Lisbon during the summer. Papa likes to spend the hottest months here. It's been a tradition of sorts for centuries since royalty moved here during the summer. The air was healthier and free of most of the pestilence that plagued Lisbon. I like Sintra very much but to see my father's lands at their best you must come in spring.'

'Is that a formal invitation?' he asked her.

Maria Eduarda noticed the cheeky grin and the twinkle in his eyes. She pretended to slap his wrist and smiling bashfully said, 'no, Mr Neale. Merely stating a fact, meaning the fields and the woods are more beautiful when the grass is green, with wildflowers scattered everywhere, and the streams are full and running. Not dry and dusty as they're now. This summer has been particularly hot so far.'

'You can say that again.'

'I suppose you're not used to such heat.'

'No. I find it difficult to cope.'

'Where're you from in England, Mr Neale?'

'Actually I was born in this country. I think I might have mentioned it before.'

She shrugged. 'Even if you did. I don't mind hearing it again.'

'All right,' he agreed, quickly summarising his life story.

Maria Eduarda listened attentively, nodding occasionally. Gerald finished by saying, 'my father eventually bought a house in London, Chelsea, and went to work for the government. He retired from public duty last year and moved to a small, rather pleasant estate he owns in Sussex, in the southeast of England, inherited from his father. My brother's now on active duty somewhere in France. He enlisted when the war started.'

'I'm sorry.'

'Don't be. It's life.'

They were quiet for a time. Maria Eduarda finished her coffee and orange juice then leaning back against the tree shut her eyes for a moment, enjoying the sun on her face and the sound of the cicadas. She felt his hand touching her arm, caressing it gently. It was pleasant. She allowed him to continue.

Something stirred. A rustling noise by her side. She didn't open her eyes. Was he moving closer to her? All of a sudden his lips were on hers. Hot. Passionate. Soft. Then it all happened very fast. His left arm around her waist, pulling her towards him. His right hand cupping her breasts over the blouse. His lips moving down her neck. Taken unawares Maria Eduarda didn't react immediately. The kisses were pleasant. But abruptly Grandmama Leopoldina's words of warning echoed in her mind. She opened her eyes wide, firmly placing her hands on his chest.

'No. Stop, please.'

But he tightened his embrace instead.

'Just call me Gerald, my love,' his voice was hoarse, his breathing fast.

Maria Eduarda pushed him away and jumped to her feet.

'No,' she repeated. Turning her back on him she added, 'we must go back.' Without another word she mounted Zuca and, urging him into a gallop with her spurs, disappeared in a cloud of dust.

Gerald remained seated, dazed. She'd fled. He could have slapped himself. Stupid. Idiot. He might have just ruined all his chances with her. Maria Eduarda was a lady, brought up to remain a virgin until married. Had probably not even kissed a man before. In future he must advance with care.

He remonstrated himself, 'what a fool.'

Stuffing the picnic remains into the saddle bags he remounted his horse and, as if it understood his haste, it leaped forward into a full gallop.

He caught up with her in the ancient woods. She'd slowed down but Gerald didn't dare ride by her side. Not a word was spoken on their way back to the house. Arriving at the stable yard he dismounted in a hurry and holding Zuca's reins said sincerely, 'forgive me, Lady Maria Eduarda. I didn't mean to offend you. Please forgive me for being so ardent and failing to respect you. I hope you will continue to talk to me.'

Still astride Zuca she gazed down with flaring eyes. The silence stretched. He pleaded, 'please, please forgive me.'

Slowly she slid to the ground and standing in front of him said quietly, 'I'm not offended. I'm just wondering what all of this means.'

He wanted to embrace her but held himself in check, instead simply declaring, 'it means I'm mad about you.'

Shaking her head she didn't reply, took Zuca's reins from him and walked the horse to the stable. Gerald followed. By the door she stopped. Glancing over her shoulder she said, 'it's all very sudden, Mr Neale. I need to think.'

With these words she disappeared inside the stable.

Gerald, frozen next to his horse, cursed himself and his actions for a second time. He must learn to wait and give her time.

The remainder of the weekend elapsed slowly, uneventfully. There were no secret conversations between Ludovico and Ricardo. No strange or inappropriate proposals to the Duke of Windsor. They, together with the ambassador, rode out in the countryside and played golf. The ladies went to Sintra's village centre to visit the National Palace and had afternoon tea together. And they all, men and women, took a trip to the Palaces of Pena and Monserrate.

Maria Eduarda maintained her distance. She played the piano and spent time with her little sister, reading her a story.

Misery didn't begin to describe how Gerald felt. He couldn't sleep and hardly ate. So much so that Sir Ronald noticed and asked him what was wrong. He excused himself with the excessive heat, saying it made him unwell as he was unaccustomed to it.

On the day of their return to Lisbon, Maria Eduarda came out with Ana Maria to say goodbye to everyone. She familiarly kissed Ricardo and his wife on the cheeks, curtsied to the Windsors and shook hands with Sir Ronald and Mrs Campbell. Him she dismissed with a nod, barely acknowledging his presence. With a resigned sigh Gerald sat at the wheel of his car, turned the key in the ignition and accelerated away, glancing in the rear mirror to look at her one more time but she had already gone back to the house. Exhaling heavily he felt sorry for himself. She hadn't even permitted him to kiss her hand in farewell.

Chapter 11 – The Language of Love

Only a few days after the weekend in Sintra, the Duke and Duchess of Windsor departed Lisbon in the early hours of 2nd August 1940, sailing to New York on the Excalibur. From there the couple would travel to the Bahamas where the Duke, however reluctantly, was to take on his post as governor.

With the departure of the Windsors life at the British embassy in Lisbon became suddenly boring. Propaganda continued, as usual to little effect. Salazar did not openly show any support for the Germans but neither did he for the British, doing business with both sides, conceding and then retracting, cunningly dealing with either faction and putting his and the interests of Portugal first. No matter what the Germans and the British threw at him Salazar seemed to emerge as the winner.

Gerald had little to do but hang around the embassy's garden waiting for orders from London. Pleasant enough. The garden was shady and fresh. A treasure in the scorching summer temperatures. He often thought about Maria Eduarda. Her image visited him during the night while he was sleeping or daydreaming in the embassy's garden. He liked to remember every detail of their ride – the kiss, her lips – and to imagine how she'd look naked. He recalled the feel of her skin. Soft. Fragrant. She smelled of roses and cherry blossom. Until the moment he'd kissed her the weekend was perfect. The conversations. Discreetly listening to her playing the piano. Staring at the stars with her. The meals. Her father's artistic treasures, especially the first edition of The Lusiads and the manuscript. The beauty and easiness of it all and nothing, no conspiracy regarding the Duke of Windsor. If there had indeed been one it was an attempt by the Germans that didn't come to fruition and neither Ricardo nor Ludovico were involved.

Gerald hadn't seen Maria Eduarda since the Sintra weekend. He looked at his wristwatch on the side table – 3.25 in the morning. Impossible to sleep. Too hot and his head full of that girl. He had to do something to still that yearning for her. His body tightened. It was painful. He must have her or he'd go mad.

But what could he do? Wearing only his underpants Gerald jumped off the bed and lit a cigarette. He stood at the window smoking, listening to the noises of the city and watching the blue smoke dissolve in the night air. He knew Maria Eduarda and her family had returned from Sintra three days ago. Her birthday was in less than ten days. Bristow, somehow always perfectly informed about everyone and everything, told him she would turn twenty on Sunday 15th September. Gerald had been playing with the idea of calling upon her at home but feared she wouldn't receive him. Perhaps he could send her flowers on her birthday. Surely it would be a good idea, an ice-breaker. Did she think about him? Or, more likely, never spared him another thought? The Sintra weekend was the past, having happened more than five weeks ago. At first he'd hoped she might write him a letter and mentally willed her to do so through telepathy or something silly like that. Wishing for it almost every single day he got himself in a bit of a state anticipating the post. But of course she didn't write. And each day he felt sorry for himself. Since her return he walked up and down the hill at the approximate time of her music lessons but to no avail. He never as much glimpsed her even for a brief moment.

Exhaling heavily Gerald told himself he must take some action. Waiting like a puppy for her to turn up as if by magic wouldn't do. Send her flowers? Or a box of chocolates? Or those little pastries she liked so much? The delicious pastéis de nata. No. Flowers. Flowers were always a good idea in his experience with the opposite sex. Or both? The pastries and flowers. No. Too much. Send flowers now and apologise for his recklessness during the ride. He didn't regret kissing or touching her. But she might be offended, believing he took her for an easy girl. Her words echoed in his head, *I'm not offended. I'm just wondering what all of this means*. And he'd answered it meant he was mad about her. Then she'd left and hadn't spoken another word with him, seemingly ignoring him. He must apologise. Yes. A girl like Maria Eduarda must receive an apology and it must sound sincere.

Crushing the cigarette butt on the windowsill he flicked it

down to the garden. What flowers to send? The first time he'd sent her a mixture of roses – red, white and pink. What about now? Red? No. Too passionate. White? No. Too pure. His thoughts weren't chaste; sometimes short of indecent. Pink? Perhaps. Neutral. Between the two. But pink was most girls' colour and Maria Eduarda was anything but. It wasn't just her exquisite beauty. She was headstrong, talented, intelligent and able to converse about matters considered a man's dominion. No. Pink was the wrong colour for her. An exquisite flower? Orchids? Sunflowers? Would he find them in the depleted florists of the Portuguese capital city? In that instant he suddenly remembered. Slapping his forehead he pushed his hair back with his fingers. How could he have forgotten? Yellow roses. Her favourite flower. It had been the second evening, at dinner, after his blunder with the kiss, the Duchess of Windsor declared she would like to see the gardens in Sintra in the spring when they must be teaming with all sorts of flowers.

'Indeed,' Rosa, Maria Eduarda's stepmother, said, 'they're a riot of colour. All types of flowers. And the fields get rather lovely too.'

'Is that where the name of the estate comes from?'

'Yes and no, Your Grace,' Ludovico had answered.

'Oh?'

'Apparently,' he had explained, 'centuries ago there were a few abandoned fields here before my ancestors bought the property and built the mansion. In spring those fields used to be covered in wild red poppies so the locals used to refer to them as Parque das Papoilas – Poppies Park. The name stuck and is still the same today.'

'Interesting, Papa,' Maria Eduarda exclaimed, 'I didn't know that. You hadn't told me before.'

'I'm sorry my dear. I hardly ever think about it. Only when guests ask.'

'Do you like flowers, Lady Maria Eduarda?' The Duchess of Windsor asked her directly.

'Oh yes, Your Grace. Very much,' she nodded graciously, then asked, 'do you have a favourite flower?'

'Difficult to say. I like all flowers but perhaps my preference goes to carnations and azaleas. What about you?'

Gerald recalled how Maria Eduarda's eyes sparkled, her face lit up with that dimpled smile and she'd said quietly, 'yellow roses. They look like they've trapped the sunlight in their petals.'

What a lovely thing to say, he had thought to himself. Yellow roses. Perfect flowers to send her. They would prove him thoughtful. Caring. Sincere. Because he remembered they were her favourite flowers. Having made his decision he ran to the bathroom to shower and dress but all of sudden realised it was still dark. Not yet four. He must wait until the morning. No problem. He had a plan. Walking back to the bedroom he threw himself, belly down, on the bed and fell almost instantly asleep.

The grandfather clock had struck three in the afternoon a moment ago. Maria Eduarda was just walking up the stairs when the front doorbell rang loudly through the quiet house. Ana Maria was having a nap and fearing her little sister might wake up, Eduarda ran back down and opened the door herself. A young man with a huge smile, workers' trousers, short-sleeved blue cotton shirt and black shoes, a brown beret on his head, stood in front of her. He took off the beret, bowed and said, 'good afternoon, Miss. Flower delivery for Lady Maria Eduarda de Arantes Silva.'

She couldn't hide her bewilderment. Flowers? Who would be sending her flowers out of the blue? Aloud she said, 'I'm Lady Maria Eduarda. Are you sure they're for me, I mean is that the name on the card?'

'Of course,' he showed her the card where her name and address were clearly written.

'All right, thank you. Wait a moment, please,' turning she shouted, 'Lucinda, Lucinda.'

A young maid came out of her stepmother's sitting room.

'You need someone, My Lady?'

'I need Lucinda. You know where she is?'

The girl nodded and disappeared through a back door. A moment later Lucinda showed up, still wearing a large brimmed, straw hat. She must have been in the garden.

'Thanks for coming so quickly, Lucinda.'

'What is it, my dear?'

'Will you give some money to this young man,' she indicated the delivery boy with a sign of her head, 'he's just brought these flowers for me.'

Maria Eduarda noticed Lucinda's cheeky grin and, giving her no time to comment, she ran up the stairs into her room, carrying the flowers in her arm and closing the door behind her. Placing them gently on the bed she admired them. It was a beautiful bouquet of about two dozen gorgeous yellow roses. Her favourite. Thrilled she picked up the envelope and looked at the address one more time before opening it. The handwriting was unknown. She tore the envelope open and extracted the card. It was a pretty card with a watercolour of yellow roses. She opened it and read.

Dear Lady Maria Eduarda,
Please accept these humble flowers as a formal apology for my behaviour in Sintra. I sincerely am sorry if I caused you any distress or offended you with my actions. It wasn't my intention. I have a genuine admiration for you and would hate myself if my reckless behaviour may have spoiled our friendship. Please forgive me.
I dare hope for a reply.
Yours sincerely,
Gerald Neale

The words stirred a turmoil in her chest. She had tried hard to forget his kiss but didn't always succeed. Touching her lips as if sensing his, Maria Eduarda read the message again. The card's handwriting didn't match the envelope's. So he must have written the card himself and the florist addressed the envelope. Eduarda felt unsure what to do. Reply? Ignore? The first time he'd sent her flowers she had discarded the message and never given it another thought. Do the same now? It'd be impolite. Rude. He sounded sincere. With a sigh she dropped the card inside a drawer of her desk to reply to it later. The envelope went in the paper basket. Then she walked out of her bedroom with the roses, fetched a vase from the music room, went to the kitchen to fill it up with water and quietly arranged the roses. Returning to the music room she placed the vase on the wall-mounted semi-circle table between the windows, under the silver framed mirror. There she could see the flowers while playing the piano. She needed to think about Mr Neale. His kiss. What to write him. And analyse her feelings. Most definitely. With this in mind she sat at the piano and began playing one of Mozart's sonatas.

At the embassy Gerald was on tenterhooks for the next four days but finally on the morning of the fifth his anxiety subsided. A messenger delivered him a letter. His fingers shook and he dropped the envelope twice before tearing it apart. Nervously he extracted one single piece of paper but, before reading it, shot back up the stairs to his rooms, wanting to savour the letter alone. With bated breath he unfolded it and began silently to read.

Dear Mr Neale,
Thank you so much for the lovely bouquet. Very thoughtful of you. Yellow roses are my favourite flowers.

I appreciate your apology. But, as you may remember, I didn't think there was a need to apologise. I wasn't offended by your actions. On the contrary, I was flattered. But a kiss is, at least for me, a serious matter. I wondered what it all meant and remember your answer clearly. You said and I quote, 'it means that I'm mad about you.'

I cannot deny that the words were pleasant to hear and that I enjoyed listening to you say them. But I still don't know what it all means. I don't know my feelings for you or whether I have any at all and I am unsure as to what you really want from me.

Roses are the language of love so I dare presume you're confessing that you are in love with me. Charming. Sweet. And I do like you. I enjoy your company and I think you generally have an interesting conversation but I am not ready for a serious relationship with a man (assuming that is what you want) just yet.

I mentioned to you before I want to study but must wait until I am of age, which is only a little over a year away. Then I won't require Papa's permission. Besides, we are living through a terrible war, though in Portugal we are fortunate to hardly notice it. It however means times are uncertain. You are British and your work brought you to Lisbon but such an assignment is on a temporary basis. You may be called back to London at any moment. I don't know whether I could embark on a steady relationship with you under such circumstances. As I said in Sintra, I need time to think and understand what I feel.

I did really love your roses – your kind and thoughtful gesture – but please do not continue to send me flowers or anything else. I promise you I will think about everything that's happened and, if I conclude I have feelings for you in the way it seems you have for me, I will write you again and we will go from there.

For now, please respect my wishes and don't try to see me or send me anything. I have no doubt we will chance upon each other sooner or later in some public place. Lisbon is a capital city with a provincial feel where everyone knows everybody, at least from sight.

Thank you again for the flowers.
Yours sincerely
Maria Eduarda

Gerald let the letter drop to the floor. He wanted to punch the walls. She liked the flowers. She wasn't offended. But still gave him nothing. Roses are the language of love. The language of love. What love? Not hers obviously. She didn't reject his feelings but neither did she accept them. Or give him any hope for the future.

He wasn't used to women turning him down. So far not one, not a single one, had said no. They found him irresistible. Yet, the one he desperately wanted didn't seem interested at all. The language of love. Puh! She needed to think and be certain of what she felt. Not ready for a steady relationship. Well, he didn't want one. He wanted to have her naked in his bed. His yearning for her was killing him. Distressing him. She said she liked him but the war, his job being temporary and whatever other stupid excuses. Wanted to study. Why? She was a woman for god's sake. She'd marry, have children. Play the society hostess. Lady Maria Eduarda, eldest daughter of the shamefully rich Duke of Beja. They would meet no doubt in some public place. Yes but he wanted to meet her now and alone in a room, naked in his bed to kiss every inch of her body. But no. Madam needed to think.

'Well, then. Think what you want. By the time you're done thinking I'll have moved to greener pastures,' he murmured to himself.

But even as he thought it he knew he wouldn't rest or get her out of his mind until he had her. Gerald snorted savagely.

'The sly little minx.'

She filled his mind, his dreams, his moments to distraction. His work suffered. He smoked and drank more than usual. He must pull himself together or the ambassador might notice and send him back to England.

Gerald exhaled. Outraged he picked up the letter, crushed it into a ball and threw it in the wastepaper basket, snarling furiously at the empty room.

Chapter 12 – Time Goes By

Gerald Neale was a man who didn't take no for an answer or kindly to a rejection – even when it wasn't a repudiation as such and simply a request for time to think. Incensed at Maria Eduarda's reply after he'd sent her the bouquet of yellow roses he wanted revenge. It took him forever and a day to forgive her and realise the letter was a message from a young woman, inexperienced where men were concerned but not naïve; a young woman who knew what she wanted but was probably unsure of her feelings for him and what they might represent for her future if she gave in.

It was good he didn't see Maria Eduarda until the end of the year. Gerald was pleased the terrible heat of the summer had gradually turned into the luminous, pleasingly warm days of autumn. He was restless, fighting inwardly with himself. Desperately wanting to see Maria Eduarda and simultaneously angry no sign came from her. Was she pondering her feelings after he'd kissed her during that fabulous weekend in Sintra? She'd said she needed to think but for how long could a person think about the same thing? Still her letter following his yellow roses was a rejection of sorts. But was it? Sometimes he thought as much and blew a fuse, being in a black mood for days. Other moments he believed she was just being normal, behaving like any honest young woman would. Probing whether he was trustworthy. Whether his intentions were serious, which they weren't. He wasn't keen on marriage. But Maria Eduarda didn't…couldn't know that.

Occasionally Gerald would pace the hill up and down for ages, pausing in front of her father's house in the hope of bumping into her or of seeing her in the garden of the villa. To no avail. He never saw her. Not a single time. Had she returned to Sintra? But no. From snippets of conversation among people who were friends with the Duke of Beja and his family, Gerald knew they were all in Lisbon. Maybe she no longer walked to her appointments, being instead driven by one of her father's chauffeurs. Try as he might she remained invisible. He didn't as much as glimpse her until the evening of 31st December.

Ricardo Espirito Santo and his wife Maria organised a large New Year's Eve party at their weekend home in Boca do Inferno, mostly for friends and family, but extended the invitations to Salazar and various ambassadors in Lisbon, including the British and the German. Baron von Hoyningen-Huene accepted the invite, forcing Sir Ronald Campbell to decline. He couldn't possibly attend a party where the enemy was also present. Other embassies followed his lead. At the same time, the British ambassador didn't wish to upset the couple who so generously had agreed to host the Duke and Duchess of Windsor during their summer visit to Lisbon for a full month. Sir Ronald therefore sent his deputy, accompanied by Gerald to represent him.

Gerald anticipated Maria Eduarda would be present and hoped to be able to spirit her away for a few minutes. As it turned out, he only managed to speak with her at midnight, after manoeuvring through the rooms to stand next to her while 1940 glided into 1941. He slid his arm around her waist and stole a hot kiss. With the excuse of greeting the new year everyone was kissing and his passion went unnoticed. Except for Maria Eduarda. He felt her body tremble. Fool's paradise as it only lasted an all too brief moment. She stepped gently away from him but her eyes told him more than a thousand words. His heart skipped a beat. He felt a lump in his throat and just wanted to leave the party with her on his arm. But any hopes of whisking her away were dashed. Gerald had observed an unknown man continuously hovering around Maria Eduarda for most of the evening. He'd left her for a couple of minutes at midnight and Gerald had grabbed the opportunity but just as he was about to propose they leave to another room to be alone the man returned. He was in his early thirties. Dark hair. Brown eyes. Medium height. Slim. Marked haughty presence. Indifferent smile, barely opening his lips. They formed a thin line, giving the impression of a continuous cold smirk. Gerald found out he was the eldest son of the Duke of Palmela. A prospective husband for Maria Eduarda with Ludovico's blessing. He took an instant dislike to the man but felt vindicated watching how Maria Eduarda didn't appear to like him at all. She hardly spared him a look, seldom addressed him and plainly avoided him, leaving him alone and escaping to her family or a group of friends. But Palmela's son was obviously persistent and couldn't be deterred from his objective. Each time she fled he quickly moved around the room until reaching her side once again.

Frustrated, irritable, Gerald left the party in the early hours of 1st January 1941, resentful of the moments Palmela's son spent with Maria Eduarda while he hardly had a chance at any quality time with her. At least he had kissed her. And she appeared to dislike Palmela's son's attentions as much as he was visibly taken with her. But then who wouldn't be? Gerald couldn't think of any man.

For the first time in months he was out like a light the moment he hit the sack. He woke up early. Shortly after six but feeling rested, relaxed. The first thing coming into his mind was the image of his midnight kiss with Maria Eduarda. Closing his eyes Gerald relived the moment. She hadn't been indifferent to his touch. Grinning like a Cheshire cat he felt certain she would eventually come round and be his one day. Just needed to give her time. Kicking back the covers he switched on the bedside lamp, then walked to the bathroom to have a shower and shave.

Once ready he remembered he hadn't written to his father for a long, long time. The old man must be worried about his lack of news, especially because his brother wasn't home either. Jonathan had enlisted at the start of the war and was somewhere in occupied France. Sitting at his desk Gerald wrote a detailed letter about his life in Lisbon and the weekend in Sintra back in the summer, taking care in describing the marvellous first edition of The Lusiads and finishing by stating,

I'm certain, dear dad, you would be as taken with the book as I was. It's exquisite. Genuine from 1572. I did ask the Duke how much he wanted for it, as I thought that between you and I we could come up with enough money to acquire it for our collection. Then we would own a real treasure. Of course we already have certain treasures but nothing like this. Unfortunately, the Duke will not sell, saying it has been in his family for centuries. He put me in contact with a book antiquarian he knows but the man couldn't find me any other edition of The Lusiads. He also asked some of his fellow antique dealers but no-one knew of such an edition for sale. A real shame. I had my heart immediately set on it and I'm certain you would too even without having seen it.

Anyway, I suppose one can say it's not meant to be. I promise however to search for one or two first editions of more modern Portuguese authors. Anything would be a precious addition, as although you've lived here so many years you've no books from this country.

I have no idea yet when I'll return to England. There is a lot of work to do here. In the meantime I hope you continue to be well. Have you had more news from Jonathan? I hope so and that he is in good health and good spirits, as his last letter to me showed.

Your affectionate son
Gerald

The new year had started slowly but 1941 turned out to be a very busy time for Gerald. Privately his head continued to be filled with images of Maria Eduarda, especially at night, disturbing his sleep. Her face haunted him. Sometimes so real he almost believed he could touch her if he stretched his arm. But for a girl like Maria Eduarda he couldn't employ his usual tactics to get her into bed. Patience was the key. So he decided to let nature take its course instead of taking action. She felt something for him of that he was certain and patience pays dividends, his former Portuguese nanny, Mena, always said. Gerald believed her. Besides, from February onward he hardly had time to think about any private matters. His job really took off and he was up to his eyeballs in work. Every minute became intense, burying him in reports, missives, meetings with informants and all sorts of planned disruption. Even his weekly visits to the Casino in Estoril were rarely for fun and nearly always for the good of his trade.

Germany had increased their business with Portugal, buying more wolfram than ever. So much so that Portuguese opportunists began leaving their jobs and turning into 'volframistas' – people who sold the mineral to the Germans, becoming rich overnight. It was Gerald's objective to disrupt such trade dealings as much as possible. In late May he had to provide support to an agent named Ian Fleming who came to Lisbon to assess various intelligence organisations in the city thus ensuring smooth coordination of Operation Golden Eye[12].

Gerald still walked up and down the hill whenever he had a free moment in the hope of seeing Maria Eduarda. He did see her sporadically but never alone. She always greeted him kindly but no chance to chat or invite her for a coffee.

On 15 September Maria Eduarda turned twenty-one and her father insisted she must accept the Duke of Palmela's son's proposal of marriage or another suitable suitor as soon as possible. Gerald learned from Bristow – how he always knew everything like any old gossip aunt was a mystery but he did – that Maria Eduarda had stood up to her father and rejected the Duke of Palmela's son's proposal. Against her father's wishes she had enrolled at university and began studying physics with the support of her mentor Professor Dr Berta de Almeida. Bristow said that Ludovico didn't like it but finally saw reason. Either of his own accord or through Ricardo Espirito Santo's influence, Ludovico had come to terms with Maria Eduarda's studies. He didn't have much choice since she was of age but at least he had stopped pressing her to accept a husband, setting however certain rules his daughter must obey while she lived under his roof. If she wanted to obtain a degree in scientific subjects and continue her music studies she must do so with a chaperone. No way out. No deviation from the rules. Ludovico had therefore employed a serious, no-nonsense middle-aged widow for the role. A dona Marieta da Silva. A small woman with a rotund figure, round face with little eyes behind old-

---

[12] See Author's Notes and Bibliography for Ian Fleming & Golden Eye.

fashioned spectacles and a special predilection for chocolates and pastries. Dona Marieta was an ever-present shadow attached to her ward. No privacy. So Gerald had to be content with a passing smile or a wave of the hand.

When Maria Eduarda had turned twenty-one he sent her flowers with a card, wishing her happy birthday and congratulating her on being her own master now she was of age. She sent him a straightforward thank you note, generic and impersonal, making no reference to his feelings and even less to her own. It could have come from anyone. Gerald chose to believe the note's detachment was down to someone looking over her shoulder while writing it. Again according to Bristow – a bottomless well of information – Dona Marieta never left Maria Eduarda alone and followed Ludovico's strict instructions to the letter. She must have supervised the note to ensure its message was proper and obeyed the rules of decorum.

From her bedroom window or the library Maria Eduarda often saw Gerald walk up and down the hill. Her heart leaped each time she glimpsed his handsome face and elegant figure. By now she understood her feelings for him were dangerously close to love but had decided to ignore them. Her independence was more important. Becoming a scientist and furthering her music studies were her unshakeable goals. She neither wanted nor needed a man, however much attraction she sensed for the good-looking Englishman. It was difficult enough to face her father, standing her ground against his wish for her to marry. Papa agreed in the end. It surprised her. All right, he had set his rules, which were not negotiable. A chaperone at all times if she wanted to continue living under his roof. And of course she did. What other option was there for the time being? She had to agree.

Maria Eduarda exhaled, rolling her eyes. Dona Marieta was irritating. She unnerved her but it was a small price to pay in order to study, gain her independence and keep relative freedom.

Gerald had sent her a bouquet for her birthday. Yellow roses again. She had almost jumped for joy, impulsively wanting to run out of the house to the embassy, fall into his arms and kiss him but of course none of that happened. A prosaic person she knew better than obeying such impulses. She might have succumbed to his charms and perhaps be in love with him but would not act upon it. Her desire for learning, for freedom and a genuine wish for a career were stronger than anything else. So, she thanked him for the beautiful bouquet and the birthday card, as good manners dictated. No more no less. No hint of her feelings or of anything that had passed between them. They occasionally crossed on the street. She would have liked to invite him for a coffee but dona Marieta's presence stopped her. Maria Eduarda would smile and he'd smile back. Frequently they waved at each other. And that was it.

The weeks after her twenty-first birthday passed so fast she hardly noticed, busy with her lectures. Additionally she had one-on-one tuition with Professor Berta de Almeida on the various subjects that formed her first semester at university. Piano, music, reading for herself and her little sister occupied the little time she had to spare, causing her to almost forget Gerald's existence. At night she slept soundly. No time to think about him, usually exhausted from a full day of learning, studying and piano practising.

And so 1941 slowly but surely approached its end. November was almost gone when her father announced this year he wanted to do something different. They would go to Sintra as always for Christmas but, immediately after, were to travel to their Alentejo estate. It was his turn to organise a New Year's Eve party. Ricardo had done it the year before. The large manor house in their Herdade do Sobreiro[13], as the estate in Alentejo was called due to its huge numbers of cork-trees, was ideal for such a celebration. There was space for dinner and a ball, and enough room to accommodate all the guests.

Without delay Ludovico threw himself and his wife into the organisation of the whole event – from travelling to food, wines, bedrooms and whatever else he thought about. He handed Maria Eduarda a list of names and asked her to write the

---

[13] Sobreiro is the Portuguese name for the cork tree.

invitations. And so, as uneventful a year as 1941 was from Maria Eduarda's and Gerald's perspectives, it was about to end with a bang. Tumultuous months lay ahead.

Chapter 13 – The Theft

The wind howled through the trees, swirling around the house. The long branch of the ancient oak bashed against the window glass panes a few times but Maria Eduarda didn't want to close the wooden shutters. The night was clear. The sky scintillated in a billion tiny lights, like a piece of delicate silver embroidery on a black velvet cloak. From her bed, with the covers up to her neck, she could see the stars designing patterns across the heavens, arches and lines of light above the house, the trees. Beautiful. What worlds could be hiding up there? Would there be a being somewhere looking down on planet Earth and wondering about the madness going on in most parts of the World? What would it think of the human race? War raging everywhere. Maria Eduarda trembled every time she listened to the stories that some of the refugees told. Bombs. Killing. Machine guns. Crippled men. More killing. Deportation of Jews and other people in Germany. Dead women. Children. Famine. More killing. And for what?

Portugal had so far managed to stay out of the war and remain a neutral country. Papa supported the policy of neutrality, as did almost everyone she knew. Maria Eduarda agreed. It was the only way Portugal could survive.

She reflected on the day. 16th December 1941 and no end to the fighting in sight. The United States had joined the war just over a week ago and she had begun her university studies two and a half months earlier. She thought the entrance of the US in the war had not changed anything so far, at least, not in Portugal. But it almost certainly would for the occupied countries and the course of the war. It must be horrible to live in a place where there was fighting, bombing, famine and fear. Not being able to go to school, to study, to buy food when needed, to lead a normal, peaceful life. She couldn't imagine how grim, how horrendous, how terrifying it must be.

'I'm very lucky,' she whispered to herself.

Residing in a country torn apart by war would have meant the impossibility of enrolling at university. She didn't want to contemplate it. The first few months were a dream. She was loving all the subjects and the special tuition hours with Berta. Maria Eduarda still found difficult to believe she had been allowed to go to university. Of course she was of age but financially dependent on her father. Almost certainly she owed his permission to Ricardo. Papa had at first said no but after a long conversation with Ricardo he'd changed his mind. She was permitted to study, as long as she agreed to attend with a chaperone. An easy decision though she didn't like dona Marieta much. Impossible to talk reasonably and rationally with her. Annoying, irritating to have her continuously looking over her shoulder. But at least at university the woman waited outside the lecture rooms in the corridor, occasionally in the cafeteria and in a different room during the music lessons. Bad. But it could be worse and, in any case, better than not studying or being forced to marry the Duke of Palmela's son. Eduarda didn't like him a bit. He was arrogant, conceited and a snob. She couldn't and wouldn't marry such a man. If she ever decided to tie the knot it would have to be for love. But she remained unconvinced by the advantages of matrimony. It meant losing independence, freedom of choice and decision. More or less becoming the property of her husband without any rights. Moving from under a father's authority to that of a husband's wasn't an attractive outlook for the future. She would not be allowed to travel or work without her husband's consent. How likely would that happen? No. It was best to remain single. To study and become independent. Marry for love one day perhaps but the feeling must be so powerful she'd feel unable to live without it.

 As it sometimes happened whenever she thought about love, her mind wandered to Gerald Neale. Her father and Ricardo said he was probably a spy but she didn't think so. Spies were dubious people, as far as she knew from her readings and from hearing the circulating rumours. Gerald was kind, gallant, tender and very handsome. Difficult to resist undoubtedly but resisted she had so far. Apart from sending her flowers on her twenty-first birthday he had been quiet and kept his distance. Maria Eduarda wondered whether dona Marieta could be the cause but concluded he was respecting her wishes or, more likely, he had too much work. She was aware of the politics surrounding wolfram, the dealings with the Germans and knew how unhappy about it the British were. Apparently they didn't mind Salazar's policy of neutrality but somehow expected him to lean more towards them than to the Germans. But then it wouldn't be neutral. Salazar was having none of it. She considered whether things would change as America had now joined the war. Probably not. She had heard Ricardo tell her father that the British but especially the US were interested in using the Azores as an airbase. Salazar could lure them with it while still continuing to trade with the Germans thus keeping everyone happy in a manner of speaking.

At the moment Maria Eduarda was looking forward to Christmas. It was a beautiful time in Sintra. Papa always went with the steward and two footmen into his pinewoods and selected a pine tree, as Portugal had no fir trees, to decorate as a Christmas tree. A tradition he had brought back from his time in England. The Christmas tree, he'd told her, had been introduced in Britain by Queen Charlotte, the German wife of George III around 1800 and made especially popular later, during the reign of Queen Victoria by her husband, Prince Albert of Saxe-Coburg and Gotha. In Portugal, the custom was to build a little nativity scene with miniature painted terracotta figures, pretend rivers, lakes, hills and sand roads. She and her family did both. Eduarda and Ana Maria would create the scene and decorate the tree together with Lucinda. Rosa might want to help. They would place their slippers by the chimney on Christmas Eve and wake up to the presents the next morning. Maria Eduarda smiled fondly. Ana Maria would be so excited. Her little sister still believed in the Infant Jesus coming down the chimney with the presents, according to Portuguese lore.

This year, immediately after Christmas, they were all leaving for Alentejo. Papa had his heart set on a huge New Year's Eve celebration at the estate. Things were in full swing; the steward and all the staff at the herdade extremely busy. Yet, with the war on, Maria Eduarda wondered if such a party was the right thing to do. Papa requested her to deal with the invitations and by now she had received most replies. Ricardo and Maria would be going of course. Salazar hadn't sent a reply yet but she doubted he would accept. Some of her father's friends had more or less said yes, or at least maybe, which in most Portuguese high society circles was as good as a confirmation. The German ambassador had accepted. Inevitably Sir Ronald declined. He couldn't possibly attend a party with the enemy but was sending his deputy and his private secretary in his place.

Mr Neale. Maria Eduarda couldn't deny she was excited about sharing the same house for a few days. A thud in her chest. Pulse accelerated. In Alentejo there would be many opportunities to escape dona Marieta. The herdade had larger, more extensive stables than Sintra. Maria Eduarda intended to ride, even though it was winter and cold. It meant avoiding dona Marieta who couldn't ride and feared horses. They were enormous and unpredictable creatures in her modest opinion, as she put it. Perhaps Mr Neale would ride with her. Kiss her again. She didn't wish to engage in a steady relationship. Marriage wasn't in her current list of things she wanted to do but Mr Neale was a very attractive man. Maria Eduarda often remembered his kisses. The memory sent shivers down her spine. Daring to be honest and admit it to herself was complicated but the truth was she longed for his lips and gentle touch. A little flirting, discreetly, so no-one would notice, especially Papa, would surely be all right. She grinned, mildly disapproving of her own thoughts.

All of a sudden a noise disturbed her. Instinctively she glanced at the window but it wasn't the wind. Glass. It sounded like glass shattering far away. Downstairs. Perhaps the gusts slashed a broken branch against a window or a door in the library, the salon or the music room. The parlour, the sitting and the dining rooms were on the ground-floor too but the same side as her bedroom so the sound would've been louder, clearer, not so distant. Maybe she should see to it. The broken pane might need covering. Rubbish or dead leaves could otherwise be blown into the house.

Maria Eduarda pushed down the covers and instantly shivered. This was the disadvantage of Sintra. Lovely and fresh in the summer but freezing in winter. The house was old and had no adequate heating. She could have a fire lit in her bedroom but disliked the smell of smoke. The previous morning there had been a touch of frost. The same would happen again. Dawn would be cold. Pale. Icy. Still two weeks until Christmas but Maria Eduarda couldn't remember a December as bitterly frosty as the present.

Another noise reached her from downstairs. More glass? A thud? She slid her feet into a pair of fluffy slippers and flinging her dressing gown over her shoulders silently opened the door of her bedroom. She glanced at the staircase. Everything was in darkness. The grandfather clock in the hall struck three. The sound echoed like an explosion through the silent rooms, startling her. Quietly and on tiptoes Maria Eduarda walked to the staircase. Leaning on the railing she craned her neck and listened attentively. There were noises she couldn't identify. Silently she walked down the stairs. The sounds came from the library. The door wasn't shut. Gently she pushed it a fraction and peered inside. A tall figure in dark clothes and a woolly beanie. A man? He had his back to her and was just escaping through one of the library glass doors that opened onto the terrace, carrying something under his arm. Not enough light to see what. She watched him run, jump onto a waiting horse and gallop away quickly, melting into the darkness of the woods. The horse seemed familiar. One of the Lusitanos. Her own. Zuca, the fastest horse in Sintra. Oh no. Not Zuca. Why had the man taken Zuca? As rider and horse vanished from view, she walked in but stopped abruptly. What she saw took her breath away.

The glass case that contained the precious first edition of Os Lusíadas had been broken. Glass splintered all over the floor underneath it, mixing with large pieces from the open door to the terrace where a glass pane had been smashed.

'Oh, no. No,' she said aloud, 'the book's gone.'

Swiftly Maria Eduarda checked the smaller glass case inside the vitrine that contained the manuscript. Gone too. The door of the vitrine stood open. Clearly it had been forced. The small glass coffer with the manuscript had vanished. Maria

Eduarda wondered who would be able to steal the precious possessions only to grasp that just about anyone could. Both book and manuscript pages were famous. The whole of Lisbon society and the press knew Papa owned a genuine first edition of Os Lusíadas from 1572 and some old pages of the same work believed to be written in the hand of the poet. She looked around carefully. Nothing else appeared to be missing. Except Zuca. Just then she heard the neighing of a horse. Zuca had returned but without the rider. The man had used one of their own horses to escape quicker through the woods and probably had a car waiting on the road nearby.

Swiftly Maria Eduarda turned around and ran up the stairs screaming to raise the alarm.

'Papa will be inconsolable,' she whispered to herself as she knocked heavily on his bedroom door.

Two hours later a constable had come up from the village to take statements regarding the theft but Sintra was a small place so, before leaving, the man had telegraphed to Lisbon asking for reinforcements. They came and canvased the whole area but to no avail. Zuca was returned to his stable box but there was no sign of the thief or of the precious items he had stolen.

Christmas was a sad affair. Maria Eduarda, little Ana Maria and their stepmother did what they could to cheer up Ludovico but barely anything worked.

Shaking his head, he said for the hundredth time, 'I don't understand why someone would steal the book and the pages.'

'The book especially, Papa, is authentic and everyone knows it's valuable. The old pages possibly are too…if anyone can prove they're real,' Maria Eduarda said.

'Yes but conspicuous. The thief won't be able to sell the book or the manuscript fast enough.'

'Perhaps he escaped to Spain, Papa. I'm sure he could find a clandestine buyer there.'

Maria Eduarda didn't know what to do or say to comfort her father. He only began gradually recovering from his loss as the departure day to Alentejo approached. They left in the early hours of Sunday, 28th December, forcing Ludovico to think about other matters.

Maria Eduarda breathed a sigh of relief. With the arrival of all the invitees at the herdade her father, forced to receive his guests and play the brilliant host, would forget about the theft if only for a few days.

Chapter 14 – Alentejo

The guests arrived on 30th December. It was a cold – for Portugal – but clear, sunny day and the undulating, green hills of Alentejo dazzled in the sunlight. Villages and towns were few and far between. One could travel for miles without seeing a house or even trees but, sprouted here and there, Gerald saw woods of oaks and holms where black pigs roamed freely. He had read the Alentejo pigs ran around like sheep or goats. Their meat was lean, tender and delicious, apparently because they fed mostly on the acorns from the oak, holm or cork trees. He saw large plantations of olive and cork trees. The latter fascinated him. Gerald had never seen a cork tree before. He knew the trees were part of the oak group and existed already in ancient times in the natural vegetation of the Iberian Peninsula. People had also been cultivating them for centuries. The cork, the bark of the tree, was cut and taken every nine years. It needed that long to grow again but its extraction didn't damage the trees. He had read all that somewhere, probably in an old book his father owned about the flora of the Iberian Peninsula in general and Portugal in particular.

The few hamlets and villages they passed on the way to the Duke of Beja's estate appeared poor. Small, crouched houses huddled together. White-washed walls, blinding in the intense light, framed with bright blue, yellow or red paint. Old men sat on benches by their front doors chatting and enjoying the warmth of the sun. There were not many women outside and Gerald assumed they were in their kitchens preparing a simple meal of boiled potatoes, cabbage and olive oil because they had little else. Here and there colourful figures were scattered in the fields, working, but small numbers. December wasn't a month for farming.

Midday had just gone when they pulled in front of Ludovico's large manor house. It was built in a classic style, resembling more a palace than a manor building, with a Palladian front. It seemed out of place in the middle of the vast estate and the thousands of cork trees – or sobreiros as called in Portuguese

– that gave the place its name. Herdade dos Sobreiros or Cork Trees Farmstead. Gerald knew that Alentejo was a region of big landowners, divided in two: Alto and Baixo Alentejo, meaning high and low, high the northern half and low the southern. Although it was the largest province in Portugal, occupying an area of 27,272 square kilometres, the land was in the hands of only a dozen or so privileged rich owners. In a small country, such as Portugal, where the mainland occupied an area of only 91,470 square kilometres, it was significant. The locals worked the landlords' vast estates in a near feudal system, living in poor, sometimes almost squalid conditions. Gerald knew some landlords were better than others and treated their people with respect. He hoped Ludovico was one of them.

Maria Eduarda, holding her little sister's hand, was at the door with her father and stepmother to receive the guests. She wore a blue skirt with a bright blue and yellow woollen jumper. Flat, sturdy shoes. Her hair was tied at the back with a yellow ribbon, forming a long, curly ponytail. No jewellery. No make-up. But she still looked gorgeous. Gerald watched her for a moment in awe. He wanted her so much it was difficult to breathe when in her presence. Exhaling he stepped forward to greet his hosts, indulging his lips a tad too long on Maria Eduarda's hand.

Footmen took the luggage and guided the guests to their rooms, informing they would hear a bell ringing twice, three minutes apart. It announced lunch, which would be served at 1 p.m. in the main dining room. Gerald looked out of his window at the wide extension of soft hills touching the horizon, and the thousands of cork trees. Voices outside his room, in the corridor, caught his attention. Opening the door a fraction he peered out to see Maria Eduarda and her little sister going into a room.

'Lady Maria Eduarda,' he exclaimed, 'is that your bedroom?'

'No,' it was Ana Maria who answered, 'it's mine. Edi's that one,' she pointed with her little finger to the door next to hers.

'I see. Thank you, Lady Ana Maria.'

The little girl beamed. 'I have to wash before lunch,' she

declared, 'Edi's going to help me. Are you going to wash before lunch too, Mr Neale?'

'Of course,' he replied with a serious face.

Maria Eduarda smiled, visibly amused at her little sister's chatter. 'Come on, hurry up. We'll see you at lunch, Mr Neale,' she said, then with one foot already inside her sister's room and glancing over her shoulder, she added, 'we can talk then.'

With those words she disappeared inside and closed the door behind herself and her sister. It was a promise, Gerald decided. A promise of something. He didn't know what but he might yet get lucky.

He was ready to go down long before the first bell rang for lunch but thought better to wait. At the second bell Gerald left and went down the stairs to look for the main dining room. Easy to find. He only had to follow the sound of voices. The room was rather large. The walls were painted in a warm pastel yellow. Various oil pictures of Alentejo landscapes and still lifes, displaying fruit, ham, types of chorizos and wines, hung on the walls. A long table was laid for twenty people. The chairs were dark oak with golden velvet upholstered seats. There were two fireplaces with lively fires cracking. The room was pleasantly warm. Large doors could be opened onto a terrace, covered with thick climbing vines. It must be pleasantly fresh and shady in the summer months.

Lunch was a light affair of a typical Portuguese soup – caldo verde, literally green soup – a smooth cream of potatoes, onion, leek, garlic and olive oil, with dark green Portuguese cabbage finely shredded. To accompany it there was homemade, warm, fresh bread with thin slices of chorizo, made from local black pigs. A light wine and water were served with the meal. Fresh oranges and pears from the estate's main orchard formed the dessert. Afterwards there was coffee.

Maria Eduarda sat with her little sister on the other side of the long table a couple of seats further to his right. Gerald stole many glances in her direction but she paid him no heed. He heard Ricardo ask her whether there was any news regarding the theft of Os Lusíadas and of the manuscript pages.

'No,' she replied, 'Papa and the police have tried everything they could but so far no clues.'

'And how's your father coping with it?'

'Not well, as you may imagine but at least for now he's thinking about more immediate matters as the house is full of guests.'

'Of course. Perhaps the book and the pages will be recovered in the new year.'

'Unlikely,' she said, 'personally I think whoever stole them, ran away to Spain and has disposed of them there, I mean has found a buyer and is enjoying his badly earned money.'

'One never knows, my dear. Don't lose hope,' Ricardo replied kindly.

'I'm sorry,' Gerald said, 'I don't mean to intrude on your conversation, Senhor Espirito Santo, Lady Maria Eduarda, but I couldn't help hearing. What happened to the beautiful first edition of Os Lusíadas?'

'It was stolen,' she replied.

'Oh Lord! And how?'

Maria Eduarda told him the whole story of the theft and repeated her view that the thief had escaped to Spain and sold both the book and the old manuscript pages there.

'I must agree,' Ricardo commented, 'though I hope the police will still be able to find both or at least, the book…for your father's sake, my dear, but there's logic in your views. The book's highly sought after. The manuscript pages perhaps not so much…at least, not without a proper authentication, but the book's famous. It's generally known that your father owns one of the few original first editions. The theft was all over the papers. The only possible explanation as to why nothing has yet been found is what you've mentioned, my dear – the thief smuggled them to Spain and found a buyer there.'

Maria Eduarda nodded, then added, 'don't mention it to Papa, Ricardo. He's in a good mood at the moment but will remember the theft soon enough, no doubt.'

'Of course, my dear. You're right,' Ricardo agreed.

Addressing Maria Eduarda Gerald exclaimed, 'I'm so

sorry about the book especially. What a terrible shame.'

'Indeed, a terrible shame but you don't need to be sorry, Mr Neale,' she declared, smiling, 'it's not your fault.'

Gerald looked at her dimples. How he wanted to kiss them first and then her lips. Unnerved he looked the other way, trying to control his desire, angry at himself.

As the meal ended Ludovico stood up and announced that, since the day was sunny, they could take a coach trip around the estate if they wished. Otherwise there were plenty of books in the library. The music room had a piano, a wireless and record player unit and plenty of records. There would be afternoon tea at five, aperitifs at eight, followed by dinner at approximately eight-thirty. As her father finished speaking, Maria Eduarda stood up and said, 'we've plenty of good horses in our stables too so should anyone fancy a ride this afternoon or tomorrow morning, I'll be very happy to ride with you and be your guide.'

Gerald hoped to be the only one lifting his hand but sadly it wasn't the case. Maria Eduarda's step aunt, Rosa's younger sister, declared she and her fiancé would like to go riding this afternoon. The four of them headed out, after Maria Eduarda chose the appropriate horses for each one. They went across fields, meadows, up and down pretty smooth hills. She pointed out names of trees and animals mostly for Gerald's benefit, adding Alentejo was charming now but one should really experience it in the spring. The meadows would be covered in red poppies, lavender, daisies and other wildflowers in a riot of colour.

'Simply beautiful,' she said, 'and in the summer there are extensive fields with golden wheat or sunflowers. It's hot and dry but a different kind of beauty.'

The ride was pleasant though Gerald had no opportunity of being alone with Maria Eduarda, except when they returned. He accompanied her to the stables while the other two went to the house.

'Would you go riding again tomorrow morning, Lady Maria Eduarda, I mean just with me and no-one else?' he asked her, gently touching her hand.

She looked up but said nothing. Handing over the four horses to the grooms she turned slowly to face him, finally speaking, 'yes, Mr Neale. That'd be lovely.'

Gerald's heart leaped in his chest. His pulse accelerated. Blood rushed through his ears. So loud he feared she might have heard it. Naturally she hadn't. Maria Eduarda walked towards the house but turning around halfway she said, 'it's winter so the sun rises late. Shall we say seven-thirty at the stables? Then we can admire the sunrise. I'll get us a breakfast from the kitchen.'

She disappeared inside the house. Gerald silently shouted to himself yes three times, feeling like jumping and punching the air. Sadly, nothing came of it. As it happened, Ludovico requested that his daughter deal with the flower arrangements for New Year's Eve. Maria Eduarda sent Gerald a note, apologising that the morning ride had to be cancelled. She spent a good part of the day organising not only the flowers but a few other aspects of the guests' comfort, playing the perfect hostess more naturally than her stepmother, still relatively new to the Alentejo estate's comings and goings.

Gerald's last day of the year 1941 was boring. He read. Wrote a letter to his father. Went out for a walk. Played hide and seek with little Ana Maria. Finally at six he went up to his room, showered and shaved. Dressed in his dinner jacket, with bow tie and cummerbund, he walked down the stairs, a few minutes before eight, just in time for the aperitifs. Later, a sumptuous New Year's Eve dinner would be served, followed by a champagne celebration at midnight and possibly some impromptu dancing to the records or the wireless. Glancing around Gerald took a white Port with ice. The long table in the main dining room was again laid for twenty people with fine china, silver cutlery and crystal glasses. The flower centrepieces were mostly red chrysanthemums, white lilies and yellow carnations with green and silver ferns – all from the estate's greenhouses. At the far end of the room the wooden sliding door was open. Through it there was a reception room with light pinewood chairs and tables, covered in white cloths, pushed against the walls. The champagne reception would be served there at midnight. Gerald could see in a corner the lovely wooden console with a radio and record player combined. So dancing was planned. Perhaps he would be able to hold Maria Eduarda in his arms after all.

A moment later Gerald noticed most men staring in the direction of the door. He followed their gaze. Maria Eduarda had just made her entrance. It took his breath away. She was a vision in a satin green dress with a delicate long shawl of silver lace around her neck and shoulders. The ensemble matched the colour of her eyes and enhanced her bronze shimmering skin. Her curls neatly framed her face, pulled on one side above her ear with a clip the same colour of the dress. She wore small emerald earrings. He felt a sting in his chest and pressed a hand to his heart. She was a temptation. Inhaling deeply Gerald desperately hoped to be seated next to her during dinner. He walked casually around the table to check his place and felt disheartened. On his left it was the duchess of Beja's younger sister who'd been riding with them the previous day and on his right Maria Cohen, Espirito Santo's wife. Her husband was next to her and then Eduarda. Gerald subtly scanned the room. Nobody was watching him. Discreetly, with a rapid gesture, he swapped Maria Cohen's and Eduarda's place cards. Smiling innocently he looked around but no-one had noticed. Now the object of his desire would sit on his right. He couldn't help but smile. Perfect.

Gerald didn't eat much. Later couldn't remember the menu. The splendid wines had all his attention. Various bottles of sparkling, white or red wines, many produced on the estate, were generously distributed on the table and bottles replaced as soon as they were empty. He had a plan of sorts, or better a hazy idea concerning Maria Eduarda. Nothing was properly delineated in his head but it entailed getting her a little drunk. Just enough so she would lose her inhibitions. He concentrated on her glasses and surreptitiously refilled them repeatedly. She didn't seem to notice, making no comments when her glass appeared suddenly full again. When midnight finally arrived and champagne was served to celebrate the New Year, Gerald gladly noted Maria Eduarda was a little tipsy.

Tradition in Portugal on New Year's Eve dictated one

must climb up a chair two or three minutes before twelve a.m., with a glass of champagne and twelve raisins in one's hands. As the clock chimed you made three wishes in silence and then ate one raisin with each stroke of midnight. Afterwards everyone kissed, embraced and danced into the early hours of the young year. Gerald helped Maria Eduarda onto the chair, holding her arm until she stood safely. Her body swayed slightly but she managed in the end. He followed her example with the raisins, standing on the chair next to hers, and was the first she kissed. She gave him a shy, sisterly kiss on his cheek when the party welcomed 1942. But he wanted more.

Ludovico had spared no expense and outside fireworks were lit up. People wrapped themselves in cloaks and coats and walked onto the terrace. Gerald slid his arm around Maria Eduarda's waist and helped her climb down but didn't let go. Instead he pulled her against his chest and kissed her mouth passionately. At first she froze, appearing dismayed, but then, to his delight, her lips opened up and she responded to his kiss. Grabbing another glass of champagne she dazzled him with a smile and ran outside to watch the fireworks.

Gerald followed after a minute, needing to recover his composure. He wanted to kiss her again. Peel that dress off her. Standing slightly behind her he pretended to watch the explosions of light and colour but his gaze was glued to her figure. He just couldn't take his eyes off her. She'd gone onto the terrace without a coat. Noticing her shivering Gerald took off his jacket and gently placed it on her shoulders. She looked up from under her velvet-like black eyelashes, then on tiptoes kissed his cheek and thanked him.

The party continued for another three hours. Records were played and everyone danced. He was able to hold Maria Eduarda in his arms for a couple of waltzes, a rumba and even a tango. She was past tipsy. Her eyes were brighter than usual. She loosened up, hugging and kissing everyone in her path. No doubt she was drunk though no-one except Gerald seemed to notice, as all guests appeared to have reached a similar status. It was then he finalised the imprecise plan in his mind. It took shape. He knew what he would do.

Shortly after three in the morning Ludovico announced breakfast would be late on the first day of the year, as the staff had also been celebrating. It'd be served at 11.30 and be a mixture of breakfast and lunch. In one word a brunch. Applause followed. Gradually everyone began filing up the stairs, retiring to their rooms.
    Gerald waited in the dark to put his plan into action, sitting on the bed, wearing only his boxer-shorts. His body was fiery hot. He waited until complete quietness descended on the house. It was ten to four. Opening his door a fraction he peered into blackness, listening to the silence. At the end of the corridor, to his right, there was a small round window high up on the wall. The silver glow of the full moon penetrated the glass, vaguely illuminating the passageway. He could distinguish the contours of the staircase and see the doors to the various bedrooms. No light escaped from under any of them. Heavy snoring came out of the room next to his. The baron something or other. Gerald couldn't remember the name nor did he care. Noiselessly he closed his door, heading barefoot to Maria Eduarda's bedroom, still only wearing his boxer-shorts. He hoped she didn't lock her door at night. It was her own house so why would she? Gently he tried the knob. Unlocked. Slipping inside rapidly he shut the door behind him and turned the key until hearing a click. Then he stood for a moment admiring her.
    She lay on her side, facing the window, her back to him. The wooden shutters were wide open. The moonlight danced on her skin, making it gleam. Gerald followed the contour of her neck, the soft line of her shoulder with his eyes. She slept. Her breathing was peaceful and rhythmical. Her left arm lay stretched on top of the blankets, sinuously covering her body. Drawing in a sharp breath he realised his whole person was aching for her. Quietly approaching the bed Gerald climbed under the covers, stretched alongside her, delicately placing his arms around her and tenderly kissing her neck. He felt her warmth. His desire grew. Maria Eduarda woke up. She turned round and faced him,

appearing confused. After a second, she seemed to vaguely grasp the unusual presence of a man in her bed, opening her mouth to speak. Fearing she might scream he placed a finger on her lips and whispered, 'shush, don't be afraid.'

Visibly muddled from sleep and too much alcohol she mumbled, 'Mr Neale?! What're you doing here?'

'I want to love you,' he murmured in her ear.

'Love me?' she echoed, slurring her words.

He began kissing her lips, her neck, her shoulders. Sliding his hand under her nighty he caressed her breasts gently.

'Oh…what're you doing, Mr Neale?'

'Call me Gerald, please.'

'Gerald,' her voice was thin, 'okay…but don't…what're you doing?'

'Do you like it?'

She didn't reply. Eyes closed, breathing peacefully she appeared to have fallen asleep again.

Gerald lifted her night-dress, to uncover her breasts. He kissed them, his hands moved down her body. He pulled off her nightie and her knickers. Threw them on the floor and knelt for a moment, admiring her naked beauty in the moonlight. Bending forward he kissed her mouth, slowly moving down her body. She opened her eyes wide.

'No,' she whispered, 'no, you shouldn't…no, what're you doing?'

Gerald smiled inwardly. He kissed the whole of her body, spending longer on what he imagined to be her most sensitive spots but she wasn't reacting and didn't seem to notice he had undressed her. He stopped for a moment, watching her. She'd shut her eyes again; seemed to be drifting into sleep anew.

Staring at her naked body Gerald experienced a hard, almost painful erection. He must have her. Throwing caution to the wind, he pulled off his shorts and covered her body with his, lowering himself, gradually penetrating her. Suddenly she was fully awake, undoubtedly grasping the reality of his actions. Her body became tense, rigid. She froze, fiercely shaking her head.

'No,' she said, trying to push him away, 'no. Stop.'

'Don't be afraid,' he whispered, 'I won't hurt you. I'll be gentle.'

'No,' she repeated. 'I don't want—'

He jammed her mouth with a kiss to keep her quiet. She pushed his head away, desperately trying to get him off her. He pulled her arms under her back, keeping them there with the pressure of his weight on her body.

'No, no,' she repeated, getting more and more agitated.

Gerald sensed a light blockage inside her but simply pushed deeper, applying more force.

'You're hurting me,' she exclaimed, as her virginity gave way.

Gerald could now move inside her more freely. No barriers. He was her first man. Overwhelmed at the feeling, his passion grew.

'No. Stop, please, stop,' she begged him.

But his desire was no longer under control, he accelerated his movements. She wiggled under him, trying to break free but only managed to extricate one arm. Fiercely she began fighting him. Trying to release herself from his grasp she scratched his neck. Her voice grew louder as she repeated, 'no, no. Stop. Please stop.'

But he couldn't stop. He held her free arm with an iron grip above her head and, fearing she might scream, covered her mouth with his other hand to keep her silent, continuing to forcibly move inside her. All of a sudden, her body lost its rigidity and went limp. Her resistance faltered. By the time he exploded, reaching his climax, there were tears quietly running down her cheeks. Taking her in his arms he kissed them dry and whispered, 'I didn't want to cause you pain. I love you. I've wanted to make love to you since the moment I first saw you. Did I hurt you?'

She didn't answer.

'Maria Eduarda I love you. Why're you crying? You didn't like it?'

'No,' she murmured, 'I didn't like it. I didn't want it. I'm scared of consequences.'

'There won't be any, my love, I'm certain.'

'How can you be?' she shouted. No sign of tiredness or alcohol vapours left in her.

'I just do. I'm careful. Don't shout. I'm sure you don't wish to wake up the house, now do you?'

She fell silent for a moment. He held her. His eyelids began dropping. He wanted to fall asleep in her arms. But abruptly Maria Eduarda seemed to recover from her shocked torpor and reacted wildly to his presence. She poked his chest with her elbow, pushed him violently away and shoved him out of bed.

'Go back to your room,' she said, averting her eyes from his nakedness and turning her back on him, 'go. Now. I don't want you here. Go.'

Gerald didn't understand. All right. He'd taken her virginity but he loved her. Didn't she grasp that? All his actions were out of love. He'd never felt such yearning for a woman. His heart, his body ached for her. He stood, hesitant whether to stay and pacify her with words of love. Now the first wave of his desire had passed he could be tender, loving. He leaned forward to give her one last kiss but she turned her face away. Puzzled he retired to his room. Perhaps he should have been gentler, taking care not to hurt her. After all he was her first man. His slight sense of guilt only lasted a minute. Soon enough he decided she'd get over it. From his perspective, it had been very pleasant. Tired but satisfied he couldn't help but smile from ear to ear. She was everything he had imagined and more. His desire fulfilled for the moment he threw himself on the bed and fell instantly asleep.

Chapter 15 – Ending

Maria Eduarda could no longer sleep. She tried to comprehend what had just happened. And how. The alcohol. She had drunk too much wine and champagne but never thought…never believed—

Was it her fault? Had she done anything…had she acted in a way that he interpreted she was asking him to…to—

Sobs choked her. Tears rolled down her cheeks. Momentarily she wondered whether it had really taken place. Switching on the lamp on her side table she kicked the covers, grabbed her night-dress and slid it swiftly down her body, ashamed of her nakedness. Moving aside she stared at the red stains on the otherwise immaculate white sheet. Blood. There was no doubt it had happened. She had lost her virginity to Gerald Neale. The immensity of the deed dawned on her, turning her into a bundle of nerves. What would Papa say if he found out? And Grandmama Leopoldina who had warned her so many times. To no use. She had allowed it all to happen. Had she? Distressed Maria Eduarda wiped off the tears with her fingers. She felt sick. Her mouth tasted sour. Bit by bit she mentally reviewed what had taken place from the moment he climbed into her bed and woke her up. Gasping for air she realised he'd taken advantage of her. And that was putting it mildly. In her own home. In her own bedroom.

The wine during the meal and later the champagne had loosened her. She forgot all inhibitions and flirted with him. True. But innocent. Never intending more than an indulging kiss at midnight. And she had indeed kissed him after the clock finished chiming. So what? She had kissed a lot of people and no-one else tried to come into her bed uninvited. She was unprepared, taken by surprise and muddled by sleep and alcohol. Gerald's first kisses and caresses were enjoyable. No denying it. But she should have been stronger and chucked him out immediately. The truth was she hadn't been thinking straight. Alcohol impaired her judgement, clouded her mind, slowed her reactions. Her eyelids had kept sinking. Fatigue had made her body dormant. All she had wanted was to sleep. But Gerald didn't let go. By the time she said no, begging him to stop, it was too late. He didn't even try. Simply ignored her plea and continued, determined to have his pleasure. Her arms hurt. She glanced down. There were bruises on them. The harsh sensation of his hand pressing her mouth was still on her lips. Bile rushed up her body. She tasted it. Running to the nearest bathroom Maria Eduarda spilled her guts out. Shivering she remembered the moment he forced himself inside her. Tears rolled down her cheeks once again. The pain was minimal when he took her virginity. The moment was hateful and against her will. She hadn't wanted it. Never in this way.

Terrified she wondered about potential consequences. Would she get pregnant? Gerald had said she wouldn't because he'd taken care. She didn't trust or believe him. As if a light bulb were switched on in her mind, Maria Eduarda grasped she felt nothing for him. Not anymore. His action had killed her feelings in the blink of an eye. Destroyed everything. He took advantage of her. A dirty trick, slipping into her bed uninvited, knowing she'd had too much to drink. Not a gentleman's behaviour. He'd forced her. Raped her. It was rape pure and simple.

Suddenly she had the urge to wash, to get clean and brush off any vestiges of Gerald Neale from her body. There was a troublesome pain somewhere in her belly. Liquid ran slowly down her thighs, staining the nightdress. She pulled it off, throwing it on the floor in disgust, then stepped under the shower. Half an hour later, cleaned, wearing a fresh nightdress she returned to bed but couldn't bring herself to lay on the stained sheets. Dragging them off she threw them on the floor, rolled them together with the soiled nightdress and lay down directly on the mattress, wrapped in the blankets. She didn't get a wink of sleep but waited in bed until hearing the first household noises. The servants were up. She rang for her maid. As the girl knocked briefly on the door and came in, Maria Eduarda indicated the pile of sheets on the floor, explaining, 'my monthly troubles came during the night. Earlier than expected so I hadn't any of my cotton cloths. I'm afraid the sheets are stained with blood and my nightdress too. Will you please take them to give the washwoman?'

'Of course, My Lady,' the girl replied and picking up the things off the floor she quickly left the room.

Gerald woke up rested. Satisfied and in high spirits. What a wonderful night. He closed his eyes and mentally reviewed every moment with Maria Eduarda in his head, getting hard in the process. He wanted more. He wanted her again. He craved her body, her full lips, her breasts, the whole of her. He must have her repeatedly.

The unattainable Lady Maria Eduarda de Arantes Silva, the Duke of Beja's eldest daughter, precious asset to her father who wanted to marry her well. And he'd had her. He, Gerald Neale, had made love to her and robbed her virginity. Wow! What would Bristow say to that? Nothing, Gerald concluded to himself. He wasn't telling him or anyone for that matter.

During that first day of 1942 Gerald tried hard to see Maria Eduarda but couldn't as much as glimpse her. She didn't come down for brunch or leave her room the whole day. Rosa, her stepmother, explained Maria Eduarda was indisposed. Women's troubles. He accepted it, thinking she might need time to digest what had happened between them. After all a woman's first time was a big deal. Or perhaps she wanted to daydream on her own, quietly reliving their moment of intimacy, secretly wishing the night to come quickly so he'd visit her again.

Gerald tried his luck that same night after the house was silent and in darkness but this time Maria Eduarda had locked her door. He couldn't enter her bedroom without causing a hell of a rattle. Obviously, a bad idea. Frustrated, he retired to his room. She didn't appear on the 2nd of January either, seemingly still indisposed. On the third the whole party returned to Lisbon. He sighted her briefly as she entered her father's car without as much as a glance back to him. Gerald was forced to accept Maria Eduarda didn't feel the same way he did after their love making. He wondered what to do. Wanted to see her. Needed to see her.

During the next twelve weeks he repeatedly sent her flowers, letters, cards. To no avail. She didn't reply to any of them, didn't even acknowledge their receipt. Gerald didn't give up easily and hated being dumped. Fine to get rid of a woman he'd tired of but none as yet – except Maria Eduarda – had ditched him. Eventually he was forced to accept she didn't want to see him ever again. Then, unexpectedly on the last day of March, he received a small note from her, delivered by hand at the embassy. It read:

Mr Neale, I want to talk to you. Please meet me tomorrow morning at nine o'clock sharp in the Patisserie Versailles. Maria Eduarda

Gerald punched the air, beaming from ear to ear. Finally. She wanted to see him. Talk to him. Must be a good sign. He might get lucky again.

He arrived punctually. The café was deserted so early in the morning. He grabbed a table and ordered a breakfast of toast, coffee and orange juice. Maria Eduarda arrived just as the waiter delivered his order. He stood up, smiling, leaning forward as if to kiss her but she simply acknowledged him with a nod and took the chair in front of his, the other side of the table. Radiant, gorgeous as ever, he thought. She wore a pair of navy blue trousers and a matching blazer, which she took off and carefully hung on the back of a chair. She placed her handbag on the floor. Gerald let his eyes slide up and down her body. She wore a pearl coloured silk blouse and a red cardigan that went well with the trousers and her complexion. No make-up. No jewellery. She ordered a coffee and looked him in the eyes, holding his gaze.

'I won't beat around the bush, Mr Neale.'

'Okay.'

Her coffee came. She sipped a bit. Then said, 'I'm pregnant. The baby is yours.'

Gerald nearly fell off his chair, thinking he had misunderstood her words.

'What?' He cried out, slowly resuming his seat.

'You heard me.'

'I did. Of course I did but…but are you sure?'

'Yes.'

She seemed so calm. So matter of fact, so casual about it.

'Hey, Mr Neale, you're pale! All colour has retracted from your face,' her voice audibly dripped with sarcasm.

'Well…it's…it's,' he stuttered, 'it's a big piece of news for a man…for a man to…to hear…without warning or preamble.'

'Indeed. But more so for a woman,' she replied.

'Maria Eduarda,' he stretched his arm, attempting to take her hand in his but she placed both her hands on her lap, out of his reach and again looked straight into his eyes, asking him, 'what do you intend to do about it?'

'Me?' he echoed pathetically.

'Who else?'

Gerald shifted uncomfortably in his chair and averted his gaze, unable to cope with the intense, loathing green stare of her eyes.

'I…I can't…I mean, I don't know. Too early to get married, don't you think? We're…we're both…we're both too young,' he paused.

Of course he could marry her if he wanted to. He was a free man. Emphasis on free. Marriage, however much he wanted Maria Eduarda, would inevitably be the end of his cheerful, adventurous life. No. Not yet. Not now.

'I can give you…yes, probably for the best, I can give you money. You can go to someone…a doctor or…or one of those women that do such things…I mean…and…and…' he stopped, unable to bring himself to say the words.

'Terminate the pregnancy?' she finished his sentence for him.

Gerald nodded, hoping she'd agree, take the money and go, allowing him to continue with his carefree life. He wasn't prepared for what came next.

She threw her head back and laughed. Loud. Her body shaking. For a moment he thought she would choke with so much laughter. Perhaps she was hysterical. Then, as suddenly as it started, her laughing ended. She stared at him with a serious but contemptuous expression.

'Do not fear,' she declared firmly, 'I don't want nor do I need your money or you to do anything. Anything at all. I've been thinking a lot about this. At first, I thought I wouldn't tell you and I didn't want to see you. You took advantage of me. I said no but you carried on. You raped me.'

He jumped off the chair. It fell backwards.

'No,' he yelled, shocked.

The waiter stared at him, raising an eyebrow. Gerald picked up the chair, sat down and lowering his voice said, 'no. I didn't do such a thing. How can you say that?'

She shrugged. 'What do you call it then when a woman says no repeatedly, tries often to push you away and you continue until you're satisfied?'

Gerald didn't know what to say. Lost for words he felt disconcerted at her almost casual tone, her composure.

'Anyway,' she resumed when he remained silent, 'I decided you should know what you've done.'

He was about to interject but she anticipated it and stopped him with an imperious gesture of her hand.

'I don't want to listen to your excuses, Mr Neale. Perhaps I wasn't completely innocent. I did flirt with you but I certainly didn't ask you to do what you did. I didn't encourage or invite you into my bed. At first you took me by surprise. I was asleep, had drunk too much earlier and was slow to react…then,' she paused and for a moment he thought she'd cry or break down but she pulled herself together and continued, 'I said no repeatedly but you just went on regardless.'

She looked at him for a long silent moment. He couldn't bear her cold stare and lowered his eyes. She spoke again.

'As I've already said, I don't want you to do anything at all. I want nothing from you or see you ever again. It's my problem, my life. You've no place in it.'

She stood up and put on her jacket.

'Goodbye, Mr Neale.'

With these words she left. Gerald sat there for over an hour. Unsettled. Perplexed. Confounded. What to do? How to react? Maria Eduarda had been clear, or had she?

He wondered whether to go after her, apologise and do the right thing. Marry her. But her cold indifference, whether real or faked, hurt him. She didn't seem to care and just wished him out of her life for good. But did she? Why had she told him about the baby? She must have felt offended when he offered her money to terminate the pregnancy. What should he do? Nothing. After all she'd said she didn't want to see him ever again. Perhaps give it a few days until she calmed down and come to her senses. Then he'd seek to see her again and talk in a civilised manner. Discuss what to do rationally. True he didn't want to get married but maybe he had to. He knew so. His father would say it was what an honourable gentleman must do. But Dad needn't know. Gerald believed the best thing for everyone involved was to convince Maria Eduarda to terminate the pregnancy. He could go with her if she wanted him to. Yes, he could tell her all that. Write her a letter first. Good idea, yes. Later call upon her or invite her to the Versailles patisserie again. Yes. Yes. That should do it.

Gerald breathed in and out, feeling calmer, paid the bill and left.

Back in his quarters at the embassy he composed what he considered a long, heartfelt letter, sending it to Maria Eduarda by messenger. To his dismay it was returned two hours later unopened. He blew a fuse. Who did she think she was? He was trying to help and she had refused to read his letter, wanting nothing to do with him. So be it. She was on her own. Her life. He had no place in it. Her words. Enraged, Gerald tried to relax pacing his room back and forward. Gradually his anger subsided. Maria Eduarda was upset. Give her time. He must give her a week or two. She would see reason. Understand they needed to talk again. Yes, he would wait several days, then contact her one more time. Visit her in person. Definitely. The best option. At that particular moment, his intentions were good. Sincere. Then, unexpected circumstances occurred that meant he did nothing.

A week after the meeting with Maria Eduarda, Gerald received a letter from his aunt Mary, his father's younger sister.

Jonathan had fallen in France. Following the news of his eldest son's death, Frank suffered a cardiac arrest but the ambulance was quick and the attendants managed to revive him. They took him to hospital. The doctors weren't sure whether he would fully recover, not yet anyway. Perhaps Gerald should come home, at least for a while. It would certainly improve his father's condition. He lay ill and crushed over Jonathan's death. He needed his other son. Gerald must request compassionate leave of absence and return to England as quickly as possible. He did so.

The ambassador granted him leave at once. But before departing Gerald wanted to see Maria Eduarda. After much thinking he had finally grasped his behaviour had been wrong and unacceptable. He must apologise. Beg her for forgiveness. Tell her he must go to his father but would return and do right by her. They would marry before the baby was due and he'd take good care of her and his child.

Full of good, honourable intentions, Gerald rang the bell at her villa, asking to see her. To his utter shock the butler dropped a bombshell, explaining Lady Maria Eduarda no longer lived there.

'She moved out?' Gerald asked incredulously.

'Yes, sir. She quarrelled with her family and left. That's all we know. All that His Grace told us.'

'Do you have her new address?'

'No, sir. I'm afraid not.'

'Could you please ask her father?'

The old butler shook his head. 'Not possible, sir. His Grace doesn't know where Lady Maria Eduarda has gone to. He said if anyone asked about her we should say she moved out and left no forwarding address or contact. Besides, His Grace is unwell. He won't see anyone and we're not allowed to enter his apartments. I'm sorry, sir.'

Gerald made a dismissive gesture and thanked the butler. The news hit a raw nerve. He felt guilty. He had made her pregnant without her clear consent. He hated the word and wouldn't say it out loud but in the silence of his mind he admitted to rape. Her disappearance and her father's reaction must be the consequence…for her and…for his freedom. He was free. No obligations. No need to do the right thing. She had disappeared and he must attend to his family. Nothing else to do. He felt elated but having difficulty comprehending the events and his own feelings he simply returned to the embassy and began packing his bags.

Later Bristow confirmed his assumption. Gerald had still no idea how the man always knew all the gossip and everything that happened in Portuguese high society without even speaking the language. Bristow said Maria Eduarda had fallen from grace. She had confessed her pregnancy to her father but refused to say by whom. Ludovico exploded. Such a situation went completely against the Duke's strong catholic beliefs. He yelled at his daughter. Called her a whore. Accused her of staining his honour and the family's. She had tried to reason with him but, enraged, Ludovico didn't listen. He expelled her, simply throwing her out on the streets, shouting she was no longer his daughter and would be disinherited. He screamed he didn't want to see her ever again. To him she was as good as dead. Then he'd locked himself away in his study. She hadn't said another word to anyone or so Bristow's informant told him, had packed a suitcase and left. No-one knew where she had gone or whether she had any money. Maria Eduarda seemed to have vanished off the face of the earth. At the insistence of his wife and his friend Ricardo Espirito Santo, Ludovico went to the police and reported her missing but after five days he told them to stop the search. His daughter was of age and could do whatever she wanted, as apparently she had or so he said. According to Bristow's source – whoever it might be – Ludovico stated he didn't care to know one way or another. To him, Maria Eduarda was dead, he repeated.

Gerald was shocked if only for a moment. Why hadn't she accepted his money to terminate the pregnancy and continue her life as normal? What were her options? He should have assumed his responsibility and marry her. Would she have accepted? No. Her words at the café were deeply engraved in his mind. They'd hurt him. She'd taken charge of her life. He didn't have a place in it. How would she get on? Might end up as a prostitute. He hoped not but she wasn't his problem. He must clear his head and forget his infatuation. With Jonathan's death and their father ill in hospital, there were pressing matters to attend to.

And so, on 15th April 1942 Gerald Neale left Lisbon for good. He boarded a BOAC plane to return to London and carry on with his life, nearly two years after first arriving in Portugal. He and Maria Eduarda would never meet again.

Part 2 – Hertie

(Germany, 1943-1956 / England, 2011)

"Ich war so müde, mir brachen die Knie,
Doch immer gingen wir weiter.

Wir gingen weiter. Mein Herz in der Brust
War klaffend aufgeschnitten,
Und aus der Herzenswunde hervor
Die roten Tropfen glitten."

Heinrich Heine (1797-1856), from strophes 9 and 10 of the satirical epic poem "Deutschland, ein Wintermärchen" (1844)

"I was so tired, my strength was falling.
And yet, we kept walking on.

On we went! Within my breast
An open wound was gaping,
And, from the depth of my wound,
Red droplets were escaping."

Translation by Joseph Massaad

Valeria's journal, February 2020

I first met Hertha Lohmeyer in July 2009. I was twenty-one, she already seventy-three.

Moving into my parents' flat in Hove I felt lucky. They had lent it to me rent free so I had a place to live while completing my degrees at the Sussex University in Brighton where, after my demise as an opera singer, I obtained a student's place. At the time the apartment was my parents' weekend home – or at least some weekends when the weather was warm and sunny and they wanted out of London. My parents owned a house in Kensington or, rather, Mum did. It was her father's wedding present. A few years before the revolution of 1974, Ludovico was clever enough to realise that with Salazar's illness, which led to his death in 1970, the old regime would not last long. So he invested in property in England – the house in Kensington and a large house in the Cotswolds that has been transformed into a luxury boutique hotel, which my parents sold three years ago, dividing the profit between my mother and her four sisters. Ludovico also moved money to a Swiss bank so, when on 25th April 1974 the fascist dictatorship ended, he wasn't completely destitute. Except for the Sintra property he lost everything else he possessed in Portugal mainland and the estates in the islands of the Azores and Cape Verde and was forced to sell some of his Sintra land. The Archipelago of Cape Verde became independent, like all Portuguese colonies, approximately four years after the revolution. As a sympathiser of Salazar's fascist regime he was a marked man. Most of his friends escaped to Brazil. Some returned to Portugal later. But Ludovico refused to leave. He retreated to Sintra with his family, living from the investments he'd made in England, keeping the money in Switzerland for an emergency.

The day I met Hertha I arrived at the Hove flat in my little car, with my cat Wonkie. A name derived from having been run over by a car as a kitten which gave her an uneven tail. Following me was a mini-van with my three brothers and my remaining possessions. A week prior I'd been there on my own to supervise the delivery of my grand piano. It wasn't one of the largest models but it caused a bit of a stir. It had to be lifted by crane into the flat through the large doors of the balcony on the top floor. There were four penthouse flats and my new home was one of them.

As my brothers and I began taking my possessions to the lift an old lady arrived with two supermarket carrier bags. She wore a turquoise blue dress with printed white flowers and a little white cardigan. Not very tall, about medium height, but slim. Hair was of a reddish golden colour in which the greys were now abundant. Skin rosy and smooth. She smiled warmly and her almost cobalt-blue eyes sparkled. When eventually finding out she was well into her seventies I was rather surprised. She appeared ten years younger and must have been a beauty as a girl. Looking at the four of us she was about to say something when one of her bags burst open and apples, pears, tomatoes, tin cans, bread, broccoli and a few other items rolled onto the pavement. We rushed to help her.

'Thank you, my dears, you're all so kind. Thank you,' she told us in a strong German accent, then turning to me said, 'you're the new neighbour, the pianist, right?'

I nodded.

'I watched the whole rigmarole of lifting your piano to the flat,' she said visibly amused, then stretching her arm she shook my hand and introduced herself, 'Hertha.'

Her handshake was firm. 'Valeria,' I replied, then noticing she was trying not to stare at my brothers, as they almost look like a copy of each other, I added, 'these are my brothers, Miguel, Afonso and Luis. They are triplets and, as you can see, at first glance they're identical,' from the corner of my eye I noticed them, clearly tickled. They were used to this kind of reaction. Then I added, 'they're helping me with the move.'

Good-naturedly she said, 'Don't think I've ever met identical or nearly identical triplets. I had three siblings, two were twins. Not identical – a girl and a boy.'

She shook my brothers' hands too, appearing perhaps curious at our names as they aren't English. So I explained our mother was Portuguese and our father British. We spoke both languages and had Portuguese names. She seemed interested.

'I'm German,' she told us, 'but have lived in Britain for forty-six years,' she paused, then grinning added, 'married an Englishman in 1958, moved to the country in 1963.'

We then helped her take the shopping to her flat and continued carrying my stuff into my new home. That same evening, after my brothers left in the mini-van back to London, I was just finishing my dinner when Hertha knocked on my door.

'I'm sorry to disturb you and please say no if you don't feel like it,' she said when I opened.

I nodded, marvelling that she'd lived in England for almost half a century. Her English was very correct but she seemed unable to get rid of the German accent. Her "rr" in particular were very strong, pronounced from the throat, as only a German would.

'You and your brothers were very kind,' she said, 'and I know they've left. I'm later than I wanted to be but I thought maybe at least you could come round to my flat next door and have a drink with me. Just to say thank you for your kindness earlier.'

I didn't have the heart to say no and so, grabbing my keys and closing my door, I went with her. What started as a politeness visit soon became rather pleasant. She had two sherries. I had a couple of glasses of Port wine. And we talked and talked until well after midnight. It was the start of our friendship. Soon we began socialising. Going for meals and walks along the seafront or visiting National Trust properties nearby. Occasionally, I took her out to concerts or the theatre in London at weekends. As our friendship developed, she began telling me about her family and her life. She didn't talk much about her childhood. It must have been difficult, possibly traumatic. It couldn't have been a bed of roses to grow up in Germany during the war and the Nazi years. Eventually she would tell me what she remembered and marked her the most. But in the beginning she spoke mostly about becoming a widow at the age of only thirty with three young children – two boys and a girl, respectively only seven, six and four when their father died.

Soon she asked me to call her Hertie. She preferred it. Sometimes, when I wasn't studying or preparing for exams, I'd play the piano for her and she loved it. I gave lessons to earn my living while studying. I started writing reviews and articles as a freelancer and it paid quite well. My parents wanted to give me a small monthly allowance but I was an adult and didn't wish to be financially dependent on them. Their generosity with the rent-free fully furnished flat was more than enough.

In June 2011, two years after Hertie and I had met and become friends, she had a bad bout of rheumatic arthritis. It took her three weeks to recover and I thought she needed a treat. So I deposited Wonkie at Mum and Dad's in London and took Hertie for a weekend in the Peak District. Surprisingly she had never visited but had wanted to for a long time, especially wishing to tour one of England's most spectacular stately homes – Chatsworth. As good a time as any, I remember thinking. I booked a twin room in a lovely, quiet country hotel for the two of us and drove up there with a very excited Hertie in the passenger seat of my little car.

It was during the night that I first became aware of Hertie's traumatic experiences during her childhood. I woke with her yelling. She was having a nightmare. Once I shook her awake she came out of it and explained it was a recurring dream she'd had for years. At my insistence she described what she felt and the ordeal experienced in the dream. In a logical follow-up step she began narrating her life. We were up all night – she telling and I listening. In the end Hertie said she intended to record her story and eventually write a book about it. As I've mentioned before, she never did but asked me to do it instead. After that night we became closer.

One day, much later, she told me her husband's deathbed confession. Amazed, we spotted an astonishing coincidence. The story of my Portuguese family, before my mother and her sisters were born, crossed indirectly with Hertie's life.

One person connected it all.

Chapter 1 – The Recurring Dream

The walls appear to curve outwards, then moving relentlessly to the centre of the room. In the middle she stands. Waiting. Panic takes hold of her body. Paralyses her. Eyes bulging, struggling for breath she searches around, trying to find a way out. There are doors. Four. All closed. Shut. She must try them. Her legs finally obey her brain's command. One foot forward. Now the other. Wobbly. Shaky. Cold drops of perspiration cover her skin. Fear chokes her throat as if icy fingers clasp her neck. Breathing is painful. One by one she tries the doors. Locked. All locked. And the walls keep moving. Will soon crush her. The window. A little window at the top. A shimmer of light. Her mother's voice. Outside. Somewhere. She wants to call out but her voice lets her down. She can't speak. The pressure on her body increases. She must scream. Then Mutti[14] will hear her. She opens and closes her mouth like a fish out of water. Please. The words form in her head but don't come out.

'I can't stay here. I'll die. Crushed. Minced into dust like a piece of meat.'

The words resonate in her head but still no sound from her throat.

She desperately pulls at her jumper. It stops her from breathing. Grabbing a stick – where did it come from? – she tries to push back the walls. Or at least to stop their unrelenting march to the centre of the room. The stick breaks in two.

'Hertie. Hertie.'
Mutti's voice.
'Hertie. Hertie. Hertie.'

Other voices. Many voices. They're searching for her. She looks up at the window. Suddenly two hands. Then the arms they belong to. She must grab them. The hands will pull her out. She jumps but can't reach them. She tries. And tries. And tries. Tears gush out of her eyes. Her body shakes. Tries again. Brushes the fingers of one of the hands. Suddenly realises the window is too

---

[14] Mummy in German.

small. They can't pull her through.

Her stomach wrenches. She bends her body in two, thinking she's going to vomit. But nothing comes out. She tastes sourness. The beginning of the end. The walls have reached her. The doors are locked. The window too narrow. The saving hands vanish.

'NOOOOO.'

A scream. A growl. Someone? Something howling in agony like a wounded animal close to death. The walls shake her. But they're softer now.

Hertie jerks upright. Opening her eyes wide she recognises her own voice and gazes into the worried face of her young friend Valeria.

'You were screaming,' Valeria says, 'are you all right, Hertie?'

She nods. Shaking uncontrollably Hertie tries to grab the glass of water on the side table. It tumbles to the floor. She hears the glass shatter. Reaching for the light with trembling hands, as if they aren't her own, she just about manages to turn on the table lamp. Valeria stands up and flicks the ceiling lights on. The brightness is soothing. A nightmare. The dream. The same dream again. Not every night but often. Too often. Gradually, holding on to Valeria's hands she manages to control her sobs. Her throbbing heart returns to normal. Her convulsive body relaxes. She can breathe normally again. Just a dream. The same dream but just a dream.

She is in her bed, in the hotel room Valeria has booked for their Peak District weekend. Nothing to fear. She glances at the digital clock. Two twenty-one. Middle of the night but she knows she'll be unable to sleep again, scared the dream may return.

'What were you dreaming that frightened you so much?' Valeria asks her.

'It's a recurring dream…a nightmare. I've had it for many years. Have been in therapy for a long time. I know why it happens now. At least that.'

'Would you like to speak about it?'

'You wouldn't mind?'

'Of course not. We're friends. Tell me.'

Slowly at first, Hertie narrates the dream. Then she begins speaking about what she remembers of her childhood. And once she starts she can't stop, talking all night, sharing with Valeria, sobbing at times on her sympathetic shoulder, unburdening herself. Swiftly her memories flood her mind. It's almost as if she were seven years old again and back in the Germany of the mid-nineteen forties.

Chapter 2 – Taken

It was an icy late November day. Frost stretched over roofs, trees, bushes and fields and a freezing wind cut through the skin. Inside the classroom was slightly warmer but not enough to take one's scarf off. Hertie lifted her gaze from her exercise-book and looked at the windows, admiring the exquisite stars and patterns the ice crystals designed on the glass panes.

'Hertha, pay attention to your work and stop your day-dreaming.'

The harsh voice of the teacher startled her. Hertie felt her cheeks grow hot and lowered her eyes to the multiplications, subtractions, additions and divisions she needed to solve. Arithmetic was boring. She'd rather read, write a composition or complete a drawing.

'Hertha,' the teacher again, 'have you finished your work?'

'No, Frau Schulz.'

'Then pay attention. If I catch you distracted again, you'll get a beating and I'll inform your mother.'

'Yes, Frau Schulz. I'm sorry.'

Hertie didn't like her new teacher. She was a young woman, married to an SS officer. Hertie didn't quite know what the SS were exactly but they wore uniforms and had guns. They were unpleasant, sullen, sometimes violent people. Uncle Siggi had told her she should stay well away from them. Frau Schulz was married to one and was thoroughly unpleasant though she was no officer, simply a teacher. Hertie had never seen her smile. She tolerated no infringement to the rules, however insignificant, and seemed continuously angry at anyone and everything. Hertie missed Fräulein Mett. Her wrinkled, good-natured, slightly plump face with tender blue eyes behind her specs and the caring, warm smile. Fräulein Mett was old, even older than Mutti or Uncle Siggi, but kind, gentle and understanding. She liked children, never raised her voice, always had time to explain and had never ever given anyone a beating. There was no need, not even for a threat. They all liked her and tried to please her. But one day they had arrived at school and met Frau Schulz instead of Fräulein Mett in the classroom. She announced herself as their new teacher. Apparently Fräulein Mett had committed a serious crime against the Führer and the state. Her punishment, if she were lucky, would be prison for life. If not, she'd be executed.

'What does executed mean, Frau Schulz?' a little girl at the back of the class had asked.

Hertie knew what it meant but said nothing. No need. Frau Schulz answered in a curt, harsh tone, 'it means she will be punished with death. And she deserves it.'

Hertie had been sad. Fräulein Mett didn't deserve to die or go to prison. She was so kind. So sweet. How could such a lady be happy in prison if she were to live? And what possible crime could friendly, loving Fräulein Mett have committed? Preposterous to think she'd do anything bad or wrong. Surely the Führer must be mistaken. Hertie didn't think he was a very nice man anyway. Papa had left home three years ago to fight for Führer and country and they hadn't heard from him for nearly two years. And now Fräulein Mett too had been arrested because of this same Führer.

At home Hertie told Mutti and Uncle Siggi about Fräulein Mett. They already knew, advising her in strong terms that it was better not to speak about Fräulein Mett again at least not at school or in front of other people. At home it was fine. She didn't understand why and asked them to explain.

'You're too young to grasp it, Hertie,' Mutti had told her.

'I'm seven years old already,' she had replied indignantly, 'not a baby anymore.'

'No Schätzchen[15], you're not a baby but you need to be older to understand. Now go and wash before lunch.'

Hertie obeyed but from that day onwards she tried to hide and listen to the conversations of the grown-ups. Eventually she learned Fräulein Mett had been hiding two Jewish children in her basement. Apparently a crime. Why? What could two children or Fräulein Mett for that matter do against a powerful man like the

---

[15] German term of endearment, translates as little treasure.

Führer? Surely nothing much. The Führer must have been told a lie. What else? Hertie was upset but followed her family's advice. She didn't want to get herself or anyone she loved in trouble. So she never again mentioned Fräulein Mett at school or in front of other people.

'Hertha.'

That hard, bitter voice again and an iron grip on her shoulder.

'I'm sorry, Frau Schulz. I'm almost finished. Honest.'

'Stretch your hand, Hertha. I warned you twice before to pay attention and stop your day-dreaming.'

Hertie did as commanded, feeling a lump in her throat. She knew it was going to hurt. Biting her lower lip she prepared herself for the pain. The large wooden ruler came down on her hand four times with all of Frau Schulz's strength. Hertie promised herself not to cry. Swallowing back her tears she stoically waited for Frau Schulz to order her to sit down again. Her hand was bright red, burning with pain. The skin had split and a thin thread of blood ran down her wrist.

'Hope you've learned your lesson. Resume your work.'

As she sat at her desk Hertie caught Amalie's compassionate, huge eyes full of tears. Amalie was her best friend. Hertie attempted a little smile and whispered she was all right. Both girls returned to their work, fearing Frau Schulz may start distributing beatings left, right and centre. It wouldn't be the first time.

At that precise moment the noise of heavy boots came from the corridor. Angry voices. No-one knocked but a couple of seconds later the door to the classroom was rudely pushed open. A group of four men in uniform with guns in their hands poured in. Hertie and all the other children shrunk in their desks, wanting to hide but there was no time. Behind them the headmistress of the school came running. She opened her mouth to speak but one look from the man who appeared to be in charge muted her. Dead silence in the classroom. No-one dared speak. You could hear a pin drop. The officer addressed Frau Schulz.

'You're the teacher of this class?'

'Yes, sir,' she replied, standing very straight.
'Name?'
'Hildegard Schulz.'
'Untersturmführer[16] Klein,' he introduced himself.
She nodded. 'I know you, Herr Untersturmführer Klein.'
'Yes. Untersturmführer Schulz and I are colleagues.'
She nodded. 'And how can I help you, Herr Untersturmführer Klein?'

He took a folded paper from his pocket and handed it over to the teacher, saying, 'it's an order to arrest the Wennike family. I've been informed their daughter is here.'

'But she's only a little girl,' came the anguished cry from the headmistress, 'please. You can't arrest a child of seven.'

Untersturmführer Klein stared at her for a moment. Hertie feared he might strike the headmistress down but he didn't. Instead he said, 'we're not arresting her. We're just taking her to join her parents. They have been arrested. Her mother is a Jew. Her father a Rassenschänder[17]. He is of pure German blood and married a Jewish woman. A serious crime. The child is a disgrace for this school. She must be taken away with her family.'

'But...' the headmistress tried to oppose him but he made a sign to one of his men who pointed the gun at her. She shut her mouth. He turned to Frau Schulz.

'Who's the little Schänderin?'

Without hesitation the teacher indicated Amalie. The girl began to cry quietly, visibly frightened. Hertie jumped up.

'No,' she screamed at the officer, 'no, you can't take my friend away. Leave her alone. You're scaring her.'

The Untersturmführer seemed amused.
'And who might you be?'
'Her best friend.'
'Do you have a name Fräulein Best Friend?'
'Hertha Lohmeyer.'
'I know your family, Fräulein Lohmeyer. Your mother's a good woman. Your father is fighting for country and Führer in

---

[16] Junior or second lieutenant in the SS.
[17] Racial violator.

the Wehrmacht, as an honourable man would and your uncle Siegfried is a good man too, sadly crippled now and no longer able to serve the Fatherland.'

'So?' Hertie said defiantly, crossing her arms in front of her chest, unsure what he was on about.

'So, Fräulein Lohmeyer, you should know better than to be friends with a little, disgusting Schänderin. You've got spirit, I'll give you that but now you must sit down and be quiet.'

'No. You can't take Amalie. She's done nothing wrong.'

Through the corner of her eyes Hertie noticed too late Herr Untersturmführer Klein's hand hissing through the air. The impact was brutal. Hertie fell to the ground. Her cheek burning. Her head buzzing. The room moved in circles around her.

'Amalie Wennike,' he said as if nothing had happened, 'stand up and come with me. We're taking you to your mother. You're both going to a holiday camp. You've no idea how lucky you are.'

Hertie saw various Amalies stand up and wipe their eyes with the palms of their hands. Gradually they merged into one – her Amalie. Her best friend. Suddenly Amalie went down on her knees next to Hertie. She put her arms around her, kissed her cheek and whispered, 'thank you and good—' her words died in her throat.

Untersturmführer Klein grabbed her arm, unceremoniously pulled her up and ruthlessly dragged her out of the room. The men disappeared. The headmistress followed them after a moment's hesitation. Hertie was still on the floor. Frau Schulz approached her.

'That's what you get for being a bad girl and befriending a lesser person, a subhuman such as Amalie. Get up and sit at your desk.'

Slowly, holding the edge of her desk with both hands, Hertie managed to stand up and slide onto the chair.

Frau Schulz returned to the front of the class and declared in a loud voice, as if fearing they were deaf, 'let this be a lesson to you all. Amalie's parents committed a serious crime. They are dishonourable, shameful and disgusting and will receive their rightful punishment.'

'Where are they taking Amalie?' Hertie whispered, 'the officer talked about a holiday camp. But why would they take them on holiday? Her mother wouldn't want a holiday in this cold and I'm sure she won't be pleased Amalie will miss school and fall behind.'

'You should know better than to speak, Hertha Lohmeyer, but you're young. So, I'll show some consideration and answer your question. Amalie and her mother, like all Jews, are going to a rehabilitation centre where they will learn respect and hard work. Her father will be imprisoned.'

Hertie said nothing further. But why did Amalie's mother need rehabilitation? From what? And Amalie? What had Amalie ever done wrong? She was kind, honest and had good notes at school. Always polite and friendly to everyone. So why?

As she got home and her mother saw her, she dropped to her knees, crying out, 'dear god, Schätzchen, what happened to you?'

She touched her face and Hertie winced away in pain. Then she looked at the old mirror in the hall. Her cheek was blueish-black and swollen.

'What happened my love? Did you fall?'

Mutti sounded worried. And suddenly, Hertie couldn't hold back anymore. She put her arms around her mother's neck and amid sobs told her the whole sad episode.

Holding her tight, Mutti spoke soothingly, 'I'm sorry you had to see that darling. You were very brave but the men who took Amalie and her family are SS. They're dangerous. Never make another one angry. Uncle Siggi's told you to stay away from them and never give a bad answer to Frau Schulz. She's married to one of them.'

'But why did they take Amalie and her family? They've done nothing. They're all so nice. The officer said Amalie and her mum are Jewish and her dad a…a…Rassen…something.'

'A Rassenschänder. You'll understand when you're older. Sadly, these are the times we live in and we must be careful.'

'Mutti…Amalie and her parents celebrate Christmas and

go to church. We saw them there when we went to your friend's baby's christening and the wedding of our neighbours' daughter. I thought Jews didn't.'

'That's true, darling. They don't. But Amalie's grandparents changed their ways and became Christians long ago. All of them were baptised: Amalie's grandparents, her mother and her aunt. Amalie too.'

'So why are they saying they're Jewish? It must be a mistake.'

'It's not a mistake, Schätzchen. The Führer and his government say it's in their blood. They say they need to be purified.'

'Is that why they're taking them to a rehabilitation centre and her dad to prison?'

'Yes, my love,' her mother was quiet for a moment, appearing to consider something important, then added, 'Hertie, promise me that you'll never mention Amalie or her family to anyone outside these walls and will not speak about them at school.'

'Again, Mutti? I had to do the same when Fräulein Mett was arrested.'

'I know, darling. But you must.'

'Why, Mutti? Amalie's my best friend.'

'Promise me, Schätzchen. Please.'

Hertie nodded. Her chest felt tight, as if crushed by giant hands. The pain inside was far worse than Frau Schulz's beating or her swollen cheek where the Untersturmführer had slapped her. Drying her eyes with the back of her hands she kissed her mother.

'I promise, Mutti. I'll go up now and play with Lottie and Sprudel.'

'Yes, Schätzchen, you do that.'

As she ran to the stairs, Hertie heard uncle Siggi enter the hall. His crutches made a thumping noise on the wooden floors. Glancing over her shoulder she saw Mutti put her finger in front of her lips, slowly shaking her head. Then they vanished into the kitchen, shutting the door behind them.

Chapter 3 – Early Night In The Peak District

Gazing up at Valeria, eyes full of tears, Hertie said, 'that morning was the last time I saw Amalie. I didn't understand then what was happening in my country.'

'Hardly surprising. You were seven years old.'

'Yes. I was too young to know. Hitler and his followers considered Jews subhuman. They distorted ideas and manipulated people to suit their twisted, criminal minds. They labelled the disabled as lesser people too.'

'Not only disabled.'

'I know but at the time Amalie was taken I didn't know what homosexuals, gypsies, so-called asocials or political prisoners were. Uncle Siggi was disabled. Of that I had experience. The Nazi sympathisers in the village mocked and insulted him for his disability, always muttering he was a burden to the state and should be taken away to some institution or other to be eliminated. Mutti was very protective of him, sheltered him and never let him go out alone. I remember her saying if she was with Siggi no-one would taunt him. My uncle ignored them but it must've been dreadful, gruesome even. As for race, I only understood much later what it meant for the Nazis and what was a Rassenschänder – disgusting word – race violator. Awful. To me then and now there are only people. Good people, nice people, bad people, etc. Nothing else matters. But I didn't understand then that Hitler had created this stupid idea of the superior race – the Aryan race. A myth. There is no superior race, there never was. The word Aryan was manipulated and misused by Hitler and his cronies to serve their own purposes. All lies of course. But Germany was in a horrible depression, with inflation at unbelievable levels – one million marks would buy you a matchbox! Also the harshness against Germany in the Versailles Peace Treaty in 1919, after the end of the First World War in 1918, contributed to the horrendous economic situation. There was among especially the working classes a dangerous feeling of resentment. Hitler knew how to speak to their hearts and he did some good things when he first came to power. So, it was relatively easy for him to win over a high proportion of the population. Then he denigrated all non-Aryans, especially Jews and made them scapegoats. Blamed them for all the suffering of the German people and the humiliation after the First World War. Not everyone believed him, there were many who tried to resist but as with all dictators, Hitler simply and literally killed all that opposed him. I only realised much later what really had happened.'

'Hertie, you were a young child. How could you comprehend all those things?'

'You're right. I couldn't. I didn't get why my friend had been taken or why Mutti insisted I don't mention Amalie or her family ever again outside our home. I came to grasp it in my mid-teens. I read books and articles in foreign newspapers narrating the horror stories that had taken place in my country. I learned about it at school too. I was shocked. Horrified and couldn't grasp how people could do such ghastly, appalling deeds to others.'

'All dictators, either left or right wing, are tyrants and commit atrocities. Hitler was one of the worst ever but he wasn't alone. Stalin, for example, carried out criminal actions against his own people, starved about two million of them to death. Or Mussolini in Italy, Salazar in Portugal and Franco in Spain. They weren't much better. In its early days, the Portuguese secret police for example was apparently trained by the Gestapo. Salazar relentlessly persecuted anyone who was against him and his ideas. He created a concentration camp for political and social prisoners and anti-fascist fighters in the former Portuguese colony of Cape Verde in the island of Santiago. It was called the Tarrafal Concentration Camp and its objective was to exterminate the resistance against the regime. It was said to be a terrifying place. Built in 1936 at first only for prisoners from Portugal, later when the wars for independence began in Guinea-Bissau, Angola and Mozambique many prisoners from those areas were also taken there.'

'You've been there?'

'No but I read a lot about it. I like history and believe that by studying the past one can better understand the present. Half of me and my family are Portuguese. So, I wanted to know more about the country. Very few people in the UK know about fascism in Portugal, the dictator Salazar and the forty-eight years of oppression and terror until the dictatorship fell. He didn't commit atrocities on the same scale as Hitler but did more than enough. The reason why Portugal was socially and economically behind most European countries for many years after the revolution of 1974 was mainly because Salazar held the country back with an iron hand for decades. He deliberately closed schools to keep the population ignorant, uneducated. Easier to control them that way. So, after the revolution, the number of people who couldn't read or write in Portugal was staggering. It took decades for the country to begin recovering from all the despotism and brutality.'

Hertie nodded, wiping her eyes and blowing her nose with a tissue. 'You're right. It takes a long time. Germany recovered very fast economically but socially it has dragged through the years. In fact, I think it's still in the psyche of the population, even the ones who were born long after the war and Nazism ended. There's often a feeling of collective guilt inherited from the past that was allowed to happen in Germany.'

'Do you feel that way?'

Hertie felt a sudden lump in her throat. Did she feel that way? Only nine years old when the war ended. She had often listened to the conversations of the adults. Didn't grasp most of it. Fragments of words and phrases remained in her head like pieces in a jumble sale but she didn't master the meaning until much later. There were vivid memories in her mind. Moments that marked her, traumatised her. Papa who didn't want to go to war but had to and never came back. Amalie being taken by the tall, athletic men in uniform to join her family for deportation. Hertie hadn't known the meaning of the word at the time. Her recurring dream was testimony to her traumas. Hunger. Running away in the middle of the night. The icy wind. The snow. The cold. Thinking her family had gone and left her, abandoned and alone in that frosty cellar, empty but for old boxes, straw and a handful of potatoes. Auntie Jutta's screams. But there were also lively, pleasant images engraved in her mind. The stars. The Milky Way when they escaped the advance of the Russian troops. The warmth and kindness of the American officer who gave her chocolate bars. A smile hovered on Hertie's lips but her chest tightened. She dried the corners of her eyes where tears threatened to flow again. Did she feel guilt for what took place in Germany? The truth was she did. Not always, occasionally though and wasn't sure why. She felt Valeria's hands holding hers.

'Are you all right? You've gone so quiet.'
'Fine, Schätzchen. Just pondering on your question.'
'Whether you feel that collective guilt?'
'Yes. And the answer is I do.'
'But why, Hertie? You were a child. If anyone was innocent it was you and all the other children.'
'I know. But I'm German. It's part of my country's heritage. I sometimes feel shame but simultaneously am also proud of Germany. It doesn't make sense.'
'Of course it makes sense. You embraced it all…and I believe everyone should do, no matter where they come from. Embracing the good and the bad that happened in one's country is important. You've many reasons to be proud of Germany – think about Beethoven to name just one. There are many good things about Germany as everywhere else. You have a terrible historical past but to understand it and remember it alongside all the glorious moments is what makes you a human being. A good person. You needn't feel guilty but it's the right thing to do to remember and to learn about all the features, good and bad events, all the collective conscious, history, art, literature, music, social welfare, etc – the whole that makes a nation, whether it's Germany, the UK, Portugal or any other.'

Squeezing Valeria's fingers Hertie said, 'you're smart and very understanding. What you say is correct. I agree with it but feelings are seldom rational and I can't help but feel guilty…for what happened in Germany. I'm German and it is part of me, my being, my personality…'

Her voice faded away. What else could she say? Valeria understood and at this moment in time that was the most important thing for Hertie.

'Tell me more, Hertie. It's good to talk.'

'You sure you want to listen?'

'Yes or I wouldn't have said so.'

'All right. It's kind of you. My recollections are one hundred per cent accurate. I remember moments or episodes that for one reason or other stuck with me – being hungry all the time, the cold, screams, crowded trains, blood, dead people. Dead people everywhere.'

Suddenly Hertie felt Valeria's arms around her. The warmth of the embrace made her feel loved. Here was someone who cared.

'Thank you,' she whispered.

'For what?'

'For wanting to listen.'

Drying her eyes Hertie patted Valeria's face and slowly resumed her story.

Chapter 4 – Hunger

Hertie was hungry. These days she was always hungry even after finishing her meals if one could call them that. With a sigh she walked into the kitchen, throwing her coat and scarf on a chair. Mutti was sitting on a bench, head in her hands, elbows on the table. Her shoulders heaved and lowered in convulsive movements. Hertie's little heart jumped in her chest. It was upsetting to see Mutti cry. Climbing onto the bench next to her mother's and sliding an arm around her shoulders she asked, 'warum bist du so traurig, Mutti?'

Gertrud turned her face slowly, drying her eyes with the back of her hands.

'Why am I so sad? I'm not sad,' she whispered, shaking her head, 'I'm just very tired, Schätzchen, and I...and I wish your father were here.'

'Perhaps Papa will come home next month for Christmas?' Hertie suggested, keen to see her mother happy.

'Yes...perhaps.'

'What're we having for lunch, Mutti? I'm hungry.'

Her mother sighed and Hertie guessed the menu. The same as usual. What she wouldn't give for a slice of bread and a piece of ham or cheese. Jumping to the floor she ran to her coat and extracted two items from its pockets. Arms stretched she returned and placed the items in front of her mother on the table.

'Look, Mutti. I wrote the best work in class today. I won the prize. Frau Jung—'

'Frau Jung?' Gertrud interrupted, 'who's Frau Jung?'

'My new teacher, Mutti. I told you last week Frau Schulz left, thank God. We don't know why. Frau Jung's much nicer. She's young and very nice.'

'Of course, my love, I'd forgotten. Forgive me.'

'That's all right, Mutti. Anyway, look. She was very pleased with me. I won the prize for the best written work and Frau Jung said we should have a small treat for lunch.'

Hertie climbed onto the bench again and, holding her mother's chin, forced her to look at the root vegetables on the table. A beet and two small turnips.

'Aren't you proud of me, Mutti?'

Gertrud smiled but Hertie noticed it didn't quite reach her eyes.

'Of course, I'm very proud of you, Schätzchen.'

'Then don't cry. There's no need. We'll help you in the house and Papa will come back. Sure of it.'

Hertie placed a kiss on her mother's cheek and ran out of the kitchen, saying she'd finish her homework before lunch was ready.

Gertrud stared at the root vegetables on the table. At least there would be something a little different. Indeed a treat. Hertie's teacher was right.

Jutta, her younger sister, entered the kitchen, holding the tips of her apron where she carried a handful of potatoes.

Placing the potatoes in the sink to wash she said, 'if this situation goes on, the potatoes won't last until Christmas. There are still plenty in the cellar but if we don't start rationing now and no food becomes available to buy we'll have miserable holidays.'

'I know,' Gertrud replied, 'I've been squeezing my brains out but I don't know what to do. At least today, we'll have a slightly better meal,' she pointed at the root vegetables, 'Hertie won them at school. She wrote the best work.'

Jutta smiled. 'Lovely. The soup will be tastier.'

'Yes,' Gertrud paused, as if gathering courage, then said, 'you think we should leave, Jutta?'

'Leave where?'

'I don't know. I met our neighbour Hilde yesterday. She said she didn't care what the orders from the army or the government were, she was leaving with her little girl. She doesn't want to be here when the Russians arrive.'

'Nonsense. The Russians won't come this far. Hilde always was a scaremonger.'

'That's what I think too. But sometimes when you start listening to other people...'

'Then don't listen, Gertrud,' her sister interrupted her.

'You're right. Besides if we tried to leave we could be caught and sent to prison or worse, shot for treason.'

'Precisely. Don't worry, sister dear, we'll manage. It's easier here on the land. We haven't bombings, as often happens in the cities. We still have some food and the woods are near. We can always find something to eat there.'

'Not so easy at the moment. This cold isn't normal. Usually November is wet but not so cold. It's unseasonable. All this snow and ice…what'll happen when we get to the end of December and the real winter starts?'

Jutta shrugged.

'Perhaps I should send the boys to fetch fallen branches from the woods. We're almost out of firewood.'

'Good idea. Shall I tell them?'

Gertrud nodded. 'Please. They can go now. It's cold but sunny. They'll have enough time before lunch's ready. Tell them to wrap themselves up.'

'Of course.'

Jutta left the kitchen shouting for her two nephews, Heinrich and Helmut, to get ready to collect wood in the nearby forest.

Gertrud remained sitting at the table, playing with the turnips and the beet. Good for the soup. It'd be the best soup in several weeks. But what should she do for the next month and especially for Christmas if the situation didn't improve? She wanted to serve a special meal at Christmas. It was the tradition in her family. No matter how bad things were, how hopeless, there was always, always something special on Christmas day. She wanted to still her children's hunger. They all looked so thin, not to mention herself, Jutta or Siggi. But what could she do? Jutta was right. They had to begin rationing the potatoes if they wanted to have any food at all during the holidays. The situation was desperate. She didn't know where to go or what to do to continue to feed her family. If nothing changed, they would starve. And she couldn't face such a terrible destiny for her children.

Hertie hid next to the tall grandfather clock in the hall when Jutta came out of the kitchen, calling aloud for her brothers. She wasn't supposed to listen to the grown-ups' conversations. Mutti would tell her off but she couldn't help it. Curious by nature Hertie liked to discover the adults' views though more often than not she didn't understand what they were on about. But Mutti had been crying and Hertie suspected she had lied about her reasons. She hadn't listened to the whole conversation between Mutti and auntie Jutta but it seemed to be related to food or the lack of it.

Her stomach rumbled. She was hungry. Always hungry. She didn't want to beg Mutti for food that she didn't have and get her sadder but it was painful to feel hungry. Hertie thought that when war had ended she would eat like a pig for several days, stuffing herself with all the delicious things she could imagine and dreamt about, especially at night when trying to fall asleep on an almost empty stomach.

Hertie didn't comprehend the war or what it really was. From her perspective it was something rather stupid. She knew people were fighting and dying. The war caused her and her family to be hungry, to not have enough food and most men to disappear. Her father being one of them. Why? Perhaps one day she'd be able to grasp the reasons but now it all seemed foolish, senseless.

'What're you doing, hiding in there?'

Hertie shook like a leaf in the wind, startled by uncle Siggi's voice. He was staring at her from the living room door.

'Shouldn't you be upstairs doing your homework?' he asked her.

Hertie nodded, feeling her cheeks redden, embarrassed Uncle Siggi had caught her in flagranti listening to the conversations of grown-up people.

'You know you're not supposed to eavesdrop,' he said in a not unkind voice.

Hertie nodded again.

'Off you go upstairs then, you little monkey,' he added in a tone that appeared amused to her ears, 'into your room and do your homework.'

Hertie shot away from him but halfway up the staircase stopped and glanced over her shoulder. Uncle Siggi was smiling. She realised he wasn't really angry. Grinning impudently she waved and stuck her tongue out at him, then disappeared into her bedroom.

Chapter 5 – Christmas 1944

Mutti had said Christmas would be different this year. Hertie didn't understand why. Christmas was Christmas. Why should it be different this year? She had secretly listened to the adults' conversations and understood more than they gave her credit for. Father had disappeared in January 1942, presumed dead at the Russian front. His body never found. Uncle Siggi had said Papa was possibly buried under the snows and below freezing temperatures of the Russian winter. Uncle Siggi was the only one of her five uncles who was home with them because he'd lost a leg when a boy in a horse and plough accident and was thus not fit to be a soldier. Mutti's other three brothers were all fighting the war somewhere and Papa's brother too. When Papa's letters stopped coming, Mutti just thought they were delayed and that he'd appear at the door one day. Now she'd given up waiting. He couldn't be alive anymore. Hertie knew in her heart her father was dead and would never return. Mutti didn't speak about these things in front of her or her older siblings but at eight years of age – close to nine, as her birthday was on 16th February – she was beginning to grasp most of what the adults said.

In spite of her father's disappearance in January 1942, they had celebrated Christmas that year. Mutti still hoped then that he might unexpectedly turn up. In 1943 they had a more subdued festivity, as Hertie was heartbroken. It was the year she had lost her friend Amalie. No idea what had happened to her or her family. Still she and her siblings decorated the Christmas tree and Mutti had conjured a duck (instead of a goose but still tasty) and homemade presents for her four children. But now Mutti seemed to have lost hope. She looked disheartened, sombre, sometimes mournful especially when she believed to be alone. Perhaps that was why she had said this year Christmas would be different. But what could be so special or not so special about 1944? The adults were distressed, more so than usual. Hertie could tell. They whispered, hurriedly shutting up or swiftly changing the subject if she or any of her siblings turned up in the room unexpectedly. What was going on? Hertie didn't know but promised herself to find out and ask her mother as soon as possible. She wasn't a baby anymore. Already eight years old though people usually pointed out she was small for her age. Nevertheless she'd be nine in less than two months. A big girl in her opinion.

Hertie dropped her rag doll and climbed on top of her bed to look out the window. Sprudel, their cat, joined her on the windowsill. She had named him Sprudel when it came to them as a kitten, four years earlier. A bubbly, fizzy, sparkling ball of fluff bursting with energy. But now Sprudel wasn't the same. He seemed sad, spiritless, sluggish as if it were too much effort to move. Too thin. Like all of them. Probably always hungry just as everyone else. For months food was lacking. No bread. Not enough grain. No meat or fish. No sugar. Hertie had forgotten the taste of cake. Most meals consisted of potatoes. Boiled. There was no butter to roast them. And the skins were used for soup. Sometimes Mutti added parsnips, turnips or a carrot or beet but hardly ever since the summer. And certainly not since November when Hertie had won the school prize for the best written work. Mutti said they were lucky to live on the land, far from a big city. And at least they had potatoes. Many people didn't even have that.

The ground was frozen. Snow covered everything. The cold was intense. Severe. Bitter. Painful and uncomfortable even inside the house. Frost and ice crystals covered most of the windowpanes. When her brothers brought branches from the woods they could light a fire and cuddle around it in the living room, otherwise just wrapped themselves in blankets when the cold gripped everything.

Hertie patted Sprudel. He purred. She had wanted to go outside and build a snowman but uncle Siggi said not today. He didn't explain why and she thought better not to ask. He appeared grumpy.

Hertie heard muffled voices from downstairs. Mutti's and uncle Siggi's. On tip toes she sneaked out of her bedroom, crouching on the floor by the staircase. A couple of thick coats hung carelessly on the banister. Cautiously, Hertie hid behind them so the grown-ups couldn't see her if they suddenly stepped into the hall. They were in the kitchen with the door ajar. She heard uncle Siggi's voice.

'You must go, Gertrud. If not immediately then in a few days. Can't leave it too late.'

Then her mother's.

'No, Siggi. You know as well as I do it's forbidden to go anywhere. The Führer has decreed no-one is permitted to leave their place of residence. And you know what can happen if one does.'

'The Red Army's getting nearer. It'll be dangerous.'

'Ach komm[18], Siggi! Our soldiers won't allow the Russians to pass. We're safe here. East Prussia is the safest place in the Reich. You know that. No bombings, like we hear in other German regions, especially cities like Berlin, Hamburg, Frankfurt am Main and so on. The schools still work. There's not much food but we've got something. Better than most places all in all. Life's still reasonable.'

'Gertrud, please. Think of the children. I'm telling you. You all must leave. The Red Army's moving fast. They've a bad reputation. Don't fool yourself about the Russians. They'll be here before you know it and then what?'

There was silence for a while. Hertie wondered if this idea of leaving because of the Russians was the reason why Mutti had said this year Christmas would be different. Were the Russians really evil, savage men as her previous teacher, Frau Schulz, had once told them? But then again, Frau Schulz found fault with anyone who wasn't a "real" German, as she put it. Mutti spoke again.

'Even if we were permitted to leave how could we go?'

'There are trains going west…or to the coast and from there you can board a ship to Hamburg,' uncle Siggi said.

'And die from the bombs? How's that better than waiting here?'

'Then take the small wheel cart for some luggage and

---

[18] Exclamation which in English would be "Oh come on!"

leave with the children and Jutta. Go west. Travel light. Only essentials.'

'And what about you, Siggi?'

'I can't walk far. If we still had the horses to pull the large cart I might attempt it. But with only one leg and crutches…I can't. Doesn't matter. You, Jutta and the children must get yourselves to safety.'

'Safety? It won't change a thing. And you know, as I've said before, it's forbidden to leave. If we still had the car…but our soldiers confiscated it. Even if not, there's no—'

'Fuel left,' uncle Siggi interrupted her mother, finishing her sentence, 'I know. No point thinking about what might have been. But in any case, I won't go and will stay behind.'

'They'll kill you.'

'I'm a cripple. They won't care about me but they'll kill the boys and…and abuse you, Jutta and the girls. Think about it, Gertrud. You don't want that to happen.'

Another extensive silence fell before Hertie heard her mother speak again.

'Perhaps me and Jutta, yes, we'll be at risk but the children? Surely not, Siggi. The Russians are people. They've got children too. Heinrich's only twelve, Helmut and Hedi eleven. Hertie eight. They're children all four of them. And with malnourishment they appear younger than their real ages. It'll be fine.'

'Remember Nemmersdorf last October.'

'I don't want to think about it. Besides our soldiers took it back. Nemmersdorf is more than two hundred kilometres away from here. I don't think the Red Army will ever get close to us.'

'Don't believe what you hear. The government…the Führer pretend they're still winning the war. Believe me, they're not. I know. You must leave, Gertrud. You must.'

'As I've pointed out repeatedly, leaving one's place of residence is forbidden,' Mutti said, 'it's treason. Even planning to escape is treason. We'll go to prison…or worse. No. We must stay where's safe.'

Uncle Siggi didn't say another word. A moment later

Hertie heard the sound of his crutches on the tiles of the kitchen. He emerged into the hall, seeming upset. Crushed. More so than usual. A dark expression in his normally kind brown eyes. Hertie pulled the coats a little down so if uncle Siggi looked up he'd be unable to see her. She wasn't allowed to eavesdrop on their conversations as she'd often been made aware. He stopped in the hall and she heard him say to her mother, 'I hope you won't come to regret your decision, Gertrud. I can only hope.'

He disappeared into the lounge and Hertie heard him throw a piece of wood into the fire. Carefully she walked downstairs and into the kitchen.

'Mutti,' she said, 'after tomorrow's Christmas day and we haven't fetched a tree.'

Her mother appeared dejected. For a second Hertie thought she was going to burst into tears but then she pulled herself together. Peeling potatoes she parted her lips in an attempt to appear cheerful and quietly said, 'there won't be a tree this year, Schätzchen.'

'Is that why you said Christmas would be different?'

'Yes. Life's more complicated now.'

Hertie nodded, deciding Mutti wasn't going to venture any further explanation. It must be the war. She hadn't seen much of it if anything at all. But she knew her father, her uncles and almost all the men in their little town, except the cripples like uncle Siggi or the very old or too young, were fighting in this war, protecting the country, dying for it and the Führer, for the glory of Germany. Hertie thought the Führer couldn't be a very nice man. Why else would he want Papa and her uncles to die for him and Germany? Only a bad man would. There was a photo of the Führer at school. She thought he was ugly. No kindness in his harsh face. Hertie avoided looking at the portrait. She didn't like him and wished the war would be over so Papa and all her uncles could return home if they hadn't died. But in her heart she thought they had. She looked at the potatoes her mother was preparing and sighed. Not potato skin soup, followed by boiled potatoes again. She'd had enough of that. For a long time now it was almost the only thing they ate.

'One day,' Hertie promised silently to herself, 'one day when I grow up and all this is over I'll never touch a potato skin again.'

On Christmas day Hertie understood why this year it would be different. The special lunch of roasted goose they had most years was only a potato soup – at least no peels on account of the day though Mutti had put them aside for another time – enriched with a small piece of meat. Mutti said she'd bought it from a neighbouring farm where they had killed their last chicken and remaining cow. Hertie wondered why they had killed the chicken and the cow. They wouldn't have any more eggs or milk. But it wasn't until much later that she discovered the meat they ate on Christmas day 1944 was Sprudel, the cat.

Sprudel had disappeared the day before Christmas. No-one paid much attention. Anguish, icy conditions, hunger were much worse problems than missing a cat. They all accepted that without food the cat had gone astray or died in the snow and ice that covered the land while trying to catch a mouse or a rabbit. Many years later Hertie, already a woman about to leave for her first job, found out the truth. Her mother told her and asked for forgiveness. She'd been desperate. Most of the potatoes had been eaten, though carefully rationed each day. She didn't know what to do, had then noticed the cat and decided there was no choice. They had to eat it or go hungry. Hertie wasn't shocked. She felt an immense sadness the war forced her mother to such drastic measures. Rage followed. Fury at Hitler and his cronies who had allowed things to become extreme. Why? For what? Not only had they killed Jews and others in the horrible concentration camps Hertie learned about at school after the war ended but they had also allowed the country to be destroyed, devastated, shattered, bombed to the ground.

Extreme necessity had demanded Mutti to kill the cat, use it as food for a slightly richer Christmas lunch. But she didn't have the heart to tell them the truth, seeing how they were all glad of the improved meal. Simple, yet better. The same usual soup, with a handful of potatoes, but a small piece of meat each. It tasted good. Mutti was an excellent cook. And after many weeks of potato peel soup and one boiled potato each, it was special.

Hertie was still hungry when they had finished but she dared not complain. Mutti told them there was a little treat. A handful of minuscule caramels as dessert, homemade by Mutti and auntie Jutta. One each. No more, no less. Uncle Siggi asked where Mutti had managed to get the sugar. She didn't say. Just shrugged, telling them to enjoy it. There was no tree. No presents. No roast. No cake. Distressing. Hertie refrained from asking why when she noticed her mother close to tears. She left her chair, walked to her mum and put her arms around her.

'Don't cry, Mutti. It doesn't matter we can't have any presents this year. We'll have more next year when Papa's back home.'

To Hertie's dismay her mother held on to her and began quietly sobbing. Hertie didn't understand and glanced at uncle Siggi for help. He tried to reassure her.

'It's all right, my love,' he said in his gentle voice, stroking her hair, 'don't worry. Your mummy misses your daddy. That's all.'

But Hertie was upset. She had made Mutti cry. It wasn't her intention. Deep in her heart Hertie knew Papa was dead but thought better not to say it because it might make her mother sadder. She didn't want that.

In the night she couldn't sleep. Hedwig or Hedi, her older sister and Helmut's twin, was out like a light but Hertie just stared at the night sky. Clear but no moon. It appeared like a piece of black satin, dotted with minuscule lights. So many unbelievably beautiful stars. Thousands. Millions. Probably more. Maybe a billion, which was an incredibly big number but her teacher had said there were much more than a billion. Hertie found difficult to imagine such numbers but believed they were real. She enjoyed gazing at the stars. So lovely. So far away. They made patterns in the sky called constellations. She had learned a few at school and tried to find her favourite – Orion. There it was. She could clearly see it. Orion, the hunter. She wasn't sure why such a name. It looked nothing like a hunter, like a man, but whatever the reason it didn't matter. It was pretty. She could see the belt formed of three stars and the sword. Would there be a little girl like her on one of those stars looking down and wondering if someone was awake looking up? Hertie smiled. She hoped so.

It had been a bleak Christmas day. Not much food. Sprudel gone missing the night before. No presents. But Hertie wasn't sad. Outside, high above, the stars twinkled like the diamond in Mutti's old ring – Papa's present many years ago – and their glow warmed her child's heart, placing a soft, unconscious smile on her lips, making her forget her hunger. Gradually her eyelids turned heavy and, after another couple of minutes, she finally fell asleep.

Chapter 6 – Escape

A Sunday in January 1945, a couple of weeks after Christmas. Four thirty in the afternoon but pitch dark. Thick snow covered everything and the temperatures were so far below zero one's lungs hurt when breathing in. All of a sudden the storm bells began ringing through the village. A booming man's voice shouted repeatedly, 'Räumungsbefehl. Removal order.'

Hertie wondered what it meant but soon realised. Mutti came running into her room, followed by her two brothers. Heinrich and Helmut appeared extremely fat all of a sudden. Then she grasped why. Mutti urgently ordered her and Hedi to get into various pairs of socks, boots and as many coats as they had. She tied two scarves around their heads and necks and commanded them to run down the stairs and join aunt Jutta in the hall.

'And you, Mutti?' Hertie asked.

'I'll be there in a second.'

Hertie watched her mother grab a few items of underwear and jumpers that belonged to her and her sister, stuffing them in a small suitcase which seemed already full.

'Mutti, what about Lottie?'

'Lottie?' Her mother raised an eyebrow and Hertie pointed at her rag doll on the window seal.

'No time, Schätzchen. We must go. Now. Run.'

But Hertie couldn't bring herself to leave without Lottie. Jumping on the bed she grabbed the doll and ran down the stairs after her mother. At the bottom of the staircase auntie Jutta stood next to uncle Siggi. She had various coats on too and held a few more for Mutti. The three of them hugged.

'Go now. Quick,' uncle Siggi said, 'you must run to catch the train.'

Mutti and Jutta had tears in their eyes.

'Come with us,' Mutti told uncle Siggi in a broken voice that didn't sound like hers, 'Jutta and I will help you.'

He shook his head. 'I'd only delay you. I might have tried if we still had the horse. I can't walk in this snow with my crutches. Now go. I'll be fine.'

'But Siggi…'

Auntie Jutta began silently to sob, interrupting whatever Mutti was going to say.

'Go. Now,' uncle Siggi repeated, 'you must hurry. The Russians are only twenty-five kilometres away.'

'They'll kill you.'

'They won't. I'm a cripple. They won't care about me. Just go. Now.'

Finally uncle Siggi writhed free of his sisters' embrace and thrust them out of the house, closing the door behind them. Mutti marched at the front, then in a single file Helmut, Hedi, Hertie, Heinrich and finally auntie Jutta. They walked fast. The snow was almost knee deep, slowing them down. The cold was brutal, raw, biting the skin, making breathing painful and eyes tearful. After only a few minutes and in spite of the four pairs of wool socks, Hertie could no longer sense her feet. Holding desperately to her doll, Lottie, she lost feeling in her hands. They were numb from the bitterly frozen air. Hertie stuck Lottie inside her coats, against her chest, shoving her gloved little hands inside the pockets of her outer layer. But it still seemed her fingers didn't exist.

'Mutti,' she cried out after a while, 'where're we going?'

'To the station to catch a train. Now, be quiet, Schätzchen. Just concentrate on walking as fast as you can.'

'Why do we need to catch a train? It's dark and so cold. And why didn't uncle Siggi come with us?'

Her mother stopped, turned and kneeled in front of her. She tried to smile but Hertie noticed the tears in her eyes or perhaps it was the icy air.

'Schätzchen,' her mother said, 'we must run away because of the war or bad things could happen to us.'

'We could die?'

'Yes, my love. We could.'

'But uncle Siggi…'

'Uncle Siggi will be all right. We'll write to him when the war's over and come and fetch him in a car. But now we must hurry and go. You understand, Hertie?'

'Yes, Mutti.'

'Good. We all have to walk a little faster. There's still a long way to the station and we don't want to miss the train. There may not be another.'

Resolutely she moved to the front, accelerating her pace. Hertie, her siblings and her aunt followed suit.

Normally the station was easily reachable after a twelve or fifteen minute brisk walk from the village but this time it took them more than half an hour. The snow and the harsh, piercing wind restricted their movements, slowing down their progress. But they were on time. The train was still at the station.

Hertie wondered why it was such a funny train. There were no carriages with seats, as she was used to when the family had travelled to a nearby town. These were freight coaches, usually transporting animals or goods but now full of people. The station's platform was crowded and Hertie wondered whether they would manage to get on the train. The carriages she could see were already brimming. A strong noise of metal scraping against other metal made her turn to look. More carriages were being added at the back of the already long train. Mutti told them all to hold hands with each other, Jutta and herself and to never let go. She led them to the back of the train where the new carriages had just been attached. Jutta jumped in and helped Hertie and her siblings climb aboard. Mutti was the last. A layer of straw covered the floor. They huddled together in a corner while more and more people scrambled to get in. Through a crack in the wood Hertie watched the platform slowly emptying then filling up again, as more people tried to enter the station. A handful of soldiers with shotguns, so young they looked like schoolboys, stopped the swarms of people, shouting orders and screaming another train was coming.

Hertie looked around the faces in her carriage. Blank, hollow, glazed eyes stared back at her. There was an unpleasant smell though the doors were still open. Hertie wondered whether it was fear. Uncle Siggi said animals could smell fear. Perhaps she could too. Or was it the lingering stench of the cattle once transported in these cars?

Hertie moved closer to her mother. She was so cold. Mutti put an arm around her shoulders, pressing her against her chest. She parted her lips, attempting to smile encouragingly but it didn't reach her eyes.

'It'll be all right, Schätzchen,' stretching one hand and touching all their faces in turn Mutti said, 'we'll all be all right. I promise.'

They crouched in their corner, snuggled together for warmth. And waited. No-one spoke. Hertie was hungry but unsure whether to ask for food. It was the twins, Helmut and Hedi, who did, whispering in unison they were hungry. Mutti gave each of them a corner of bread, telling them to chew it slowly and make it last. Hertie noted neither Mutti nor auntie Jutta had a piece. How much longer until the train began moving? They waited. And waited. And waited.

Jutta asked the time. Mutti said just after midnight. They'd been sitting on the hard floor of the train for over six hours. It hadn't moved a millimetre and still more people kept arriving. The soldiers must stop them, Hertie thought, frightened. There was no corner left in their carriage. Surely the others must be the same. If they allowed more people to climb in they would have to sit on top of each other. Just then a potent, authoritative man's voice sounded outside. He shouted something about trucks that Hertie didn't understand. Seconds later the head of a soldier appeared at the carriage's door. He glanced around, then shouted the new information. Hertie thought his voice echoed strangely in the confined space. Flat. Detached. Weary.

'Trucks are arriving in a few minutes to take people to the coast. There you can board the ships sailing west to Kiel and Hamburg. There's no other train coming after all and not enough space for all,' the soldier announced.

He moved on to the next carriage. Hertie heard him speak again in the same monotonous tone. She didn't understand the words but presumed he was repeating what he'd told them. Mutti looked at auntie Jutta.

'What do you think?' she asked her sister, 'should we take

a truck to the coast? Board a ship?'

'And then where would we go, Gertrud?' Jutta questioned, 'I thought we'd take the train to get to Elsa's. It stops in Belgard and from there it's only half an hour hike to the village where Elsa's farm's located.'

'But this train doesn't seem to be going anywhere,' Mutti pointed out.

Auntie Jutta shook her head vigorously.

'I don't want to go on a ship,' she said, 'we could all get seasick, perish in a storm. The train's safer. I'm sure it'll move soon once the trucks arrive and the soldiers start allocating people more effectively. And think about it, Gertrud, what would we do in Hamburg or Kiel? We know no-one there.'

Aunt Elsa was Mutti's and Jutta's older sister. She had married a farmer and had two teenage sons who, along with their father, were all forcibly enlisted in the army, fighting somewhere for Führer and country. Hertie didn't understand very well why but it seemed stupid to her. Why should so many people leave, abandon their wives, children, families to fight for one man and the country? To die? She didn't grasp the meaning but it made no sense in her head. Auntie Elsa now lived alone with her daughter in their small farm at the edge of the village. Perhaps she'd be happy to have them. They could help in the house or in the fields and with the animals.

Mutti nodded at Jutta's words and said nothing further about getting into a truck and aboard a ship. On the train they continued to wait. In silence. No-one talked aloud or with anyone outside their own little group but Hertie heard whispers. Seconds later, some of the last arrivals in the middle of the carriage stood up and moved to the door. A woman called out to a soldier and said they'd be happy to go in a truck. The soldier helped her down, then the old couple and the two children who were all part of her group. A moment later a family of five followed – two women, three children. Then a group of four people – one old man, two old women and a child. They left for the trucks. The carriage was roomier now. They could stretch their legs. Helmut and Hedi fell asleep under auntie Jutta's tender embrace.

Heinrich leaned his head on Mutti's shoulder and was soon napping. Hertie was too scared. She wished the train to move. But after a while she too rested her head on Mutti's lap and fell asleep, hungry, cold, exhausted from the walk in the snow and the long hours sitting in the carriage.

A jolt. Hertie woke up. The train was slowly beginning to move. Finally. The door was still open. Hertie gazed at the clear, starry sky and glimpsed the constellations. They glowed and twinkled brightly, as they always did when the heavens were cloudless, as if nothing had happened. Hertie wished for wings to fly out of the carriage, toward the stars. The wind through the open door increased as the train gained speed. Biting cold. Painful. An old woman and a boy stood up and slid the door shut. The wind stopped. It was pitch dark inside. Hertie sighed. She could no longer see the stars.

Chapter 7 – The Journey

The train rattled through the night. Hertie woke with a sudden violent tug. Her body jerked forward against her mother's knees. She opened her eyes. Dawn had broken. She could see light through the cracks in the wood. Her stomach rumbled. She wondered whether Mutti had any bread left.

The heavy door of the carriage slid open. A soldier looked in briefly, then shouted, 'alle aussteigen. All must alight. There's a problem with the locomotive. We're trying to fix it but might have to stay here a while.'

Hertie jumped off the train, rolling down the snow embankment along the railway lines. She laughed. Other children followed her. And for the first time since they had caught the train there were sounds of joy. It was still bitterly cold. The sun shone brightly in the clear blue sky but it gave little warmth and yet the children's laughter playing in the snow warmed people's hearts. The adults relaxed. Some smiled, watching the kids' snowball battles. For a few brief but precious moments hunger, fatigue, desperation and the harsh winter were forgotten.

Hertie ran back to her mother and Jutta, feeling happy. Her cheeks were red. She beamed. Her intense blue eyes sparkled.

'Enjoying the snow, Schätzchen?' Mutti asked her.

She nodded, pausing to gain her breath and look around. It seemed they were in the middle of nowhere. Whiteness. Pristine, luminous snow as far as the eye could see, seeming to dissolve into the blue sky at the horizon line. Scattered here and there a few evergreens but they too were covered in snow. In the distance, four or five hundred metres away, two buildings. A fence. Mutti said it must be a farm.

'Perhaps they'll give us some food,' exclaimed an old woman standing next to them, 'if I were younger I'd go there and ask but my old legs won't move fast enough in the snow.'

'We'll go,' two young women from another group announced. A boy in his early teens joined them and another woman with a baby. Hertie turned and asked, 'Mutti, may I go too? I can bring food for us.'

'All right but don't get distracted and stay with them,' opening her rucksack she took a corner of bread and handed it over, 'eat this Hertie and—'

'I know,' Hertie interrupted, rolling her eyes, 'chew it well and slowly. We haven't got much left.'

Gertrud smiled. Jutta laughed. Thrilled to see her adults happy, Hertie ran and joined the small group heading for the farm. It took them longer than ten minutes to reach the buildings. The snow was thick, making it difficult to walk. Moving tired, weakened limbs through the powdered, deep whiteness was a laborious task. Out of breath when they reached the farm they glanced around in hope of finding food. There was a gate on the fence, hanging open on only one hinge. No animals or people in sight. They walked into the yard and the woman with the baby shouted, 'hello? Anyone home?'

Silence answered them. They searched the barn first. It had no door. Nothing inside except a couple of old, dirty straw bales. They cried out again, hoping someone would turn up but nothing. Only noiseless, cold snow. They walked to the house. The door was wide open but they knocked before entering, shouting hello one more time. The place was deserted. Abandoned. They walked in, searching for food but someone had already taken everything. The kitchen ransacked. Nothing to eat. Not even a morsel of bread or a handful of potatoes. The boy walked out and a couple of minutes later came back running.

'I went round the house,' he said, 'there's a coal cellar. A tiny window's open and I looked. I think I saw potatoes in a corner. Perhaps we can go in from inside the house and get them.'

Everyone nodded and separated in two groups to probe every door in the house. But nobody found the right one. They noticed a floor latch, which might lead to the coal cellar, but it was locked. Impossible to break in without tools. There were none. Soldiers must have confiscated them, as they did with nearly everything nowadays. The small group met outside, disheartened and tired, staring at the tiny window. It resembled more a horizontal slit in a sentry's box than a window. Each at a time they knelt on the snow and peered inside. They all agreed there were potatoes in the far corner.

'I'll try to get in,' the boy said decisively.

Hertie thought it a good idea. The adults wouldn't fit the opening so they agreed. The boy was thin, a tad smaller than the three women, but seemed strong. He slid his head into the opening to inspect how he could climb down to the floor of the cellar and pass the potatoes out to the others.

'There's a small pile of coal, a couple of straw bales and a few empty boxes just by the window,' he announced, 'I can easily climb down and then back up.'

With these words he attempted to squeeze through the opening but it was too narrow. He tried again. And again. And again.

'Shitty thing,' he shouted in frustration, 'I can't get my shoulders through. Who builds such a stupid slit on the wall instead of a proper window?'

His question didn't require an answer but one of the women said, 'it's just for the coal to be dropped in when delivered. Nothing else. That's why it's so small.'

'There must be a way of getting in from the house.'

'We looked. We didn't find it and we need to go. The locomotive might be ready any minute now.'

The boy and the woman with the baby stared at Hertie.

'What about you?' they said in unison.

'Me?' Hertie exclaimed, sudden butterflies in her stomach.

'Yes. You're small enough. We'll help lower you to the boxes and the straw. You can jump to the floor or run down the coal pile and get to the potatoes, then pass on as many as possible. We'll help you out when you're done,' the boy said.

Hertie didn't like the idea. The baby had begun to cry. The mother whispered with tears in her eyes, 'he's hungry. I haven't any milk left. It's dried. I've forgotten when I last had a proper meal.'

'Go on,' the boy insisted, encouraging Hertie.

She could reach the potatoes. She could help still everyone's hunger. Her family would be delighted. Mutti proud of her. Her heart in her mouth, Hertie finally nodded and easily slid through the tiny window. The boy held her feet and let go once Hertie shouted she was firmly on the straw and could clearly see the potatoes. Before jumping to the floor, Hertie examined the coal, the bales and the boxes to decide how she could climb back up. It wasn't difficult if she used the straw and the boxes but the others would need to pull her up through the window. She could reach it on tiptoes from the top of a box, placing it upside down on the straw bales. But she wouldn't be able to lift herself unaided.

Slowly Hertie slid to the floor and ran to the pile of potatoes. She removed one of her scarves and loaded it with potatoes, then climbed back up and stretched her arms with the booty. The others gratefully received it and returned her scarf. Hertie ran back and forward, repeating the operation five times. She could see the pile of potatoes physically reducing. It was pleasing. Satisfying. She felt proud of herself.

Assessing the number of potatoes for a moment she decided another three or four trips would suffice to take them all out. Just then one of the women outside shouted something that Hertie didn't understand. It was difficult to hear anything in there above the screaming baby. She began placing more potatoes on her scarf. Then the boy's voice from the window.

'Come up. Now. Leave the rest of the potatoes. Doesn't matter. Come now. The locomotive's repaired and ready to leave. Come. We must return to the train fast.'

'Okay.'

Hertie left the scarf and ran, carefully climbing up the straw bales. She arrived at the upside down box and climbed on top of it, then reached out with her arms, stretching her little hands, touching the edge of the tiny windowsill.

'Now, pull me up,' she said.

No-one replied. No-one slid their hands through the opening.

'Hello?' Hertie cried out. 'Help me up, please. I can't do

it alone.'

Silence.

Hertie's heart began flapping in her chest. Where were they? Where had everyone gone?

She held the ledge firmly with her fingers, attempting to pull herself up but couldn't. Then jumped, trying to hold on that way but it only caused the box to fall. Now even on tiptoes she was unable to reach the edge.

'Please,' she shouted, 'one of you must stretch your arm to reach me and pull me up. I can't on my own.'

No sound. Only quietness and the wind. Hertie stifled a sob. The others had run back to the train and abandoned her. She would die, imprisoned in this cellar. No water. Only raw potatoes. Tears began streaming down her cheeks.

'Mutti,' she whispered.

Standing on the snow embankment, ready to climb into the carriage, Gertrud saw the three women and the boy approaching, running as fast as they could. The baby was screaming. Where was Hertie? She couldn't see her. Her heart missed a beat. Walking briskly toward the oncoming group she asked them, 'where's Hertie? Where's my daughter?'

One of the women asked, 'the little girl that went with us?'

Gertrud nodded.

Glancing over his shoulder the boy began, 'well, she's behind…' he stopped talking abruptly, recognising there was no-one else trailing him.

'Where is she?' Gertrud repeated, attempting to control her growing anxiety.

'I…I don't know,' the boy said, 'I thought she was behind me. She…she went into the house's coal cellar and got the potatoes out for all of us.'

'She was the only one that fitted through the tiny window,' one of the women said.

'And where is she now?' Gertrud shouted, attempting to keep her anger in check.

They shrugged.

'You left her there?' Gertrud wanted to hit them.

A booming voice interrupted them.

'Einsteigen. Alle bitte einsteigen. Wir fahren gleich los. Climb aboard. All aboard. We'll depart soon.'

'Noooo,' Gertrud yelled in panic, 'no. My daughter's missing. We must look for her.'

'We can't wait, Madam,' the soldier said, 'the train's already delayed. We're in danger of being caught up by the Red Army.'

'Please,' Gertrud implored on her knees, 'please, she's only a little girl, eight years old.'

The soldier hesitated, then exchanged a few words with another man, older, standing a few paces away, who seemed to be in command. The soldier returned and helped Gertrud to her feet.

'All right, Madam. Der Kapitän says ten minutes. No more.'

Gertrud nodded relieved.

'Thank you, thank you,' she murmured, 'then turning to Jutta and her other children she said, 'Hedi, stay with aunt Jutta. Heinrich, Helmut with me.'

'I'll go too,' the boy from the group who'd gone to the farm said, 'I've been there. I know the way and the entrance to the cellar. It'll be quicker.'

'Okay…I don't know your name,' Gertrud said.

'Oskar Kaufmann,' he replied, running ahead of them.

'Gertrud Lohmeyer,' she said but doubted the boy had heard her.

It didn't matter. Gertrud ran after him with Heinrich and Helmut alongside her.

Hertie sat on the straw, crying quietly. From time to time she looked up, hoping to see a pair of hands or hear a voice. But nothing. Not even a bird or any other animal. The wind had also stopped. Silence. Only silence. The sun was still shining but it was winter. It would get dark soon. Hertie rubbed her eyes. She could glimpse a small blue rectangle of sky. Would she be able to see the stars when night descended? Sobbing she hoped she would. The stars would comfort her. She wouldn't feel so alone. So forsaken.

Crunching sounds on the snow. Had she just heard steps? Hertie swallowed her tears and listened attentively. Nothing. But no. There it was again. And voices.

'Hertie. Hertie.'

Mutti's voice.

'Hertie, Schätzchen, where are you?'

Frozen and frightened, Hertie was unable to move or stand up. Wiping off her tears and her runny nose to the sleeve of her outer coat she began shouting as loud as she could, 'Mutti, here in the cellar. Mutti.'

The sound of grinding snow under boots became stronger. Faster. People running.

'Mutti,' Hertie yelled at the top of her lungs.

More voices. She couldn't grasp what they were saying but then a clear voice.

'No. I'll stretch on the ground and put one arm through the opening,' Hertie recognised the boy who'd been with her and the women earlier, 'I'm smaller than all of you.'

'All right, Oskar,' Mutti said.

'Your two boys can hold my legs. You wait till we pull your little girl out.'

He seemed to be in control and no-one minded.

Hertie was surprised that Mutti didn't protest. On tenterhooks, she looked up and saw a hand. An arm. Then a face.

'Hertie,' the boy said, 'it's Oskar. I was here with you. Remember?'

She nodded.

'Hertie,' he said, 'we're going to pull you up. Your mother and your brothers are here but you must stand up or I can't reach you.'

Hertie nodded again. She heard Oskar speak over his shoulder.

'She's scared stiff, Frau Lohmeyer.'

Then Mutti's voice.

'Hertie, Liebling, we're here. We won't leave without you. Breathe in and out, Schätzchen. Begin to move slowly. We're here and we'll stay until you're out, my love.'

She did as Mutti told her. Then, stifling her last sobs, closing her eyes she concentrated on moving her legs and jumping to her feet.

'Come on, Hertie,' it was Oskar, 'come on.'

'You can do it,' her brothers' voices.

Hertie stood for a moment. First her legs were wobbly. She leaned on the wall. Glancing up she saw Oskar's hand. Then his face, smiling at her. Gathering all her strength she stood on her toes and stretched. Oskar grabbed her left wrist.

'I've got her,' he shouted, 'I've got her.'

Gradually, Hertie felt her feet leave the straw. A moment later her head emerged. She stared into Oskar's brown eyes. He grinned. 'I've got you,' he said again.

She saw Heinrich and Helmut each holding one of Oskar's legs and pulling him out. Soon Hertie was lying on the snow. Mutti knelt and picked her up. She hugged her, pressing her against her chest. There were tears gushing out of her eyes.

'Oh, Hertie, Schätzchen. For a terrible moment I thought I'd lost you.'

Her brothers knelt and they all hugged.

'There'll be time for that later,' Oskar interrupted energetically, 'soldier said only ten minutes. We must hurry to the train or it'll leave without us.'

'You're right, Oskar,' Mutti said, then turning to her asked, 'can you run, Hertie?'

She nodded. Her fear had gone. She was cold. Hungry. Thirsty. But she was out. Mutti, her brothers and Oskar were all with her. They began running. In the distance they saw a soldier waving them to hasten. As they reached the train, it had jolted slowly forward. The soldier helped Mutti in, then threw Hertie into her arms before helping the three boys and pulling himself up just before the train gained speed.

Chapter 8 – Aunt Elsa's Farm

The train sped through the night, stopping many times. No-one knew where. Nobody knew why. There was no information. The few soldiers said nothing, simply preventing people from alighting and repeating that every single person must stay inside the carriages. Once, in the back of beyond, blackness engulfing them, the soldiers allowed people out to relieve themselves in what seemed like a huge empty field. Men and boys older than ten to the left of the train, women and all other children to the right. Hertie gazed up at the sky, as she jumped off the carriage with her family. The bitter cold took her breath away. She pressed a hand to her chest. The pain of breathing in the biting, icy air was harrowing. Her stomach rumbled loudly. It felt as if glued to her back. Hertie ignored it. The agony of continuous hunger had vanished, her body grown accustomed to it. The norm now was to feel hungry.

    Hertie took comfort in the stars, as she gazed at the velvet cloak of the night dotted with twinkling lights. Stars. Planets. Comets. What other things might be up there? So beautiful. The heavens reminded her of a large midnight blue shawl embroidered in silver thread and tiny crystals she had seen once, adorning the shoulders of a ballerina at the theatre. Hertie had been a very little girl, only three or four. It was before Papa went to war. They had gone to see a ballet called Der Nussknacker[19]. She had loved every minute of it. The dancers were wonderful, handsome, graceful, elegant. The costumes colourful, luminous and the music transported Hertie into another world. A world of beauty and warmth where everything was magnificent and people were marvellous. Unwittingly, her lips parted slightly at the memory. She gazed at the stars one more time. Their beauty comforted her. It eased her chest and breathing felt no longer painful.

    A loud voice interrupted Hertie's reverie.
    'Alle aufsteigen. All aboard. Train leaving.'

---

[19] The Nutcracker.

The stop had lasted less than ten minutes. Hertie sighed, disappointed to leave the stars and her dreams outside. She was so tired of it all, the cold, the smell of unwashed people herded together, the rattling of the train, the uncomfortable carriage, the hardness of its floor. So, so tired. And hungry. And thirsty. And cold. She just wanted to arrive somewhere. Didn't matter where, as long as this infernal journey ended. She cast another sigh and moved slowly up the snowed embankment to return to the train.

Quietly, no words, no whispers, just the odd sigh of desperation or sadness or fatigue escaped someone's throat, as they boarded it again and the train went on its way.

Hertie hoped the next stop would be the town of Belgard. Their stop. Where they could finally leave the blasted train. She fell asleep. Her head on her mother's lap. The only way to forget about the hole in her stomach. She hadn't asked Mutti for anything to eat or drink. Her lips were dry, cracked from the cold. But she knew there was nothing. No food. She had eaten a chunk of snow to still her thirst while they were out. The last of the bread had long gone. They had eaten a cold raw potato each at some stage after dark. Hertie guessed it would have been dinner time. Her eyelids dropped. Seconds later, she was flying high, hopping from star to star, looking down to Earth and its people, behaving like lunatics, staring at the ground instead of looking up and allowing their minds to take wings.

When she woke, it was morning and the train pulling into a station. An overcrowded platform greeted them, full of people trying to get in. Hertie wondered where they could fit. There was no space left in the carriage. Every centimetre was occupied. To her great relief she heard her mother's voice.

'Come on,' she was saying, 'we leave the train here. It's Belgard. We can walk to auntie Elsa's. Then we'll be able to rest and have something to eat.'

They set up in a single file. Mutti at the front, auntie Jutta at the rear. It was another radiant sunny but bitterly cold day. The wind picked up once they left the relative shelter of the town houses and marched across the fields. Biting. Painful. Harsh. Walking was laborious. The snow had hardened in places, making it easier to move, but softer under the trees or on the paths. They followed a country road. Mutti knew the way. Hertie's feet were wet or frozen from the snow. She didn't know. Only that she couldn't feel them. It was so cold she wanted to cry, drop to the ground, curl up and sleep until she could rise from this icy nightmarish landscape. After forty minutes she grumbled.

'Mutti, I can't walk anymore. My feet...my legs. I just can't.'

Her mother picked her up and pointing ahead said, 'we're nearly there, my love. See the houses in the distance?'

Hertie nodded, too exhausted to speak.

'That's the village. Auntie Elsa's place is just one kilometre after the last houses down there,' she pointed at the end of the road.

Hertie said nothing, leaned her head on Mutti's shoulder and shut her eyes, happy to be carried.

They walked slowly through the main street of the village. Saw no-one. Not even a cat or a dog. Gertrud began to wonder whether something was wrong. She looked to her left toward the dense woods only five hundred metres from the edge of the village, straining her eyes, trying to catch sight of people among the trees. No sign of a living person. Glancing around she noticed many houses had their doors wide open. Probably abandoned. Ahead to their right was the church. There was movement by the side of the building. Instinctively she slowed down her pace. Someone. A person. A moment later an old woman, leaning on a crude stick to help her walk came fully into view. Her back arched, bent forward, her eyes on the ground she dragged her feet through the snow, barely lifting them.

Gertrud stopped and addressed the woman, 'gnädige Frau, bitte, dear lady, please, where's everyone?'

The woman lifted her head and gazed at Gertrud through weary, expressionless pale blue eyes. Her face grey, like creased cardboard. She lifted her left arm in a gesture that included the whole village, then said in a weak, jaded voice, 'all gone...all that were left, which weren't many…women…children. Most men already been taken.'

'Taken?'

'Yes. A few weeks ago, just before Christmas, a battalion of our soldiers came round. They forced all men who weren't old or crippled – not many left, mind you – and boys as young as thirteen to enlist.'

Gertrud glanced scared at Heinrich and Helmut. They would have been taken if she had waited with Siggi. She felt lucky to still have all her children around her.

'Then,' the woman continued speaking, 'they confiscated the few horses, cows and sheep still around and departed, saying that everyone had to do their bit for country and Führer. The devil take our scheiss Führer. He disgraced this country, killed everyone. Murderer. Murderer that's what he is.'

'Don't say that. It's treason.'

'Puh! And who's going to arrest or kill me? I'll be dead soon anyway.'

'What happened after our soldiers left with the men, the boys and the animals from the village?'

'Women, young children and those men or boys who were too old, too young or too ill to fight were left behind. Earlier this month, an officer and a small group of soldiers came by and gave order to leave, remove the whole village. Everyone left for the train in Belgard. Some in trucks for the coast to get on the ships to Kiel or Hamburg. There's only a handful of us left – too old or too ill to move. We're waiting for death.'

The woman went quiet for a moment. Then lifting her gaze she asked, 'why're you here? There's hardly anything left to eat. Go to Belgard or the coast with your family, take a train or board a ship. Escape while you can. The Russians will be here sooner rather than later. You don't want them to find you.'

Gertrud was lost for words. After a long challenging silence she said, 'we're going to my older sister's. She and my niece can join us, then we'll leave together.'

'Who's your sister?'

'Elsa . She's Hans Baumann's wife.'

'You won't find her. Hans and their two sons gone a long time ago, to fight in the war...' she paused, shaking her head, then added, 'what a waste of men, young men,' she sighed, shaking her head again, 'anyway,' she resumed, 'when the Räumungsbefehl came Elsa and her daughter left. Her farm's deserted but I guess you can rest there for a few days. There might be wood and potatoes left in the house. I don't know where Elsa and Gerdchen headed to. The girl wasn't very well. She'd a spot of flu. They might have gone for the train or the ships. No idea but left they have.'

Gertrud thanked the old woman and resumed walking. The situation was desperate. Hertie had started coughing and sneezing. She glanced at Hedi, Jutta and the boys. They could barely walk. Exhausted, hungry, thirsty. There was no food or water left. They must reach the farm and rest there for a few days. Give everyone time to recover and Hertie to get healthy again. Then they would return to Belgard and take a train or a truck or whatever was available and leave this frozen hell behind forever.

As the old woman in the village had told them, Elsa's farm was deserted. The front door to the house was shut but unlocked. They went in and Gertrud was relieved to find a sack of potatoes, a jar with herring and another half full of raspberry jam in the larder. In the kitchen there was some wood left. They could cook and warm up. Jutta started a fire while Gertrud placed Hertie on the couch in the living room and went searching for blankets in the upstairs bedrooms. There were enough.

'We'll light a fire in the living room and we'll all sleep there. We'll bring the mattresses from upstairs,' Gertrud said, 'so we can keep warm. Tomorrow we can look for wood in the forest and perhaps you two,' she indicated her sons with her head, 'can try and hunt a couple of rabbits or something. The woods on the edge of the farm and the village are extensive and shelter many small animals. I remember Elsa telling me that Hans went there in the autumn and winter, hunting for partridges or hares. I'm sure you'll find at least some voles – small and possibly not very tasty but at the moment anything to restore our strength will be welcome to land in the saucepan.'

As it turned out they couldn't leave the farmhouse for the next two days. There was a storm. The blizzard continued unabated. The wind and snow only died down in the early hours of the morning on the third day that dawned clear and bright. Blue skies, with sparkling sunshine above the white landscape. But still biting cold. The snow appeared like powder or sand made of tiny shimmering crystals. One could notice the minuscule ice stars on the sleeves of a coat when throwing a handful of snow up in the air. Hertie watched her brothers and sister play for a bit. She wasn't allowed out. Her cold hadn't completely healed and Mutti didn't want her to get worse. She heard her mother talking to auntie Jutta.

'There's one more bag of potatoes in the cellar. About five kilos perhaps. But it won't last for long. I'd say another day or two. Should be enough. Hope by then Hertie will be fully recovered and we can return to Belgard for a train or whatever.'

'All right,' auntie Jutta agreed.

Then Mutti called out, 'Hedi. You and I are taking the wheelbarrows and going to fetch wood in the forest. Boys, the two of you come too and try to catch a few rabbits. Set a trap. You learned to do that, didn't you Heinrich?'

'Uncle Siggi taught me and Helmut too.'

Hertie hovered by the door to the living room. 'Mutti,' she said, 'can I go too? I could help gather wood.'

'No, Schätzchen. You'll stay home with auntie Jutta. You have a cold to nurse.'

Hertie sulked but said nothing. She knew Mutti wouldn't change her mind.

'Don't worry, Liebling,' auntie Jutta said, 'you and I shall give the house a clean and start peeling some potatoes.'

'I guess,' Hertie replied with a disappointed shrug.

For a moment she and auntie Jutta watched the others go from the porch but soon went back inside. Too cold. Hertie had heard Heinrich say it must be minus 18 or minus 20 out there even in the sun. She didn't understand very well what it meant but, anyway, it sounded icy.

The others had gone half an hour when Hertie heard footsteps outside. A child's voice shouted something that neither she nor auntie Jutta understood. Then someone banged on the door. It was a boy, about the same age as Helmut. He was slightly out of breath and had obviously been running.

'The Russians,' he shouted, 'the Russians are coming. Hide.'

'How do you know?' Jutta asked him.

'A soldier in Belgard. I can run fast. He sent me to tell people in the village. I have. You were the last. Hide.'

'But where? Where are the Russians?'

'Only four or five kilometres away the soldier told me. Hide. I've to run back to town. My family's waiting for me to leave for the…'

His last words were lost in the air, as he'd begun running. Jutta looked at Hertie.

'What shall we do?' she asked her rhetorically.

'He said we should hide.'

'But the others…your mum, the boys, Hedi, they're in the woods.'

'They can hide there.'

'You're right, Hertie. They can and they will when they notice Russian soldiers around here.'

Jutta began pacing the hall, talking aloud to herself.

'Perhaps we too should run to the woods. But you're still unwell. Where can we hide in this house? The cellar? No, they'll look in there first.'

It was then Hertie heard voices. Men's voices. Shouts. Boots crushing the snow. She glanced out of the window.

'Auntie Jutta, I think it's the Russians.'

Jutta ran to the window and looked out briefly.

'Oh dear God, already? They must have been closer than the boy said. It's them. We must hide.'

'The chimney has a ledge,' Hertie said, 'I hide there when Hedi, Helmut and Heinrich play hide and seek with me. They never find me but…but you're too big to also hide there, auntie Jutta.'

221

'Never mind me, Liebling, you go and hide. Make no noise. And Hertie, no matter what you hear you don't get out. Understood?'

Hertie nodded. Her little heart jumped in her chest. She ran to the chimney in the living room – luckily, the fire was out – and skilfully pulled herself up. Standing on the rim she pressed her body against the wall as far back as possible. It was dark and the ledge wide enough. The tip of her feet didn't stick out. If any of the soldiers put his head through the fireplace opening to look up the chimney, he wouldn't be able to glimpse her.

Hertie had only ever prayed at school. Her parents didn't go to church except for weddings, christenings and funerals but she prayed now, begging God to help auntie Jutta find a good hiding place and keep Mutti, Hedi and the boys in the woods until the Russians had left.

For a time there was silence. Hertie thought perhaps the Russians had marched on instead of stopping to see inside the house. Then all of a sudden she heard shouts and someone banging heavily on wood. The front door. Were they trying to bring it down? It took a while. Glass breaking. The windows. Perhaps they were trying to get in through the windows. Then a harsh noise of wood splintering. She heard their heavy boots on the floor of the living room and held her breath. It sounded as if they were dragging the furniture around. Then the noise and their footsteps withered away a little. Perhaps they had left the lounge. She heard their voices. They were speaking to each other but Hertie didn't understand what they were saying. She assumed it was Russian. She had never heard the language before. Very different from German. More glass breaking. Shouts. Thuds. Doors opening and shutting. More shouts. Then laughter. And a scream that congealed Hertie's blood. A scream as if from a wounded animal. A terrified voice in German. Begging.

'No. Please no. No.'

Auntie Jutta. More laughter and shouts from the men. Hertie's heart raced in her chest. It was beating so loud she feared the Russian soldiers might hear it. Auntie Jutta carried on screaming. The men laughed. Should she leave her hiding place and try to help auntie Jutta? But Auntie had said no matter what she heard she must stay hidden. Besides what could she do against a bunch of grown-up men?

Hertie pressed her body further against the wall, trying to make herself invisible. The voices of the Russians appeared excited. Noises she couldn't identify. What were they doing? She couldn't guess. Auntie Jutta continued to scream, then abruptly she stopped. Was she dead? A moment later the men went quiet. Hertie heard a powerful, grave voice. A voice used to being obeyed. Another Russian. She didn't understand what he said but whatever the soldiers were doing they stopped. She heard thunder. Thunder? No. A shot. Someone had fired a gun. She remembered the sound, had heard it before when uncle Siggi fired his rifle up into the air to scare a fox away and stop it from grabbing a chicken, years ago when they still had animals.

Hertie heard the sound of boots on the floor, then on the snow, fading away. Silence. But she didn't know whether the Russians had left; dared not move from her ledge. She lost sense of time. No idea how long she had stood there, shaking. Frightened. Where was auntie Jutta? She couldn't hear her. Had the Russians taken her? Were they still outside?

All of a sudden, she heard people.

'Auntie Jutta. Auntie Jutta?'

Heinrich.

'I think she's dead, Mutti.'

Helmut. Then her mother.

'No. She's still breathing. Jutta? Jutta can you hear me?'

Mutti. It was Mutti's voice.

'Jutta, where's Hertie? Did they take her?' It was Mutti again.

A whisper.

'What? Say it again, Jutta, please,' Mutti said.

Hertie wanted to climb down from the ledge. Wanted to scream she was well and had been hiding. But her legs, frozen, didn't obey her head. She opened her mouth to shout but no sound came out.

'I'll look for her.'

Hedi. But Hedi didn't know about the ledge. No-one knew. She must say something or they would go and leave her behind, thinking the Russians had taken her. Then she heard auntie Jutta's voice. Weak. Just a thin thread of sound.

'Chimney,' she said, 'ledge.'

And then it all happened very fast. Hertie glimpsed Heinrich's and Hedi's faces looking up. Hedi disappeared, screaming, 'she's here Mutti, she's here and she's alive.'

Then Heinrich reached out to her, his arms stretched. Hertie let herself fall. He held her and carried her out of the chimney.

'She's fine, Mutti,' he said, 'just scared but fine.'

Mutti had tears in her eyes. She hugged Hertie with one arm. Auntie Jutta had her head on Mutti's lap. Her eyes closed but her chest still heaved up and down, slowly. Then Hertie noticed auntie Jutta had no clothes. They were torn apart in a pile next to her. Her naked body was full of bruises. There was blood coming out of her abdomen. Her legs were spread. A pool of blood between them.

'Helmut,' Mutti said quietly, 'the blanket, please.'

Her brother fetched a blanket abandoned on the floor by the sofa. The furniture had been moved around. Chairs and tables upside down. Drawers opened or thrown on the floor. Glass everywhere from the windowpanes. Mutti covered auntie Jutta with a blanket and held her tight, saying quiet words, singing a lullaby. Hertie held on to Heinrich. They stood looking down at Mutti and auntie Jutta. Hedi sobbed. The boys were crying. Mutti continued to sing, rocking auntie Jutta gently. Hertie didn't know how long they stood watching Mutti on her knees, cradling auntie Jutta. She couldn't speak. Hertie wouldn't in fact say a word until several weeks later after they had settled down, near Hamburg.

Eventually, Mutti stopped singing, staring silently at her sister. Quietly she began to cry. Auntie Jutta was no more. Hertie understood she had died but only fully grasped what had really happened years later, as a young woman. Jutta had been gang raped by the Russian soldiers, then shot before they were ordered to leave.

Mutti and Heinrich buried Jutta in the yard, under the snow. The ground was frozen solid. Too hard to dig a proper grave. Quietly Mutti gathered their few possessions and ordered them to dress in as many coats as they could just like before when they had left their home.

Hedi told Hertie they had seen the Russians arriving at the farmyard and remained hiding in the woods until they had left, hoping she and auntie Jutta had been able to conceal themselves. Hertie sobbed for auntie Jutta, killed by the Russians. Her body forever left in auntie Elsa's abandoned farmyard but she remained mute. Often opening her mouth to speak she was unable to bring a sound out and left wondering whether she would ever recover her voice.

Mutti cooked the two rabbits the boys had caught, mixed the meat with boiled potatoes and made them eat. She packed raw potatoes in her rucksack, a jar of potato skin soup and two flasks with water. Then they marched back to Belgard in a single file through the main street of the village. Hertie saw corpses, including the old woman who had talked to them when they first arrived. It seemed years ago but was only a few days. They continued to walk in complete silence. It suited Hertie. Mutti didn't shed any more tears or speak a word until they reached Belgard's train station. The last train travelling west was about to leave. They found space in the last carriage and huddled in a corner but the train didn't move. Later they heard engines. Trucks. Someone shouted they must move to the lorries. The train wasn't leaving. It couldn't pass ahead. There was a military column. Hertie didn't know whether of Russians or their own German soldiers nor did she care. She followed the others.

Quietly, orderly, weary and without any energy to panic people left the carriages and climbed onto the trucks. The lorries travelled through the night, braving the darkness in a single file, heading for the coast. Ships were ready to take the refugees to Hamburg or Kiel. From there people could travel further if they so wished or get shelter in one of the refugee centres created to accommodate their numbers.

The cold was grim. Harsh. Hertie couldn't feel her hands

or feet. The truck didn't have a cover. The wind, increasing with the speed of the vehicle, made their eyes tearful. Breathing made her chest ache severely. They continued to move through the freezing night air, across the white landscape, glowing silver in the fading light of the crescent moon. Hertie looked up. Somewhere up there, it was beautiful. There was no war. She gazed at the stars. Perhaps there were angels flying between them, sliding down their paths of light. Hertie smiled. She would like to think so. She hoped it was so.

Chapter 9 – Peace

They reached Hamburg on 5th February 1945. Hertie hardly remembered the journey on the ship. The night drive in the open truck made her worse. Burning with fever as they disembarked Mutti carried her. She was too weak to walk and still did not speak.

As refugees, Hertie and her family stayed for a few days in a centre for arrivals from East Prussia. As there were four children they were soon allocated to a small farm, with a large family house. The owners, an old couple, were prepared and glad to receive them. Kurt and Ingrid Weisenbach, both in their seventies, owned the property located in the area south of the river Bille, referred to as Billwerder, a little over fifteen kilometres southeast of the Hamburg city centre.

Kurt, 73, had suffered a severe attack from a bull as a young man and lost an arm. It saved him from fighting both in the Great War and in the present one. The downside being he had since been prone to depression. His disability dominated his life, dictated his personality and meant he often felt sorry for himself.

Ingrid, 71, was her husband's complete opposite. A resolute, capable woman with a kind heart, weather-beaten skin from working in the fields, sad grey eyes and grey hair tied in a bun at the back of her neck. After their children had left home, Ingrid carried out the work on the small farm, planting and harvesting potatoes and all types of vegetables. They had six apple trees, which she picked herself whenever they gave any fruit. Their animals, especially the horses, had been confiscated by the army but they had managed to keep an old cow and an ewe that sporadically still trickled some milk, and one hen that occasionally laid eggs. The food their little farm produced was enough for both of them. But Ingrid was worn out, ravaged by the war and the suffering it had brought her. She and Kurt had lost three of their five children. Kurt, with only one arm and his frequent depressions, was little or no help and Ingrid was beginning to find it hard to cope. Volunteering to take refugees from East Prussia seemed like a good idea. The house would be full again and Ingrid could have the support she needed.

The Weisenbach couple had produced five children - two daughters and three sons. Marlies, the youngest girl, was a nurse, working in one of Hamburg's hospitals. Johanna, the oldest of the five, had died a few months earlier during a bombing of the city centre. Their three sons, Kaspar, Bastian and Holger, like almost all able-bodied men, had either voluntarily enlisted or been forced into the army. Bastian, the oldest, and Holger, the youngest, had been killed in battle. Kaspar, the middle boy, had been captured by the Red Army during one of Germany's offensives into Russia. He was a prisoner of war somewhere in a Russian camp. Who knew whether he was still alive or if he would ever return.

Kurt and Ingrid warmly welcomed Gertrud and her exhausted children. Hertie had no recollection of the first week in her new home. Later someone told her Mutti and Ingrid had given her a hot bath, taken her to bed and made her eat a vegetable broth for strength. She retained little in her mind but vaguely remembered dreaming things that didn't make sense. A woman on her knees thanking God for their safe arrival. Someone shouting about their good luck for escaping the Russian submarines that patrolled the East Sea. Once Hertie remembered waking up, screaming that a submarine wanted to kidnap and drag her to the bottom of the ocean. That was the day her voice returned, several weeks after the attack on Jutta. Hertie couldn't recall what happened next. Apparently her mother held her, comforting her until she had fallen asleep again. Then there was this image of a different woman. Tearful. Crying out the Russians had torpedoed a ship full of refugees. Thousands had perished in the frozen waters of the East Sea.

Three weeks after their arrival at the farm, Hertie finally woke free of temperature. She had recovered her voice during the illness. Felt weak but relieved and realised for the first time that her feverish delusions had a foundation of truth. Heinrich told her the Russians had indeed sunk a ship named Wilhelm Gustloff on 30th January. Nine thousand people had died in the freezing waters of the East Sea.

Hertie turned nine on 16th February but her birthday passed unnoticed. Still bedridden with temperature and no clear notion of her surroundings, she only met Kurt and Ingrid once able to leave her sickbed. Exactly nineteen days after her arrival at their home.

The month of February approached its end when Hertie managed to rise unaided for the first time. Weak and extremely thin, it was the comeback of the vivid cobalt-blue light to her eyes that announced her return to health. She smiled at the old couple, taking immediately to them both and instantly charming them. In Kurt and especially in Ingrid, she was reminded of her maternal grandparents who had lived with them in East Prussia before their death when she was five.

Life in the little farm was relatively quiet. Gertrud and the boys worked outside as the snow began to melt, farming what they could, supporting Ingrid. Hedi and Hertie helped inside the house or cleaned the shed of the single hen. Kurt did little. True enough every task was arduous with only one arm. Nevertheless, Hertie thought he didn't try hard enough. Having solely one leg – a worse fate than Kurt's in Hertie's opinion – uncle Siggi had never shied away from any kind of work. More often than not his determination succeeded. Kurt spent most of his time reclining on a sofa, which had seen better days, listening to an old wireless device or trying to read between the lines in the newspapers he could get. Always spare with words but affectionate.

Hertie thought about uncle Siggi often. Left alone in their home in East Prussia how could he cope? Would he be all right? Had he managed to hide from the Russians? Did their pretty little house survive? And the farm, once her father's pride and joy? Her chest tightened. Heart in her mouth she considered uncle Siggi might be dead. Sorrow crept up imperceptibly. Her skinny, weakened body shook like a leaf in the wind and Hertie began silently to cry.

Nearly undetected, time passed. Night succeeded day. Day succeeded night. Lethargically. The weather improved. Life in the Weisenbachs's farm remained unchanged. Quiet. Sluggish.

They planted vegetables, collected the infrequent eggs from the hen, struggling for nourishment. No respite. No break. No end to the fight.

Once recovered from her illness, Hertie began relishing her time on the farm. At night, from her bedroom window, she could watch the stars, silently naming the constellations to herself. During daylight there was a continuous stream of planes flying overhead towards the city centre and the harbour of Hamburg. British and American planes mostly, someone told her. Enemy planes. At first, Hertie excitedly followed them with her eyes, wondering how it would be to see the world from up there but soon they started to frighten her. In the distance she could hear the clamour of the bombs. Explosions. Blasts. Annihilation. Destruction. Sometimes the aircraft crossed the dark skies above the farmhouse at night. Giant, soaring monsters like dinosaurs or dragons of old, roaring, spitting fire and death. Mutti had managed to salvage in their reduced luggage an old book of fairy tales with such drawings. They stuck in Hertie's mind though she wasn't scared. The pictures weren't real. But the planes were. She hated them for disturbing the soothing stillness of the stars and feared them for she knew what they brought. Covering her head with the feathered pillow in her bed during the night, attempting to muffle the sound, she felt lucky to live outside the city limits in a scarcely populated, tranquil area. No bombs were dropped on them. Grateful and innocent Hertie prayed to whatever god or guardian angel might be looking after her and her family, floating in the middle of the glowing stars she loved so much.

During April they began hearing news of German troops surrendering. Hertie's most intense memory of that month however was not the surrender of the troops, the bombing upheaval or the procession of wounded soldiers and civilians on stretchers on the roads around the farm. Weirdly, what stayed embedded in her mind vividly forever was the image of her mother uncontrollably sobbing by the radio. Hertie questioned her why but she only shook her head, saying Hertie was too young to understand. Years later, she learned her mother's tears were for the horrors committed against Jews especially but also homosexuals, disabled, gypsies and others during the Holocaust. Mutti had been listening to the news of the liberation of prisoners from the Nazi concentration camps where millions had been killed in abhorrent ways. Not even when Papa didn't return from the front or when they were forced to leave their home and uncle Siggi in East Prussia had Hertie seen her mother so sombre, so sorrowful, so guilt ridden as if she herself had sent all those people to the camps. Surprisingly, amid her tears, her mother cursed aloud.

'I hope this bloody stupid war will soon end and that goddamn Führer rots in hell.'

Hertie gawked at her mother. She couldn't remember Mutti ever swearing before.

A glimmer of light appeared on the horizon when news of Hitler's suicide reached them. Then, on 8th May 1945 the end of the war, with an overall surrender of Nazi Germany to the Allies, was finally broadcasted. At the tender age of nine, Hertie didn't fully understand what it all meant, except that there was to be no more war. The adults seemed happy in a subdued manner. She remembered Mutti saying things could only get better in spite of having foreign powers ruling Germany.

With the advent of peace life took an unhurried turn for the better. The bombs stopped. Hertie, her brothers and sister were able to go to school. They all hitched a lift with Mutti in an old, rattling army truck to Hamburg, travelling to place official written requests with the authorities so they could search for their relatives – Papa, uncle Siggi, auntie Elsa and her daughter Gerdchen, plus all other uncles.

Hertie's shock at the state of the city left her frozen, rooted to the ground for a moment. Words failed her. She'd never seen so many ruins, dilapidated buildings, debris, piles of stones and rubble like crumbs from tons of giant bread loaves but made of solid stone and bricks. Hardly a house stood intact. Destitute people, refugees, children who'd lost all their relatives lived among the wreckage, sometimes under an oil skin stretched between what was left of two walls. No hope. No place to call their own. Hertie's heart withered in her chest. Tears flooded her eyes. She felt sorry for all those people – mostly women and children, some old men. How fortunate she, her siblings and their mother were to live on the Weisenbachs's modest farm. A proper roof over their heads and thick walls that didn't bear the weight of the bombs or display fighting scars.

Mutti submitted the official applications to find their relatives' whereabouts, then queued for rationing. She wanted to get some meat. It had been announced there would be some in a shop nearby. She carried all their rationing cards, hoping to secure a slightly bigger portion. Hertie had forgotten how meat tasted…or fish or sweet foods. She wondered whether they'd find sugar to bake a cake or do some caramels but Mutti said not this time. Hertie sighed. One day, Mutti kept saying, things would be normal again. They'd be able to buy whatever they wanted and eat as many cakes as they liked. Hertie smiled at the thought of it. She was always hungry.

To deviate her mind from the needs of her stomach Hertie asked Mutti when they would find out about Papa and the rest of the family. Her mother shrugged. She didn't know nor appeared hopeful they would track them down but searching was important. She needed the certainty. Somehow Hertie understood. She wanted to know for sure too.

By the summer, early July, there were still no news of their relatives but a change happened. Mutti decided she needed to earn a steady income instead of solely helping Ingrid on the farm. She applied for a cleaning job three times a week in a former aristocratic house in one of Hamburg's noble quarters. Those beautiful areas of the city, where the rich had once lived, had been spared the bombing. Hertie heard such houses were now occupied by officers of the allied military powers and transformed into their resident headquarters, their base for the job ahead – cleansing Germany of Hitler's influence and Nazi ideology. The Allies had divided the country in four zones, each occupied respectively by the British, the Americans, the French and the Russians. Berlin, the capital city, split into four sectors. Hertie wondered whether it was possible to determine the exact path of the bombs, to precisely know where they would fall. She reasoned if so the allied countries might have left such lovely houses standing on purpose. Because they knew that, once they had won the war, they would need comfortable, refined accommodation while in Germany. She said as much to her mother. Gertrud told her off, warning her to keep quiet and never say such things in front of the foreign soldiers.

Her mother cycled the circa fifteen kilometres from the farm to the city for her cleaning job three times a week whatever the weather. Mondays, Wednesdays and Fridays. The work was well paid. Many of the army officers were kind but not all. Some were arrogant, high-brow and conceited, believing themselves superior and the owners of everything to do with as they pleased. They respected nothing and no-one. Their views being the Germans had lost the war so they must put their heads down and cope with whatever was thrown at them without complaining. The victorious powers reigned supreme. Hertie thought it was unfair but simply followed her mother's example, behaving properly and quietly doing as commanded.

Occasionally, once school finished for the summer, Mutti took Hertie with her on the bicycle. She would sit at the front in what used to be the shopping basket. She fitted right in. Too small and skinny for her age.

In one of the pretty houses there was an old American colonel – tall, grey hair, pale green eyes behind glasses with metallic frames, wrinkles on forehead and round the eyes, ready smile – whose name Hertie didn't understand. She just called him Herr Offizier. He seemed happy each time Hertie was around, his eyes smiling warmly at her. He spoke to her in broken German and allowed her to play in the garden of the villa, watching over her, so none of the other officers would have reasons to give her a tongue-lashing. One day he crouched in front of her and gave her a chocolate bar. Hertie thought that when a person died and went to heaven, becoming an angel, they must feel how she did as she took the first nibble. A marvellous sensation, the delicious, sweet melting of a chocolate square on her tongue. She'd never been so joyful in her entire short life. Impulsively, throwing her arms around the old colonel's neck, she whispered, 'danke schön, lieber Herr Offizier, thank you, dear Mr Officer.'

He pressed her against his chest and when Hertie stepped back, jumping up and down, delighting in her chocolate, she noticed the old man's kind gaze was full of tears behind his specs. Later Mutti told her his granddaughter had died of an inflammation of the brain, called meningitis, at the same age Hertie was now, before the war began. He was still grieving. Hertie had touched his heart and reminded him of the little girl he had lost. On that day Hertie made a silent but solemn promise to herself. She was going to learn English just so one day she would be able to converse with the colonel in his own language. She felt certain it would delight him.

Summer passed in the blink of an eye. Before Hertie noticed, it was Christmas again. At school, the teachers were making a big fuss about it being the first Christmas in peace. For the first time in years no-one needed to darken their windows. No aircraft alarms would sound. No bombs would drop. People should celebrate. Hertie supposed they were right but was there really anything to celebrate? Hunger. Disease. Missing their loved ones. Not knowing their whereabouts, whether alive or dead. There was no fuel for the cars or buses. No electricity was yet being produced. They sat by candlelight in the evening. It would be a dismal, sombre Christmas. But, as always, somehow Mutti managed a miracle of sorts.

When she wasn't working, Gertrud spent hours in the endless rationing queues. Sometimes, as her turn finally arrived, the shopkeeper would be hanging a sign explaining whatever people had come for was no longer available. Perhaps tomorrow. Or next week. Dejected and weary she would cycle back to the farm, hardly able to pedal. Hertie felt sorry for her. Mutti worked too hard and barely made ends meet. It wasn't her fault. The shops were empty of food or otherwise. So Hertie knew there wouldn't be any presents. They had a little money but there was nothing to buy. If the old colonel were still in Hamburg he would gift each one of them a large chocolate bar but he had returned to the United States in November and wouldn't be coming back.

Hertie had his address. He asked her to write him and tell him about school or her daily life. How they were all doing. She made him a solemn promise to write and send letters, sensing it was the proper thing to do but uncertain whether able to keep it. The old man seemed happy.

One icy day, in mid-December, Hertie noticed her mother wasn't wearing her pure gold wedding ring. She asked her.

'I've lost it while cleaning, Schätzchen,' her mother explained dismissively, 'it must've dropped somewhere and I didn't notice. It was loose on my finger anyway. I'm too thin.'

Two days later, Mutti's gold stud earrings – Papa's present a long time ago – also vanished. Hertie wondered. She happened upon Mutti and Ingrid, chatting in the kitchen, and couldn't help but eavesdrop on the two women's conversation.

'Got a pound of sugar, a full slab of butter, a small pork joint to roast, a chocolate bar and half a pound of flour. We've eggs, potatoes and parsnips. I can cook us a lovely Christmas dinner.'

It had been Mutti speaking.

'That all you got?' Ingrid had asked.

'Yes. Thought it was a good bounty so to speak. Don't you?'

'No…I mean yes, of course. It's just I think you should've got more for solid gold stud earrings and a wedding ring.'

Hertie heard Mutti's saddened, dispirited voice.

'Black market for you. What else could I do?'

Hertie had moved away and did not listen to anything further, grasping the fate of the little jewellery Mutti had left. All traded on the black market to be able to give her family a better Christmas. For the rest of the afternoon Hertie buried herself in her bedroom with the excuse of a headache. Her mother came to check on her but Hertie pretended to be asleep. She didn't want Mutti to notice her tears.

Christmas Eve, 1945. No heating. No tree. Mutti and Ingrid lit up candles around a couple of fir branches and twigs. All of a sudden the room seemed warm and pretty. Then her mother walked proudly into the lounge, carrying the platters with the food. In Hertie's view Mutti had managed to cook a prince's meal. They each had a slice of roasted pork, one potato and parsnips but the true marvel was the dessert. Gertrud had conjured up a chocolate cake with the items canvassed in the black market. The best cake ever. Hertie had never tasted anything so good, except perhaps for the chocolate bars the old colonel used to give her. And Ingrid, in the kindness of her heart, had found time at night before bed, to create a little present to everyone. She knitted scarves out of old socks where the pair was missing and out of old wool leftovers. Each scarf embellished with embroidered tiny patterns of different colours to make them look pretty and special. For her troubles Ingrid received lots of hugs and kisses. Thanks to her and Mutti's sacrifices they spent a quiet but not desperately dismal Christmas celebration.

The happy moments didn't finish with the lovely time at Christmas. Unknown to Hertie and her family, the end of 1945 would unexpectedly become memorable. A letter, addressed to Mutti, arrived on the last day of the year.

Uncle Siggi was alive. Residing in Hamburg since mid-February he'd been given accommodation in one of the city's refugee centres. The peculiar thing was that he had disembarked from a ship at the city's harbour only two weeks after themselves. All this time no-one had any idea of his whereabouts. Mutti visited him immediately on the first day of the new year but couldn't bring him to the farm at once. There was no fuel for the general population thus no cars or buses and naturally, she couldn't transport uncle Siggi on her bicycle.

The occupying forces and military personnel had fuel. Their jeeps and lorries the only ones circulating in the city. Mutti appealed to a young, kind British lieutenant, housed in one of the beautiful mansions she cleaned. He agreed to drive her and her brother to the farm. Uncle Siggi arrived on 2nd January of the new year, beaming from ear to ear at Mutti's side. Stormy hugs and kisses followed. Uncle Siggi, carefully balancing on his one leg and a crutch, nearly lost his footing under the overwhelming welcome of his nieces and nephews.

In the evening, by candlelight – electricity not yet available for the majority of the population – they huddled around uncle Siggi and listened to his story.

After Gertrud, Jutta and the children had all left for the train station in their East Prussian village, he had sat alone in the house, considering his options. It just happened that their friend, Maria Keller, stopped at their farm, announcing she was fleeing West with her children – a little boy of four and a girl of six – and wanted to ask them whether they should travel together. Maria and her kids were on a cart, pulled by a donkey, successfully concealed from the German soldiers when they were on a mission to confiscate vehicles and animals. As the others had left three days earlier, Maria told Siggi he could travel with them. She helped him climb onto the cart and together they reached the next town, two days ahead of the Russian army. Maria headed Southwest in an attempt to join her sister who lived close to Frankfurt-am-Main.

There were lorries stationed in the town, waiting to transport people to the coast. Uncle Siggi aided by a young soldier – a boy, a child of fourteen – climbed into one of the trucks, heading North to the nearest harbour where ships waited to take the refugees to Hamburg and Kiel. Hungry and thirsty uncle Siggi was dependent on the kindness of others but he didn't starve or freeze to death. There was solidarity in misery. People shared the little food they had and their blankets with him. He had disembarked in the Port of Hamburg on 18th February. Checked in by some sort of official he was conveyed to a centre for refugees from East Prussia who had fled ahead of the Red Army. And there he remained until being told his sister Gertrud Lohmeyer was alive and had submitted an application to find him. Siggi's letter to Mutti followed shortly.

And here he was. United with the family. Hertie felt emotional. After a while they were all crying tears of joy, even Kurt and Ingrid. Only one thing cast a shadow on the happiness of their reunion. Uncle Siggi asked about Jutta. With a sob and an obvious lump in her throat, her voice failing, Mutti explained

Jutta had died. A victim of the Russian military in Belgard before they could leave Elsa's abandoned farm.

Chapter 10 – The Stepfather

With Siggi's arrival in January 1946, life for Hertie, her siblings and her mother slowly returned to the kind of routine they had grown accustomed to. The years ahead were quiet, peaceful. At times boring. A blessing after everything they had been through, as Gertrud often commented. And they were privileged. Living on a small farm meant they were a little more self-sufficient than people in the city. They now had two hens thus enough eggs. Gertrud and Ingrid planted potatoes and parsnips, occasionally a few carrots and cabbage. Somehow Gertrud managed a treat from time to time. Either on the black market or from the officers' kitchens at the beautiful houses where Allied forces had set up their headquarters. She queued with her rationing cards and those of her children to obtain food, candles and oil. Electricity had returned but more often than not it failed for hours when darkness fell.

Gradually Hertie forgot the days of hunger and cold. Unconsciously she suppressed the memories of fear, of the terrible experiences of the last few years. Instead she began to have scary dreams. Nightmares. Sometimes she woke up screaming but when Mutti ran to her bed to soothe and rock her gently she would say she couldn't remember what had frightened her in the dream. It was true. She couldn't. Once awake all she recalled was feeling scared, spooked by something. Her conscious memories vanished though the unexplained nightmares didn't disappear but became less frequent.

Hertie liked to listen to the conversations Mutti had with Ingrid, occasionally with Kurt. The grown-ups discussed the rumours of a new currency – D-Mark or Deutsche Mark – to replace the old Reichsmark. Hertie didn't understand the implications but some adults said life would become better, the economy prosper and people would be able to buy not only food but whatever merchandise they fancied. It sounded good, Hertie thought, but didn't comprehend why changing from the Reichsmark to the D-Mark would be any different. Why was it needed for pleasant things to happen again?

The new currency didn't officially arrive until 20th June 1948. Hertie noticed the changes in the shops. In people. From one day to the next things were available to buy – clothes, shoes, books, meat, cheese, sugar, butter. The air smelled sweet. A sense of optimism appeared to float around, enveloping each person with a glow of joy and an unconscious smile of delight. Hope for life. Space for dreams in a new democratic, peaceful country. Warmth filled hearts once frozen by despair. Hertie didn't fully grasp the transformation but didn't care. Seeing her siblings and mother happy, made her jubilant. She began to enjoy life. The horrors experienced in the last few years were pushed further and further back to the recesses of her mind. All she remembered was the trip in the open truck and the images of the stars. The constellations she had learned at school, punctuating the crystal clear, glacial sky like abstract embroidery designs. Inexorably life continued to move on.

The year before the new currency arrived, 1947, Hertie and her family received a piece of bad and a piece of good news. Werner Lohmeyer, their father, was finally confirmed dead, after five years of uncertainty, fallen in battle on the Russian front during the winter of 1942. His body never found. Sadly, all their uncles had the same fate. The good news reached them with an official letter stating Elsa and her daughter Gerda were alive and well, residing in Munich. Elsa's own missive to her sister dropped through the letter box two days later. That evening they celebrated the best they could. Heinrich had caught a large fish in the stream that cut through the farm. They had a feast, treating themselves to a watery soup with parsnips, boiled fish and potatoes with butter sneaked from the officers' kitchen in one of the houses Gertrud cleaned in Hamburg. Even Kurt was less gloomy and enjoyed the special meal. After dinner, before the children cleared up, Ingrid gave each an apple from the tiny orchard, if one could call six trees an orchard, at the far end of the farm where hers and Gertrud's hard work had finally paid dividends.

Biting her apple, juice running down the sides of her mouth, Hertie looked at her mother. For the first time in years she saw a genuine cheerful smile illuminating Mutti's pretty face and lovely blue eyes. Her chest swelled. For a moment it appeared to burst with happiness. Life could be good. While they did the washing-up, Mutti sat at the dining table and began writing a letter, replying to her sister Elsa in Munich.

December 1947 brought comfort and joy to the old Weisenbach couple. Their middle and only surviving son, Kaspar, was finally released from the prisoners of war camp in Russia, returning home after nearly six years of captivity and in time to celebrate Christmas with his parents. Hertie didn't know it then but life would radically transform with Kaspar Weisenbach's arrival.

 Kaspar was a tall man, painfully thin from years of deprivation, forced labour and poor nutrition. He was only three years older than Mutti but at thirty-eight his hair had greyed prematurely, with only a few streaks left of the former rich chestnut brown colour. His muted blue eyes stood out in his face where the skin stretched over the bones, lending him a slightly macabre appearance. He was moody and taciturn at first though embracing his parents with genuine warmth and emotion. Hertie felt touched because they all cried together, but his haggard, ashen appearance frightened her. Like a skeleton, as pictured in a science book at school, but alive. Unlike the pile of bones in her book Kaspar had skin, clothes, moved and talked.

 For his first few months at the farm Kaspar was sparse with words. He talked only if spoken to and in monosyllables. The only person he uttered more than two words in a row to was his mother. He slept for hours during the day, rarely leaving his room. Ingrid said he was too frail to get out of bed and took him his meals on a tray. Eventually, he emerged from his bedroom a different person. Had gained weight. Looked handsome. Still quiet but his eyes were no longer dull. His smile reached them, making them sparkle. He began working on the farm, taking the heavy load off Mutti and Ingrid. Hertie felt pleased. Mutti could accept more hours cleaning for officers thus earning more money. Half of it she deposited in the bank in a special account designated for their education. She wanted her four children to learn a profession and one day stand independent in life. The other half she divided in two. One part she kept, the other handed over to Ingrid to help with their keep.

One day, after her twelfth birthday in February 1948, Hertie heard a conversation between Ingrid and Kaspar that sent alarm bells ringing. She was sitting at the bay window in the lounge doing her school homework. Her brothers and sister were in their rooms also busy with their schoolwork. Mutti hadn't yet returned home from the city. Uncle Siggi was doing his slow daily walk outside to exercise his sole remaining leg. Hertie preferred to sit downstairs rather than in her bedroom. There was more space and she could look out of the window at the nearby trees. Kurt was sleeping on the couch but his light snoring didn't disturb her concentration. Kaspar and Ingrid were in the kitchen cleaning the various fish he had caught in the river that morning. The doors to both rooms were ajar but, from the kitchen, the bay window corner where Hertie sat wasn't visible. Besides, mother and son must have assumed the four kids were all upstairs. They spoke freely with each other. Obviously they believed the only person able to hear them was Kurt and he didn't count. Always sleeping or staring into the distance watching nothing at all.

'Now you're better, mein Schatz, you should settle down. Find a good woman. Have children.'

Ingrid's voice.

'I don't know, Mutter. Won't be easy.'

Kaspar replying.

'If you were a woman, no, it'd be difficult. But for a man in his prime…well…There's plenty of single or widowed women everywhere. However, hardly any men your age. You're not yet forty. Good-looking. With the farm you can take a wife, support her and form a family.'

'Perhaps.'

'What about Gertrud?'

Ingrid's direct question hit Hertie like a bolt from the blue. Stretching her neck, ears alert she stopped writing and paid attention. Was Ingrid suggesting Kaspar should marry Mutti? That was crazy. What the hell was Ingrid thinking?

'What about her?' Hertie heard Kaspar ask in return.

'She's a good woman. Hard working. Pretty, honest and a widow.'

'She's already got four kids.'

'So? She's only in her mid-thirties. Young enough to bear you more children.'

'I don't think she likes me that way.'

'Gibberish. Do you like her?'

There was silence. From Hertie's perspective far too long. Then, Kaspar's voice.

'As it turns out, yeah. I find her attractive.'

'She is and, as I've just said, also a good, honest, steadfast woman. Already here, at the farm. Knows what it takes to keep it going, doesn't shy away from hard work. Propose to her.'

'She's got a job in Hamburg. Seems pleased with it.'

'Because there wasn't any other option. Forced to run away from East Prussia with nothing and four young children she had to work. What else could she do? Husband dead. Brothers dead, except one and he's a cripple.'

Heart in her mouth Hertie quickly glanced outside, fearing uncle Siggi might have heard them. But he was far away from the house, having reached the big oak tree at the far end of the courtyard. Ingrid had continued to speak.

'Gertrud had no choice. She had to find some sort of job to sustain herself and the children while still helping me around here. Don't think Dad and I would've survived if we hadn't taken her and the kids on board. Was a good decision.'

'You think she'd accept me?'

'Why wouldn't she?'

'Don't know. She may not like me.'

'What's not to like, Kaspar? You're a handsome man with means. This farm is yours. Your only surviving sibling, your sister Marlies is a nurse. She cares nothing for farming and doesn't want anything to do with it. But once Dad and I are gone you can't be here on your own. You need a woman.'

'If I marry her, she must stop working in Hamburg. No wife of mine's going to have a job in the city. I want her here looking after the family, keeping house for me and our future kids.'

'Gertrud's a sensible woman. She'll grasp you're a good catch. After everything she's been through she'll be happy for security, stability and safety for herself and her children. I'm sure after considering pros and cons she'll say yes if you propose.'

'Perhaps you're right.'

'I know I'm right. It's the next logical step for both of you. We already know and like her. She's aware of what being a farmer's wife entails. Grab her while you can, Kaspar. With her job in the city among all those fine foreign officers who knows? One may take a liking to her and if one does, she won't refuse the chance for a better life even if in another country. I'm certain of it.'

'I'll have a think, Mutter. But I hear you. And you're giving me good advice.'

'Just don't take too long to think.'

Hertie heard him laugh briefly – he didn't often – and then say, 'I won't. Don't worry.'

She wondered what to do. Should she tell Mutti? Warn her? What about if Mutti actually liked Kaspar as she had liked Papa once and wanted to marry him? Hertie didn't know. Perhaps she should talk with Hedi first. Her sister was already fifteen. She knew about these things. Or even Heinrich. He'd turned sixteen and had a girlfriend at school.

As it happened, Hertie said nothing, thinking perhaps Ingrid and Kaspar hadn't seriously meant he should marry Mutti. Or they had thought better of it. Hertie banned it from her mind, forgetting all about it until over a year later. In the spring of 1949 her mother called them all into the lounge. Hertie wondered what could be so important for Mutti to want to speak simultaneously with all of them. Some good news, perhaps. But what?

Hertie followed her siblings into the room. Helmut and Hedi sat on the couch next to Ingrid and Kurt. Uncle Siggi at the table. Heinrich and herself on the floor. Then Mutti, holding Kaspar's hand and smiling radiantly, announced they were getting married in the summer.

With bated breath, her gaze glued to her children, Gertrud waited for their reaction. She feared their disapproval. They might think Kaspar was replacing their dad. Never. But she felt lonely. The children would soon have their own lives. Werner had disappeared, presumed dead, in the Russian winter of 1942. She had waited and waited for years, hoping he would return. But after his death was finally confirmed she wept quietly, alone in her bedroom, deeply grieved there wasn't a grave to go to. Nowhere for the kids to place flowers and remember their father. She had kept his memory alive in their hearts. They wouldn't forget him. But they were growing up. Would leave home. She'd be left behind. Lonely, old, tired. Kaspar's interest flattered her at first. What woman didn't enjoy it? Gradually, she came to like him. She didn't love him. Love was what she had with Werner, but Kaspar was kind, attentive. He would make a good companion. A thoughtful, courteous husband. She didn't demand more. Didn't require more. But she wanted…she needed the children to like him or at least to understand her reasons and be happy for her. Werner was the love of her life but she was still young and felt the need for male company. The children remained quiet. No smile. No words. Their silence began tearing at her heart. Then an almost imperceptible movement. Heinrich, her eldest, always affectionate, gracious, reliable like his father, stepped forward. Smiling.

'Congratulations, Mutti. Great news,' he said.

His tone genuine. His hug sincere. The twins followed his example. Then Siggi. Hertie came last. She seemed more reluctant than her siblings or her uncle but she came and kissed her cheek. A weight lifted off Gertrud's heart. They had accepted her decision.

For the first time since they fled East Prussia, Mutti appeared happy. Hertie wouldn't dare say anything but felt uncomfortable with Kaspar. He didn't frighten her as in the beginning. He no longer gave the impression of an ambulant skeleton but she had a sense of unease whenever alone with him in a room. Not only that. A few times when he didn't know she was watching, Hertie noticed he stared at Hedi in a weird sort of way. Her sister, now sixteen, had turned into a very pretty girl. When he thought no-one was around, Kaspar glared at Hedi as if he wanted to eat her. Like a hungry wolf. Creepy. Hertie didn't like it but kept quiet, certain Mutti or the boys would dismiss it as a child's silly imagination. They still thought her a little girl.

For the first three years of the marriage Kaspar seemed content with their mother. Hertie watched them sometimes fooling around like a pair of young kids. Her impression of her stepfather improved a little. But one day, in the autumn of 1952, she found her sister in her bedroom, face buried on the pillow, sobbing.

'Hedi,' she exclaimed, 'what's the matter?'

Hedi lifted her red, swollen eyes.

'Didn't hear you come in, Hertie. What do you want?'

'Never mind. Why're you crying?'

At first, Hedi shook her head and said nothing but Hertie knew her sister well. She wouldn't cry without a reason.

'It's Kaspar,' Hedi finally blurted out.

'Kaspar?'

Hedi sat on the bed, wiping off her tears with the palms of her hands. Her sobs subsided. She regained some composure. After a long silence, appearing to consider what to say or do next she began talking, 'you're sixteen now, Hertie. You know what happens between a man and a woman, right?'

'Well, I've never even kissed a boy but, yes, I know what happens. Why?'

'Kaspar's been trying his luck with me,' her voice faded and tears gushed out of her eyes once again.

'What?' Hertie was shocked, 'you mean he tried to do with you what he presumably does with Mutti, as his wife?'

Hedi nodded. Incapable of speaking Hertie took her sister in her arms and rocked her.

'It's more than a year now,' Hedi whispered between sobs, 'that he's been staring at me in a funny way. For the last two months he's tried to force himself on me when he caught me alone and there's no-one else in the house, except his father who's always snoring on the couch anyway.'

'What did you do?'

'I pushed him away and said I'd tell Mutti but he...'

'He?' Hertie nudged her gently.

'He threatened to ridicule me, beat you and Mutti up and throw out the boys. We needed to learn who wears the trousers around here. Who's the man in the house.'

'He said that?'

Hedi nodded. 'His precise words. I'm afraid of him.'

'He can't throw out Heinrich or Helmut. They left home last year. Share a small flat with two other boys in Hamburg. You don't need to worry about them, you know that. Heinrich's working. Helmut will get a job as soon as he finishes his apprenticeship.'

'Yes but you and Mutti are here. I'm scared if I continue to push him away his threats may materialise.'

'You really think he'll do something?'

'He came into my room three nights ago when Mutti stayed in Hamburg with Heinrich and Helmut, as she'd been invited for the christening of her friend's baby. It was difficult to get him off me. He covered my mouth with his hand when I threatened to scream and wake everyone else in the house. He touched me and I hated it. I bit his hand. He called me bitch and tried to hit me across the face but I managed to run out of the room. I locked myself away in the bathroom and he didn't dare make a scene. So he went back to bed. When I returned to my room I locked the door. But I'm frightened. I don't want to tell Mutti. She'd be devastated but I can't take much more of this and I fear what he may do next.'

'We must find a solution for this without opening up to Mutti.'

'Have you got any ideas?'

Hertie was quiet for a long time. All of a sudden her face lit up.

'What? You thought of something, didn't you?'

Hertie nodded. 'Listen, Hedi, you're nineteen. You can do

what you want. Didn't auntie Elsa say in her last letter to Mutti she needed someone to help in her shop?'

'She did. I could go to Munich. Live with auntie Elsa. Work for her in the shop. I don't care whether she pays me. If she allows me to stay, provides me with meals and a bed it'll be fine. She said she wanted to expand her small business from selling magazines and tobacco to sell books too. I could help her do it. Perhaps later I can find another job or, if the shop does well, auntie Elsa will be able to pay me a steady salary. Gerdchen has a job as a teacher in a local primary school so she's got no time for the shop.'

'Write to auntie Elsa and ask her. No need to tell her about Kaspar.'

'No. I'll just say I'd like to stand on my own two feet and am tired of life in the farm.'

'Good. Do it now. At once.'

'I'll miss you and the boys. And Mutti.'

'I'll miss you too but if you don't want to reveal this ugly truth, I can't see any other solution.'

'I can't face Mutti,' tears filled Hedi's eyes again, 'I can't make her unhappy. Can't tell Mutti her husband is a slimy bastard. I'm scared of him and that he'll...he'll force me if I continue to deny him what he wants.'

'Write to auntie Elsa now...' Hertie paused, considering another option, then added, 'or actually better, just go to the post office and put a call through to auntie Elsa's shop. She's got a telephone there. The number's in one of the letters she wrote Mother. I'll get it for you. I know where she leaves her letters.'

Hedi nodded. They travelled to the city together and Hedi phoned auntie Elsa from the post office. There was no phone at the farm but even if there were they wouldn't have used it, fearing Kaspar might hear them.

As it turned out, auntie Elsa was over the moon to take on her niece. Enthusiastically she said she'd prepare Gerdchen's room straight away for Hedi. Their cousin was living with two other girls who taught at the same school. Auntie Elsa said Hedi could travel next weekend if she was ready and her mother agreed. And so it came to be.

Hertie saw her sister off at Hamburg's main train station. Neither girl knew whether Mutti suspected the true reasons behind Hedi's departure. They didn't think so. Mutti was sad but seemed to accept Hedi's wish for independence. Auntie Elsa's offer was a rather good option.

Seeing her sister leave Hertie's heart sank in her chest. What now? Would Kaspar lash at her and Mutti out of revenge? She hoped not.

'You've a face like a wet weekend, Hertie,' Ingrid said as she returned home, 'what's the matter? Missing your sister already?'

She nodded and locked herself in her room for the rest of the day.

Kaspar didn't take the revenge Hertie feared. He didn't beat up their mother but Hertie noticed that the hungry, lustful looks he had once thrown at Hedi were now directed at herself.

A week later, fearing a similar situation with Kaspar as her sister had experienced, Hertie packed her things and moved in with her brothers in the city. The flat had only three bedrooms but Heinrich and Helmut shared one; the other two boys the second. The third and smallest room they used as storage but were happy to arrange it for her. Her mother wasn't particularly impressed with her move. Hertie was still a minor but in the end Mutti accepted her excuse. Commuting between the farm and the city every day of the week took too much time and didn't help her studies. Heinrich was a sensible young man, already twenty, with a job. Helmut, one year younger, was nearing the end of his apprenticeship and would soon find work. They were both happy to look after their youngest sister. Without questioning Hertie's reasons they helped her convince their mother to agree. It was reasonable. Made sense. Gertrud wanted her children to do well. Hertie had banked on it. Her mother wouldn't oppose a move painted as advantageous for her studies. And so at sixteen Hertie went to live in the big city. She dedicated her time to becoming a translator and didn't return to the farm except for visits but never alone, always with her siblings. Mutti had no idea about the real reason why Hedi had left to work with auntie Elsa in Munich or why, shortly after, Hertie had gone to live with her two brothers.

Just like Hedi before her, Hertie didn't have the heart to tell her mother the truth, keeping it for herself. No-one knew. It was hers and Hedi's secret. Hertie passed her exam to enter the translators' school with flying colours.

A few months after Hertie had moved out there were some sad news. Uncle Siggi slashed his good leg on the tractor. He refused to see a doctor or go to hospital. The wound infected. A few weeks later he died of septicaemia. The funeral was a sad affair. Hertie felt sorry for her mother who seemed inconsolable to lose the only brother she had left. But, to her relief, Mutti pulled herself together soon enough so Hertie didn't feel obliged to return to the farm and keep her company. She remained in the city and continued her studies.

In 1956, at the age of twenty, Hertie obtained her translator diploma, finishing top of her class. Soon after she applied for and obtained a job in the headquarters of the British Foreign Office in Berlin. Elated she took the bus home to the farm to inform her mother.

'Do you have to go to Berlin, Hertie? It's so far away.'

Her mother's pride was palpably tinged with sadness. Hertie's heart sank to her feet.

'It's a great job, Mutti,' she said and it sounded forcibly cheery even to her own ears.

'I know,' her mother exclaimed, appearing disconsolate, 'but…it's just…well…all my children are far away. Hedi's in Munich, working for Elsa. Has gained her trust and is about to become her partner. Heinrich's gone to Frankfurt with a new job as an accountant; Helmut's in Cologne, working for a bank—'

'I thought you'd be happy for them, Mutti.'

'I am. It's all wonderful news…it's just…' she paused seemingly dejected, then added, 'I'm proud of all of you but always thought…' a sudden sob forced her to stop. Hertie watched her swallow back a few stubborn tears and felt dismal for causing her mother pain.

Gertrud resumed speaking, 'I'd always hoped that you... you of all people, Hertie, my youngest, my baby...you'd stay in Hamburg to be closer to me.'

Hertie groaned inwardly but putting on a brave face she said, 'I'm sorry, Mutti. I didn't mean to disappoint you—'

'You haven't disappointed me, Schätzchen' her mother immediately interrupted, 'it's just...Berlin's so far away and...and...it's...' she stopped talking but Hertie guessed.

'Too close to the Eastern zone and the Russians?' she finished.

Nodding, her mother murmured, 'remember our escape from East Prussia.'

'Mutti,' Hertie replied decisively, 'East Prussia's in the past. Besides, I'll be working for the British in the Allied occupied zone, the western side of the city. The Russians are on the eastern side. What can they do to me? Nothing. We have peace. The war ended more than ten years ago.'

Gertrud went silent, appearing resigned. Hertie hugged her long and tight.

Mutti and Kaspar accompanied her to the train station on the day of her departure to Berlin, her new job and her new life. A flicker of anger appeared in Kaspar's eyes after Hertie said goodbye and climbed onto her third class carriage with a one-way ticket to Berlin. Brandishing a handkerchief in the air, heart clenched, Hertie leaned out of the carriage's window until Mutti and Kaspar disappeared from view. Then, pressing her forehead against the glass she wept. There were no more young women at the farm. No more temptation, as Kaspar had called Hedi and herself, implying it was their fault for being attractive. Never his. She hoped Kaspar would now behave and treat their mother well.

After drying her tears and recovering her composure, Hertie went to find a free seat. It wasn't easy but she found one next to a sleeping old man. As the train jolted forward, she breathed a sigh of relief. It was the beginning of her life. Her proper, independent life. Her own. A new life in a new city. Unwittingly a smile hovered on her lips. Butterflies in her stomach. What would be waiting for her in Berlin?

Chapter 11 – Late Night In The Peak District

'I had great hopes for Berlin and the job,' Hertie said, looking up at Valeria, 'work was stimulating. I enjoyed it. Then I met my husband. Things changed, I expected for the better. Time would prove me wrong but it'd take a few years.'

Tears flooded her eyes. She swallowed them.

'Don't cry. You've a good life now,' Valeria said.

Amid the wet fog of her gaze Hertie's lips parted, 'du bist so lieb zu mir, Schätzchen,' she whispered.

Valeria said in a gentle voice, 'I'm touched you think me so kind. I care for you and really like it when you call me Schätzchen.'

'Mutti called me Schätzchen. I think about it with fondness. And you're very dear to me. Thanks for listening.'

'Always.'

Hertie felt lucky to have such a good neighbour and friend. It was thrilling to be able to converse with Valeria in German. The girl was good with languages, perhaps because she'd been brought up bilingual in English and Portuguese. Her German was excellent. And she was a warm, intelligent young woman. Hertie would have liked one of her children to be like her – artistic sensibility, hard-working, determined, strong, tough but with a big heart.

The mixture of a Portuguese mother and a Scottish father made Valeria's looks different from the average British person. She wasn't a beauty. At first glance there was nothing unusual about her. Her features were subtle, fine and once one began talking to her or noticed the smile, Valeria became pretty. Classic face. Delicate nose. Sympathetic brown eyes, long lashes, dark brown hair with a reddish shimmer in the sun. Cheerful, affectionate, sunny smile that could brighten up a room. Everything about Valeria was suave. Understated. Serene. Unknowingly, she radiated warmth, tolerance, goodness. It was this that made her pretty. Hertie's lips curved slightly upward. It was a joy to have a young friend and Valeria had turned into one of the people she cherished the most, almost as if she'd known her all her life. The age difference didn't seem to matter but, after revealing details of her troubled childhood, Hertie worried Valeria might be upset with some of it. What if she was? Unnerved she allowed a few tears to escape down her cheeks, saying in a shaky voice, 'I hope you weren't shocked when I told you we ate the cat. After all, you have a pet cat – little Wonkie.'

Valeria said quietly, sincerely, 'I'm not shocked you ate the cat. I'm shocked at the situation that forced you and your family to eat the cat. That's what I'm shocked about.'

Hertie's tears ran freely. She breathed in and out a few times, accepting the tissues Valeria handed over. A little later, more composed, she said, 'thank you. I'm sorry I've been sobbing and telling you all this. You haven't slept because of me.'

Valeria replied graciously, 'doesn't matter. I'm interested. I write. I love good stories and yours is extraordinary. Tell me more if you don't mind.'

'Are you sure?'

'Yes, hundred percent. This dream of yours is frightening but it seems obvious to me why you have it. The episode with the potatoes in the coal cellar of the abandoned farmhouse where you couldn't get out on your own, for one; then hiding in the chimney while the Russian soldiers gang raped your aunt. Horrible, traumatic events for anyone but especially for an eight year old girl.'

Hertie nodded, then added, 'definitely traumatic but the thing is I forgot everything or so it seemed. Unconsciously I didn't. I pushed it all back. According to Skye, my psychologist, it was my brain's way of coping with the shock. For years I didn't understand my nightmares, especially the recurring one. To be honest I was afraid to find out. Eventually, a few years ago, encouraged by my grandson, I decided to book an appointment with Skye. Xavy went with me for the first two sessions. I feared going on my own,' pausing she shook her head, 'not sure why but I did.'

'Xavy? Have you mentioned him before?'

'Of course. Perhaps you forgot. Xaver or Xavy, as I call

him, is my favourite grandson. We're very close. He's my daughter's only boy. She's got two girls but we don't get along so well.'

'And your sons have no boys, right?'

'Doch[20]! My eldest has two but I don't see them often. One's married, lives in Scotland. The other went to the States. My second son has no children.'

'I'm sorry, Hertie.'

'For what, my dear?'

'Forgetting you'd already told me all that some time ago.'

Shrugging Hertie replied, 'don't be silly, I've told you so many things since we first met, you must've forgotten some. Only human.'

'Thank you.'

'Nothing to thank me for, Schätzchen, I'm the one who should thank you.'

'No need. Just go on telling me your story. I find it compelling.'

'I will. By the way, you'll meet Xavy at some stage. He'll visit when he's next on holiday—'

'Of course.'

'Anyway,' Hertie resumed, guessing Valeria was more interested in her story rather than her grandson's, 'Xavy booked me the first appointment with Skye. She came highly recommended by a friend of his. Skye is indeed excellent. She did wonders with me and helped me remember what caused my nightmares. I know why now. The reasons are exactly what you said – those horrible events in my life when I was a child. The escape from East Prussia, the hunger, the violence, the depravation. The fear in that cellar when I thought the train and all my family would leave without me. It was frightening to think I'd be abandoned in that icy cold, terrifying little basement. Skye said and it's true, the nightmares, the recurring dream would seldom happen once I understood them but could occasionally take place, triggered by illness, fatigue or stress. As you know,

---

[20] German for yes, used instead of "ja" when the question is made in the negative.

I've been ill recently – the crisis of rheumatic arthritis made me anxious, which caused my blood pressure to shoot up. I'm still recovering.'

'I know. That's why I suggested this break.'

'You're a dear. So I guess that's why the recurring dream happened. I'm not quite well yet and when I have these attacks I get stressed, sleep badly, feel exhausted. It adds up. I was looking forward to this weekend with you, Valeria and now…' her voice faded.

'What?'

'Well, I'm spoiling it all for you.'

'No, you're not spoiling anything. Your story's fascinating and I'm sure it's good for you to talk about it.'

Hertie agreed silently.

'Tell me more. Did your mother ever find out about Kaspar?'

'No. Mutti never suspected why Hedi went to Munich to work for auntie Elsa or why I wanted to put as much physical distance as possible between myself and Kaspar.'

'How can you be so sure?'

'If Mutti knew he'd tried to force himself on Hedi, she would have left him right there and then.'

'Perhaps, it would've been better?'

Hertie reflected for a moment, then shaking her head said, 'I don't think so. After we left, he was good to her. And when she fell ill with motor neuron disease, he stayed by her side, cared for her and looked after her in a kind, loving way.'

'When did your mother die?'

'In 1961, only forty-eight. She married young and had my older brother, Heinrich, at nineteen. A harsh life. Painful. Not much to enjoy I think,' she shuddered, 'poor Mutti. Anyway, I couldn't go to the funeral. I was in Kenya with my husband – he'd been placed there – and pregnant with my daughter, my third child, in fact she was born two months after Mutti died. Tough on me but I just couldn't travel. When at last I could go, I visited all my siblings in turn. Helmut took me to Mutti's grave. I placed some flowers and finally grieved her loss.'

'When did you meet your husband?'

'Shortly after I arrived in Berlin. My job was as translator for the British Foreign Office and Gerry—'

'Gerry as in?' Valeria interrupted.

'Gerald. Gerald Neale, his full name, which is naturally why, as his widow, I still use the name Neale, instead of just Lohmeyer, my father's name. Neale's my children's name too. Makes sense. Actually he preferred people used his proper name, Gerald. I've forgotten why I always called him Gerry. He worked at the British Foreign Office in Berlin too.'

'As a translator?'

'No. Gerry was MI6. He'd had other placements before Germany. His first was in Portugal actually. He spoke the language like a native. Your mother's Portuguese so you may find the story interesting.'

'There's a story?'

'Oh yes. My husband wasn't the loyal, honest, lovely man I believed him to be. He had a vindictive streak about him and was a womaniser. I began to grasp it two or three years after our marriage. He was hateful to a man who once worked with him while in Portugal and later in England. He had affairs with all sorts of women, lied about them, though always kind to me, maintaining he loved me. I indulged him. Not quite sure why. I loved him, I suppose, but…well…then, it was the thing to do. If it were now, I'd have divorced him,' she shrugged, 'but his "Portuguese" story in a manner of speaking, I only discovered shortly before his death.'

'What did he do?'

Hertie sighed heavily. 'What didn't he do,' she murmured, then she began, 'Gerry was based at the British embassy in Portugal from 1940 to 1942. The Royal Navy representative there at the time was a man named Edwin Thorp with the rank of Rear-Admiral. He didn't take to Gerry, thought him too young, inexperienced and too crazy about women and partying. He complained to the ambassador but unfortunately, Gerald overheard it. He then discovered Thorp was gay and blackmailed him into silence. But he held on to his grudge and did worse later. After the war, Thorp left the navy and joined MI6 with a high ranking. He was supposed to come to Germany with Gerald and Gerry would be reporting directly to him. Gerry was upset. So, he revealed the truth about Thorp's sexuality thus destroying his career and landing him in prison. Homosexuality, as you probably know, was only decriminalised in the UK in 1967. Apparently two years after being arrested, Thorp committed suicide in prison. Gerry destroyed his life.'

'That's a terrible story.'

'Indeed. I never met Thorp but I was very sorry for him. It was difficult to forgive my husband.'

'And did you?'

'Not deep in my heart, no, but I told him I had,' she shrugged, 'he was dying.'

'I think I understand.'

Hertie lifted her gaze, then added dismally, 'but there's more.'

'Worse?'

'Equally harmful, wrong and distressing.'

'Tell me.'

'When Gerry grasped he was dying he burdened me with his confessions. First, his despicable actions against Thorp and then, what he did to a young woman in Portugal. It's a disgraceful story but, from his perspective, also pathetic.'

'What do you mean?'

'He died without knowing the end.'

Hertie watched as Valeria raised an eyebrow. Heavy-hearted she explained, 'Gerald never found out whether he had a child in Portugal or what happened to the girl he got pregnant. His behaviour wasn't the best, to put it mildly. Utterly dishonourable. Although he never called it rape, once I'd heard his full confession, I think that's exactly what he did. He raped the girl in question. He told me he'd been crazy about her. Apparently she was a beauty. He wanted her, had to have her or so he said, and forced her to have intercourse with him. He liked to say he seduced her but I believe in calling things by their names. It was rape. I'll tell you everything if you like. I'm sure you'll agree with me.'

'And even after you knew the full truth about your husband, you didn't leave him?'

'What for? As I said, he was dying.'

'What did he die of?'

'Lung cancer and heart disease, due to years and years of excesses – smoking, drinking, partying, women. He died three weeks after his confession. I had our children to think about. Three still very young kids. They didn't need to know their father wasn't exactly what they believed him to be. Gerald was an extremely handsome man, utterly charming, attentive, kind when he wanted to be and a good, dedicated father to the children. To me, he was a considerate lover though showing me little respect through his numerous affairs. But they never lasted long. It was almost as if he needed them to feel alive…and I was in love with him. I stayed with him until the end and that's that but my feelings for him died with his confession.'

'Do you regret it?'

'No. What would be the point?'

'Was he your only man?'

'Yes. I had other admirers but Gerald was my first and only man for many years. After he died I had the children to think about. Men were at the end of my list. Anyway, Gerry was much older than me. Very experienced with women. I assume he found it easy to make me fall in love with him. I met him shortly after I arrived in Berlin. I was twenty, he already thirty-eight but…' she heaved her shoulders, 'still devastatingly attractive, charismatic, elegant. Somehow, I couldn't resist him.'

Chapter 12 – Under the Berlin Sky

She arrived in Berlin on a blustery day, late September 1956. A heavy shower fell just before the train reached its final destination. Glancing through the window of her third class carriage Hertie watched the first sights of the city. A high number of buildings appeared neat, well-kept. However, alongside them she could still see the scars of the war and, occasionally, small piles of rubble. Obviously, care had been taken to restore and rebuild many of the city's areas but the full objective was not yet fully met. There were trees everywhere, some old, bearing beautiful autumn colours. Trees that dropped copper, yellow and red leaves to the ground and the river. Tears for the loss of summer, briefly crossed Hertie's mind. It was a bit like she felt, this being the first time in her still young life that she would be without her family. Alone. No-one to rely on but herself. Excitement had ruled her heart most of the trip but now, as the train approached the station, she felt frightened. What would lie in wait for her?

Stepping out of the train, her small suitcase in one hand and handbag in the other, Hertie wished she had never have left Hamburg. There was a buzz in the air, a kind of electric current humming around her. She sensed a tension, a strain as if something alarming was about to happen. Her stomach clenched. Berlin was a busy city...and a dangerous city, full of foreign agents, spies and war criminals trying to hide and cover their tracks. Hertie had heard conversations and read reports but ignored whether they were true. Hesitating she stopped and looked around. The station was crowded. Men in brown or grey suits and hats running to catch a train, newspapers under their arms. Others in the uniforms of the occupying western forces – the US, Britain and France. No Red Army soldiers that she could see but they must all be in the eastern sector of the city. Hertie knew the western foreign powers didn't mix with their Russian counterparts. Not anymore. The Soviets had put strict controls in place between East and West Berlin because too many Easterners were moving to the western zones with no intention of going back.

Hertie noticed more women in uniform than in Hamburg but also many in plain clothes running, possibly for their jobs after a longer lunch break, fearing they would be late. School children moved around. Young men, selling newspapers, shouted out the headlines. She wondered where to go. Someone was supposed to pick her up. She had no idea who. He or she could be wandering around the bustling station searching for her. How would she know who to address?

A woman with wavy brown hair and hazelnut eyes beamed at her, waving her hand. Hertie glanced around to ensure she was the gesturing woman's subject and not someone else. A second later, feeling certain she was the recipient, she smiled shyly.

'Are you Hertha Lohmeyer?' The woman asked, approaching fast, her lips parting warmly.

Hertie said nothing at first, carefully observing the woman who wore a long dark green, good quality wool overcoat, elegant black shoes and a matching handbag. The coat was unbuttoned, allowing Hertie to glimpse a well-tailored light green and beige tweed suit with a pencil skirt and a short, belted jacket. The collar of a beige blouse emerged from it. She wore a graceful small hat in the same colour of the overcoat on her carefully frizzed hair. Looking down herself at her out of fashion grey coat, once Hedi's, and her worn-out shoes which had seen better days, Hertie felt shabby. She had no hat decorating her red-blonde hair and had never entered a hairdresser's salon. Mutti cut her naturally wavy hair regularly and Hertie invariably wore it tied at the back in a simple ponytail. She felt scruffy. Ugly.

'Excuse me,' the woman spoke again, possibly thinking Hertie hadn't heard her. Pulling off her pretty, dark green gloves she repeated, 'are you Hertha Lohmeyer?'

Hertie finally found her voice.

'Yes. I'm sorry. I'm a little distracted…everything…is…so new to me.'

'Perfectly all right. I'm Emily Swift. Miss. I head the translation department at the British Foreign Office in Berlin.

You'll be working under me.'

'You're English?' Hertie was genuinely surprised, 'but you speak perfect German.'

'My mother was German. She married an Englishman at the end of the first war and moved to the island after I was born. I grew up speaking both languages.'

At close range, Hertie noticed Emily Swift wasn't as young as she appeared from a distance. She must be in her early forties. Her own boss had come to fetch her. Hertie felt a little intimidated.

'Thank you for picking me up, Miss Swift. I'm grateful,' she said timidly.

'Oh well, there was no-one else available. Anyway, you come highly recommended. Top of your class, hey? Impressive. English only?'

'No. French too and…and a little Russian.'

Miss Swift made a dismissive gesture. 'Russian's mostly irrelevant but French may come in handy,' she glanced at Hertie's suitcase and handbag and making a sign with her head asked her, 'all of your luggage, Fräulein Lohmeyer?'

'Yes.'

'Very well. I've a car parked outside. I'm taking you first to the office so you can meet your flat mate and some of the people you'll be translating for most of the time.'

'My flat mate?'

'Didn't they tell you back in Hamburg?'

'No, Miss Swift. Herr Direktor Schmidt from the translators' school only said my application for a job here had been successful and he'd arranged everything, so I'd be picked up and then given further information.'

'I see. Well, there're a good number of girls and a few men working in the translation department at the British Foreign Office. Most English agents, officers and government officials from the British Isles don't speak German or any other foreign language for that matter – they speak only English. So, they require a small army of translators. Mostly translating German documents into English and English into German; sometimes

French into English or vice-versa. Occasionally one of us may be asked to accompany an official to some meeting with the German government or Chamber of Commerce or something similar and serve as an interpreter. Rarely other languages are required; however, we've had an instance or two where Russian was needed. So, who knows? Your knowledge of the Soviets' language may yet come in handy.'

Miss Swift turned, telling Hertie to follow her. As they reached the car, Hertie noticed it was a British army vehicle with British number plates. A young, baby-faced soldier sat at the wheel. He stepped out and greeted her in English.

'Good afternoon, Miss. May I take care of your suitcase?'

Hertie nodded. He held the back door open for them, then placed the suitcase in the boot and resumed his seat. Glancing over his shoulder he asked, 'where to, Miss Swift?'

'Headquarters. Thank you.'

Emily Swift turned to Hertie and said, 'anyway, regarding your accommodation, as you're young and single, we thought you'd be better off living with a similar aged girl who knows the city well. She's lived here for several years. You'll meet her in the office and you will go home with her. Her name's Bettina Ascher, twenty-two...' she paused, then asked, 'you are?'

'Twenty.'

'Ah, yes. I remember now, I saw your birthdate on your application form – 16th February 1936, correct?'

'Yes, that's right.'

'Hmm, yes, young. Very young,' she said as if recalling an obscure past event that only she knew about, 'anyway, Fräulein Ascher's twenty-two. She works mostly with French translations, occasionally English. As mentioned, lives in a small flat in Spandau – a Berlin borough – and has been searching for a flatmate to help her pay the rent. We suggested you and she agreed. I'm sure you'll like her. She's a good girl, knows the ropes of the job and the city very well so she can help you fit in.'

Hertie nodded in agreement. 'Thank you, Miss Swift.' she added for lack of something better to say.

The drive through the city fascinated Hertie. So different

from Hamburg. The city centre was clearly wealthier. No ruins left from the heavy bombings in the final years of the war. Perhaps not that surprising. Eleven years later, Hamburg's rich quarters and city centre had also none left. A visitor from the outside could be forgiven for thinking the war had spared the city. Away from the main avenues and boulevards, Hertie again glimpsed rubble here and there. Some façades still displayed the scars of the metal fragments that had hit them, possibly a consequence of violent explosions or debris scattered from the blasts' shockwaves.

They were driving along what seemed a glamorous avenue. Hertie thought it might be the celebrated Ku'Damm – the Kürfürstendamm, Berlin's most famous street. She had seen photos in some magazine. Just then, to her left emerged a dramatic, impressive ruin of a church. The remains of a tall tower, part of a nave and a spiral. There was a tragic, melancholy aura about it. Hertie felt a lump in her throat. The ruins of the church were like a sombre, mournful, burnt finger pointing at the sky – a compelling reminder of her country's recent past.

'We've just come up the Ku'Damm – you've heard of it, right?'

Hertie nodded.

'And that,' Miss Swift pointed at the ruin, 'is what's left of the Kaiser Wilhelm church. It was quite a spectacular, elegant church before being extensively damaged on the night of 23rd November 1943 after an air-raid. It could be rebuilt or demolished and a new church built in its place. But Berliners want the ruin to stay as a memorial to remember the horrors that happened in Germany during the Nazi regime and as a tribute to all its victims. There were plans for a new church to replace the remains of the previous one but, after public outcry, the new church will incorporate what's left of the old.'

'I see. I agree. It should be a memorial.'

'People here call it the Gedächtnis Kirche, the memorial church. It's right in the heart of the city. So, yes, I too think it's fitting it stays there and becomes part of the new church. It'll be a reminder of what happened but also that Germany's recovering and the country is different now. The Nazi past is firmly in the past.'

Miss Swift introduced Hertie to Bettina Ascher once they arrived at headquarters, as she called the building where the British Foreign Office had its base in Berlin. Bettina was a lively, rather pretty girl. Blonde. Bright blue eyes. Mouth shaped like a heart. Ready smile. Voluptuous body. Her silhouette enhanced by the tight, navy blue wool dress and light grey cardigan she wore. Shaking Hertie's hand firmly she said, 'pleasure to meet you, Hertha. May I call you by your first name? I'm just Bettina. After all, we're going to be flat mates.'

Hertie smiled and nodded. She liked Bettina's extrovert, easy manner. Good to be paired with someone who appeared so self-confident, assured of herself. Hertie was shy and quiet but always enjoyed the company of people who were her opposite.

Miss Swift left her with Bettina who took her around the office, introducing Hertie to a lot of different people whose names she instantly forgot. Then she showed her the desk she would occupy and explained how the work was divided between the various translators. Sometimes something unexpected or urgent might turn up and Hertie would be asked to prioritise it. But mostly it was routine.

Bettina obtained permission from Miss Swift to finish work early so she could take Hertie to their flat and help her settle down. It was around four in the afternoon when they took the bus to Spandau where the flat was located. Hertie thought Berlin was an attractive city. She liked what she saw from the dirty window of the bus. To get to Spandau, the bus crossed the borough of Charlottenburg, an area with spacious, wide avenues, noble buildings and the remains of the Charlottenburg Schloss. Infrequent piles of rubble could still be seen. Specks in the landscape. Burnt fragments of debris breaking up the harmony of the boulevards. The palace was closed, Bettina told her. A lot of it ruined from the bombings and not enough money to restore it. But the city would eventually get there in a not-so-distant future. Hertie admired Bettina's optimism about everything. It was refreshing and made her feel good.

'It's much better than in the Soviet sector on the East side of the city,' Bettina explained, 'but some things in West Berlin are more expensive,' she seemed to examine her hair and to glance briefly at her clothes, 'no offense, Hertha—'

'None taken I'm sure but call me Hertie.'

'Okay, if you like. As I was going to say, I don't want to offend you but you'll need to go to the hairdresser and get smarter clothes...or have you any in your suitcase?'

'No. My clothes aren't great. We didn't have much money and I've never been to a hairdresser in my life.'

'Hah! We must correct that. I'll take you to East Berlin, to my hairdresser. It's a lot cheaper to have your hair done there. As for clothes, you can shop for some in the East too. Again less expensive than here.'

'Can we enter East Berlin at all? I read there were strict controls—'

'Yes,' Bettina interrupted, 'from East into West Berlin. We'll need our West Berlin personal ID cards. Have you got yours by the way?'

Hertie nodded. 'Miss Swift left it on my desk. It has my photo and your address.'

'Our address,' Bettina corrected her with an amused grin.

'Yes, our address, you're right.'

'Anyway, Hertie, as I said I'll take you to East Berlin but to start with, you may borrow a couple of things from me for work. We're about the same size.'

'That's very kind of you.'

Bettina shrugged, smiling. 'We're flatmates, Hertie. We need to help each other. I know how it is to arrive in a large, unknown city where you don't know a soul. Daunting. But you're not alone. I'm here. We're a team now.'

'Thank you,' Hertie felt touched, then asked, 'you said the controls are from East into West Berlin. Not the other way around? So we as West Berliners are permitted to travel to the Soviet sector?'

'Yes but the Easterners can no longer come to the West. Many people have come to the American, British or French sectors and stayed. So if you're a resident of the East side of the city, it's nearly impossible to come here. But we, as long as we've proof we're West Berlin residents, can go there for shopping or visiting relatives.'

'I see. Is it scary?'

'No. It's just an area occupied by a different foreign power than the west side. But don't worry, I wouldn't let you go by yourself.'

Hertie nodded. She wasn't particularly keen on travelling to the Russian sector but didn't want to disappoint Bettina who obviously meant well. She made a mental note to never tell her mother about visits to the East side. The bus was just passing through the borough of Charlottenburg and Hertie couldn't help but mention how pretty it looked.

'Was even more beautiful before the war and the bombings destroyed everything. But slowly it's being rebuilt. The palace,' Bettina pointed to the right and Hertie saw the remains of a pretty façade and a dome covered in scaffolding, 'was fully destroyed. The roof collapsed, most rooms reduced to rubble and there was no money to rebuild it. But they've received some funds now and have begun restoring it. I read in the *Berliner Morgenpost* that the dome should be ready next year,' she shrugged, 'but who knows.'

Hertie nodded and decided to step out of the bus one day in this area and walk around to admire the pretty boulevards, gardens, trees and noble façades.

They arrived at the flat after a forty-minute ride on the bus. The apartment was on the first floor of a newly rebuilt house, destroyed to the ground during the bombings. It wasn't large but it had two reasonably sized bedrooms, a small sitting-room, tiny bathroom and kitchen. More than enough for the two of them. Everything looked very clean and tidy. She looked out of her bedroom window, as Bettina left her to unpack. The street was relatively quiet and mostly neat. There was the rest of a wall at the far end and an old pile of rubble in front but, just like at the Charlottenburg palace, there was scaffolding so it seemed those last remains of the war would soon vanish.

On her first Saturday in Berlin, Bettina was as good as her word and travelled with her to East Berlin. Hertie noticed there were more ruins and piles of rubble in the Soviet sector of the city and a higher number of soldiers patrolling the streets, especially close to the crossing points into West Berlin – the Soviet army. The uniforms were different than what she remembered. On some streets she heard more Russian than German. But Bettina was right. The hairdresser was excellent and inexpensive. He cut her hair in a modern way, allowing her natural waves to frame her face. Hertie had never felt so pretty. They bought two skirts, three blouses and the same number of cardigans, one jacket in neutral grey and beige colours that would go well with both skirts – one brown, one black. They found a navy blue wool overcoat that fitted Hertie, contrasting her red-blonde hair nicely, with a matching small hat and pair of gloves. All for a third of what she would have paid in one of the fancy shops of West Berlin. Hertie was pleased with herself and felt certain her mother would have approved.

The return to West Berlin wasn't as easy as she had assumed from Bettina's words. There was a queue of people attempting to cross. Four were turned down and not permitted to leave. Apparently their documents were not in order. One, a young man, with ash blonde hair tried to run towards the west side but one of the soldiers sent a warning shot into the air and went after him. Frightened, he stopped and was taken back in handcuffs. The scene brought unwanted memories into Hertie's mind. A flicker of Russian voices and the screams of her aunt Jutta. She shuddered, feeling suddenly very cold. Her tension grew. What if the soldiers stopped her? What if they didn't allow her through? What would she do then? She felt sick and wished never to have come into the Soviet Sector, cheaper prices or not.

Bettina went first. She glided through, followed by an appraising smile from one of the soldiers. Heart in her mouth, Hertie followed. The man said something in Russian. She shook her head and he repeated the phrase in German.

'Ausweis bitte.'

'Of course.' Nervously, with shaky hands, Hertie fumbled

in her handbag searching for her ID card. She didn't find it immediately and began perspiring. Cold sweat covered her skin. Her stomach contracted. She tasted bile. For a terrible moment she feared they might take her away in handcuffs like the young man with ash blonde hair. A little ahead, Bettina glanced over her shoulder, gave the soldier a dazzling smile and said, 'it's in your porte-monnaie, Hertie, come on.'

The soldier returned Bettina's smile and when Hertie, with trembling hands, finally handed over her West Berlin ID card he barely looked at it, waving her through. Breathing a sigh of relief she promised herself to never travel to East Berlin again. Better safe than sorry, as her mother used to say. It was better to pay a slightly higher price and buy less but avoid another stressful experience.

Hertie settled quietly into her new life and soon felt at home. The job took most of her time but there were always days off, as well as most evenings. Bettina was a pleasant, lively, extrovert girl. Hertie liked her and felt comfortable by her side, losing some of her natural shyness and gaining in self-confidence. Bettina was out most evenings, particularly on Saturdays when she would go dancing at some fashionable nightclub, with a never-ending string of boyfriends who seemed to change often. One of them was always escorting her somewhere. Sometimes she spent the night with the flavour of the month young man, always arriving home before daybreak and openly telling Hertie her adventures with the opposite sex. Hertie often wished she wouldn't. It made her feel awkward at best and at worst, a misfit for still being a virgin in more ways than one. She hadn't as much as kissed a man yet.

One Saturday, five weeks after Hertie's move to Berlin, Bettina invited her to go to the British Club. On that particular evening Bettina had no partner, having sent her latest boyfriend packing. Nevertheless she wanted to dance and wasn't prepared to stay home. Hertie reluctantly agreed to go. She feared no-one would notice her and dreaded being dumped, ignored in a corner. No-one to dance with or talk to. It had happened before. The boys circled Bettina like flies around the honey pot but hardly noticed her. Quiet, shy and pale she looked unremarkable and dull next to Bettina. Or so she thought of herself.

'Hertie? Are you ready?' She heard Bettina's voice outside her bedroom and opened the door.

'Yes.'

Bettina stared her up and down with a critical look. 'You're going in that?' She finally asked, pointing at her outfit and appearing startled.

Hertie's heart dropped to the floor. 'It's my best skirt and my prettiest blouse,' she said dispiritedly.

'Well, it won't do. Perfect for work but not to a club, least of all the British Club. It'll be full of officers, officials and their wives. You need an evening gown.'

'I haven't got one,' Hertie whispered, disheartened.

'We'll soon fix that,' Bettina said, placing an arm around her shoulders, 'come into my room. You're about my size so it won't be a problem.'

Half an hour later Hertie could hardly recognise herself in the mirror. Bettina's silver shimmering navy blue dress fitted her like a glove, enhancing her graceful figure, cobalt blue eyes and red golden hair. It fell in a cascade of soft waves to her shoulders pulled on one side above her ear with a silver-plated clip. Wearing Bettina's glass earrings, high heel shoes and lightly made up Hertie thought herself pretty for the first time in her life.

'There,' Bettina said, visibly satisfied with her creation, 'you look stunning. Let's see how many British hearts you're going to break.'

Amused, Hertie smiled and watched Bettina chuckle at her own joke in her typical dirty laugh.

They made quite an entrance at the British Club. Hertie felt her cheeks tingle, perceiving men's admiring gazes and not only for her friend but directed at herself too. Unintentionally she smiled, positively glowing.

Gerald Neale stood at the bar, talking to a mate when the two young women arrived. He knew Bettina Ascher well, having tried to seduce her unsuccessfully a couple of times. She told him bluntly she didn't like men almost old enough to be her father. He'd given up adding Bettina to his list of conquests. But who was that radiant creature next to her? Perhaps she liked older men and the experience they could offer. Gerald needn't despair of his age. At thirty-eight, fit, elegant and still with striking good looks he was very much aware of his attraction to women of all ages. Excusing himself to his mate he approached Bettina.

'Miss Ascher,' he said, 'you look ravishing as usual.'

'Mr Neale,' she replied, her voice dripping sarcasm, 'you're flattering and amorous as usual.'

He smiled, amused. Glancing at Hertie and picking up her hand he asked, 'and who might you be, dear lovely lady?'

Colour suffused her cheeks and Hertie didn't know what to say. Bettina came to the rescue.

'She's my flat mate, Hertha Lohmeyer. You must've seen her around headquarters, Mr Neale, she works with me as a translator in the same department.'

'I don't think I've seen you before, Miss Lohmeyer,' he paused for effect, then added, 'I'd remember you.'

'Yes...well,' Bettina said, 'Hertie, this is Mr Gerald Neale – one of the British officials from whatever Foreign Office Department he works for in his country,' she smiled ironically and warned, 'beware of his charms, Hertie. Mr Neale's a bit of a womaniser.'

'Seriously, Miss Ascher? You're staining my reputation and painting me in ugly colours in front of your friend,' he said in a pretend scandalised voice.

'I'm telling the truth, Mr Neale,' Bettina shrugged, gave him a dazzling smile and grabbing Hertie pulled her away.

'Will you give me a dance later, Miss Lohmeyer?' He shouted after them.

Hertie's lips opened. Amazement all over her face. He wanted to dance with her. She had never been on the receiving end of a man's interest, especially not one as handsome. Nodding she replied softly, 'perhaps. Probably. I mean yes, Mr Neale.'

Trailing behind Bettina she watched him as he stayed

glued to the floor until they disappeared from view into the ball room.

'You don't like him much, do you, Betti?' Hertie asked her friend, a little surprised with her reaction, 'yet he seemed charming to me.'

'Oh, he's charming all right and very handsome but you can't trust him. He's always running after a pretty face.'

'So, he isn't married?'

'No, but I don't think it would make a difference.'

'How old is he?'

'Old. Thirty-eight I think. Old enough to be your father.'

Hertie smiled. 'My father was already thirty when he married my mother. She was eighteen and had my eldest brother at nineteen. But I thought Mr Neale was younger than thirty-eight. He looks…I'd say about thirty or so and not a year older.'

Shaking her head, Bettina told her, 'just be careful, that's all I'm saying.'

Later, when finally dancing with Gerald Neale, Hertie's heart swelled in her chest. It was as if she were up in the air, close to the ceiling, looking down on the dancing couples, herself and Mr Neale gliding around the room. He was a good dancer and a very charming man. By the time the music ended and he'd thanked her, placing a soft kiss on her hand, Hertie felt hooked. He was glamorous, charismatic and seemed attracted to her.

Before returning her to her place, he asked whether she'd give him one more dance and accept a drink. She nodded. Appearing encouraged by her reaction he invited her to go with him to the ballet. It so happened he had two tickets. Flattered, she answered yes but didn't tell Bettina, not wishing to hear her words of caution. While dancing with him for the second time, Hertie's pulse accelerated. Her heart skipped a beat. As if assaulted by a high tide, she felt the attraction grip her whole body.

The icing on the cake came the week after with the ballet visit. Tchaikovsky's Swan Lake. She'd never seen anything so beautiful. Dazzled by the dancers' movements, the music, the lights, Hertie felt as if floating on cloud nine. Gerald kissed her, leaving an ardently sweet taste on her lips. And in that instant she fell hopelessly in love.

Chapter 13 – Unfinished Story in the Peak District

Staring past Valeria at some invisible point on the wall, Hertie concluded, 'six months later, I'd lost my virginity. Our relationship became more intense but I was naïve, had no idea I could have taken precautions. Gerald should have done so but he obviously didn't think about it or didn't care. One year after I'd arrived in Berlin, in September 1957, I realised I was pregnant. Bettina was furious, not with me but with Gerald. She wanted to go to him and tell him what she thought of an experienced, older man who seduced young, innocent women such as me.'

'And did she?'

Hertie looked up at Valeria. They were both still sitting on her bed, talking or, rather, she was talking and Valeria was listening.

'No. She didn't. I didn't allow her. I said I wanted to talk to Gerald myself.'

'You told him you were pregnant.'

'I did. We married in May 1958 just two months before my first child was born.'

'Were you still in Berlin when the Wall was built overnight on 13th August 1961?'

'No. Gerald was transferred to a post in Africa, in Kenya and we left with the baby in the winter of 1959.'

'You got married quickly, so presumably he reacted well when you first told him you were pregnant?'

'Better than expected. At first, I thought he was going to break up with me and leave me to deal with the baby. He seemed aghast, almost amazed it could have happened. Then, a palette of emotions passed through his face, his eyes. After a minute or two, he turned to me and said, "don't fear, my darling, I'll do right by you." And he did. We married,' she shrugged, 'but when he said those words I didn't quite grasp the implication. What he meant when he said he'd do right by me. Later, I realised he was thinking of a similar situation years before when he wronged someone badly.'

'The girl in Portugal you mentioned earlier?'

'Yes. Her name was Maria Eduarda, an exotic beauty, daughter of a Portuguese Duke and a native Cape Verdean woman. Gerald met her in the summer of 1940 when he was sent to Lisbon as an MI6 agent. She was nineteen when he met her but turned twenty at the end of the summer. It took him a while to get what he wanted from her. She wasn't just beautiful, also independent and intelligent. He couldn't chat her up and seduce her in the way he was used to do with most women. He'd never met one who resisted his charms but Maria Eduarda did until he couldn't hold his desire – his feelings or so he said – any longer and in December 1941, in Alentejo, while a guest at her father's estate, in her own bedroom, he raped her. As a consequence, she got pregnant but refused him, left her parents' home, after her father apparently threw her out on the streets. Gerald left Portugal in the spring of 1942 and never knew whether Maria Eduarda had the baby or what happened to her.'

Hertie stared at Valeria for a moment. The girl seemed strange all of a sudden. Her face was very pale, enhancing her chocolate brown eyes. She was rubbing her hands and shaking her head ever so slightly. Then, she murmured, 'no, it's just not possible.'

'What, Schätzchen? What's just not possible?'

Looking directly at Hertie, an emotional earthquake visibly rocking her body and mind Valeria answered, 'what a strange…actually serendipitous situation.'

'I don't understand.'

'Maria Eduarda who got pregnant by your husband, Gerald Neale, is my aunt. Or actually my half-aunt. She's or was my mother's eldest half-sister.'

'No!'

'Yes. My maternal grandfather was the Duke of Beja, Ludovico de Arantes Silva. I never met him. He died when I was still a baby. Ludovico married three times. His first wife was Cape Verdean. With her he had a daughter, Maria Eduarda. With his second wife he had a son who died still a child and a daughter, Ana Maria. His third wife my grandmother, Rosa, gave him five daughters. My mother is the youngest one. Anyway, going back to his first daughter, Maria Eduarda, we know that she got pregnant in December 1941, a few months after her 21st birthday. She refused to reveal who had fathered her baby. Ludovico, a staunch catholic, expelled her from home and disinherited her. None of her half-sisters know what happened to her. They know of her but never met her and while he lived Ludovico refused to talk about her. We don't know whether she's still alive, whether she had the baby or what happened to her.'

Struck dumb Hertie opened and shut her mouth without a sound. To describe her feelings as surprised or astonished was an understatement. She didn't believe in coincidences. Nevertheless, coincidences did indeed happen, however infrequently and rarely they took place. Mentally she reviewed Maria Eduarda and Gerald's story, every detail her husband had told her on his deathbed and realised something else. There was an opportunity of correcting some of the wrong he had created. Turning to Valeria she held her hands and said, 'we've a lot to talk about. I now know Gerald connects me to you in an odd way, almost like the famous six degrees of separation. I must tell you everything about him and Maria Eduarda, what he did to Thorp I've already mentioned and his secret…but not now. Tomorrow's another day.'

Valeria agreed and Hertie added they should finally get some sleep.

Chapter 14 – Gerald's Confession

'Gerald died in late spring 1966 about a year after returning to England,' Hertie said, glancing at Valeria and speaking quietly to the digital recorder.

They had returned from their break in the Peak District several weeks ago but Valeria had had to travel to London. One of her singer friends, a young tenor who was due to perform a recital of Schubert's Lieder at Cadogan Hall, called her. His accompanist had been involved in a car crash and lay in hospital with a few broken bones. With less than two weeks to spare, the tenor asked Valeria whether she could step in and accompany him at the piano. Valeria knew the material and said yes. Nevertheless, she needed to practise intensively before the concert and was therefore unable to pay attention to anything else. Hertie wasn't upset, using the time to refresh her memory, organise the stories in her head and jot down a few key topics.

Hertie's grandson had sent her a digital recorder on her birthday, back in February, but she hadn't touched it since. Once Valeria returned from her stint in London and taught her how to use it, she was ready to narrate Gerald's story and her own memories.

She sat comfortably on the large sofa in her lounge, her feet up, with the little recorder in the middle on the coffee table and Valeria the other side of it. Two tall glasses of mineral water in front of them. Hertie began to speak.

'It was a Saturday at the end of May – 22nd I think. It rained all day. It was dark. Four in the afternoon but the lights were on. The rain was so thick I couldn't glimpse the sea from the lounge windows. Our house then was on the seafront in Worthing but the sea, the sky and the pebbles were all a blur through the heavy curtains of rain. I remember standing by the door to my husband's bedroom, gathering my courage to go in. It pained me to see him in the state he was in – a shadow of his former self. He'd been given only a few weeks to live and didn't want to go into a hospice. He wanted to die at home. So, I was looking after him full time though a nurse came twice a week and

I could phone her whenever needed if Gerry got suddenly worse or was in agonising pain. The children were staying with our best friends – a couple who lived only six miles away, in Shoreham-by-Sea. I didn't want the kids to see their father like that. Painfully thin, dark rings around his eyes, his body nearly disappearing under the covers. coughing and wheezing most of the time,' she exhaled, 'I finally went in with a cup of tea and a soft bread cream cheese sandwich. He ate little and slept most of the time but was awake when I went in. With a sad smile he asked me whether I was busy. I said I wasn't and did he need anything. I remember he shook his head and, after a pause, added he'd been thinking a lot since being bed ridden.'

'About what?' Valeria interrupted.

'Exactly what I said,' Hertie replied, then resumed the story, 'Gerald was silent for a while, as if analysing something from all angles, then, patting the bed gently, urged me to sit by his side, stating there was something important he must tell me…'

Hertie's voice faded. She looked at Valeria, tears in her eyes, then breathing in and parting her lips slightly she felt ready to continue, 'I agreed to sit with him for a time. It was the start of his confession. It lasted several days…about a week, I think. Speaking tired him. He could only talk for minutes at a time or the wheezing and coughing became more intense and were too painful. He took my hand in his. I remember his bony fingers, long and hard. The skin appeared to hang from them. He was so thin. Then, he spoke these exact words, *I know I'm dying and don't have much time. I want to go with a clean conscience. I've done things in my life I'm not proud of…in fact, things I regret and want to confess. But I'm not a religious man…so, all I can do is tell you the truth, my darling, hoping you'll forgive me.* I'll never forget his little speech for as long as I live. Then, he was forced to stop. A violent coughing attack shook his body. It seemed his lungs would explode and his ribs pierce his skin and tear his chest apart. It was distressing. I remember touching his forehead with my cool hands. It seemed to provide him some relief if nothing else than emotionally. He looked pitiful.

Struggling to breathe, to calm down and control the convulsions. I waited, swallowing back my tears. So, so painful to watch him and being unable to help. I felt useless. I could do nothing to make him more comfortable.'

Hertie reached for her glass of water, sipped a bit and cleared her throat. Valeria remained silent giving her time and Hertie felt grateful for it.

'First,' she continued, 'Gerald talked about Rear Admiral Edwin Thorp and maintained deeply regretting his vile behaviour,' pausing Hertie organised her thoughts for a moment, then addressing Valeria directly she added, 'my husband was a rather conservative man though most of his views were the norm in the forties and fifties. Some still prevail today among narrow-minded circles. What I'm saying is that Gerald couldn't accept a homosexual man. He'd a grudge against Thorp, wanted to destroy him, savour revenge. Stupid, childish and really intolerable in my view. I've told you what he did to Thorp. I remember feeling wretched, as if I were about to vomit. It disgusted me to know my husband…my charming, loving husband could be so horrible, so cruel. I knew he had casual affairs with other women but what he did to Thorp was on a different level. Despicable, to say the least.'

'What did you say to him once you knew?'

'I said I wasn't sure I could forgive him. I found difficult to pardon his actions towards Thorp. And, to my amazement, Gerry wept. I'd never seen him shed a tear. His repentance appeared genuine. I suppose knowing death's coming does that to a person. So, in the end, I felt pity and forgave him. There was nothing to atone for his actions but he seemed to find comfort in my compassion. As I've mentioned before, deep in my heart I couldn't absolve him or accept what he'd done but didn't want him to know. What would be the point? Torturing a dying man? I'm not that callous. I told him I forgave him and he relaxed, beginning to confess the case with Maria Eduarda.'

Glancing at Valeria, Hertie paused the recorder and asked, 'before I go on, should I make us some sandwiches for lunch?'

'What a good idea. I'll help you.'

They ate in silence. Then had some fruit and coffee before Hertie resumed her husband's story. Gradually she revealed the full extent of Gerald's perfidy against Maria Eduarda. When she finished she asked Valeria, 'don't you think it was rape?'

Valeria nodded sadly.

'Definitely,' she agreed, 'What else could it be? After all, he confessed he entered her room without her knowledge and climbed into her bed without her consent. He caught her by surprise. She didn't ask for it. He forced himself on her while she said no. He told you that himself.'

'Yes. There's no doubt in my mind it was rape.'

'An ugly word but truthful.'

'Indeed. Gerry called it seduction but, to me, seduction implies Maria Eduarda wanted it, was happy to allow him to do what he would with her and she did not.'

'And you forgave him...yet again?'

Hertie shrugged hopelessly. 'What else could I do? He was a condemned man.'

'I understand.'

Valeria wasn't judgemental. Hertie appreciated that about her. For a moment they were quiet, lost in their own thoughts, then she exclaimed, 'Gerry's despicable revenge on Thorp and odious rape of Maria Eduarda weren't his only shameful actions. There's more.'

'Like what? I can't think of anything worse...short of murder.'

'No. No murder, but criminal nonetheless.'

'Tell me.'

'Gerald's confession of his wretched behaviour to Thorp and Maria Eduarda lasted about four days if I remember correctly. He had much difficulty speaking for long periods but he was in a frenzy to confide in me. I think he feared he mightn't have enough time left. As it turned out he lived for another three weeks. Anyway, on the fifth day I went in with tea and a soft biscuit. He had another violent bout of coughing before being able to speak. His eyes were closed as he attempted to breathe calmly. It wasn't easy. His wheezing had got worse. I helped him drink some tea. He seemed happy about it, saying it was soothing. I dunked the biscuit in the tea but he refused it. He'd lost his appetite...the illness and the strong medication, I suppose. After ten minutes or so he was able to resume his tale. Unexpectedly he asked me whether I remembered his father's first editions collection. I said that I did but thought the question was curious. What could the collection have to do with anything?'

'And did it?'

'Yes. It was related to Maria Eduarda. Her father owned a beautiful book, a first edition – a genuine 1572 edition of the epic poem Os Lusíadas by possibly the greatest Portuguese poet who ever lived, Luis de Camões or so Gerry told me. The book wasn't just lovely to look at but also very valuable. Ludovico kept it in a specially built glass case in the library of his Sintra mansion. On the weekend when the Duke and Duchess of Windsor visited his Sintra estate, he proudly showed the book to his guests. Besides this first edition and other artistic treasures, Ludovico also owned four pages of an ancient manuscript, guarded in a glass coffer on display inside a vitrine in the same library. Those pages contained some strophes of the The Lusiads. Eduarda's father wasn't certain whether they were part of the original manuscript by the hand of the poet himself but confirmed they were very old and been in the family for centuries though he'd never bothered getting them authenticated...unlike the book, which was certified. Famous. There were...or are – I actually have no idea, just repeating what Gerry said – only six original genuine first editions left and, at the time, everyone knew one was the property of the Duke of Beja.'

'This collection, is it the one in your spare room, Hertie?' Valeria asked her.

'Yes. Gerald inherited the full collection, including those two Portuguese items, from his father upon his passing away. Gerry always said they were his most prized possessions.'

'Must've been rather expensive, I mean your husband or his father must have spent a lot of money to acquire them.'

'That's the thing,' Hertie said, 'they didn't or Gerald

didn't. His father had no idea.'

'Weird!'

'To say the least. Anyway, Gerry had another terrible episode of coughing and could only go on with his confession a day or two later once he recovered a little. By then he spoke in quiet whispers. To hear his words I had to lean forward, with my ear close to his lips or I couldn't understand him. Gerry said he told his father he'd bought them but actually the first edition and the manuscript were free!'

'Free?'

'Yes. Exactly my reaction, Valeria.'

'How come?'

Hertie exhaled. 'He stole them.'

'Stole them?'

'You're beginning to sound a bit like a parrot, my dear, but that's precisely how I too reacted. I kept repeating his words. I was shocked. Yet another criminal act from my husband whom I believed so honest, kind and charming.'

'So, how did he do it?'

'He first had the honest intention of buying the book and asked Ludovico how much he wanted for it but the Duke said it wasn't for sale. Apparently later, Maria Eduarda told Gerald that her father might sell almost any treasure in his various mansions but never the book or the manuscript pages. Gerald said he couldn't stop thinking about the two precious items. He wanted them, felt he must have them – a bit like the way he treated Maria Eduarda...Anyway, he added he thought it wasn't fair that the Duke owned so many precious items. Paintings. Sculptures. Porcelain. Ancient books. Antique furniture and whatever else. So he devised a plan. It'd be an adventure. Risky, daring. Just the sort of thing Gerry enjoyed in those days. So, he broke into the house and stole the two precious items, feeling certain the Duke wouldn't care and eventually forget they'd gone because he owned plenty of valuable possessions.'

'How did he do it?'

'In his own words, he concocted an audacious plan. He'd noticed during his visit escorting the royal guests that neither the book nor the manuscript were particularly secure. The glass case and the vitrine were locked and of course Maria Eduarda's father had the keys at all times but the glass was easy to shatter, simple, common glass; no safety or armoured glass. During his visit with the royal guests, Gerry had time to get to know the mansion and its grounds well. He knew where to go and exactly what to do.'

Hertie paused for another drink of water. Then she picked up the story's thread again, 'one winter night, in mid-December 1941, my husband drove to Sintra in an old embassy car, which he was allowed to use. As long as it wasn't the ambassador's limousine, no-one controlled who took the motors out, especially if these were to be scrapped at the end of the year. Gerry drove one of those. He parked the car, leaving it hidden from casual passers-by on the road close to the mansion. It was around three in the morning and unlikely anyone was out and about but he didn't want to risk it. Under the cover of darkness and the thick woods that formed part of the estate, he walked to the house and went directly to the stables, leading out a fast horse – Maria Eduarda's favourite animal. Gerry saddled him and walked in silence across the back garden, guiding the horse to the rear terrace. The library opened onto it, on the ground floor. The horse made no noise and was calm, he remembered my husband from his summer visit. Gerry left him by the terrace, climbed the steps and smashed one of the glass panes of the library door, which made it easy to open. Then he simply walked in, cracked the glass case open and took the book, did the same with the vitrine, grabbed the small glass coffer containing the manuscript, wrapped book and coffer in a large piece of linen he'd taken with him for the purpose, ran out and jumped onto the horse, disappearing in the woods. After reaching the road he wiped the saddle and reins of his fingerprints, letting the horse go. The animal would of course return home. Gerry climbed in the car with his bounty, drove back to Lisbon through the night and entered the embassy before daybreak. No-one the wiser. He hid both items under socks, pants and undershirts in the drawers of his private embassy quarters. Nobody suspected him. At the time of returning to England, he placed the book and the small coffer in his suitcases and dispatched them. Being part of the diplomatic corps, officially the private secretary of the British Ambassador in Lisbon, no-one checked his luggage.'

'And no-one saw him?' Valeria cut in.

Hertie shook her head. 'No, but he was lucky. Maria Eduarda heard noises, got up and walked downstairs. She peered in the library, saw the glass splinters on the floor, the open door and glimpsed the back of a man jumping onto her favourite horse and disappearing in a fast gallop in the woods.'

'How do you know that?'

'As I've said, Gerald was one of the invitees to the New Year's party in the Duke of Beja's estate in Alentejo. That's where he forced himself on Maria Eduarda. Anyway, the theft was just a couple of weeks earlier. She, her family and friends spoke about it. They told him what had happened. Gerry played the innocent, of course, pretending to be distraught at the loss of such precious items.'

'And Maria Eduarda wasn't suspicious?'

'How could she be? Apparently she wasn't even certain the figure she'd seen fleeing on her horse was a man. She said it looked like a man but she wasn't sure. Gerry took precautions. For example, he'd covered his conspicuous platinum blonde hair with a black woolly hat and was wearing a worker's clothes. The horse returned later but there was no sign of the man. The police found nothing. Gerry said he'd been proud of himself, though when he confessed his crimes to me he said he regretted everything he'd done.'

'What did you tell him?'

Hertie's shoulders dropped. Turning her palms up with a resigned sigh she asked rhetorically, 'what could I have told him?'

'You forgave him yet again?'

'On the surface, yes, I forgave him everything,' she paused and breathing out added, 'but I showed him my disapproval, my disgust and disappointment. I told him that not only had he disgraced a girl, he'd also stolen from her father. I said it was criminal and that I didn't really know the man I'd been married to all those years – he was a stranger and a felon and such a man was the father of my children.'

'How did he react?'

Hertie wiped off a tear with her fingers, a feeling of heaviness oppressing her chest. Quietly she replied, 'he begged me not to tell the children. I just shook my head and he grabbed my hand and pleaded with me, urging me to forgive him. He said he'd confessed his actions…' she parted her lips in sadness, 'he never called them crimes, just ill-advised actions. Puh! As if. He added he wasn't proud of what he'd done but he thought his agonising death, far too early, at only forty-seven, was punishment enough. Then he implored whether I couldn't find it in my heart to forgive a dying man.'

'And presumably you did,' Valeria placed a comforting hand on her shoulder and Hertie felt grateful for her sympathy.

'I did forgive him, yes. What else could I have done? He was right. To die at the age of forty-seven of such a harrowing disease, suffering excruciating pain was punishment enough. The thought of leaving his three children fatherless and not be able to watch them grow up devasted him. The illness had ravaged his body and his sadness was very near desperation. He no longer was the Gerald I'd fallen in love with. So I promised him I'd never tell the children and that in my heart, I still loved him and had forgiven his many sins to me and others. He died in peace.'

Valeria's Journal, March 2020

I was astonished when Hertie told me of her husband's deathbed confession. Gerald Neale got Maria Eduarda pregnant by forcing himself on her, but it wasn't the only thing he did. There was so much my family and I were unaware of. And Hertie was determined to put right some of the wrong her husband had done. No-one knew what had happened to Maria Eduarda. At least my mother and my aunts had no idea. My grandfather might have known the whereabouts of his daughter in the last years of his life but whether he did or not, he never breathed a word to anyone. Not to Rosa, my grandmother. Not to any of his daughters. By all accounts Maria Eduarda disappeared without a trace. I don't know whether my aunt Ana Maria knew anything. But we never met her. The family had lost contact with her. She was the daughter of Ludovico's second wife, sixteen years younger than Maria Eduarda. She emigrated to the States and married there before we were born. She didn't come to her father's funeral because no-one had a current address for her.

It was strange to say the least that the man who got my mysterious aunt pregnant had later married Hertie who was to become one of my best friends. I'm not one for coincidences. They hardly ever exist. I don't believe in fate or destiny. But what else can I call this reality? A peculiar coincidence is the only fitting description.

Before beginning on her husband's confession, Hertie asked two favours of me. I remember being surprised and wondered what she could possibly want. In her straightforward manner she said, 'the first is that you'll try to trace Maria Eduarda, find out what happened to her and, if she no longer lives, to find her descendants. When you do I'd like you to take me to Portugal or wherever she or her heirs might be living to meet them. Promise?'

I was intrigued.

'Why, Hertie? Why is it so important?' I asked her.

'You'll understand when I tell you what I intend to do with the items Gerald stole. Now, do you promise?'

'Yes, of course I do.'

'Thank you.'

'What's the second favour? You mentioned two.'

I had no idea what to make of it all.

She quietly whispered, 'As you know, I've been using the digital recorder my grandson gave me,' she paused, visibly mulling over something, then resumed, 'I've been recording what I know about Gerald, as well as my own memories of the war in Germany but from my perspective, I mean from the eyes of the child I was at the time.' She stopped for another moment then added, 'one day I'd like you to use my notes and write a book.'

My jaw dropped. I was speechless. Hertie stared visibly anxious at me, perhaps fearing I might say no.

'But why me?'

'I trust you. You're a dear friend, Schätzchen.'

I remember swallowing to clear the lump in my throat, touched at her confidence in me and my abilities. Gradually I recovered my voice and managed to utter quietly, 'it'll be an honour.'

She smiled, visibly happy. 'I'd prefer you to write it as if it were a novel,' she told me, 'and change the names. People in the family or close friends will guess but others don't need to know. You can do it, can't you?'

I nodded. 'I think so and am truly honoured with the confidence you have in me and my abilities.'

'That's music to my ears, Schätzchen, thank you.'

A comfortable silence fell between us. For a moment I wondered whether to ask her the question ruminating in my head. In the end I did. I had to.

'Why don't you write the book yourself, Hertie?'

She seemed amused and replied in her tranquil, honest way, 'I'm not a good writer. I haven't a book in me but you do…and more than one.'

I was touched.

'You told me,' she continued, 'you lost your voice and had to give up your career as an opera singer…' she halted, as if not sure what to say next, then grinning added 'but I've a hunch it was for the best. You're a natural writer and I believe you'll make a good, solid career out of it. So, you see, I couldn't entrust my stories to anyone else.'

Our friendship became stronger after this and was to become tighter through a third person. I didn't know it then. I only met Hertie's grandson a few months later.

Part 3 – Connecting Dots

(Germany and England 2011-2017)

"The unexpected always happens."

Proverb, late 19th century

Chapter 1 – Xaver

As the plane slowly descended to London Gatwick airport, Xaver glanced out of the window and could see nothing but grey clouds, announcing wet, colourless weather. He recalled the view towards the sea and the promenade from his grandmother's Hove penthouse. Beautiful on a sunny day; featureless and dreary when it rained. However much looking forward to spending Christmas with Oma[21] he dreaded this type of English weather. Earlier in the evening he'd left Munich covered in a blanket of pristine snow, cold but with clear skies. It had snowed during the night, making the city glow in the early hours of the morning as he looked out of the window of his top floor flat overlooking the Englischer Garten – the enormous park in the heart of the city.

In normal circumstances he wouldn't have time off over the holidays. He'd been scheduled to dance the Prince in Tchaikovsky's The Nutcracker but his swollen ankle meant inactivity for at least two weeks. A stupid accident – skidding on ice on the pavement right on his doorstep and twisting his left ankle. It hurt when he put weight on his foot. An x-ray showed it was nothing major but it meant resting. He must regularly apply ice, massage with an anti-inflammatory, wear an elastic bandage when walking and above all must not dance. Miffed at his own clumsiness he decided he might as well make Oma happy, which saw him catching a flight to England on the evening of 22nd December to spend the festive season with her.

The other members of his family might visit on Christmas day but Xaver wouldn't mind if they didn't. He cared about his mother but she was different when his stepfather was around and he would be. Xaver had tired of listening to Darren's disapproval of his career choice and while keeping silent as a teenager so Mother wouldn't be upset, after becoming an adult Xaver answered back. What annoyed him the most was that when Darren was present Mum sided with him.

---

[21] German term of endearment for grandmother, can be translated as Granny or Nana.

Xaver had fallen in love with ballet a long time ago. He was five. His mother took him and his older sisters to a performance of The Nutcracker at Christmas. Their father played the clarinet in the orchestra of the Royal Opera House and could always obtain good tickets for the family. This time they were sitting in row B of the orchestra stalls. Xaver was transfixed and standing on his seat at the end of the Prince's solo in Act II shouted loud and clear, much to his mother's embarrassment, 'I want to do what he did.'

There was laughter from the audience and the artists at the sound of the child's voice. The dancer performing the Prince was German and a guest principal with the Royal Ballet at the time. His name was Roland. He walked to the front of the stage, searching for the child he'd clearly heard at the end of his solo. The lights went on and he could see the little boy, still standing on his seat, his face glowing, his eyes shining in wonder, beaming at him. Smiling Roland bowed to Xaver and said, 'come and see me after the performance,' and turning to his mother added, 'I'll arrange it with the stage door.' Then he thanked the audience for their applause, the lights went out and the ballet resumed.

Xaver went into Roland's dressing-room with his parents and his sisters. The conversation that followed saw Xaver being enrolled into local ballet lessons and a few years later into the Royal Ballet School. Eventually he gained a scholarship to the famous Mariinsky in St. Petersburg in Russia, returning to the Royal Ballet at its end, easily ascending through the company ranks; then moved as First Soloist to the English National Ballet. He had kept in contact with the man who'd inspired him as a child and the same Roland, artistic director of the Bavarian State Ballet in Munich, invited him to join as a Principal. Xaver accepted. After his parents' divorce – he was only ten – Roland had been paramount in supporting his dancing career and Xaver looked up to him professionally and as a kind of second father figure. Their friendship continued.

In contrast and right from the start Darren was vocal about his disapproval of a career in ballet for a boy. The disliked stepfather had come into his life two years after his parents' divorce. Xaver was twelve when his mother married Darren. Throughout his teenage years he endured Darren's sneers; the mildest being that 'ballet was for sissies'. His jeering, belittling ballet dancers, ended when Xaver turned eighteen. By then he was taller than Darren. His body strong and athletic. No longer afraid of Darren's bullying Xaver asked him whether he could lift his mother above his head. Darren laughed in his face, saying lifting a skinny woman up in the air wasn't a way of measuring a real man. Xaver wasn't an aggressive person but the glass, already spilling through years of insults, simply exploded. He lost it and punched his stepfather on the nose, flattening him on the floor.

'Who's a sissy now?' he shouted, his voice dripping with sarcasm.

From that day onward their relationship deteriorated further. Because of his mother, Xaver spoke to Darren when absolutely necessary. He didn't wish to upset her but couldn't help feeling elated when for family occasions Mum came on her own. Sadly it didn't happen as often as he'd like.

Yawning Xaver wondered whether his uncles were coming to Oma's on Christmas Day. He didn't mind them. They were all right. The younger would probably turn up with his wife. The older would as usual be away over the holidays to be with his eldest son and his first grandchild, born only seven months earlier. Xaver's cousin lived in Scotland with his family. The other cousin wouldn't leave the States. He never did. As for his own sisters, they might turn up but they didn't get along with Oma, thinking her too sentimental. Something Xaver believed to be simply silly. Oma was a tender, caring and loving woman. She showed her emotions. Nothing wrong with that. He liked and enjoyed it. The year before his sisters had spent Christmas with their respective boyfriends and their families. What they would do this year was anyone's guess.

The plane shook as it touched down, jolting him out of his reverie. He returned to the rainy reality of England, hoping Oma had done all the necessary shopping. With his injured ankle he'd be little help and didn't really want to walk or drive much. Resting was key for recovery. He wanted to dance again as quickly as possible. Hobbling, he emerged into the arrivals hall and searched for a person bearing a sign with his name but saw no-one. Cursing in silence Xaver took a seat in the nearby chairs from where he could see the terminal's doors to the exterior. His mobile peeped. A message from the taxi driver. There had been an accident on the M23 Northbound just before the airport junction and he was stuck. It would probably be another fifteen minutes or so.

Xaver stood up and limped to the café behind him. He ordered a coffee and a pastry and sat at a table keeping an eye on the terminal entrance, watching the crowds for entertainment. His gaze came to rest on a young woman, probably mid-twenties, with dark hair and a soft profile, eagerly concentrating on the doors from where the passengers emerged as if willing whoever she was waiting for to come out quickly. She wasn't alone. Next to her there were three tall, dark-haired men, possibly in their early thirties who looked remarkably similar. Triplets? Unusual. The woman turned to speak to one of them and Xaver glimpsed a pair of clear brown eyes and a smile he thought radiant. She wasn't a beauty but there was something about her – warmth. Yes, he thought, warmth. And that smile made her pretty. Just then the doors slid open and a large group of people – men and women, young and old, teenagers and three young children – walked out with their luggage. The young woman with the radiant smile jumped up and down, excitedly waving both her arms up in the air. The three men waved but stopped short of jumping. The children saw them first. Beaming like cute Cheshire cats all three ran towards them. The young woman with the radiant smile dropped on her knees and simultaneously hugged all three kids. Then the two little girls and a boy let go of the woman and in turn put their arms around the legs of the three men. There was a lot of embracing and cheek kissing between the large group that had just arrived and the four waiting for them. Everyone seemed to be speaking at the same time, gesticulating with hands and arms. Xaver had never seen anything like it. He felt touched. There was so much obvious joy, love, warmth and tenderness among them that Xaver couldn't help but feel envious. He wished that large family were his own. His Oma aside there were hardly any manifestations of affection in his.

He continued to watch, observing much confusion, excited gestures and loud speaking before they appeared to know what to do next. For a moment Xaver thought they might be Russian due to the numerous "sh" sounds he could hear when they spoke but, paying closer attention, he realised it wasn't a Slavic language. He recalled his colleague from Portugal at the Bavarian State Ballet, his soft accent was similar. The language they were speaking was Portuguese. He should've guessed it straight away. He didn't speak it but knew French, German, Russian and Spanish and it really didn't sound like any of them. Besides, the whole family definitely looked Southern European – dark hair, dark eyes.

Since his driver hadn't yet turned up and Xaver was enjoying watching the group so much, he decided to follow them for a bit while they left for the car park. With his faltering steps he needed to look where he placed his feet. Another fall would be dreadful and aggravate his injury. He heard one of the children say something, then the other two joining in a sort of chorus. Xaver looked up and at that moment, without warning, the young woman with the radiant smile turned and bumped into him. He lost his balance and had to lean against the nearby pillar in order not to fall.

'Oh, I'm so sorry,' she said apologetically, looking up into his eyes with that luminous smile, 'I didn't see you. Are you okay? Did I hurt you?'

There was a musical quality to her voice. He immediately grasped why he thought her so attractive. She radiated goodness, sympathy, affection. It seemed to flow out of her and float through the air directly to his heart as she smiled.

'I'm fine. Don't worry,' he said.

'Oh good. So sorry again. I need to get drinks for the children before we leave and was in a hurry. I should've looked where I was going but must admit I didn't.'

'No harm done,' he smiled back, tempted to add that lovely girls such as her could bump into him any time. She had no accent when she spoke English and sounded well-educated. Perhaps born and bred in this country but with family in Portugal, he decided. From a distance Xaver watched as she returned to her family with drinks for the three kids. He hopped slowly to the car park behind them. They had four minibuses and split themselves and their luggage evenly and orderly between the four. Once everyone was accommodated comfortably and seatbelts fastened, the girl and the triplets each slid into the drivers' seats. As they drove slowly away Xaver found himself wondering whether one of the triplets was her husband. But she had no wedding ring. He'd checked. Perhaps boyfriend or partner then.

What did it matter, he thought? He'd never see her or the family again. Dragging himself back to the terminal he resumed his seat in the waiting area. After another twenty minutes he finally spotted a man running in and holding a sign with his name – Xaver Du Vergier – as usual misspelt. Few people used the correct French Duverger. The downside of having a non-English father. His grandfather had immigrated to France from the French-Guyana and married a girl from Marseille. Xaver's father was the sole remaining offspring of the union. There had been a sister who died as a child. His grandparents never spoke about her and his father didn't remember her. Xaver's granddad was black but his grandmother was a very pale white redhead with eyes so light blue they appeared the colour of ice. Even though his father was mixed race, he'd inherited the red hair of his mother and the dark brown eyes of his father. His skin had a light colour, appearing tanned rather than black. Xaver took after him except for his hair – brown rather than red. People were often surprised to learn his grandfather was a black man. Not that Xaver cared one way or the other. He was proud of his heritage and the mixtures in his blood – Guyanese, French, German and English.

Hertie was over the moon when she finally hugged her grandson. Kissing both his cheeks she stepped back to look at him properly.

Nearly eighteen months since she'd last seen him. He didn't appear to have changed. Gazing up she lifted her hand and touched his hair, then his face.

'Oma,' he exclaimed taking her into his arms for a second time, 'it's so good to see you. I've missed you.'

Hertie's heart leaped. He was the only one of her grandchildren that called her by the German term of endearment for grandmother – Oma. And she loved it.

'I've missed you too,' she replied in an emotional voice.

She and Xaver exchanged e-mails, messages and phone calls regularly but none of it was remotely similar to having him physically there, in front of her, able to touch, hold or hug him. In the interminable, dark winter evenings Hertie frequently longed for her grandson. His elegant movements, pirouetting around the flat to the sound of music or his off-key singing cheered her up immensely. She found joy in looking at his soft eyes and brown hair often dishevelled or watching the graceful movements of his hands. She craved his dear, loving smile but, most of all, deeply missed their conversations. Xaver would discuss any subject with her. It made her feel young and relevant.

'You know where your room is,' she told him.

Smiling he rolled his suitcase towards the bedroom.

'You're limping,' shocked, Hertie stated the obvious, 'what happened? That crazy woman with a fixation on you? She attacked you again?'

'No, Oma, not for a year now. No sign of her since the court restraining order.'

'Good. When I think she could have killed…' Hertie's voice faltered. She found hard to even contemplate that Xaver might have died. The woman in question had started waiting for him at the stage door after each of his performances. At first he hadn't noticed her. She followed him home several times and began leaving messages in his letter box, stating how much she loved him. And one day, as he was walking out of a restaurant with his then girlfriend, the woman attacked the girl, pushing her to the ground but fortunately causing no injuries. Then she had brandished a pistol at Xaver and screamed she'd kill him if he dated other women. Two men passing by were able to subdue her. It turned out the gun wasn't real, although a good imitation. Simply a water pistol. Fearing it could escalate Xaver pressed charges. The woman spent a few months in a psychiatric clinic, then was obliged to carry out community service and finally received a court restraining order. She wasn't permitted within one hundred metres of his person or risk imprisonment. Hertie asked, 'so if it wasn't her, what happened?'

'A simple accident, Oma. I slipped on black ice outside my door.'

'So you can't dance.' It was a statement rather than a question but Xaver answered.

'Not for two or three weeks. I've been replaced for the festive period.'

'Oh, Xavy. I'm so sorry, darling. You must be really upset.'

'It's okay,' he said graciously, 'It wasn't a new role and besides, if I hadn't injured myself I wouldn't be here to spend Christmas and New Year with you. Everything has a bright side.'

Hertie beamed at him. Xavy was a treasure.

Chapter 2 – Oma's Tale

One morning after the festive days were over, Xaver woke to the noise of the coffee machine. Oma was preparing breakfast. Stretching, he thought how nice it was to be with her. She pampered him. Sometimes too much. Meanwhile, with such a great deal of love and care his ankle had recovered. Three days earlier he managed to complete some basic ballet exercises in his grandmother's spacious living room. After warming up he felt no pain so decided to try a few more complicated movements. First he did a series of simple sautées[22] and feeling no strain or lack of strength ventured into a few entrechat quatres[23], beautifully achieved. It made him confident enough to resume daily training, naturally in a reduced format since he was limited to Oma's lounge. He had another nine days with her. Lovely. He'd be fully rested by the time of his return flight to Munich, scheduled for Saturday, 14th January.

Listening to the noises of his grandmother laying the table for breakfast he yawned and stretched again. Christmas and New Year had been all right. Better than expected. The family came for lunch on Christmas Day, including one of his sisters but for once there were no arguments. His stepfather had been unusually muted and not mentioned Xaver's career a single time. Grateful but surprised he wondered why Darren was so quiet and asked his mother when Darren went out to walk their dog.

She told him there were redundancies in Darren's firm and he was worried for his future. Xaver didn't wish his stepfather ill but the news came with a positive. Darren kept his mouth shut thus Christmas went by in peace and harmony. New Year had been an even quieter affair, just himself and Oma. Rather enjoyable. Relaxing. Something Xaver had missed in the last four months. Too many guest appearances across Europe and

---

[22] sautées – simply means jumps in classical ballet.
[23] entrechat quatres – in classical ballet means interweaving. It describes when a dancer jumps into the air and beats their legs by changing the position of their legs and feet to the front or back of each other. The number at the end indicates how many times they do it. So quatre is four times.

performances in Munich. He hadn't told Oma yet but the Royal Ballet had invited him for twelve months as an on and off special guest artist, starting at the end of April. He knew they were keen to have him as principal and perhaps this invitation was a lead up to the more formal job offer. Xaver wasn't sure if he wished to leave Munich. He liked Germany and loved the city. His German was now fluent and he'd made many friends among the company but also outside of it. The time with the Royal Ballet as special guest artist would be a good experience. Not a permanent position; he'd continue to perform with his Munich company, commuting between the two countries, as well as whatever guest appearances might come his way. But at the end of it he would have an accurate idea of what it meant to be a principal with them. If the offer came he'd have his answer ready. New York was also lined up. Four weeks in the summer with the American Ballet Theater for Don Quixote. No hesitation there. He had immediately accepted and was looking forward to it. A brief knock on his bedroom door interrupted his thoughts.

'Xavy, you awake?'

Grinning he replied, 'yes, Oma. I'll be right out.'

'Good. Everything's ready.'

Shortly after he entered the kitchen wearing only his pyjamas. Oma, in her dressing gown, was already sitting at the table. She poured coffee, pushed yoghurt, cereal and fruit in his direction and asked whether he'd like some toast. Agreeing he began spooning the contents of his bowl and watched as she placed bread in the toaster. A moment later Xaver stopped his spoon mid-air.

'What's the matter?' his grandmother asked him.

Lifting his finger he said, 'you hear that?'

'What?'

'Piano. Someone's playing the piano...or listening to piano music. Nice. Pretty good, actually.'

'Oh, yes, of course. She's back. I'd forgotten.'

'Who?' Xaver asked, puzzled, 'who's back?'

'Valeria. She must have returned yesterday. I think she mentioned she'd be back soon after New Year's day, once her family had flown home.'

'Valeria? Your new friend? The lady who's moved into the penthouse next door?'

'That's right. Her lounge shares a wall with mine. That's where she's got the piano so we can hear her play. Even here, in the kitchen.'

'Plays well,' Xaver said appreciatively.

'She does. In fact that puts me in mind. You're still here this coming Saturday, aren't you?'

'Yes. Why?'

'I'd like you to meet Valeria. I thought I could invite her for dinner while you're still around.'

He wasn't enthusiastic, had no interest in meeting her friend, but didn't want to upset Oma. She mentioned the woman in most of her e-mails.

'What does she do besides play the piano,' he asked, resuming eating.

His grandmother told him what she had learned of Valeria's history.

'So she still plays,' he said as she finished.

'Oh, yes. She loves it too much.'

'Valeria's an unusual name. Is she British?'

'Yes…well, I suppose you could say fifty-fifty. Her full name's Valeria Silva-Strachan. Father Scottish; mother Portuguese.'

'Uh-huh,' he replied, his attention turning to his mobile as a little jingle signalled a new message.

Hertie was keen for her grandson to meet Valeria, certain he'd like her. Xavy was the apple of her eyes and the girl had become a dear friend. Dinner it would be. Hertie knew Xaver would be polite if only to make her happy. After breakfast, while he was in the shower, she rang Valeria's doorbell and issued the invitation. Her agreement thrilled Hertie, leaving her cheerful for the rest of the day.

Later that evening, having a nightcap with her grandson, Hertie decided it was time to tell him hers and his grandfather's story. Xaver never met his grandfather. He'd died when Xaver's mother was a young child. But Valeria was now familiar with the facts and Hertie felt it was important to make her favourite grandchild aware, hoping he would support Valeria with the enterprise.

'Xavy,' Hertie said, 'I'd like to tell you something. You know your grandfather's book collection?'

'You mean the first editions?'

'Yes,' she said, nodding.

'How could I forget? I love books, like you. I appreciate your decision that one day the collection will be mine.'

'Yes. Not only the collection. When I die this flat will be yours—'

'Oma,' he interrupted, 'that's too generous. I think—'

She stopped him. 'No. Don't oppose me. I made the decision a long time ago. It's written in my will. Other possessions will go to my children but the flat is to help you in your life, your career. As for the books, that's in the will too. I think you're the only one in the whole family who loves books the same way I do…and perhaps, yes, also as your grandfather did.'

'Thank you, Oma. It's really generous of you.'

'No more than I think you deserve.'

'And what's this you want to tell me? Is it about the collection?' he asked, his voice betraying his emotion.

'To a certain extent,' she paused, searching for appropriate words, 'it's a long story.'

He grinned. 'You know I like long stories. And we've got all the time in the world.'

Delighted, Hertie asked him, 'will you get me another Port, please, mein Schatz? My throat will need some lubrication. I'll be speaking for a while.'

Once he'd returned with two full glasses Hertie said, 'the story might shock you even though you never met your granddad. He wasn't the man the family thought him to be but…' she paused, then grabbing his hand said, 'Xavy, you must promise me that everything I'm about to tell you will stay between us. I don't want your mother or your uncles…no-one in the family to find out.'

Bewildered he agreed, 'I promise, Oma. You can trust me.'

'Good.'

Hertie sipped from her Port then added, 'the story also concerns Valeria and—'

'Your new friend? The pianist next door?' He sounded puzzled.

'The very same. She already knows the whole story. Now it's your turn and it'll stay between the three of us…at least until I die. After that, anyone may know. And when I've finished my tale I need a favour too.'

'Goes without saying.'

Xaver felt suddenly worried. Oma appeared rather serious. Nervous. Perhaps upset. What could possibly be so wrong about Grandfather? Had he harmed anyone? Committed a crime? Done something immoral? Xaver had no idea but it must be grim. Oma's eyes were full of tears. He stood up, placed his glass of Port on the low table in front of them and knelt on the carpet, leaning his head on her knees, as he had done as a little boy when she read him a story. Quietly he waited for her to speak.

She took another sip and began. Xaver could hardly believe his ears. Of course he had never known Gerald. His own mother hardly remembered him, being only four years old at the time of his death, but Oma had always said he was a wonderful man. Listening to his infidelities was bad enough but the shocking story of Thorp, of Maria Eduarda and the horrors of Oma's childhood at the end of the war in Germany left him speechless. The connection to Oma's friend Valeria was also surreal.

He held his breath as she continued to speak. What had happened to her was appalling. The escape from East Prussia, the hunger, the cold, all the horrible events in Germany must be unimaginably traumatic for anyone, particularly a child. Astonishing really that Oma had turned out as she had.

It was nearing midnight when she ended her narrative. Baffled, rattled at everything he'd heard, Xaver turned to hug her.

'Oma,' he said sincerely, 'you're an extraordinary woman. I'm glad I never met Granddad. What he did to you and especially to that Maria Eduarda and his colleague Thorp was just despicable.'

'He never treated me or the children badly.'

'But he didn't respect you. That's awful.'

'You're right but at the time...well...anyway it was all a long time ago,' she shrugged, then added, 'but there's something more.'

'More? Good God, what else did he do?'

'No, it's not about your grandfather,' she paused and Xaver waited for her to continue.

'I've asked Valeria to write a book about all this, which I'd like her to publish one day after I'm gone.'

'Is she a good writer?'

'I'm certain of it. The other thing is I've also asked her to try and track down Maria Eduarda and if she does—'

'But Oma,' he interjected, 'you said Maria Eduarda was only two years younger than Grandfather. She'd be now...what?'

'Ninety-one.'

'You think she can still be alive?'

'I've no idea, Xavy, but it's possible.'

'Anyway, carry on. You've asked Valeria to try and track down Maria Eduarda...'

'Yes, or her descendants. If she gave birth to Gerald's child and he or she is alive I want him or her to have the book. It's theirs by right. Your grandfather stole it. And the manuscript. If there's no-one and Maria Eduarda's dead, I think both should go to Valeria and her family. They don't belong to us.'

Xaver considered the matter. Oma was right. It was the proper thing to do, as a way of mildly atoning for all his grandfather's wrongdoing.

'I agree.'

'I'm glad, Schätzchen.'

'You mentioned needing a favour too?'

'More of a request, really.'

'Which is?'

'If or when Valeria finds Maria Eduarda or her descendants, I want to travel to Portugal or to whatever place they might be with her and I'd like you to go with me—'

'But of course,' he cut in.

'Haven't finished yet. The other thing's when Valeria starts writing the book. I'd like you to help her with it. I'd like you to organise my notes – it'll make things easier for her – and I want you to sort out the photos. There are some I think she should include.'

Perplexed Xaver couldn't help but ask, 'you don't trust Valeria to do it on her own?'

'Of course I trust her. It's not that.'

'Then what?'

'It's a lot to ask of a friend. The family should help her...with anything that might be important,' she seemed to waver but at last added, 'in our family, the only one I implicitly trust to carry out the task and do it well, is you, my darling.'

Deeply moved, Xaver said, a lump in his throat, 'thank you for your faith in me, Oma. I promise to do as you wish.'

She seemed pleased and held his face between her hands. Gently pulling his head down she placed a kiss on his forehead and announced it was time for bed.

Chapter 3 – The Woman with the Radiant Smile

The morning broke grey. Cold. The lack of light was depressing. Xaver stretched and looked at his mobile. New e-mails in his inbox. He'd check them after showering and having breakfast.

Half an hour later, as he switched on his laptop, his eyes rested briefly on Oma's desk calendar. Why had she circled the day and scribbled a time – 19.00 hrs? Saturday, 7th January 2012. No special date he could think of. So, why... but then it dawned on him. The dinner with Oma's pianist neighbour and friend.

Xaver had to admit to being mildly curious about this Valeria. Oma spoke of her so affectionately. He decided to google her but couldn't remember her surname and didn't want to ask his grandmother, fearing it might unnerve her he was trying to check out her friend.

The day went on lazily. He helped his grandmother with the shopping, exercised during the afternoon and after another shower, sat to read until it was time to help with dinner. He could hear the piano next door. Valeria was practising. First she seemed to only be doing scales and arpeggios, probably warming up her fingers but then she began on a piece he recognised. It was a Lied – the first in Schubert's song cycle to Walter Scott's Lady of the Lake, consisting of seven songs composed in 1825. She played extremely well. He wondered why she was practising the piece but then remembered Oma had said Valeria sometimes accompanied some of her friends' recitals. It must be it then. He also knew she wrote on a freelance basis reviews about music and conducted interviews with classical artists. Her way of subsidising her studies. Sensing his eyelids dropping Xaver decided to do a few more exercises, unwilling to fall asleep on the couch. Later he helped prepare dinner.

Punctually at seven in the evening, the doorbell rang, echoing throughout the flat. Xaver shouted to his grandmother in the kitchen, 'I'll get the door, Oma. I've finished laying the table. Check whether it's to your liking.'

'Okay. Thank you, Schatz.'

Opening the door Xaver said, 'good evening, you must

be…' but then stopped abruptly, startled. The woman with the radiant smile stood in front of him. The one from the airport. And she was smiling. At him. She seemed puzzled at his reaction. Only then did Xaver realise his absurd behaviour.

'Forgive me,' he said, 'I was expecting someone different. Are you Valeria?'

'Yes. You must be Xaver.'

'I am. Please come in. Oma…I mean Hertha's in the kitchen.'

Valeria gave him again that wondrous radiant smile. 'I know Oma means Granny or Nana in German. I speak it too. I think it's lovely you address your grandmother as Oma. It sounds so tender, caring.'

'Thank you,' he said pleased, realising she was prettier than he remembered. Her eyes were warm, chocolate brown and her hair was dark, neatly cut at mid height, touching her neck. She wore black flat shoes, black jeans with a black cotton turtleneck and a bright red cashmere cardigan. Fused glass earrings in red, matching the cardigan, brightened her face. She wore no make-up, except for a whiff of mascara. Her skin appeared smooth, fresh like a peach ripened in the summer sun. His grandmother came out of the kitchen saying everything was ready and he could serve the aperitifs. She kissed Valeria on both cheeks and they hugged affectionately. After the drinks, they sat at table to begin their meal.

As a starter there was a prawn cream soup with lightly toasted bread and salted butter. It was delicious and Xaver commented sincerely, 'you exceeded yourself with this, Oma. One of the best soups I've ever eaten.'

'Thank you, darling.'

'Xaver's right, Hertie, it's truly fantastic.'

It was followed by a roasted seabass fillet stuffed with fine herbs, accompanied by roasted potatoes and cauliflower, washed with a lovely Portuguese white wine from the Douro Valley. Conversation was soon flowing.

'Valeria,' his grandmother asked, 'have you received any work? You mentioned before Christmas you were expecting some good stuff early in the new year. And you look happy, relaxed.'

Valeria beamed and Xaver was left gazing at her in pure delight. Lovely woman. He'd like to know her better.

'Yes,' she was answering Oma, 'as a matter of fact, I did. Paid work all of it. Feel very lucky. I got requests for three reviews of classical concerts, an interview with a pianist and a recital series where I'll be accompanying one of my singer friends in concerts of Schubert, Wolf and Schumann's Lieder. Good money. I'll have to miss a few lectures but that won't be an issue. I can catch up in the evenings.'

'Is your friend singing Schubert's cycle of seven songs to Walter Scott's Lady of the Lake by any chance?' Xaver asked her.

Raising her eyebrows Valeria seemed surprised.

'How do you know that?'

'I heard you practise this morning,' he replied, 'and recognised the first song in that cycle.'

'Oh. Do you like Schubert?'

'I do and the reason why I know that particular cycle so well is because in Munich I danced in a modern ballet, choreographed by our Munich choreographer in residence to that music two years ago or so.'

'I'd love to see it.'

'You appreciate ballet?'

'Immensely.'

'And opera?'

She remained silent for a moment. Xaver remembered Oma telling him Valeria had wanted to become an opera singer but had lost her voice through illness. Calling himself stupid for his lack of tact he regretted asking the question. Too late. But she didn't seem upset and answered graciously, 'I adore opera. Becoming an opera singer was my first career choice. Sadly, it didn't work out. But it's okay. I've accepted it and moved on to other professions. I love to write and translate so what I'm doing fulfils me too and my degrees, once completed, will help me obtain more and better work. Besides, I didn't leave the music behind.'

'Of course not. You're a talented pianist,' he said sincerely, 'you could make a career out of it.'

'I know...and I enjoy doing it occasionally for former colleagues or friends who are singers...but otherwise I'd rather not. It wouldn't have the same flavour,' she grinned and added, 'I'm rather fussy about flavours.'

Oma laughed. Xaver thought Valeria was adorable. Then, out of the blue, she asked him whether he'd give her an interview.

'You want to interview me?' he exclaimed, unable to hide his surprise.

'Yes,' she confirmed and glancing at his grandmother added, 'Hertie spoke often of you, your passion for ballet and the rather neat, cute tale of how you decided you wanted to become a ballet dancer. I found parallels to my passion for opera. Your story seems interesting. So – and I hope you don't mind – I googled you. I know you're a principal with the Bayerisches Staatsballet in Munich. I found photos and videos of your performances, which I thoroughly enjoyed watching. I must compliment you on the quality of your dancing. Your elegance, the beauty of your movements and your technical prowess impressed me. You appear to dance as a guest artist all over the world, which I believe vouches for your supreme talent. And I read a few reviews and articles about you, one interview and even a brief report on your stalker. It all confirmed you'd make an engaging subject for an interview. I'm sure I could get one of the digital magazines I write for interested.'

Caught unawares Xaver decided he must pay her a compliment too. He'd already praised her playing and wondered whether to tell her something else but decided against it, not knowing her well enough for a more personal tribute.

'Well, thank you,' he finally said, feeling simultaneously excited and flattered, 'you're rather good at tickling the ivories yourself if I may speak informally.'

She laughed. 'Naturally.'

'I'll be honoured to give you an interview,' he said, taking her hand and pretending to kiss it in a delicately gallant gesture.'

Her gaze sparkled, appearing thrilled with his agreement.

'I'll keep you informed once I've proposed my idea for an interview with you to the people who sometimes commission work from me.'

He nodded, noticing not for the first time the twinkle in his grandmother's eyes. She knew. She always did. Perceptive and in tune with his taste and moods she had grasped he was becoming very fond of her friend. Xaver looked at her and smiling shook his head almost imperceptibly. Valeria didn't appear to notice the exchange of glances between himself and Oma. She was still speaking about the magazines that might be interested in publishing her interview with him. Feeling a little awkward he stood up, began taking the plates and announced dessert was Oma's delicious baked apples with brown sugar and cinnamon.

'Accompanied with a glass of Port,' his grandmother added, 'not because you're half Portuguese, Valeria, but because I love it.'

They all laughed. Xaver walked to the kitchen and Oma followed him. Valeria remained at the table.

Hertie began portioning dessert into the lined up plates, glancing sideways at her grandson carefully pouring Port in the glasses and preparing the espresso machine for coffee. A cheeky glimmer in her eyes she said matter of fact, 'she's lovely, isn't she?'

'Sorry, didn't catch what you said,' he replied, without looking her in the eye.

'It's her smile, isn't it?'

'Who're you talking about, Oma?' He seemed surprised.

'Oh, I think you know.'

To her delight, Xaver appeared a little embarrassed as if unsure where to look. He stopped the bottle of Port mid-air, lifted his gaze and grinning said, 'you're so naughty, Oma,' then shaking his head added, 'yes, she's lovely. Yes, I find her attractive and yes, I like her. Happy now?'

Hertie laughed aloud, throwing her head back, then

suddenly turning serious commented, 'you seemed bewildered when she came in. Did you expect her to be different?'

'No…well, yes, I guess. The thing is I've seen her before and found her and her family engaging. Just didn't expect to ever see her again.'

'Really? What're you talking about? And how would you know her family?'

'I don't know her family and I didn't know her until she came here. I said I'd seen her and her family before.'

'Oh? Tell me.'

Xaver related the episode at the airport while waiting for the taxi driver to pick him up, finishing with, 'I thought her good-looking, charming and the whole family just so…lovely and interesting. They seemed to get along really well and to genuinely love each other. I remember thinking that apart from you, Oma, I've never seen anyone in our family show half as much affection for each other as Valeria and her family at the airport.'

Hertie smiled. 'I'm an affectionate person. So glad you think I show it openly, mein Schatz.'

'It's true, Oma.'

He went quiet for a moment, resuming his task pouring the Port. Getting the coffee machine ready he appeared to hesitate, debating with himself.

'Something on your mind, darling?' Hertie asked, without glancing at him and pretending to give her full attention to the already full dessert plates.

Xaver's silence lasted for another second or two, then shrugging he said, 'oh what the heck…I'd like to know if one of the triplets I saw with her at the airport is her husband…or no, no. She doesn't wear a wedding ring, but her boyfriend, partner perhaps?'

Amused, Hertie replied, 'no. The triplets are her older brothers. They look almost identical. Small differences apparently. They are all the same height and build but, according to Valeria, Afonso's cheekbones are higher than Miguel's or Luis's which means his smile has apparently a bigger impact than the other two and Luis has thicker eyebrows and longer eyelashes than Miguel or Afonso. I didn't notice any of it. To me they looked exactly the same but then I haven't been with them often,' perceiving her grandson was about to open his mouth, she added, 'and to answer your next question, no, she doesn't currently have a boyfriend. There was someone once – years ago but apparently he died in a car crash.'

'How awful.'

'She doesn't talk much about it. I know he was a colleague while she was studying to become an opera singer. They were together throughout her illnesses and the loss of her voice. Then the accident happened and he died. I don't know how or where it took place. I didn't ask. I thought if she wanted to speak about it, she would.'

'Does she still miss him? Mourn his loss?'

'I don't know for certain, Xavy. I don't think so but could be wrong,' Hertie was quiet for a moment then added, 'in any case if you like her, show her you like her, get to know her better. Women like Valeria don't come along frequently.'

Beaming he said amused, 'Oma, you're priceless. If I didn't have you, I'd have to invent you.'

Hertie laughed. 'You silly sausage. Let's go back to the dining room, take the pudding and Port. Valeria may think we've deserted her otherwise.'

Chapter 4 – Next Steps

Dessert and Port ritual completed Xaver began serving the coffee and Hertie decided it was time to talk about serious matters. Turning to Valeria she said, 'I assume you remember Gerry's first editions collection he inherited from his father, plus what he added himself, right?'

'Yes, of course, how could I forget? The walls in your larger spare room are lined with shelves full of books organised by year and then alphabetically. It's a bookworm's paradise,' Valeria grinned as she spoke the last words.

'I'll say,' Xaver commented, 'I've got to sleep in the smaller room. Oma transformed the other into a library.'

Rolling her eyes Hertie resumed, 'anyway what I wanted to say is although I've revealed Gerry's secrets to both of you, secrets I've carried with me for a long time, I haven't shown you the two *real* precious items,' she stressed the word real, 'after his death, I placed the stolen book and manuscript in a secure location and showed them to no-one. It's time you both get to see them.'

Xaver seemed surprised. 'You mean you've got them here, in the flat, Oma?'

'Yes…in the wall safe in my bedroom.'

'You've a wall safe?' Xaver exclaimed, 'wow! Each time I visit you I learn something different.'

Hertie chortled, then turning serious added, 'it wasn't my idea but my predecessor's. The old man who lived here before me, so I've been told, was a miser of sorts. He didn't trust banks or credit cards, not even cheques, only cash. So, he had all his money at home and had a safe built in the wall for the purpose. It used to be opened and closed with a key but your uncle Tobias,' turning to Valeria she said, 'my middle child,' then continued what she'd intended to say, 'who's very security conscious, told me I should upgrade the safe to something more modern with some sophisticated code,' she shrugged, 'so I've done it and keep the book, the manuscript and my jewellery in there.'

Leaving the lounge Hertie glanced over her shoulder at

the two young people. They had easily fallen into relaxed conversation. Unexpectedly she found herself thinking it'd be charming if those two ended up together. Play matchmaker?

'No, no Hertha, bad idea,' she whispered to herself, 'let nature take its course. Don't interfere and don't be a meddling old bat.'

Entering her bedroom, Hertie removed the picture depicting a reproduction from a famous Claude Monet painting – Bridge over a Pond of Waterlilies, based on his garden at Giverny. She punched the code and the safe quietly opened. With great care she took the parcel containing the book and the clear plastic folder with the manuscript, placing them gently on the bed, then closed the safe and replaced the painting on the wall. Returning to the lounge she told her grandson, 'will you please clear the table? Then we can use it to look at the items properly.'

Nodding he stood up, followed by Valeria and together they quickly took everything to the kitchen while Hertie unwrapped the book, packed in various plastic bags, placed it on the table and the manuscript next to it.

'Gerry never touched the book with his bare hands hence these white cotton gloves,' Hertie explained as she pulled them on.

All three of them stood reverently around the table staring at the first edition. Hertie opened it. A moment later Xaver broke the silence.

'Oma,' he said, 'you're sure this is genuine? Perhaps Grandfather invented it all to…I don't know…to impress you.'

'No,' Hertie replied, firmly shaking her head, 'he was dying,' she paused, then added adamantly, 'no-one tells lies on their deathbed.'

Before Xaver had a chance to retort, Valeria jumped in.

'Oh, it's real all right. I've—'

'How do you know?' Xaver interrupted.

'Let her finish, Xavy,' Hertie admonished him, slightly annoyed with her grandson.

'Okay, sorry,' he replied.

'I know it's the real thing,' Valeria resumed, 'because

after you told me the whole story,' she glanced at Hertie who nodded, 'I did some research on various Portuguese websites and digital archives of newspapers of the time Gerald stole the book and the manuscript.'

She lifted her eyes, possibly wondering if Xaver would have another question, Hertie thought quietly. Aloud she said, 'go on.'

Pointing at the book, opened on the first page, Valeria continued, 'if you look at the top of the page, above the title and the poet's name, as part of the decoration you can see a bird – a pelican – its head is turned to the left from the reader's perspective. That's the genuine first edition.'

'There's another?' Xaver asked, appearing surprised.

'Well, as far as I could discover, there was another edition that appeared later in the same year – 1572 – where the pelican's turned to the right. Apparently, for many years there was controversy as to which was the true first edition until it was confirmed that this one, with the pelican looking left, is the most perfect of the two so it must be the one overseen by the poet himself. The other was done without his consent and he didn't revise it, so it contains mistakes, discrepancies. There are allegedly only five or six copies of the real first edition and this is one of them.'

'Wow. I'm impressed.'

Hertie smiled. 'Yes, it's a shame we can't keep it. I want to return it to the rightful owner – Valeria's unknown aunt, Maria Eduarda.'

'If she's still alive,' Xaver commented.

Valeria shrugged. 'We don't know whether she is but, as Hertie must have told you, she'd like me to find out.'

'But Maria Eduarda's your aunt. How come you and your family don't know whether she's still alive?'

'I assume your grandmother told you the whole story?'

'I did,' Hertie confirmed and then with an amused smile added, 'sometimes he's a bit forgetful.'

'So,' Valeria carried on, 'you know that after telling her family she was pregnant, Maria Eduarda disappeared. Her father, my granddad, threw her out. After that no-one knows what happened. There hasn't been any contact.'

'I see. Did you find any further information about the book? And on the manuscript?' Xaver pointed at the old pages inside the clear plastic document holder.

'I found nothing about the manuscript. But I did find accounts of the robbery in some newspapers of the time. They report a precious first edition of Os Lusíadas and pages of a manuscript believed written in the poet's own hand – so Camões,' she pointed at the name on the page, 'were stolen from the Duke of Beja's collection in his Sintra mansion in the early hours of 16th December 1941. The police were baffled. Couldn't find any clues or trace the whereabouts of the items. After a couple of weeks, the newspapers lost interest but still published a couple of articles venturing the book and the manuscript must have been taken secretly across the border to Spain and sold there.'

'Rather fascinating,' Xaver said.

'Isn't it just?' Hertie commented, then turning to the two young people she asked, 'so what're we going to do about it?'

'I thought hiring a private detective in Portugal might be a good idea to trace Maria Eduarda and/or her descendants,' Valeria said.

'Hmm, yes, so did I,' Hertie agreed.

'And how'll you go about it?' Xaver questioned, looking in turn at his grandmother and Valeria, 'will you ask your family to help?'

'No. I don't think so.'

The answer was quick and assertive. Hertie could see her grandson seemed irritated so she explained.

'Valeria and I talked about this before, darling. She doesn't want…and I agree…to tell her family until we know whether Maria Eduarda's still alive. After that, we can reveal the truth. If she still lives, I'll return the book and manuscript to her. If not, to her descendants and if there are no descendants then to Valeria to do as she pleases. It belongs to her and her family.'

'I doubt Maria Eduarda can still be alive,' Xaver

commented, 'how old would she be…what? Late eighties?'

'She'd be ninety-one and turn ninety-two come September,' Valeria said.

'Unlikely don't you think?'

'No. My grandfather lived nearly to a hundred. He died at ninety-nine years old, two months short of his one hundredth birthday.'

'Oh, well then, she may still be alive.'

Hertie changed the subject to what mattered. She wasn't interested in speculating whether Maria Eduarda lived or not.

'The important thing is,' she said, 'Valeria's got a friend in Lisbon who's a detective sergeant in the criminal police force and could help her find a reliable, trustworthy private detective. I thought it a good idea and when we've got one I'll pay for his fees and expenses.'

'Hertie,' Valeria interjected, 'we agreed we'd share the costs.'

'We'll see about that, Schätzchen.'

A long silence followed while they simply stared at the two precious items in front of them on the table. Xaver was the first to speak.

'I can help with the manuscript,' he said, 'if you'd like to find out more about it.'

'You can?' Hertie echoed perplexedly.

'Yes, Oma. Do you remember Luke?'

'Luke? You mean Luke Sinclair, your school friend?'

Xaver nodded.

'What does Luke know about old manuscripts?'

'Nothing but his older brother, Oliver, is curator of old documents and illuminated manuscripts at the British Library.'

'Oliver Sinclair? The wild, handsome one always chasing after pretty girls?'

'The same but he's calmed down. After finishing his degree with honours, he found this job at the British Library and leads a quieter life.'

'Is he married?'

'No. Does it matter, Oma?'

317

'Of course not. At least not for the purpose of the manuscript. I was just curious.'

'Then, all's settled,' Xaver concluded, 'I'll speak to Oliver or ask Luke to do so, Valeria will contact her friend in Lisbon to help find a suitable private detective and you,' he turned and hugged her, 'my darling, dearest Oma, will sit quietly at home and wait for results.'

Pretending to be angry Hertie slapped his wrist and said, 'impudent boy!'

Valeria's journal, April 2020

I offered to take Xaver to the airport on that cold Saturday morning, 14th January 2012. He seemed delighted at the suggestion. I was thrilled. I liked him…a lot. There was something about him that pulled me irresistibly towards him. I felt the attraction surge and spread throughout my being when I first met him at Hertie's dinner. His natural elegance, the unconscious grace of his movements, second nature to most ballet dancers, were undoubtedly seductive but it was what I sensed behind the charm and the style of the man that attracted me – his passion for the ballet, his desire to dance from the heart, sharing his feelings with an audience. I knew that type of passion. I'd felt it for singing and opera. The urgent need to do something so powerful it takes your breath away. I had to overcome it and find another due to illness but Xaver had realised his dream, making it real each time he danced on stage. And it was this that drew me unstoppably to him.

He hugged Hertie lovingly, saying goodbye before we left for the airport. His affection for her was obvious. I found it beautiful and moving. He added she should visit him in Munich soon. Not only to see him dance but also to visit her sister Hedwig.

'You're right,' Hertie agreed, 'I should. I haven't seen Hedi in what…six, seven years, I think, at Helmut's funeral,' turning to me she added, 'he died of cancer. Hedi was devastated. Helmut was her twin. They were always very close.'

'What about your older brother?' I asked her.

'Oh, Heinrich? He's still alive and well. Continues to live in Frankfurt where he went for a job back in the fifties. Again, last time I saw him was at Helmut's funeral.'

'About time you went back to Germany, Oma, don't you think?' Xaver commented.

'You're right, mein Schatz, you're right.'

'You could go with me,' I blurted out.

Xaver stared at me, obviously not understanding but how could he? I hadn't told anyone. So, visibly startled, he enquired, 'you're travelling to Munich?'

'Yes. I meant to tell you both earlier. There's a digital magazine I occasionally write for interested in publishing an interview with you, Xaver. They'll pay for my flight and hotel expenses in Munich.'

'Lovely,' he said, seeming sincere, 'I can't wait.'

'Thank you. So, you could go with me, Hertie. Much nicer than on my own.'

'Yes, Oma, please do.'

'It's not a bad idea.'

'It's a brilliant idea,' he exclaimed, then glancing at me asked, 'what are your plans?'

'The magazine suggested in about eight weeks to coincide with your role debut as Romeo in Romeo and Juliet.'

'You're well informed.'

'I try to be,' I grinned.

As I drove him to the airport I remember he asked me at some stage why I wanted to interview him. I wasn't going to tell him I found him attractive. Besides, in the first instance, it had nothing to do with attraction. I hadn't met him but his tale, as told to me by Hertie, had made me curious. I said as much, adding, 'she's very proud of you. You're the artist in the family.'

He smiled vaguely, appearing a little disappointed but didn't comment. And I thought that maybe, just maybe, he felt attracted to me too.

Two days before leaving for Munich with Hertie, I travelled briefly to my parents to leave Wonkie with them. My cuddly, lovable cat would be better off with my family than in some cattery.

And so eight weeks and a couple of days after delivering Xaver to London Gatwick Airport, Hertie and I arrived in Munich. Xaver's flat was on the edge of Maxvorstadt, popular with students, near the underground station of Giselastrasse, looking over the famous park called The English Gardens. He picked us up at the airport in his little VW-Up, dropped me at my hotel nearby, taking his grandmother to his place.

I completed the interview with Xaver on my second day

in the city. On the third, fourth and fifth days I went with Hertie and met her sister Hedwig. The three of us travelled around to visit some of Munich's most beautiful sites – Marienplatz and the famous Glockenspiel in the Rathaus, Town Council's building, which looks like a cathedral, followed by the beautiful royal residence in the city centre, with the stunning Cuvilliés Theatre where Mozart premiered his opera Idomeneo. Naturally also the English Gardens, the pretty Theatiner church, the famous streets, Schwabing, the various wonderful museums, the university, the fountains dedicated to the Scholl siblings who were killed by the Nazis after having created the resistance movement called the White Rose, the Olympia Park and of course one of the jewels in the crown – the gorgeous Nymphenburg Palace and grounds. We would leave in the morning after Xaver had gone to class, rehearsals and whatever else belongs to the hard daily training of a ballet dancer, only returning in the evening. Exhausted but happy.

Then, out of the blue, on the fifth day as we finished our coffee and cake in one of the lovely Marienplatz cafés, Hertie declared she wanted to visit the former concentration camp in Dachau, located close to the city and now a memorial to the victims of the Nazi atrocities in Germany.

Chapter 5 – Dachau

Shaking her head, Hedwig said, 'I'm not going with you, Hertie. I've visited Dachau twice before, years ago. I was sick for a week. Not going again.'

'I understand, Hedi. But I've never been…and I think…' Hertie glanced away, something brewing inside her head. Looking back at her sister she continued, her voice emotional, 'I think that I owe it to all the ones who were killed in such camps and their surviving families to visit such a place…lest we forget.'

Valeria, standing by her side, seemed moved by her words but Hedi just shook her head for the second time reaffirming her intention of never setting foot in that damned place again. Hertie grasped Hedi's feelings but remained firm in her resolve. Turning to Valeria she asked, 'will you go with me? Please.'

The answer was immediate, 'of course I'll go with you.'

Hertie was pleased. She felt it was her duty to visit such a place and pay her respects to all the victims of the Holocaust but sensed she couldn't do it alone.

Early the next morning, after Xaver had left the flat to go to class, Hertie met Valeria at the Giselastrasse underground station. They travelled on the U3 line to Marienplatz and once there took the S2, the S-Bahn[24] line towards Altmünster, which would stop at Dachau station twenty-six minutes later. From there they needed to get the bus 726 directly to the KZ-Gedenkstätte, then walk approximately two minutes to the memorial site. Hertie was well informed. The evening before she had asked her grandson to search for directions on the internet and write down the information for her. She knew exactly where to go.

As the S-Bahn left Marienplatz, Valeria turned and said to her, 'may I ask you something, Hertie?'

'Of course.'

'Why haven't you visited Dachau or another

---

[24] Schnell Bahn – trains in big cities that connect the city centre to places in the outskirts. They are fast and when in the heart of the cities go underground and work like the common tube.

concentration camp before?'

Hertie shrugged. 'I don't know. I guess...' she paused, then repeated, 'I guess it was never the right time somehow. After Gerald and I married, we left Germany and went to Africa. His work for the foreign office meant we moved frequently. First he was transferred from Germany to Kenya, a couple of years later to South Africa but only for twelve months, then we lived in Bahrain before coming to England for good, mostly because of the children. I seldom travelled to Germany for one reason or other – too far away, trip would take too long, pregnancy...lots of things. I visited my family two or three times with the kids. They never came to England...and otherwise I visited because one of them had died. I couldn't go to my mother's funeral though I visited later. I travelled when my aunt Elsa passed away and of course seven years ago when my brother Helmut died. But none of those few visits left me with any spare time to do this.'

'You could've asked Xaver before to take you there or even this time. I'm sure he'd do it.'

'Oh yes, he would, which is why I didn't ask him.'

Valeria appeared surprised. Raising an eyebrow she exclaimed, 'I don't understand.'

'This is my first visit to Xaver in Munich,' Hertie explained, 'he always comes to England and stays a few days with me.'

'But you didn't ask him to come today.'

'No. He's preparing for his debut in a great role. Romeo is a fantastic part to dance. I've seen the MacMillan production in London with the Royal Ballet. The music is also wonderful and I don't want Xavy to experience something like this. I don't want him to have negativity, horror images inside his head when he dances. He needs to feel love, to put his heart completely into it. Only then will he be able to give an outstanding performance as Romeo. I wouldn't forgive myself if it'd be anything less due to the impact of such a visit on him. Xavy's a young, sensitive man.'

'You adore him, don't you?'

'Yes and he has enormous affection for me. We've a close

relationship which's why I knew if I'd asked him to take me to Dachau he'd go out of his way to please me and go with me. As mentioned, I couldn't have that and risk being the cause of a bad performance. Actually I'm happy about this.'

'What?'

'You coming with me. I'd hoped you would,' she said, smiling warmly.

There was a bus already outside when they came out of Dachau station. A few minutes later they stood in front of the site. It was March but a cold, grey day. The forecast informed that snow wasn't out of the question later in the day though the calendar was closer to spring than winter. A glacial wind whistled around their ears, funnelling amid the buildings. Hertie adjusted her scarf around her neck, buttoning up her coat and wishing she'd brought a woolly hat. The world appeared to have lost all colour. The weather was closing in as if any sign of gaiety or intense glow would be offensive to the victims of the horrible crimes committed in Dachau and other such places.

Hertie stood silently staring at the letters intertwined in the iron bars of the large gate, forming the slogan "ARBEIT MACHT FREI" – work sets you free. Cynical to say the least. Nothing could have been further from the truth. Her chest tightened. For a moment she couldn't breathe as if an enormous wave was crushing her to death, drowning her. Then she felt a warm hand holding hers, an arm sustaining her dead weight. Her legs failed her but a gentle voice brought her back to reality, 'Hertie, are you all right? You look very pale.'

Naturally Valeria standing by her side, gazing at her with a worried expression. Hertie swallowed the lump in her throat and held on to her friend's arm as if for dear life.

'Fine,' she whispered, 'fine,' pointing at the slogan she added, 'how can people be so cruel, cynical, heartless? Mocking the prisoners in such a vicious, evil way. It was impossible to be set free no matter how hard you worked. The only way out was death.'

Still leaning on Valeria Hertie began walking in. They entered the camp greeted by the biting, relentless wind and wandered first into the building where the prisoners had been received when they arrived. They were stripped of their clothes, jewellery, photos, any personal items and their names. They would hand over all their items, including their identity, standing at the long tables in the arrivals' hall. They became a number. Were addressed by their number. Their names never used again.

Hertie approached a steward with a name tag on his navy blue jacket. Heiko Weber she read silently, then greeted him using his surname, asking whether he knew the number of prisoners killed in the gas chambers at Dachau. The young man shook his head slightly and explained, 'although there's a gas chamber here in Dachau it wasn't used. Prisoners who were to die in that way were pushed to other concentration camps usually in the seized countries like Poland for example. The government didn't want the civil population to suspect people were being executed in the gas chambers so such prisoners were sent to the camps in the occupied regions specialised in terminating lives with the use of gas. However, many people were killed here but in different ways. There were also massacres of war prisoners.'

Hertie's throat felt suddenly very dry. Breathing in deeply she asked, 'I assume families were separated here when arriving at this building – men to one section of the camp, women to another and children pushed away in another corner without their parents.'

'That is accurate of many concentration camps but Dachau was for men. All sorts of male prisoners were brought here, including prisoners of war.'

Heiko Weber made Hertie and Valeria a sign to follow him. He stopped in front of a large vitrine containing a colour coded table, with symbols and words printed in the old German alphabet, always used by the Nazis.

'You can see here,' he said, 'the various categories in which the prisoners were classified, the symbols and colours they were forced to wear on the uniforms besides their number. For example, here at the top you can see Political Prisoners, Professional Criminals, Emigrants, so-called Asocial Prisoners with the symbols and colours below but within these there were other special sub-categories, as you can see on the left: Badges for Relapses – I must admit I'm not quite sure what these people were or had done – for Jews and then some special badges for the so-called Rassenschänder, meaning the ones who were considered to have shamed their race by marrying or having sexual intercourse with people from different races or at least seen that way by the Nazi regime. Here,' he pointed at the bottom of the table, 'you can also see some symbols for prisoners by nationality – P for Poles for instance – and the white circle with a red circle inside which was for prisoners thought to be a flight risk, meaning they would try to escape. Sadly, as far as I know no-one ever escaped and anyone who tried was caught and executed.'

Hertie felt an instant sympathy towards Mr Weber. A young man but very professional and capable of explaining things in a factual, clear manner. They, all three, stared together at the colour-coded table for a long time. As a child during the war, Hertie had learned the old German alphabet at school. She was able to decipher most letters but gathered that Valeria was probably struggling.

A moment later, Hertie thanked the young man for his detailed explanations and moved on to another part of the building where high up, twenty or thirty centimetres below the tall ceilings, square holes had been fashioned, suggesting something – perhaps a large plank – had once been fixed there. There was an explanatory note inside a vitrine. Hertie read it, confirming her suspicion. Once there had indeed been sturdy, solid wood crossbars with hooks and iron chains hanging from them. A common torture for prisoners was to force their arms behind their backs, chain their wrists and pull them up, leaving them dangling from the hooks for hours. It caused terrible pain and horrific injuries to muscles, bones and nerves. Hertie's chest ached acutely. She sensed tears in her eyes. Better to move outside, she thought, as she heard Valeria, who had stayed behind, chatting to young Weber. She was saying, 'your job must be rather difficult to do. You're confronted with evil every single day, must remain professional and explain facts in a straightforward, objective, non-emotional way.'

Glancing over her shoulder Hertie saw Heiko Weber's lips part in a sad smile. She listened to his words, 'yes, it's a difficult job, made harder when we've visitors who were concentration camp survivors or their descendants but I believe,' he paused as if to gather his feelings, swallowing hard a couple of times, 'I believe what happened in Germany during the Nazi years was appalling…in fact there aren't words bad enough to describe it but I'm German. It's part of my historical heritage and we mustn't ever forget what took place in this country. I think what I do is important to help people remember and understand that it must never happen again.'

His voice was emotional when he finished. Hertie moved away. Outside she noticed a couple by the gate, staring at the hideous slogan. The woman was saying, 'the bastards. I wish Germany had sunk, consumed by an earthquake or something and never emerged again.'

'Well,' the man commented, 'in a sense they did. The country was bombed to the ground. There was nothing but ruins and rubble.'

'Yes but they came back.'

'It's a completely different country now, Elsbeth.'

'My grandfather was here in Dachau, later was sent to Auschwitz where they killed him in the gas chambers. My grandmother died in Treblinka and I'm only alive because they had the good sense of entrusting my father, then still a boy, to his former French nanny who took him to Switzerland—'

'Yes, my dear, I know the story,' the man cut in, 'your dad was thirteen or fourteen and stayed with the nanny in Switzerland until the end of the war when they, along with other refugees, immigrated to the States.'

They were speaking in English and Hertie could tell from their accent that they were Americans. The woman at least was perhaps of Jewish descent. With tears in her eyes, Hertie felt a sudden urge to apologise. A desperate need to say she was sorry for everything her country had done. With small, hesitant steps she approached the couple and said in a quiet voice, 'I don't mean to intrude but couldn't help hearing your conversation.'

'Yes. So?' The woman, Elsbeth, said curtly.

'Are you Jewish?'

'We both are,' the man replied, 'but I come from a family who left Germany long before the Nazis came to power. My wife, as you heard, lost part of her family in the concentration camps.'

'Termination camps. That's what they were,' Elsbeth said, visibly raging.

'It's true,' Hertie said, 'and I am so sorry for your family and everything that took place in this country.'

Elsbeth frowned. 'You should be since you're German. I can tell from your accent. You German bastards have a lot to answer for and—'

Her husband placed his hand on her shoulder interrupting her influx of furious accusations. In a kind voice he asked Hertie, 'how old were you when the war ended?'

Hertie lifted her eyes full of tears to him and murmured, 'nine. I turned nine in February 1945.'

He took her hand gently and said almost affectionately, 'you were a little girl. Couldn't do anything whatsoever or even understand what was going on. You've nothing to apologise for, dear lady.'

'Thank you for your gracious words.'

His wife opened her mouth but, turning to her he said, 'it's all right, Elsbeth. You can't forget what happened to your family but this lady was a child. It was never her fault. She was as much a victim as the members of your family.'

'Perhaps,' she seemed to concede and, after a long silence, added, 'I didn't mean to be rude.'

Hertie nodded.

The woman's sympathetic husband commented, addressing Hertie, 'you know, dear lady, I believe that yes many Germans knew what was going on and did nothing. Others had no idea. But in charge of the country was an iron-handed, cruel dictator who can only be described as mad otherwise no-one can explain the atrocities. When a country gets in such a grip there isn't much the population can do. I know there was resistance in

Germany in the beginning but they were all killed, wiped out. Hitler ruthlessly and methodically eliminated anyone and everyone who was against him or dared to defy him and his acolytes. God help us when dictators take charge.'

'You're right, Mr?'

'Rosenthal. David Rosenthal. And my wife, Elsbeth.'

Hertie stretched her hand, 'Hertha Lohmeyer-Neale,' she said.

He shook her hand firmly and cordially. After some brief hesitation, his wife also gave Hertie a friendly handshake. Then they both said goodbye and disappeared inside the building.

Valeria came out and asked Hertie about the couple. Quietly, she narrated the whole episode to her friend.

'Oh, Hertie,' Valeria exclaimed, 'you're such a generous person. You of all people don't have to apologise to anyone. You were a little girl during the war. What could you have done?'

'Nothing,' she replied with a shrug, 'but I sometimes wonder if the grown-ups at the time could have.'

They moved to see other buildings and the sheds – they could only be described as sheds or cabins – where the prisoners had resided. The beds were like large boxes over each other, with the minimum space available between them for people to move in and out. Mostly there were three bunk beds in rows of ten or more sets. A note on the wall explained that the prisoners had to keep the beds properly done, the linen stretched and neat. If one was messy, the prisoner would be punished and beaten up. It stated that often the SS officers would come in when the prisoners were already out doing their forced labour tasks and disarrange several of the beds, then shout at the prisoners they were disgusting pigs, dirty and unable to make a bed. Thus having a legitimate excuse to execute their abuse and beatings.

Hertie and Valeria walked out of the sheds. Hertie felt as if her body had shrunk. All energy drained out of it like a shell where there was nothing but sadness, grief and sorrow. The temperature had dropped while they were inside and though only one in the afternoon, it was overcast and dark. A few, scattered snowflakes drifted in the wind. Hertie felt frozen inside and out.

'As if it's snowing in my heart,' she thought to herself. Turning to Valeria she said aloud, 'I think we should go. I can't stay in this place for another minute.'

As they moved towards the exit, her eyes passed through the barbed wire of the fences and the bars of the gate. Slowly she lifted her gaze to the leaden sky above and wondered whether on clear nights, the prisoners had looked up at the stars just like she had as a little girl, escaping East Prussia, questioning herself whether somewhere up there in another world another being was looking down on this planet. Would they think the people who inhabited it were savages, killing and torturing each other? Or did they simply see the distant pale blue dot as a world neither special nor spectacular among so many others in the immensity of the universe and the emptiness of space?

Hertie didn't know. But inside her heart there was the hope that the prisoners might have found comfort in looking up at the skies just as she had as a child in Germany, for without darkness people could not see the stars.

Valeria's journal, April 2020

After the visit to Dachau, Hertie was pensive for several days. Hardly surprising. The experience was harrowing for me but must have been chilling and excruciatingly painful for her. She told Xaver and me she needed to digest everything. Didn't want to discuss it, at least for the time being. So I returned to my hotel room that evening, after the visit to the concentration camp and buried myself in work, as I'd neglected my uni studies a little.

On the afternoon of the day after the trip to the camp, I received a message from the digital magazine stating they were pleased with the interview I'd conducted with Xaver and would publish it at the weekend. They asked if I could write a review about Xaver's debut as Romeo in Kenneth MacMillan's choreography to Prokofiev's beautiful ballet *Romeo and Juliet*. They added that if I couldn't obtain a press ticket – too short notice – they would be pleased to pay for one. I messaged back that Xaver had kindly given me a ticket.

The performance started at 19.00 hours. He left early for the National Theatre that housed both the Bavarian State Opera and the Bavarian State Ballet. Hertie, Hedi and I arrived at the theatre one hour before the performance and enjoyed a glass of champagne. I remember the evening very vividly. It was the first time I saw Xaver dance live on stage, just a few metres away from me, and it was the night I fell in love with him.

I had found him attractive from the moment we met but never anticipated falling for him, least of all so quickly. After Aidan, my soulmate and boyfriend of four years, I consciously walked away from relationships. The pain of his loss in the car crash wouldn't allow me as much as to look at other men. The frustration of being unable to pursue my career of choice added to my lack of interest in relationships. It hurt to have lost my voice and it ached to think of Aidan. It happened one late summer night. Aidan and his older brother, John, were driving home after a visit to their grandparents in the North of England. John was at the wheel of the car. It was pitch dark, raining heavily. John said afterwards that suddenly, out of nowhere, an animal materialised on the centre lane of the motorway, three hundred yards or so ahead of the car. A fox? He wasn't sure. They saw the animal frozen scared on the middle of the road, eyes glowing in the headlights. John hit the brakes and steered to his right in order not to hit it. There was hardly any traffic but the road was wet. The car skidded. Aquaplaning, John lost control. Unfortunately the car rolled, jumping the central barrier and landing in the path of a large truck travelling the other way. Aidan was hit first and died instantly. John had to be cut out. He survived but lost one arm. And I took refuge in music and writing to be able to cope. I don't like to speak about it but I've learned to live with the pain. I've got used to it. Until meeting Xaver I thought I'd never fall in love again and then, I simply did.

From the moment he made his first appearance on stage, a long cape floating away from his shoulders, I was hooked. Magnetic with an aristocratic bearing, I remember thinking to myself that no Juliet could ever resist such a Romeo. Taller than most ballet dancers, at 1.86 metres, he easily stands out but told me in the interview that being tall means he has to work twice as hard as most dancers. Steps, pirouettes and especially jumps become more difficult with height. It may well be true but, personally, I find a tall dancer more alluring, captivating. The height gives Xaver a rather special elegance. It is difficult to describe in words how he dances. There's a radiance in his flawless movements. He's luminous. Perfect alignment of shoulders, arms and legs in his arabesques[25], splendid outline in his attitudes[26]. His pirouettes are so superb it appears his foot is glued to the floor as he rotates. His impeccable execution of all jumps and an easiness at elevating himself in the air that almost defies gravity are simply breath-taking. His technique is

---

[25] An arabesque is a classic ballet body position in which the weight of the body is supported on one leg while the other is extended back with the knee straight.

[26] An attitude is a classic ballet position where a leg is lifted in the air to the front (devant), the side (a la seconde) or the back (derrière). The leg in the air is bent in a 90-degree angle, often turned out so the knee is higher than the foot. The supporting leg is straight and on pointe or demi-pointe.

immaculate, embedded with a pure classicism. All his training and ballet studies were of outstanding quality but I perceive his two-year scholarship at the Mariinsky in St. Petersburg. It shows through in the exquisite refinement he gained. Smoothly, as if it were the easiest thing in the world, he displays with every step and position the astonishing grace and the beautiful seamless flow of motion so peculiar to Russian ballet dancers. Topping all this technical and athletic prowess, Xaver is eloquent and ardent. Every step, every move of the arms or hands or head, each jump or turn or when he effortlessly lifts the ballerina up in the air are heartfelt. There is fervour. Sincerity. Passion. We feel and see his joy, his pain, his love. He makes it look uncomplicated, simple, straightforward. It is almost as if he is inviting one on to the stage to dance alongside him, readily and perfectly executing the same steps, experiencing ballet the way he does.

I was stunned. It dawned on me I didn't know how to write the review. For how can one describe in words the sheer beauty expressed by a dancer of Xaver's calibre? I would struggle. It would be the most arduous review I'd have ever written. But as he moved across the stage and the scenes succeeded one another I sensed a transformation inside me. Just a hint at first. An intimation of a surge of emotion. It became stronger as I watched. Deeper. My chest tightened. I felt a lump in my throat. I opened my mouth, finding it difficult to breathe normally.

The exquisitely charming, touching balcony scene where all of Romeo's intense feelings for Juliet pour out of him and out of her for him made something burst inside me, exploding in a thousand multi-coloured emotions – desire, excitement, affection, happiness, despair, sentiment. I was Juliet, loving him with all the power of my heart, flying through the air in his arms, held delicately, joyfully as a precious jewel that love created. And I had to admit to myself I'd fallen in love with Xaver. For what else but love could this contradictory, powerful feeling pulling my heart, my very being in all directions, be? Yes. The balcony scene was the moment of realisation. I was in love with Xaver. I wanted him whole, as I'd wanted Aidan once, as a partner, a companion, a friend, a lover. It surprised me. My chest ached. I pressed my hand against it. I had believed I could never love another man as I had loved Aidan and yet suddenly, out of nowhere, here it was – that overwhelming, mighty, all-powerful feeling. How could it be? I didn't know. Love is unforeseen. It lurks in the least expected corners of the mind, ready to bounce you. And it did...me.

Hertie told me later my face had changed as I watched. She had guessed what I was feeling but said nothing. Waited to see how it developed. I ignored it but she already knew her grandson was attracted to me. Being discreet, Hertie only commented on our feelings once Xaver and I had become an item.

At the end of that first performance Xaver took Hertie, Hedi and me to the Premiere's party. After a glass of champagne to everyone and a couple of speeches, waiters and waitresses walked round with canapés before a cold buffet opened. I was nervous. Not certain why. Actually, not true. I knew why. I was nervous because I had realised my feelings for Xaver. I wanted to tell him but was unsure how. What if he felt nothing of the sort for me? What if he rejected me? I grabbed as many glasses of champagne as I could. Drank them in one go, one after the other, until my inhibitions vanished, my head got a little fuzzy and a silly grin of happiness sat on my lips.

I finished my fifth and last glass of champagne. In that glorious moment, Xaver pulled me aside, asking me what I'd thought about the performance in general and his in particular. I remember I replied something along the lines that the production was excellent, beautifully danced. Orchestra gave a fine interpretation of Prokofiev's gorgeous score. I was sincere in my praise. Then I turned to him, gazing up into his eyes.

'As for you,' I said, noticing I was slurring words a little, 'well, you dance like a god. Breath-taking and...' I paused, thinking of a suitable word to say, finally adding, 'luminous. Yes, in two words: You're terrific and your performance was luminous.'

He appeared moved and whispered thank you in my ear.

His voice tingled my skin and sent a shiver down my spine. A wave of attraction surged through every fibre of my body, my being. I couldn't stop myself, pulled his head down and kissed him fully on the mouth. It was an ambush of sorts, I suppose. At first he took a step back, appearing bewildered but it only lasted a second. Intensely looking into my eyes he slid his arms around my waist, held me tight against his chest and returned my kiss passionately. And that was it.

Under Hertie's indulging grin Xaver left her at his flat and walked with me to my hotel. He stayed the night and made love to me the same way he danced – delicately, with elegance and overwhelming passion. I remember thinking I'd died and gone to heaven. We had five more days of bliss together. I had to return to England for my studies, already neglected for more than enough time. Our separation wouldn't last long. Xaver had accepted a twelve-month position as principal guest artist of the Royal Ballet in London in addition to his position in Munich. He'd be commuting between the two cities, thus we would be able to see more of each other.

Munich was bathed in sunshine when Xaver and I said our temporary goodbyes at the airport. I felt that fabulous, beautiful city was celebrating our being a couple, dressing itself in its most gorgeous colours, glowing in the sun. I remember smiling to myself. Munich had become my favourite city in the whole wide world. Xaver affectionately hugged his grandmother, saying, 'thank you for your visit, Oma. I'll see you soon and will visit more often from now on due to the Royal Ballet position.'

Hertie kissed his cheek, pulled back the strand of hair that kept flopping onto his forehead and added with a cheeky twinkle in her eyes, 'and to see a certain brown-eyed girl.'

Xaver chuckled and shook his finger at his grandmother, pretending to be angry. Then he gave me another quick kiss and waved at us as we disappeared inside the terminal.

The weather forecast for London, unlike Munich, wasn't pleasant – rain and wind – but Hertie and I would have a lot of interesting news waiting for us. The ending of Maria Eduarda and Gerald's story was about to begin.

Chapter 6 – The Manuscript

Hertie had enjoyed her time in Munich and was increasingly elated with the developments between her grandson and Valeria. Ecstatic, she hugged both heartily when Valeria, appearing a little embarrassed, told her everything. But Hertie was genuinely gratified. She cared dearly for Valeria and adored her grandson. In her mind they made the perfect couple. Silently, during Xaver's performance as Romeo at the ballet's opening night, she had observed the changes in Valeria's face, her body language. Spellbound Valeria had watched Xaver move across the stage in that natural, easy, smooth way that made his dancing so appealing. By the end of the performance, Hertie knew. Cupid's arrow had hit Valeria badly and once she realised Xaver was anything but immune, her joy was complete.

Two weeks had passed since their return from Germany when the voicemail materialised. Hertie listened to it quietly. It was from Oliver Sinclair, Xaver's friend and curator of antique manuscripts at the British Library in London. Back in January Xaver had visited him and taken the manuscript Gerald had stolen from Maria Eduarda's father, intending for Oliver to provide an evaluation. Oliver was calling to advise he had news, would she please go see him in London or send someone on her behalf. The message caused a stir and Hertie promptly rang Valeria's doorbell.

'When are you next travelling to London, Schätzchen?' she asked immediately, as Valeria opened the door, without bothering to greet her first.

'As a matter of fact this coming weekend. Going Friday evening to see my family and…' Hertie noticed colour suffused Valeria's cheeks and guessed the reason before she resumed, 'and…staying until Sunday. Xaver's flying in from Munich on Saturday for an informal chat with the Royal Ballet's director.'

'I see,' Hertie grinned all-knowingly, then added in a serious tone, 'you think you can fit in a visit to Oliver Sinclair at the British Library?'

'He called?'

She nodded. 'Left a message on my answering machine. I'd prefer you to go and since you're travelling anyway...'

'Of course. Give me his number. If he can see me Friday afternoon, I'll leave earlier for London. May I also ask you a favour?'

'Look after Wonkie?'

'Please.'

'No problem. I like your cat. She can keep me company.'

'Thank you.'

It turned out that Oliver had time on Friday afternoon. So, after leaving her car at her parents' Kensington house, Valeria took the tube and arrived at the British Library at the agreed time of three o'clock. Oliver was waiting for her at the main entrance. She guessed it might be him from what Xaver had told her. Tall, dark, a square jaw, curly hair pulled back with gel, tiny scar above his left eyebrow caused by a push bike accident as a child, and always smartly dressed. Valeria noticed him immediately. He was handsome, wearing an impeccable white shirt and an elegant navy blue suit. No tie. Not the type one imagined a curator of old manuscripts.

'Mr Sinclair, I assume,' she said, adding, 'I'm Valeria, coming to talk about the manuscript on behalf of Hertha Neale and your friend Xaver Duverger.'

He displayed a row of perfect white teeth, smiling at her and stretching his hand.

'Pleasure to meet you, Valeria. Just call me Oliver or Olly.'

She nodded and followed him to his office on the top floor, with large windows and a striking view over the city.

'Please sit, Valeria,' he told her, as they entered his office, pointing at a chair the other side of his desk, then added, 'would you like anything to drink? Coffee? Tea? Or perhaps some mineral water?'

'Water, please.'

He opened a small fridge in the corner of the room, took two bottles of mineral water and two glasses from the cupboard above it, returning to his desk. Once they were settled, Valeria asked, 'I won't beat around the bush, Oliver, have you found anything interesting about the manuscript?'

'I have. Mrs Neale and Xaver I believe will be pleased.'

'Good. So what can you tell me about it?'

'I can tell you it appears to be really very, very old,' he paused to glance at his notes then continued, 'I've sent it this morning to our specialist team where our historians, scientists, archivists, conservators and I will be thoroughly analysing and testing it. It's a long process and I'll explain it in a moment but the reason why you're here is that I did a preliminary examination – superficial but nevertheless important. At first glance, the type of paper and the deckle edge appear to indicate it's handmade and possibly what would have been used in the 16th century.'

Valeria's heart leaped a beat. Excitedly she said, 'the original owners of the manuscript thought it might have been written by the hand of the poet himself which ties in with the period you just mentioned.'

'Yes. Xaver told me the story…apparently some people believe it could be part of the original manuscript of The Lusiads, which Camões saved during a shipwreck he suffered.'

'Well, I guess he did save it somehow and that's the story, yes. I'm not sure it's real but…even if it is, I don't think it can ever be proved.'

'It's difficult but not impossible. When our team is finished with it, I want a scholar…an expert in Portuguese literature to also have a look at it. If everything fits in we may be able to authenticate it and declare the manuscript as the real thing, handwritten by the poet himself.'

'But wouldn't it imply the need for a certified sample of Camões's handwriting to compare and be certain?'

'That'd be ideal, yes. But after a thorough analysis if all the bits fit in, it can still be authenticated even without a genuine writing sample from the poet.'

'It'd be marvellous,' she paused, as something occurred to her, then added, 'I suppose, as you said, you may still be able to prove Camões wrote it even without a writing sample but the other thing, meaning swimming only with one arm and the other high up in the air above the stormy sea to save the manuscript, surely is unprovable.'

Oliver had a slightly smug look about him.

'One never knows,' he said, 'I did a basic, quick test on a microscopic sample of the paper. There are plant fibres, indicating the paper was handmade and,' he seemed to waver for a moment then visibly delighted added, 'I also found a faint trace of sodium chloride—'

'Salt,' Valeria interjected breathlessly, 'the ocean. It would appear the legend is confirmed.'

Oliver smiled indulgently. 'Maybe but not unavoidably. It proves it was in contact with salt water…'

Valeria was about to interrupt him again but he lifted his hand, stopping her.

'The traces of salt,' he resumed, 'could be from saltwater drops in a kitchen or even from tears. It could also mean it might have been close to the sea at some stage but it doesn't prove that the author of the manuscript verses was a victim of a shipwreck.'

'You're right, of course. Still, it's exciting and a possibility.'

'With that I must agree.'

'You mentioned the analysis process is quite long. What does it entail?'

'I'll send you…or Mrs Neale, an attachment in an e-mail with a report explaining the process in detail but in a nutshell this is what happens…' he paused to sip some water.

Valeria smiled and said, 'good, I like explanations in a nutshell.'

Oliver stared at her for a moment. His eyes were intensely dark, almost black. He grinned and she didn't quite understand his expression. Then, unexpectedly he told her, 'you've got a lovely smile, are you aware of that?'

For a moment she didn't know which way to look but, deciding to ignore the compliment simply exclaimed, 'you were saying the process in a nutshell…'

He turned serious. 'Of course. So, there are three types of analysis that we must do – stylistic, historical and scientific.'

'Okay and what happens in each one?'

'In the stylistic analysis we try to determine the place, the period and the purpose of origin. These are three very important steps to establish whether a manuscript is the real thing or whether it could be a clever fake.'

'Right. I get it.'

'In the historical analysis we need to find out whether a manuscript is made with materials and techniques consistent with its style, meaning with the place it originated, the period it belongs to and its purpose. Is it just a sketch? Was it part of a whole document? And so on.'

'Okay.'

'In the historical analysis we determine the paper making techniques. For example, I've already told you I made a preliminary test on a microscopic piece of the paper and it appears to be handmade in line with what was common in the 16th century but we need to be sure so more detailed tests have to be carried out. Paper as early as this was made by beaten plant fibres, first dispersed in water, then cast randomly on a papermaking mould. That needs to be established. We also need to analyse the materials and techniques of media. Finally, there's the scientific analysis which entails actions like illumination, radiography, magnification, elemental analysis and property measurements.'

'I'm not sure I understand what you mean by illumination or elemental analysis.'

'An object's size, shape, texture or optical properties like colour or gloss for example, can be revealed through different wavelengths of light. That's very simplistically the definition of illumination.'

Valeria nodded.

'Elemental analysis is analysing the elements by using a variety of instruments for identifying both organic and inorganic elements. A graph is created, which serves as a fingerprint of an unknown component to be matched with that of a known material.'

'Seems complicated.'

'Yes but it's not as bad as it sounds.'

'And what do you measure in the properties measurements step?'

'Chemical and physical properties of materials change upon exposure to oxidative, hydrolytic or mechanical forces. These properties can be measured and characterised. Some are for example, colour, gloss, opacity, strength, acidity among others.'

'Fascinating.'

'Yes but it takes time. So, final results won't be ready in the next couple of months. May take six months or a year, sometimes longer. And you should bear in mind that dating a paper object, such as the manuscript Mrs Neale entrusted us with, is next to impossible. There are techniques to date organic materials such as radiocarbon dating and a lot of other technologies I won't go into detail here, but none of these techniques is particularly applicable to paper though they can be used. So the best results for the authentication of a manuscript like this one come from the kind of collaborative efforts I explained and have set in motion.'

'Thank you. Very interesting and enlightening. I really had no idea.'

'Most people don't. Why should they? It's a specialist's work.'

'Of course. Is there anything else?'

'No. As I mentioned earlier, I'll send you a report in an e-mail with more detailed explanations of the processes we'll be going through.'

Valeria stood up and reached across the desk to shake his hand. 'In that case, Oliver,' she said, 'thank you very much for everything so far and most of all, on Mrs Neale's behalf, thank you for carrying out all this work for such a small, nominal fee.'

'My pleasure. I've always liked Xaver's grandmother. She's a lovely lady.'

'Indeed she is and a very dear friend to me. Anyway,

goodbye now.'

He grabbed her stretched arm, holding her hand firmly for a moment, then asked her, 'are you staying in London tonight?'

Valeria raised an eyebrow. What did he care? Aloud she answered, 'yes. Why?'

'Have dinner with me.'

'Oh, well…that's very kind but—'

'But no?' He cut in.

'Yes.'

'Ah, it's a yes then?'

Valeria shook her head vigorously. 'No. It's a no. I can't.'

'Why not? You married?'

'No.'

'Then why?'

'I came this weekend to London to visit my family and meet with my boyfriend.'

He dropped her hand. 'I see. Lucky man. I'm sorry if I came across as too pert.'

'It's fine. Goodbye Oliver. I look forward to the final results of all your analytical efforts.'

With these words Valeria turned hastily away and walked out of the office before he could say anything further or try to escort her to the exit.

Chapter 7 – The Detective

Hertie looked out of her window towards the sea. If she didn't know any better she would say it was the middle of November instead of early July. The sky was murky. Colourless. The water grey. Rain fell heavily. People walked with raincoats, hoods over their heads or huddled under umbrellas. She hoped the weather would improve at the end of the month. The London Olympic Games were starting on 27th July. It wouldn't be nice under such downpours.

Languishing she moved away from the windows, sitting on a sofa, feet up, picking up a book only to readily put it down again. Finding a suitable, trustworthy detective to locate Maria Eduarda or her grave was proving difficult. Valeria was drowning in work. Busy with exams, flooded with offers of work after the success of her interview with Xaver but not only those. Rave reviews of her performance as a pianist accompanying her opera singer friend in Schubert's Lieder had put her name on the map. It meant no time as yet to find and hire a detective. Xaver had tried to help, making a stopover in Lisbon on his way to New York for four weeks to dance the lead male role of Basilio in Ludwig Minkus's *Don Quixote*.

His relationship with Valeria was going well. Hertie had never seen him so much in love. It seemed for real this time. She hoped so.

Xaver's two days in Lisbon did not bring much progress. He met with Valeria's friend, a young man by the name of Marcelo Faria, a detective sergeant in the Polícia Judiciária, the Portuguese criminal police. Marcelo had promised to check the credentials of various private detective agencies in the country and come up with a recommendation for Valeria. So far, nothing. Would it be better to engage someone in England and pay for their trip to Portugal? No. Not good. Unlikely such a person would speak Portuguese. The search for Maria Eduarda must start in Lisbon where she had been seen for the last time seventy years ago. An impossible task. If she wasn't dead, she could be anywhere. Might have left Portugal as a young woman. Never to return. Who knew? There were multiple possibilities. Maria Eduarda would not…could not be found. Hertie was thus convinced even if they hired the best detective in the world.

Abruptly there was a loud noise. Shuddering, confused, Hertie opened her eyes, glancing around. The room had darkened. Twilight and a hint of pink lining the clouds. She must have dozed. Looking at the clock on the mantelpiece Hertie jumped to her feet. Eight twenty in the evening. She had slept for three hours. The rain had stopped. She heard the loud noise again, finally identifying it as the doorbell. Sleep muddled she gradually managed to get her legs in gear and walk to the door. Opening it she saw Valeria smiling at her.

'I was beginning to think you were unwell, Hertie,' she said, 'took you a long time to get the door.'

'I know. Sorry. I fell asleep but I'm fine. This murky weather tires me.'

'May I come in?'

'Of course. You needn't ask.'

Valeria headed for the lounge and sat down while Hertie shut the door and followed slower behind. As soon as Hertie was comfortably installed in her favourite sofa, beaming Valeria blurted out, 'I've got news.'

'About the detective?' Hertie hoped it would be. Judging by the smile on Valeria's face it had to be.

She nodded. 'I've just had a video call with her.'

'Her? The detective's a lady?' Hertie couldn't hide her surprise but it was absurd to be surprised. Why wouldn't a woman be a private detective? There were female detectives in the police force and women in the military.

'Yes,' Valeria was saying, 'her name's Renata Monteiro. Seems nice. Comes highly recommended. Marcelo, my friend, said her credentials are impeccable. She runs a small agency – herself, two other women detectives and a young man who does admin work. They apparently have a very high rate of success, specialising in locating missing people but also do other detective work.'

'Sounds ideal.'

'Believe so. We talked for quarter of an hour just to give her a flavour of what we require and I've organised another video call for tomorrow morning at ten. I'd like you to be present, Hertie. See what you think, your gut feeling. Then, if we're agreed, we can hire her.'

Hertie nodded, raring to go. How could she manage the hours until meeting with the detective albeit virtually? But manage she did. When the time arrived Hertie, bright eyed and bushy tailed, sat next to Valeria in her study, patiently waiting for the laptop's screen to come alive.

Renata Monteiro, the detective, appeared to be in her early fifties and distinguished. Dark hair, streaked with grey, framed her face in a neat, modern cut. Hazelnut brown eyes behind frameless glasses. She wore an aquamarine blue jacket and white blouse, with matching stud earrings. Introducing herself for Hertie's benefit Renata displayed a professional smile and quickly described the work of her agency in rather good English. Hertie liked her instantaneously. Renata Monteiro inspired confidence, seemed serious about her work, well organised and methodical. As she finished her introduction, Hertie asked her to explain the steps taken to locate a person.

'Nowadays,' Renata answered, 'we tend to start with an online investigation, researching various social media. We also carry out google searches and visit the places where the person was last seen or known to have lived. Whatever leads or clues come out of it, each is followed to the end thoroughly.'

'The woman we're looking for,' Hertie explained, 'disappeared seventy years ago. Do you think you've got a chance of finding her?'

'Well,' Renata replied, 'I won't know until I begin.'

Hertie's lips parted. She liked the reply. Amusing and clever. Aloud she said, 'good answer, Ms Monteiro.'

'Honest. It's the simple truth. But tell me, after seventy years, is it likely this woman is still alive?'

'You tell me.'

'In my experience, after so many years even if we find the person, he or she is almost always dead. Having said that, I had a case two years ago and another four years before where the people in question had disappeared 47 and 63 years earlier respectively. We located them. Both were still alive albeit one very ill and who sadly died just six months later.'

'Had they disappeared of their own accord or was anything criminal involved?'

'Slightly one of them but not the other. No abduction or anything like that. The first was given for adoption. The mother and a sister wanted to find him. The other had run away due to debt, living in Brazil under a false identity. I'm afraid she's in prison now.'

'Interesting, don't you think, Valeria?'

'Yes, definitely.'

'Mrs Neale,' Renata said, 'this woman you'd like to find do you know why she disappeared?'

'Yes. She got pregnant at I believe twenty-one. Her father was a prominent man and a strict catholic. He threw her out and after that no-one ever heard from her again.'

'And why would you like to find her now if I may ask.'

'You may. The man who got her pregnant was the same who several years down the line married me. He died in 1966 but before his death he confessed the sins of his life. Some related to this woman. Strangely enough there also are links to my friend sitting here next to me,' she indicated Valeria with her head, 'the missing lady is…or was my friend's aunt. She and my friend's mother are half-sisters – same father, different mothers.'

'I see.'

'There's much more to it than what I've just said and I'm happy to entrust you with all information so you can attempt to locate this lady. Would you be willing to take the case? And if yes, could we get an estimate of costs and time?'

'I'm willing to take the case. At first glance, it seems intriguing. I can provide an estimate but each case is different and bearing in mind the person has been vanished for such a long time, I can't really tell how long it may take us or how much it would cost. From past experiences I'd say, at least a year to eighteen months, probably more and of course there's no guarantee that we'll find her after spending your money.'

'I'll take the risk,' Hertie said decisively, glancing at Valeria who nodded and appeared in agreement.

'All right,' Renata concurred, 'then may I please ask you for some specific information so we've somewhere to start. I'll try to prepare an estimate but it'll really be more of a guess.'

'It's fine. So ask away.'

'First, what is this woman's full name?'

It was Valeria who answered, 'Maria Eduarda Gabriela Leopoldina Teresa Livramento de Arantes Silva.'

'Goodness! Can you send me that in an e-mail?'

'Of course.'

'From all those names I'm deducing this Eduarda was a member of the aristocracy?'

'Correct. My aunt was the eldest daughter of Ludovico de Arantes Silva, Duke of Beja, who died in 1989. Her mother was—'

'You mean *the* Duke of Beja, once a trusted friend of the dictator Salazar?'

'The same.'

'I see. That should make things easier. Who was then Eduarda's mother?'

'A commoner, daughter of a Cape Verdean employee and a Portuguese woman.'

'Do you know her name?'

'Yes. Gabriela Santiago do Livramento.'

'That'll be helpful too. Again, can you please send it in an e-mail?'

Valeria nodded. 'I'll do it straightaway from my phone. Just carry on talking.'

'Eduarda was born on?'

'15th September 1920.'

'And you said she was pregnant when her father threw her out?'

'That's correct.'

'The name of the man who was responsible?'

It was Hertie who replied. 'Gerald Joseph Neale. He was

British and my husband. But I only met him many years after he'd left Portugal. When he was there and before he assaulted…before he got Eduarda pregnant, he stole a precious first edition book and a potentially also valuable antique manuscript which should have been Eduarda's once her father died. This is one of the reasons why I'd like to find her, preferably alive, so I could make right some of my husband's criminal actions.'

'Okay. Gripping. What was this precious book?'

'A real first edition from 1572 of Os Lusíadas by I believe one of your greatest Portuguese poets—'

'Luis de Camões,' Renata interjected, 'dear Lord, you can put precious on that. What about the manuscript?'

'The Duke of Beja suspected it might be in Camões's handwriting and a fragment of an early draft of the same epic poem.'

'Wow! Potentially priceless.'

'Indeed. It was never authenticated before but Valeria and I,' Hertie glanced at her, 'have now taken it to an expert to try and find out whether it's the real thing.'

'Fascinating. I definitely want the case, Mrs Neale. I'll assign it to myself and my senior detective. This was a good preliminary conversation. I'll get right on to it. My admin will put together an estimate…or as mentioned, it'll be more of a guess but it'll serve as a guideline for you. Agreed?'

'Absolutely. Thank you, Ms Monteiro,' Hertie said, looking at Valeria who seemed to concur.

'Great. Shall we book another video call, say in three or four weeks' time? And I'd need a deposit to secure our engagement.'

'I'll do that,' Valeria said, 'would a PayPal payment be acceptable?'

'Of course. I'm used to it. I'll send you an invoice and the invite for the video call.'

'Perfect. Thank you.'

The screen went blank. Hertie stared at Valeria and asked, 'what do you think? Have we done the right thing?'

'I think so. We've set everything in motion. I can hardly wait for the results from Oliver Sinclair regarding the manuscript and anything that may come from Ms Monteiro about Maria Eduarda.'

Hertie remained silent, nodding pensively. She had mixed feelings. Excitement on the one hand and apprehension on the other. What if Renata Monteiro discovered anything unpleasant, grim or evil? Hertie exhaled, admonishing herself at once. Of course there wouldn't be anything of the sort. What a notion. Ridiculous fears from an old woman with a tendency to worrying about nothing.

'Everything's all right, Hertie?'

'Yes, Schätzchen, everything's fine.'

Two and a half weeks passed. Hertie had received nothing from the detective or Oliver Sinclair and knew Valeria had not been contacted either. In that instant her e-mail made a peeping sound. The laptop's screen showed her inbox. Hertie placed her reading glasses on her nose. Her heart leaped a beat. A message from the detective. It must be important or Ms Monteiro would wait until the next fast approaching video call. Hertie opened the mail and read:

> Dear Mrs Neale
> We've started our enquiries and our preliminary investigation has already given some results.
> Please find my report attached below. I also have cc-ed your friend Valeria. We can discuss any questions you may have in our next Skype in five days.
> Kind regards
> Renata Monteiro

Hertie stared at the PDF icon at the bottom of the message. She hovered the mouse over it, hesitating whether to click it open. For some reason she couldn't quite explain Hertie felt scared. Nervous. What if she didn't like its contents? And why should she care? Short of murder nothing could be worse than what

Gerry had confessed. The only solution was to download and print the document. It'd be easier to read from the printed page. Exhaling deeply Hertie put her thoughts into action.

The report was short. One page, containing bullet points. Hertie read aloud to herself:

- Maria Eduarda Gabriela Leopoldina Teresa Livramento de Arantes Silva will be referred to hereafter as Eduarda for simplicity's sake.
- We decided in this case to start the investigation in more conventional places – registry offices, electoral roll, naval records at the ports and so on. If Eduarda lives, she'll be over 90 years old. We reasoned an old lady would probably have none or little presence in the social media.
- Eduarda's birth was registered in Sintra on the date given me – 15th September 1920. We found no entry of her death. Neither in Sintra nor in any registry office in Lisbon. It does not necessarily mean that she is still alive.
- On 15th June 1942 Eduarda made an official request to change her name at a registry office in the island of Santiago in Cape Verde. The request came to the central in Lisbon and was granted on 1st July that same year. From then on her name was very much simplified – Maria Eduarda do Livramento. It appears she really wanted to cut all her ties with her family or at least with her father.
- I consulted the naval records at the Port of Lisbon and found out that Eduarda, still under her original name, had set sail to Cape Verde on 29th April 1942. We couldn't find out when she actually arrived or where she lived while in the islands, however we established that Maria Eduarda do Livramento (her new name) returned to Portugal in the summer of 1943, on 17th July. She stopped two days in Lisbon but then took another ship to

the city of Porto. According to the records she was travelling with an older lady named Leopoldina do Livramento, presumably a relative. We assume this lady to be her maternal grandmother, as by then the Dowager Duchess, her paternal grandmother, had already passed away.

- We dug into the registry offices in Cape Verde but didn't find any indication of her residence or whether she had a baby. However, at the time, Eduarda's father owned a big coffee plantation estate in Cape Verde. Her maternal grandmother resided there so presumably Eduarda, with or without her father's knowledge, went to stay with her. This is proved by the following facts: We checked in the city of Porto and found that Maria Eduarda do Livramento presented the registry office there with the birth certificate of a boy, born on 28th September 1942. The certificate had been issued in the island of Fogo, Cape Verde. Hence the conclusion she was living at the coffee plantation her father owned there. As mentioned, he may or may not have known. During the war years he had little or no contact with the stewards running his properties outside of mainland Portugal. A common fact during the time span of WWII.
- The boy Eduarda gave birth to was registered under the name of Jorge Eduardo do Livramento. Mother: Maria Eduarda do Livramento. Father: Unknown.

Hertie looked up from the piece of paper, staring blindly at the landscape painting on the wall in front of her. So Gerald did have a son with Maria Eduarda. Born in 1942. The boy... the man, would be seventy next September. A few years younger than herself. He must still be alive. Perhaps had children. Would they know their origins, their roots? That they had relatives in Portugal and England? She returned to the report. There wasn't much more information. Just two further bullet points and the next steps.

- Eduarda enrolled in Physics at the University of Porto in the Autumn of 1943. She graduated with honours at the end of the educational year 1947-48 and won a post-graduate scholarship to Harvard University in Boston, United States. She sailed to America in the spring of 1949, accompanied by her son and a Professor Berta de Almeida.
- It appears her grandmother Leopoldina returned to Cape Verde a month after Eduarda left for America. In the naval records of the Lisbon Port there is an entry for Leopoldina do Livramento who took a second class cabin and set sail on a ship headed for Cape Verde at the end of May 1949.

Next Steps:
- investigate thoroughly at the University of Porto's archives, attempting to locate address in the city where living before departing for the USA. If successful carry out interviews with people who may have known Eduarda – although not much hope here since so many years have passed,
- request information from the United States,
- establish whereabouts of Eduarda's son who must still be alive, as well as any descendants he may have had,
- consult electoral roll,
- start on social media for Jorge, Eduarda's son, and his potential descendants.

Hertie placed the detective's report on the table. Then picked it up and read it a second time. It wasn't much but it was a start. And not a bad one. Gradually her lips parted. Her eyes sparkled.

A certainty took shape in her mind. Maria Eduarda lived. They would meet and she would return the book and the manuscript to her, their rightful owner.

Valeria's journal, May 2020

Hertie hoped the analysis of the manuscript and the search for Maria Eduarda would be fast. Quite the opposite, in fact. As it turned out we waited short of a year for the results on the manuscript, until the end of March 2013. The full investigation of Maria Eduarda's whereabouts was to last not months but well over two years. Unfortunately, Ms Monteiro and her senior detective were caught in a motorway pile up, which meant they were both hospitalised for three months, requiring a long recovery period after being discharged. The good news is they were eventually restored to full health and able to resume the investigation. Without its two main detectives the agency was overwhelmed so the two remaining employees breathed a sigh of relief when Hertie told them she did not wish someone else to handle the case, preferring to wait. To please her I agreed.

In the meantime my relationship with Xaver became more serious and intense. We were practically living together. Whenever he visited his grandmother more often than not he would share my bed. We talked several times about moving in together for real. Perhaps London. My work took me there most of the time and he spent long weeks in the city whenever performing with the Royal Ballet. But Xaver loved Munich and Germany and wasn't sure he really wanted to leave. So we compromised and met whenever he could between his travels to New York to the American Ballet Theatre where he also became a principal, Munich where he continued to be principal of the Bavarian State Ballet and London where he carried on his role of principal guest artist. Add to these his guest appearances around the world and it's easy to conclude we didn't meet that often. When I took time off I'd go to stay in Munich with him or we'd travel together to the many places where he had been invited to dance.

Thinking back it was great to journey around together for his performances. It is May 2020 now and the world – or most of it – is in lockdown. Covid-19 is everywhere and at the moment there is no treatment or vaccine. Theatres, concert halls, opera houses are all shut. Culture is in lockdown, as are sporting events and hospitality. It is particularly difficult for Xaver. He misses performing but that isn't the major issue. As a classical ballet dancer he must keep fit. Be ready to jump onto the stage and deliver a great performance as soon as they are allowed to do so again. I can work from anywhere, as long as I have a good broadband connection, but for Xaver it is complicated.

After Hertie's death, on 5th May 2018, he inherited her flat and, as stated in her last will and testament, he could either live there or sell it should he need the money. By then I'd finished my studies and was established as a writer and reviewer. Xaver preferred Munich to London and so he sold the flat. With the amount he received and my savings we bought a pretty little house in Munich-Pasing. We were lucky. It's a popular area, approximately twenty minutes from the city centre with the S-Bahn. Commuters like it. It's expensive, as is almost anything in the Bavarian capital. Our house is spacious but needed a new bathroom and kitchen and the walls painted. We had it all done before we moved in. It has become a cosy, comfortable home. The lounge is large, with the staircase going from its side. It is extensive enough and with a high ceiling for Xaver to exercise. So, as the pandemic began and with it lockdown, we transformed the widest section of the lounge into Xaver's training room – a square corner of three by three metres with a mirror and a barre. Meticulously he practises four to five hours a day; has lost nothing of his flexibility or movement power.

I'm writing in one of the bedrooms upstairs, converted for me into a home office. I listen to the recorded piano music coming up from the lounge. Keeping my door open I can hear Xaver. After warming up and completing his barre exercises he starts his unbelievable sequences of entrechat quatres or the jumps with various rotations in the air. Sometimes I notice the squeaking of his ballet shoes on the polished wooden floor during his interminable fouettés[27] and pirouettes. Once he finishes, he

---

[27] fouetté en tournant (its full name or whipped turning in English) is a spectacular turn in ballet, usually performed in series, during which the dancer turns on one foot while making fast outward and inward thrusts of the

comes up, sweaty, tired but happy. Smiling he pauses at my door, waves, then disappears into the shower. After that we have a light meal. It's our new pandemic routine. It works and we enjoy each other's company all the more. But I'm getting distracted. Back to writing the story.

---

working leg at each rotation.

Chapter 8 – Results

It was on a frosty, clear morning at the end of March 2013 that Oliver Sinclair's phone call distracted Valeria from piano practising. She remembered thinking it was too cold for the time of year. Oliver's voice sounded excited when she answered her mobile.

'Have you got good news?' she asked him.

'I'd say so though perhaps not as good as you'd like. There's a potential minor disappointment. Anyway, I'll send you a detailed report but would you like to hear the summarised version now?'

'Of course.'

'As I explained when you came to my office, we carried out detailed stylistic, historical and scientific analyses. The type of paper and the deckle edge are definitely handmade and in line with what was used in the Portuguese India of the 16th century, meaning it corresponds with the time that Luis de Camões was there. The ink used is undoubtedly of the period too and appears to have been a cheaper type made in India rather than the more expensive one transported from Portugal for use by the Viceroy and his court. All other required steps, which I explained to you when you came, were carried out and all results match with what was expected in the 16th century. So the manuscript is authentic and not a clever fake. A more detailed analysis revealed also further traces of sodium chloride…I mean salt.'

'I know. Are you saying it was definitely in contact with the sea?' she interrupted.

'Possibly. Difficult to confirm without a doubt but the more logical explanation.'

'Okay. What about the actual text?'

'That's where the potential disappointment lies.'

'Oh? How do you mean?'

'Three independent scholars have examined the text once we were certain the manuscript was the real thing. They all came to a similar conclusion…'

Oliver paused. Getting impatient Valeria questioned, 'and

that is?'

'The text definitely is an extract of Os Lusíadas. It isn't a sketch but three sequential pages of the same epic poem.'

'Good news, right?'

'Yes, but they can't tell whether it is part of the original manuscript written by the poet himself or if it is a copy of the original made by the hand of someone else.'

'I see. A little disappointing, yes…but more would be over ambitious or too optimistic.'

'Perhaps. I suppose we won't ever know if it's part of Camões's original manuscript, written in his own hand, which he managed to save during the shipwreck or a copy in another person's hand – a friend of the poet, an admirer…who knows? However, you'll get a certificate that the manuscript is authentic and of the correct period.'

Valeria thanked him and went straight to Hertie who seemed over the moon with the results, stating she had never expected proof beyond a shadow of a doubt that Camões was the manuscript's author. She added that to know for sure it was a genuine 16th century document was far more than she'd ever dared hope for.

The document was returned to Hertie's wall safe together with the authentication certificate and a copy of Oliver's final report. Then began the long wait for the detective's findings to arrive.

Renata Monteiro's results reached Hertie and Valeria in early 2015, once the work was complete and the detective's long recovery from the accident behind her. The investigation concluded, Ms Monteiro decided to travel to England to deliver the information in person. More effective than over a video link. Valeria agreed. They met at Hertie's on 5th February 2015 over tea, coffee and home-baked scones to hear about Maria Eduarda.

Fidgety all morning Hertie moved continuously around the flat in a hyper state of excitement, waiting for the detective to turn up with her news. Xaver was in England for a stint with the Royal Ballet and had a few days off. He had come down to Hove, borrowed Valeria's car and driven to Gatwick airport to pick up

Ms Monteiro and bring her to Hertie's. Valeria and Hertie were waiting for their arrival. Hertie had baked scones in the morning. She began eating one.

Grinning Valeria pointed out, 'I thought you baked for Ms Monteiro!'

Hertie shrugged. 'I didn't have lunch. I'm hungry.'

'You said you couldn't eat because you're so anxious and excited.'

'I know, Schätzchen, but my stomach has other ideas.'

Valeria laughed. Hertie turned serious.

'Why did Ms Monteiro have to come all the way here? Couldn't she just tell us over the phone?'

'I don't know, Hertie,' Valeria replied, 'she said she'd rather give us the news in person.'

'But why? Are they so bad?'

'No idea. Perhaps she had to come to England anyway for some other business and decided to kill two birds with one stone.'

'Maybe,' Hertie was quiet for a moment, then added, 'and she told you Maria Eduarda's alive?'

'Yes but that's all she confirmed.'

Hertie walked back and forth. Back and forth. Back and forth. Stopping by the window she turned brusquely to face her friend, questioning rhetorically, 'But why? I can only imagine bad news.'

'Calm down, Hertie, you'll dig a path in the carpet if you carry on like that. We'll know soon enough. Be positive. The news doesn't have to be bad,' Valeria said, stressing the negative.

Hertie sighed. 'I know,' then dropped onto the couch only to jump up again, shouting, 'she's here,' hearing Xaver unlocking the front door.

Xaver came into the lounge followed by Renata Monteiro. After exchanging pleasantries and asking about her recovery from the accident they took their places around the low table. Once everyone held tea or coffee and a scone Hertie, unable to contain herself any longer, blurted out, 'so, Ms Monteiro, you said Maria Eduarda's alive, now tells us everything.'

Renata Monteiro smiled, visibly diverted at Hertie's

excitement. Placing her cup and plate carefully on the table she began, 'Eduarda's indeed alive and well, residing in Portugal,' she paused, then added, 'I told you before we thought it made no sense to search social media. We speculated an old lady like Eduarda wouldn't have any presence on such things...' the corner of her lips curled up in obvious amusement, 'well, we were wrong. Eduarda's all over the internet, has her own website and a Facebook page. She's a professor doctor in astrophysics and has various published books to her name. Naturally, she's retired from her professorship at Harvard University in Boston now but she still carries out consultancy via video link, writes scientific articles and is currently collaborating, as a consultant expert, on a series about the universe for America's PBS TV channel.'

'Wow!' Valeria heard Xaver exclaim, 'that's amazing,' then looking at her he asked, 'how old is she now?'

'I think ninety-four. She was born in September 1920,' Valeria replied.

'That's right,' Renata agreed.

'Her mind must still be very active and sharp,' Xaver couldn't hide his admiration.

'Indeed,' Valeria said, making the detective a sign to continue the story.

'Eduarda lived in the States for most of her life,' she resumed, 'but returned to Portugal a few years ago. I don't know why. She didn't say and I didn't think it was my place to ask. She lives in a pretty property – a small estate – on a quiet location in Alentejo, south of the village of Porto Covo on the coast.'

'Is it her father's former Alentejo estate?' Valeria enquired.

Renata heaved her shoulders. 'Don't think so but don't know for sure. I believe her father lost many of his properties after the revolution of 25th April 1974, as he openly supported Salazar and the fascist regime. I think she bought this property herself.'

'Hmm. Probably, yes, makes sense...also, as they weren't in touch – as far as I know – he wouldn't have mentioned her in the will...I suppose, as he had disinherited her,' Valeria commented.

'Does Maria Eduarda live alone?' Hertie jumped in.

'No,' Renata replied, 'she lives with her half-sister Ana Maria – a widow with no children. There's a resident couple – young, the girl is Maria Eduarda's great-grandchild; her young man is from Portugal – they manage the estate and look after the two old ladies. Eduarda's sister is quite a bit younger than her, nearly sixteen years. She's seventy-nine.'

'Yes,' Valeria interjected, 'I've never met her but I know that my aunt Ana Maria was the daughter of my grandfather's second wife. Maria Eduarda the child of his first marriage and my own mother the youngest child of the five daughters he had with his third wife.'

Renata Monteiro nodded and Hertie, clearly impatient, jumped in before anyone could speak again. 'You mentioned the girl in the young couple is Maria Eduarda's great-grandchild. So did she have a baby from my husband or only later?'

Ms Monteiro's lips parted in an indulgent but not unkind smile. She said, 'Eduarda, as I've told you before, did indeed give birth to a son. I've also mentioned his full name – Jorge Eduardo do Livramento, born on 28th September 1942. From the date's perspective, it could be right. He could be your husband's son. Anyway, Jorge, his American wife, two children and five grandchildren all live in the States. He and his two children have dual nationality – Portuguese and American. The grandchildren and one of the two great-grandchildren are only American. The other, the girl who lives with her partner in Alentejo, also has dual citizenship. Eduarda only had the one son. As I said, he could be your husband's child, Mrs Neale, but I think you'll have to ask her yourself. She never married and had no other children but I couldn't find out who fathered Jorge. Didn't think it was my place to ask her.'

'You talked with her?' Xaver asked seemingly surprised.

'I did,' Renata answered promptly.

'Do tell,' Hertie begged, plainly anxious.

'After I traced Maria Eduarda and her descendants' whereabouts I thought you'd like me to talk to her and understand whether she'd be happy to meet you.'

'And?' Valeria gently nudged. Her turn to feel nervous.

'She said yes. She and Ana Maria seemed rather excited at the prospect of meeting you,' Renata Monteiro looked at Valeria, then added, 'but also you, Mrs Neale. I saw Maria Eduarda's expression when I mentioned you had something, stolen by your husband, you'd like to return to her.'

'You told her what it is?' Hertie asked.

'I mentioned the book – Os Lusíadas – and she seemed at first surprised, then overjoyed.'

'So,' Valeria concluded, 'she'll be happy for us to visit, right?'

'Yes, they all are. She wrote a letter to you, Miss Valeria, and suggested I hand it over personally. She thought about writing an e-mail but then decided the first approach would be better on paper, in her own words more personal,' Renata picked up her briefcase and extracted a light blue, sealed envelope. She handed it to Valeria with the words, 'here you are. Please read it at your leisure. I know Eduarda added her contact details and I had the impression she'd be looking forward to a reply.'

Nodding Valeria said, 'of course. It goes without saying.'

'I think,' Renata continued, 'Eduarda would like to hear about you, your family, particularly your mother and her sisters. You're the part of the family that both Ana Maria and Eduarda lost contact with, so—'

'Did they tell you why?' Valeria interrupted, 'I mean, we know Maria Eduarda disappeared without a trace after my grandfather expelled her from home once he found out about her pregnancy. We also knew Ana Maria immigrated to the States and married there. After which there was no further contact.'

'I don't know the details, Miss Valeria, but I'm sure they'll tell you when you visit.'

'Sorry. I interrupted you before. You were saying?'

'Nothing much. Just going to add that I thought the two old ladies would be very happy to meet you both,' glancing at Hertie, Renata added, 'Eduarda said it'd be interesting to share stories. I'm guessing she means about Mr Gerald Neale, as you both knew him well, but she didn't specify,' she looked at Valeria, Hertie and Xaver in turn, then smiling said, 'that's all really. I've given you the letter and told you everything...' she paused, 'unless you're interested in the details of my investigation and the steps taken to eventually trace Eduarda.'

'It'd be good to have all that in your final report and invoice, Ms Monteiro,' Hertie said, 'but for now this suffices. Thank you for coming all the way here to tell us, I mean, you could've done it via video link or the phone and posted the letter.'

'True but I've business in London on another case so thought you'd prefer a personal meeting and, as I said before, Eduarda also suggested it.'

'It was the right thing to do, Ms Monteiro, thank you,' Valeria said.

She stayed for another hour, then Xaver drove her to the station so she could take a train to London. Valeria and Hertie began immediately planning their visit even before reading Eduarda's letter. As Xaver returned Valeria was in the middle of jotting down bullet points on the things needed to be organised for the trip. He stated he'd like to go with them and requested Valeria to plan the trip for when he had time off in the summer. She agreed. He then wanted to know what Eduarda's letter said.

Valeria looked at the envelope with her handwritten name. The handwriting had a vigorous swing and elegance. Not like an old lady's handwriting. Opening the envelope she extracted one folded sheet of paper and, as she did so, a small note fell to the floor. It was for Hertie who picked it up and read aloud.

Dear Hertha,

First, I hope you will forgive me the familiarity of addressing you by your first name and would be very happy if you'd accept it. I'm too old to worry about such minor, unimportant social niceties.

Second, you're very welcome in mine and my sister's home. We live in the lovely countryside of Alentejo, my favourite region of Portugal, by the coast in a quiet isolated small estate south of the little village of Porto Covo. I feel you will enjoy it. I am eager to recover the first edition of Os Lusíadas, share my story with you and hear yours. I haven't thought about Gerald Neale for many years. You may have guessed he's the father of my son. He couldn't have told you because we never saw each other again and he didn't know I gave birth to a boy. My world fell apart when I realised I was pregnant. For a brief moment I was scared but then decided I wouldn't let it bring me down. And in the end I turned my life around, coming out on top. We will talk. For now, I just wish to thank you for partnering with my niece Valeria and hiring a detective to find me. Meeting you both will give me the closure I've longed for before my life eventually ends.

Please feel free to bring someone from your family with you if you so wish.

I look forward to your visit.
Maria Eduarda

'Well, she seems nice,' Xaver said, 'it's a brief but kind message. She doesn't appear to hold a grudge against Grandfather, Oma.'

'Possibly not. It all happened such a long time ago. Besides, as she tells us herself she turned her life around and came out on top.'

'You can say that again, Hertie,' Valeria commented, 'professor doctor in astrophysics by the University of Harvard. If that isn't the wow factor, I don't know what is.'

Hertie grinned. 'You're right. Anyway, have you read your letter?'

She nodded.

'Is it nice? Will you read it for us?'

'Yes and of course,' she replied.

Xaver moved to sit next to her, placing his arm around her shoulders. Valeria cleared her throat, then began reading aloud.

Dear Valeria,
I am so, so happy to finally address one of my many nieces and nephews directly. I can't wait to meet you in person.

It's a long time coming and it's my fault. I could have reached out to my five younger half-sisters after Dad died and especially after Rosa, your grandmother and his third wife, passed away. I didn't. There are reasons why but I will tell you when we meet and can talk in person.

You may be surprised to hear that I knew of my half-sisters' existence though they weren't yet born when I left for good. I also knew about my nieces and nephews, and logically about you and your triplet brothers before the detective, you and Hertha hired, traced me. Again, I'll explain when we meet in person.

I lived in the States for a long time. My son married an American. My life was there. I didn't think I would ever return to Portugal but after retiring I began missing the places of my youth. I wanted to see them again. So I came and when by accident I found the property where I now live I simply decided I had to buy it and would stay. Ana Maria joined me after her own retirement and her American husband's death. She has no kids and just wanted to live with me. We were always very close.

Ms Monteiro may have told you that my great-grandchild Ellie (her full name is Eleanor but she prefers Ellie) lives with us. She came to visit me one summer and met Miguel on the plane. He is from Porto Covo and his parents still live nearby. Miguel and Ellie fell in love and she didn't' want to return to America. Once Miguel finished his degree in agriculture, I offered him a job to run my estate. Ellie and he moved into the bungalow adjacent to our house. Ellie is good with numbers and obtained a degree in accountancy. She's become an excellent accountant. Handy. Ana Maria and I pay them both a small salary, which is topped up with the profits from the estate. They look after us and manage the estate together. We lead a quiet but happy life. I feel I can speak for all four of us.

Your mother and her sisters know nothing about me, I assume. Dad made sure of it and your grandmother, Rosa, didn't mind one way or the other. I believe she felt relieved when I left. I am not certain it'll be a good idea to meet the whole family but I can decide after you've visited us.

The detective told me what she knew about you and your work. As a follow-up, I researched you on Google. Finding many of your articles I promptly read them. You write well and are very knowledgeable about music. That much is clear from the very positive reviews of your work as an accompanist to some opera singers' recitals. Additionally, I read a few interviews you conducted with a variety of artists. I particularly enjoyed what you wrote about the dancer Xaver Duverger. To me it seemed to come from the heart.

Xaver interrupted her reading and kissing the tip of her nose, a cheeky twinkle in his eyes, commented blatantly, 'of course it came from the heart. You'd fallen hopelessly in love with me.'

Valeria pinched his arm.

'Ouch. That hurts.'

'Serves you right for being such a shameless, big-headed—'

'Adorable, handsome, smart, loving man,' he interjected with a cheeky smirk.

'Idiot,' she muttered, laughing and unable to resist him.

'Now, now children,' Hertie said, pretending to be angry, 'I want to hear the rest of the letter so behave Xavy.'

'Me?'

'Yes, you,' she said, trying to remain serious, 'and don't you look at me wide-eyed, feigning innocence. I know you're not.'

Xaver chuckled and mildly shaking her head Hertie made Valeria a sign to resume reading.

I'm an astrophysicist but, like you, I play the piano and besides the stars, music is my greatest passion. I learned to play as a child – mostly because then young society ladies were supposed to – but I loved it and never stopped playing throughout my life. Music and the piano picked me up and consoled me through many a trying time. It fills me with joy to know we share a love of music. I hope when you visit we can play together. I have two pianos. You're welcome to use one of them as you see fit during your stay.

'Rather sweet of her,' Xaver cut in, 'don't you think?'

'Yes,' Valeria agreed, 'she sounds kind.'

'I don't know about you two,' Xaver commented, 'but I can't wait to meet her.'

Valeria and Hertie both acknowledged in unison. Valeria resumed the letter.

I just want to repeat how you are all very welcome here. I'm eagerly anticipating yours and Hertha's visit, my dear Valeria. I don't know whether you're married or have a partner but if you do please don't hesitate to bring him or her with you. I'm sure we will have a lot of fun all together. Alentejo is the hottest region in Portugal so, depending on whether you all enjoy and have no issue with the heat, you may visit in the summer, otherwise in the spring or autumn. However, Alentejo is to my mind beautiful no matter the season. The winters are mild so you can come in the winter too.

I can't wait to meet you. In the meantime, please write. Now that we have found each other we should stay in touch. With love,

Your aunt,
Maria Eduarda

Valeria was touched and could see Hertie was too. Xaver apparently bursting with excitement said, 'it's all perfect. She tells Oma to take a relative and you to take your partner. I am both so I believe I'm ideal to accompany you two.'

They indulged him. It was the truth anyway. He could hardly wait to book flights and organise the trip. As it turned out, it had to be postponed until March 2017. In May 2015 Hertie had a bad fall on the staircase in her building, slashing her right leg below the knee and needing a hip operation. It took her nearly a year to recover her mobility. But, just as she believed she was getting better, the wound on her leg started hurting. The cut was deeper than initially thought. It had infected. Hertie needed another stint in hospital. Valeria especially visited her often. Xaver had to attend his numerous dancing commitments and performances but travelled to England whenever he had a couple of days to see his grandmother. She kept suggesting Xaver and Valeria should travel without her in the summer of 2016, after the notorious referendum on membership of the EU in late June that same year. But they thought it'd be too hot and neither of them wanted to go without Hertie.

Eventually the date for the trip came around. Somehow Xaver managed twelve free days in the middle of his busy schedule. He didn't explain how. Hertie and Valeria didn't care. The fact he could go with them was music to their ears. Once again Valeria had to take Wonkie, her cat, to stay with her parents before leaving. She wondered whether the cat minded, as it always seemed happy to see her when she arrived home. Her parents were happy about it. They liked Wonkie and accepted Valeria's explanation at face value, telling them she was taking Hertie and Xaver to Portugal on holiday, as none of them knew the country. And so, after exchanging many e-mails with Maria Eduarda, Valeria, Hertie and Xaver were finally on their way and arrived in Portugal on Thursday, 16th March 2017.

Part 4 – The Visit

(Portugal, 2017)

"De todos os cantos do mundo
Amo com um amor mais forte e mais profundo
Aquela praia extasiada e nua,
Onde me uni ao mar, ao vento e à lua."

Sophia de Mello Breyner Andresen (1919-2004), "Mar", Mar Poesia, Editorial Caminho, Lisboa, 2001

"From all the corners of the world
I love, with a more powerful, profound devotion
That ecstatic and exposed shore,
Where I merged with the sea, the wind and the moonlight core."

Translation by M G da Mota

Chapter 1 – Driving Through Alentejo

It was a sunny day with clear blue skies when the plane landed at Lisbon's Humberto Delgado International Airport. The temperature, according to the pilot, was 22 degrees Celsius. Hertie was pleased, telling her grandson and Valeria it was ideal, especially after the rain and greyness they had left behind in England.

Valeria had booked a hire car with sat nav. After passing passport control, collecting their luggage and completing the car formalities they headed south of the Portuguese capital with Valeria at the wheel.

Hertie sat quietly in the back, staring out of the car window at an unfamiliar landscape. They had crossed the elegant and long suspension bridge over the river Tagus, named Vasco da Gama after the great Portuguese explorer, to move onto the A2 motorway half an hour ago, leaving Lisbon behind. Alentejo's rolling hills extended on both sides of the road, green and fresh. Isolated trees seemingly seeded at random, scattered the land here and there. Only the olive groves betrayed the presence of humans, planted in neat well-planned rows. Hertie was surprised. Alentejo was an arid region, in places almost a desert, according to her readings, but this here was green and covered in wildflowers.

'I didn't know Alentejo was so vividly green. So many flowers,' she said to Valeria who glanced at her through the rear mirror.

'When it rains in Alentejo it turns green overnight and the flowers blossom in a riot of colour. They've had a rainy February. As soon as the sun comes out, spring arrives.'

Looking back at the passing landscape Hertie murmured, 'it's beautiful.'

'The area where Maria Eduarda lives,' Valeria went on, 'is perhaps even more gorgeous. Porto Covo is a pretty little village and the coast south of it is wild. Stunning. Even in the summer the beaches are quiet. But now we should be able to admire them in all their glorious rough, ragged beauty. Long stretches of white sand between high cliffs and steep crags, white crested rolling waves, deep green waters. You'll like it.'

'I'm sure.'

Hertie leaned back, tired and enchanted in equal measure. Xaver looked over his shoulder.

'Are you all right, Oma? You look pale. Would you like us to stop for a bit so you can rest?'

'No,' Hertie said, 'I'm fine, Schatz, don't worry. Just admiring the landscape.'

'Okay, but you'll tell us if you need to stop, right?'

'Of course, my darling.'

She did feel tired but wasn't ill, just weak from the time in hospital and months and months of therapy and pain. But she was healthy again and excited about the days ahead in a country she didn't know, meeting interesting people. Her eyes wandered to the scenery. She noticed the first cork oaks for which Alentejo was famous.

'Valeria, Gerry told me Alentejo was a region of big landowners, with tens of thousands of cork trees, pigs that roam free and where the locals work the landlords' vast estates in a near feudal system, living in poor, sometimes almost squalid conditions. Is it still so?'

'The part about the pigs and the cork trees is still true,' Valeria replied, 'but the revolution of April 1974 that ended the fascist dictatorship also ended the reign of the feudal landlords. Most lost their properties and were forced to flee the country. They went to Brazil. The estates are now in the hands of either big corporations who have to obey strict employment laws, or they're managed by a cooperative of workers. Some of the owners recovered their estates but they were forced to employ agriculture and cattle experts, proper business managers, salaries, sick pay and holidays to all workers, including the ones working the land. The situation is completely different now. One of the many good things to happen after the revolution. My grandfather lost almost everything he had but refused to leave Portugal. He realised the revolution was coming so transferred money to Switzerland and invested in properties in England. It turned out to be the right move.'

'We know so little about this country. And it's so fascinating.'

'Who's we?' Valeria asked.

'We in England, in Germany, probably in most European countries.'

'Have you been reading about it, Oma?' Xaver enquired.

'Yes. I didn't want to appear totally ignorant in front of an educated, intelligent woman like Maria Eduarda.'

She noticed her grandson and Valeria exchanging an amused, tender glance. He turned round and touched her hand. 'You're a treasure, Oma. I'm sure Maria Eduarda won't be upset if your knowledge of Portugal is limited.'

'That's not the point. Anyway, Valeria, I wanted to ask you something.'

'Okay.'

'Do you know why the revolution of 1974, which you've just mentioned, was called the Carnation Revolution? I know the army had carnations in the gun barrels but was there more to it? I mean, why were they there in the first place?'

'I know the story, yes. It's actually rather touching. Would you like to hear it?'

'Oh yes, please.'

'As you know, on 25th April 1974, the armed forces in Portugal revolted and ended the then 48-year-old fascist dictatorship in the country. They were tired of the guerrilla wars in the African colonies, which had been going on for years with no end in sight, unless the dictatorship was terminated. In the early hours of that morning, troops from all over the country travelled to Lisbon. The signal was given at midnight on the radio where a revolutionary song entitled *Grândola, Vila Morena* was played. Grândola is a town in Alentejo in an area that particularly suffered under the exploitation of big landowners. The song was written by a singer-song writer named José or Zeca Afonso. His songs were forbidden under the dictatorship and each time he published one he landed in prison and was tortured by the PIDE – the secret police. It didn't stop him. He possessed a beautiful voice. So, his song sung by him was an appropriate sign to start a revolution. It was a memorable revolution because there was no blood, no shots and no-one was injured.'

'But what about the carnations?'

'Getting there, Hertie. In 1974 a woman called Celeste Caeiro was 40 years old and lived in a rented room on Largo do Carmo – Carmo Square – in Chiado, a borough of Lisbon, with her mother and daughter. She worked in a different borough, on Braancamp Street, cleaning a restaurant called Franjinhas, which had opened a year earlier on 25 April 1973. The restaurant's owner wanted to celebrate his establishment's first anniversary by offering flowers to his customers. He'd bought red carnations and had them in the restaurant, ready for lunchtime later in the day, when he heard on the radio that a revolution had begun in the city. He sent everyone home, fearing fighting on the streets and told his employees, "take the flowers with you, it's a shame if they stay here withering away." Celeste took the underground to Rossio – a famous square in the heart of Lisbon – and there she saw the chaimites – Portuguese armoured vehicles. She asked a soldier what they were for. The soldier, who'd been there since the early hours of the morning, didn't answer and asked for a cigarette instead. Celeste, who didn't smoke, offered him a carnation. The soldier put the flower into the barrel of his shot gun. The gesture was seen by others who asked for a flower from Celeste and imitated their comrade. On the way home, on foot, to Largo do Carmo where she lived, Celeste offered the rest of her carnations one by one to the soldiers on the street and they put them in the barrels of their guns. Soon the people and the soldiers were copying the gesture. That's how the Portuguese Revolution of 25 April 1974 that ended the 48-year-old fascist dictatorship became known as the Carnation Revolution.'

'Very moving,' Hertie exclaimed, 'but is it true?'

Valeria shrugged. 'My cousin says it is. He works in a newspaper and even showed me a photo of this lady with her arms full of red carnations. I believe it.'

'Thank you for telling it so well. It really is lovely.'

Hertie went quiet for a moment, reflecting on what she

had just heard. Dictators and dictatorships wrecked countries and people, causing so much suffering. She remembered all the horrors she and so many others had lived through in Germany. It had taken a punishing, brutal war to finish it off. At least the Portuguese dictatorship ended without bloodshed or additional suffering. Warmth crept over her. It was good to be here. To feel the sun. To admire the beauty of the region. Focusing her eyes on the landscape parading past the car windows she noticed the lean, black pigs roaming around. The sunflower fields now dormant looked a bit sad while patiently waiting for the early summer to bloom their yellow exuberance. So bright it almost defied sunlight. The cork oaks fascinated her. The bark had been harvested from many. They had large numbers painted on the trunk where the cork was cut and removed. What did the numbers mean? Curious, Hertie asked Valeria whether she knew.

'The numbers are the years.'

'The years?'

'Yes. Once the cork is cut and removed, the tree needs nine years to fully regrow the bark and be in a condition to have it harvested again. The farmers paint the last number of the year on the cork, so they know exactly when a particular tree can have the cork cut and removed again without damaging it. For example, a five means it was cut in 2015, a six, last year in 2016 and so on.'

'But doesn't the number disappear as the bark grows again?'

'No. It fades a little but doesn't vanish. It's painted immediately after the cork was taken and when it begins to grow it remains on the surface of the bark.'

'Fascinating,' Hertie replied sincerely, 'and how do you know all this?'

Valeria seemed amused and smiling through the rear mirror said, 'you forget I'm half Portuguese. I've family here and we often visit.'

'That's true. Your English is so impeccably British I often forget your mother's Portuguese and you're bilingual.'

'I feel privileged to have grown up bilingual. Makes it a

lot easier to learn other languages.'

'Exactly how many languages do you speak?' Xaver intervened.

'Fluently?'

'Yes.'

'One more than you. You speak English, German, Russian and French. In my case, besides English and German, there's Portuguese, Italian and French. My French isn't as good, not to the same degree of fluency. The Italian I learned when I travelled there for music studies and singing courses.'

Caressing the back of her neck with his fingers he said in a loving voice, no hint of irony, 'you're an adorable, rather impressive woman.'

'So are you,' Valeria exclaimed in the same tone, 'not woman naturally,' she added chuckling at her own joke.

Hertie's chest swelled. It was wonderful to witness them revelling in each other's company. Aloud she said, 'we've been driving for just over an hour. It appears there's a motorway petrol station with a café approaching. I saw the signs. Could we stop for a moment? I could do with a cold drink and I need the loo.'

'Of course. I need a coffee, water and the loo as well,' Valeria agreed.

'Coffee would be lovely and maybe a bite to eat?' Xaver added.

'Good idea.'

'Are we still far from Maria Eduarda's place?' Hertie asked, as Valeria signalled to the right, indicating she was turning into the petrol station.

'About another hour, or perhaps a bit longer. The estate isn't in the village of Porto Covo itself. It's by the coast, in the middle of nowhere, south of the village and about halfway between it and the town of Vila Nova de Mil Fontes. So what I'm trying to say is that it may take a little longer. I don't know whether the driveway's easy to find.'

'Didn't you put the coordinates in the sat nav?' Xaver asked.

'Yes, but it may not be obvious.'

Valeria parked the car and Xaver went around to open the door for his grandmother. Hertie held on to his hand, climbing out with some difficulty. He offered her his arm and she gladly accepted. They walked slowly to the café. Hertie narrowed her eyes to protect them from the intense sunshine. It was warm. A gentle, pleasant breeze blew, caressing her skin and touching her hair. Life was made of simple pleasures. Suddenly she laughed brightly.

'It feels like summer,' she exclaimed, 'and I feel happy.'

Chapter 2 – Arrival

They had passed the signs for the village of Porto Covo twenty minutes earlier. No glimmer of the estate or its driveway.

'Perhaps we drove by and didn't notice,' Hertie ventured.

Valeria stopped the car. Xaver looked at the sat nav. She pulled up her phone to read Maria Eduarda's directions sent on a WhatsApp message and commented, 'I think you're right, Hertie. We need to turn back. Did any of you see a brown sign with the estate's name?'

'What's the name?' Xaver asked.

'Quinta das Estrelas.'

'What does it mean?' Hertie wanted to know.

'Farm or Estate of the Stars.'

'Pretty.'

'Yes and appropriate for an astrophysicist,' Valeria agreed, 'anyway, Maria Eduarda says that after passing the signs to Porto Covo we continue ten minutes on the N120. Then we'll find a brown sign with the estate's name on the right-hand side. We turn right immediately after onto a small, paved country road. We drive along that little road five minutes or so. After a sharp bend with the ruin of a windmill, we'll see the ocean further ahead. Approximately eight hundred meters after that there's another brown sign with the name of the estate. There we turn onto an unpaved, gravelled wide boulevard-like alley, with ancient, tall trees on both sides. That's apparently the driveway. We'll reach the house after one kilometre in a straight line.'

'Okay. Let's do it. It'd be good to arrive before dark,' Hertie commented.

Valeria made a U-turn, saying, 'remember we're heading north now, as we've done a u-turn, so the sign will be on the left, not the right.'

'Obviously,' Xaver commented with a smirk.

He and Hertie kept an eye for the brown sign on the side of the road. He saw it first.

'There it is,' he cried out, 'Quinta dash Eshtrelas,' he pronounced in a slow, exaggerated manner.

The sun was gradually lowering in the horizon, painting the sky and the sea in a palette of reds, oranges and yellows when they finally found the driveway. As they approached the house, it began slowly to darken. Getting out of the car they stood staring for a moment. To the west the sun set in a fireball, unhurriedly sinking into the sea, tracing a crimson path of light on the water from the horizon to the coastline. Hertie heard the distant sound of the ocean, of waves crashing the sand. She smelled salt and seaweed. Spellbound from Nature's spectacle she nearly forgot where they were. Xaver's voice brought her back to reality.

'Beautiful,' he exclaimed, voicing what they were all undoubtedly thinking.

Hertie turned and looked at the house. It was two-storey, in the architectural style of Alentejo, whitewashed walls – glowing orange and pink from the left-over light of the sunset – framed with blue. Red tiles on the roof. Three hundred metres or so to the right of the main house she saw a bungalow in a similar style. Evidently both buildings had been thoroughly renovated and modernised, with large, double-glazed windows and state of the art shutters. Three exterior lights were on – one above the front door; two next to the trees marking the end of the driveway or the beginning, depending where one was heading. Bright light came through some of the ground-floor windows where the shutters were up. The bungalow lay dark. Someone must have heard the sound of the car on the gravel because the front door opened and a tall young man stepped out and walked towards them. His hair was brushed back in dark, unruly, almost wild curls contrasting his serene hazelnut brown eyes and welcoming smile. He stretched his arm to Hertie, shaking her hand firmly.

'You must be Mrs Hertha Neale,' he said in impeccable English.

'Yes,' Hertie replied with a nod.

'I'm Miguel Andrade. Welcome to Quinta das Estrelas,' turning to Valeria he added, 'you must be Edi's, I mean, Maria Eduarda's niece and—'

'I am,' Valeria interrupted him, 'and presumably you're Ellie's partner?'

'That's right.'

Taking Xaver's arm Hertie said, 'this is my grandson Xaver, also Valeria's partner.'

Introductions completed Miguel made them a sign to follow him, explaining they could fetch the luggage later. They entered a large hall with a mirror hanging on either side and a wide variety of coat hooks. Wellington boots, in various sizes and colours, were lined up on a long wooden box, obviously built for the purpose. Miguel closed the door, saying, 'they're in the back sitting room. We can have a leisurely drink. We never eat before 8.30 pm. Then, after dinner, I'll show you to your bedrooms upstairs.'

Hertie walked slowly behind the three young people, looking around her with an approving eye. The staircase was wide in polished dark wood. She noticed a cage-like lift to the side. It seemed completely out of place however practical it might be. Maybe the two old women had difficulty walking up and down the stairs. She knew she did. Pretty, bright watercolours and oil paintings of mainly seascapes lined the walls. Hertie sensed happiness hanging in the air. The house had a heart. It was clearly loved by the humans who inhabited it. Smiling inwardly she called herself silly. Houses were not living things. Ahead the others were already in the sitting room. Hertie heard the rustling of clothes on chairs as undoubtedly their occupants stood up to receive their guests. She stepped into the room, glancing around. Pleasant first impression. Spacious, with a wide window and patio door. Must have a lot of light during the day. The furniture was simple, almost rustic, light coloured pine wood, bright red chairs with painted flowers in yellow and blue, modern couches in deep red with navy blue cushions. More paintings and a couple of enlarged photos of what Hertie thought were galaxies on the walls. A welcoming room. To her right, standing in front of a chair there was a woman. A marking presence, remarkable deportment. She knew how to carry herself – Maria Eduarda, no doubt. Next to her another old lady and further right a girl, sitting in a wheelchair. Maria Eduarda's great-granddaughter Ellie? It had to be. No other people lived in the estate. So, was the lift for

Ellie's benefit?

Discreetly while smiling and shaking hands Hertie observed Maria Eduarda. She was dressed in a pair of knitted navy blue trousers, a white cotton turtleneck and a turquoise cardigan, wearing black slippers. The skin of her face was smooth and little wrinkled for her advanced years. Curly white hair, neatly cut, shining silvery in the lights. A natural grace and elegance enveloped her, an inherent aristocratic bearing. Unwittingly one's gaze was drawn to her. Behind the stylish, frameless glasses Hertie noticed the grass-green eyes that had so much turned Gerald's head. Still bright. Still lively. She stood erect in front of the armed chair, no walking stick to help her, smiling warmly at them. Hertie noticed the dimples. And all of a sudden she saw the young Maria Eduarda in front of her. A stunning vision of striking, exotic beauty. In a flash she understood why Gerald had so hopelessly fallen for her and wanted to have her. Naturally, no excuse for what he'd done. He, like all men, had the obligation of controlling his desires, however strong they might be, especially if a woman said no.

Hertie remembered how he had persistently chased attractive women until they had given in to him. He must have been crazy about Maria Eduarda. At ninety-six she was still a remarkably handsome woman. An arresting presence. At twenty she must have been memorable, stunning and almost irresistible. Her sister Ana Maria faded in comparison. White hair, slightly plump and shorter than Maria Eduarda she had a similar innate aristocratic aura but lacked the elegance. Her eyes were dark blue, sparking warmly behind her specs. She too smiled kindly at them, leaning on a black walking stick with a silver top. The young Ellie was a rather pretty girl, with dark brown eyes and classical, delicate features. Like her great-grandmother two cute little dimples appeared on her face when she smiled. Hertie wondered why she was in a wheelchair. Recovering from a recent accident? Or something more serious and permanent? Sad. A young person should always be able to move energetically around.

Maria Eduarda and Ana Maria dropped their hands and

hugged each one of them instead.

'Valeria, my dear niece,' Eduarda said, 'I'm thrilled to finally meet you. How lovely you are,' turning to Hertie she continued, 'Hertha, welcome to mine and my sister's home, so happy to receive you and talk,' then moving on to Xaver she embraced him too, saying, 'the famous Xaver Duverger. I've read and heard a lot about you. Hope you'll grace us with at least a few ballet steps to the sound of a piano.'

Hertie's grandson seemed impressed and greeted the grand lady with a balletic bow and hand kiss, causing her smile to widen and the grass-green eyes to twinkle.

Later, after dinner, Miguel stood up and said he would show them their rooms. Xaver went out with him to get the luggage from the car. Hertie's room faced the back and was close to the stairs. She thought Miguel and her grandson had decided to take the lift for her benefit but made no comment. She glanced over her shoulder before entering her room and saw that Valeria's and Xaver's room was at the end of the corridor facing the front of the house. She stepped in, closing the door behind her and looked around. A spacious bedroom. Comfortable. Two large windows. Double iron bed. White wardrobe with painted blue flowers. A matching chest of drawers. A couple of blue chairs with small white patterns on the back. A comfortable looking chaise longue in blue fabric. Pictures of seascapes hanging above the bed. A dressing table with an oval mirror. A glass shelf with framed photos above the air-conditioning device embedded in the wall. She remembered someone mentioning the house had been equipped with central air-conditioning – warm in winter and cool in the scorching Alentejo summers. Hertie switched off the light and opened one of the windows. She looked out. To her right there was a pretty balcony with canvas chairs and a small table. The shutters were down and only a little shimmer of light escaped through them. Hertie remembered Maria Eduarda had opened the door before hers. It must be her bedroom.

Hertie's eyes took a while to adapt to the darkness. She looked up. The sky took her breath away. Elegantly curving above her an arm of the Milky Way. Constellations she knew and other countless unfamiliar groups of stars punctuated the night. Hertie hadn't seen such a sky since her childhood in Germany when at night no lights were allowed to shine and windows were covered with thick black cloth. She remembered the icy firmament glimpsed from the train and the trucks during their escape from East Prussia. The memories had faded. Time taken its toll. Almost as if they weren't hers but some other unknown little girl's. The luminous beauty of the stars, however, was the same.

Hertie sensed tears at the back of her eyes. She looked down to earth. In the middle of the field behind the house and the bungalow there was a structure. It was round and with a dome, barely visible in the darkness but the dome clearly silhouetted against the night sky. What could it be? Her curiosity awoken she decided to ask Maria Eduarda or Ana Maria the next morning. And about Ellie. Why was the girl in a wheelchair? Would probably be bad manners to ask. At least in front of the girl. Hertie sighed. She felt touched at the obvious love with which Miguel looked after Ellie. When it was time to retire to their bedrooms, he gently sat her on a sofa in the living room, taking the wheelchair outside and returning to carry her. With great care he placed her in the wheelchair and they headed to their bungalow.

The evening had been a quiet one. By mutual silent agreement no-one touched the stories of the past during the various conversations. Better to leave it for later when they were rested from the travelling exertions. Tomorrow was another day. There would be plenty of time to talk and most of all, to return the stolen items to their legitimate owner.

Hertie breathed in the night air. She could smell the salt from the ocean and hear the distant waves breaking up on the sand or against the rocks. There was peace in this place. Peace. Love. Warmth. Her lips parted instinctively. She liked it here. Lifting her eyes to the heavens for a second time she lost her gaze in the contemplation of the stars. Her skin gained goosebumps. She shivered. It was getting chilly. Turning her back to the night Hertie locked the window and flicked on the light switch.

Chapter 3 – Photographs

As the ceiling light shone brightly, Hertie's eyes caught a glimpse of its reflection on the glass shelf above the air-conditioner. Her gaze rested on the framed photos arranged on top of the ledge and one caught her attention. The face was familiar.

She approached the corner and picked up the blue wooden frame with painted stars, containing a portrait in old-fashioned colour – like the Kodak films she used in the sixties to take pictures of the children. The photo depicted a young man with dark curly hair flopping carelessly over his forehead. Bright eyes, smiling at the camera. An appealing glimmer of mischief, of cheekiness twinkling in his green irises. Handsome. Extremely attractive. She had a light bulb moment. A brunette version of Gerald. It must be his and Maria Eduarda's son.

Hertie pressed her right hand to her chest, feeling a sudden pang. Naturally she knew the story of how Gerald had abused Maria Eduarda's trust and hospitality…really how he'd raped her but somehow it didn't feel real. Not her own reality. Simply part of Gerald's deathbed confession. Now it stared her in the face. The indisputable proof that Gerry had fathered Maria Eduarda's son. Unmistakable likeness. Replace the dark curls with straight platinum blonde hair and the eyes with blue rather than green and Gerald materialised in front of her eyes, exactly as he must have been when a young man.

Hertie wondered about the age of the boy at the time the photo was taken. Opening the frame she removed the picture and looked at the back. Her guess was right. There was a date and a place. Boston, November 1961. Jorge…was his name Jorge? Or Eduardo? She made a dismissive gesture to herself. Didn't matter. He'd been born in September 1942 so he was nineteen in the photo. Must be an old man now. She calculated his age in her head. Seventy-four. A few years younger than her. She had turned eighty-one just a month earlier. It would be nice to see a current photo of him and imagine how Gerry would have looked had he survived to old age. At first a need, the idea soon became an urge. She felt compelled. Must see a current photo of

Eduarda's son.

Remembering she had seen photo albums in the back sitting-room Hertie decided to go downstairs and page through them. She opened her bedroom door and peered outside. Landing and staircase were dark. She closed her door silently and furtively descended in darkness, hoping no-one would detect her. Music came from the library as she arrived at the hall. Someone played the piano. Light escaped under the door. Gently Hertie opened it a fraction and peeped inside. Maria Eduarda sat at the grand piano. A charming, graceful tune escaped the keys under the elegance of her gliding fingers. Something by Mozart? Perhaps. Hertie's knowledge of music was limited. Why was Maria Eduarda playing alone at this time of night? Maybe she couldn't sleep. One slept fewer hours when old, as she very well knew.

Hertie hovered by the doorframe for a moment. Eduarda and the piano seemed to have merged into one single entity. The sound so beautiful it made her heart ache. The experience so transcendent, so sublime Hertie thought people who believed in God must feel that way. She shook her head in mild disapproval of herself. Intruding on an intimate musical moment between her hostess and her piano was wrong. Noiselessly, so she wouldn't disturb Maria Eduarda, Hertie shut the door. On tiptoes she headed to the back sitting room, slipped quickly inside and turned on the light. She was right. On top of a little table, next to an upholstered chair, rested five photo albums.

Hertie sat down, picked the top one and placed it on her lap. There was a label on the hardcover with handwritten dates – 1950 to 1955. Hertie placed it on the floor. The second stated 1940 to 1945. The third 1955 to 1960. The fourth 1960 to 1965 and the final one 1935 to 1940. No current photos of Maria Eduarda's son in these albums for sure. It occurred to her they might be in Eduarda's laptop. Everything was digital nowadays. Why did she even want to see a pic of someone who, had he lived, might resemble Gerald in old age? Gerry was dead. Buried years ago. He had often made her life miserable. So why so keen to see photos of someone who resembled him? Perhaps she wanted to have an idea of how unattractive he'd have been as an old man. It was interesting that her children with Gerry didn't look as much like him as Eduarda's son. Her own genes must be stronger. Hertie smirked. It served him right.

Feeling curious she picked up the album marked 1940 to 1945. Gerry had been in Portugal from 1940 to 1942. Perhaps there were images of Eduarda as a young woman and of the people Gerry had talked about during his confession.

The photos were all in black and white. Maria Eduarda appeared in some. Dear God, Hertie exclaimed silently to herself, how amazing she looked. Maria Eduarda was a real stunner as a young woman. So beautiful. So exotic. Hertie looked at a picture of her in an evening gown, her hair decorated with what seemed like tiny diamonds. Shame it was just black and white. She would have liked to see the colours. Eduarda was on the arm of an older rather distinguished looking man. She stood on his left and smiled directly at the camera. There was another young woman on the man's right. She was greeting someone else and hadn't noticed the photographer. Everyone depicted was in evening dress. Underneath the words: Papa, Rosa and I – July 1940, Ricardo's dinner at his home in Boca do Inferno for the Duke and Duchess of Windsor. Gerald had really told her the truth. That was where he'd met Maria Eduarda. The story seemed realer, more palpable to Hertie now. More authentic. She continued paging through the pictures and soon found photos of the Windsors with other people. One in particular caught her attention when she scanned the caption: Papa, Ricardo, the Duke of Windsor, Sir Ronald Campbell and his private secretary, Gerald Neale, at Ricardo's dinner, July 1940.

Hertie adjusted her spectacles, then glanced around the room, believing to have glimpsed a magnifying glass somewhere. Sure enough there it was, resting on one of the bookshelves. She fetched it and sat down again with the album, examining the photo carefully. The Duke of Beja was a remarkable presence. She perceived that Eduarda's aristocratic elegance had visibly been inherited from her father. Ricardo must be Ricardo Espirito Santo, the Portuguese banker Gerry had mentioned. An elegant, handsome man with obvious charm. She recognised Edward,

Duke of Windsor easily, having seen many pictures of him. Sir Ronald Campbell, Hertie remembered, was the British ambassador to Portugal at the time and then there he was – her husband Gerald Neale. He looked young, actually he was young then – only twenty-two. And so gorgeous. Hertie had met him when he was thirty-eight. Slim and devastatingly handsome, she remembered thinking.

She admired the twenty-two year old Gerald through the lenses of the magnifying glass. Stunning. No man had the right to be this handsome. And what a marvellously beautiful couple he and Maria Eduarda must have made standing next to each other. Shame it didn't work out but then if it had she wouldn't have married Gerald or met Maria Eduarda. Laughing at her own thoughts Hertie noted she was very tired. Not just that. Sadness and guilt engulfed her. By preying on Maria Eduarda's old photo albums she had been intruding in her private sphere. It was wrong and she must stop. Her chest ached. All of a sudden a lump in her throat and an inexplicable urge to cry swamped her. Poorly disguising a sob she stood up. Abandoning the albums and the magnifying glass on the floor Hertie walked to the door. She opened it, simultaneously switching off the lights. Footsteps. She heard footsteps on the staircase. The music from the library had stopped. No light escaped under the door. Hertie guessed Maria Eduarda was walking up the stairs, heading to her room to sleep.

Hertie waited until the footsteps faded. She heard the sound of a door opening and shutting on the first floor, then tiptoed up the staircase in the dark, vanishing inside her bedroom, exhaling, relieved no-one had witnessed her incursion into the past. Flicking on the light she fetched the photograph of Eduarda's son, holding it to the beam to better see it. She stretched her fatigued body on the inviting chaise longue and stared at the smiling face on the photo for a long time. Her mind wandered to the face of the other man. Gerald. The man in hers and Eduarda's past – the father of her children and the father of Eduarda's son. Her kids had a half-brother they didn't know existed. Xavy and her other grandchildren a great uncle. Hertie wondered why she was thinking about Gerald and the past. After telling the whole story to her grandson and Valeria she had hardly given it another thought. Except now. The similarities between Jorge and Gerald were remarkable. Perhaps that was the reason. She inhaled, leaning her head back.

Without warning her life began swaggering in front of her eyes. Papa going to war. Her uncles going to war except Siggi. With his wooden leg he had to stay behind. Mutti crying, as Papa didn't come home for the first Christmas after he'd been sent to fight. Or next Christmas or the one after that. Mutti sobbing in aunt Jutta's arms, whispering she didn't know what to do for food.

The school. The primary school in East Prussia. Her little friend Amalie. So quiet. So sweet. So kind. Those horrible men in uniform. They had taken her. Hertie had never seen her again. Amalie disappeared without a trace because of being Jewish. Later, as an adult, Hertie had searched for Amalie in the concentration camps registers but had never found her or her parents. Killed probably. All of them. And that horrible woman. The teacher. Frau Schulz married to an SS officer and always talking about the people who committed crimes against the Führer and the Fatherland like Fräulein Mett who could never have done anything wrong. So kind. So friendly. Always.

Russian soldiers. Coats. Scarves. Walking in the dark to the station. Uncle Siggi couldn't go. The train. The cold. The ice. The snow. Strudel, the cat that had landed on their plate. The interminable potato skin soup. Each day. Every day. Mutti. Uncle Siggi. Frozen feet. Numb with cold. The pain in her chest when breathing in the glacial air. The cellar with the potatoes. Fear. Terror of having been abandoned. Mutti. The boy who'd helped save her. What was his name? Oskar. Oskar Kaufmann. She hadn't thought about him for ages. Why now? She'd never seen him again. No idea what had happened to him. The train. The village. The old woman in the village. The dead. Auntie Elsa's farm. The noise of boots. The screams of auntie Jutta. The fear. Making herself invisible on the chimney ledge. The fear. Mute. Her voice had gone. She couldn't speak. Auntie Jutta covered in blood, agonising in Mutti's arms. The tears freezing on their faces. The open truck. The polar, raw wind. The fear. And the stars. Always up there the beauty of the twinkling dots. The cold sky covered in stars. And over it all the fear.

Vividly her recurring dream came back. In all its terror, making her anxious. For a heartbeat Hertie couldn't breathe. Then a face. A kind face. Of course. Ingrid. And Kurt. The farm near Hamburg. Uncle Siggi who had miraculously survived. Mutti. Hedi. Helmut. Heinrich. The first Christmas in peace. Mutti and her wizardry in the kitchen with lack of food and ingredients. Ingrid's imaginative scarves – their first Christmas present after the war.

Herr Offizier – the nice American colonel who gave her chocolate. Because of him she had become a translator. But that was later. Mutti had a job and they met the old colonel. Kaspar's return. Taciturn. Menacing. Ingrid suggesting he ask Mutti to marry him. Mutti announcing they would marry. Hedi's fear of him. Her departure to Munich. Her own anxiety about Kaspar. Mutti couldn't know. Mutti mustn't know.

Departure from Hamburg. The ruins of a church. Faces. A pretty, friendly girl. Bettina. Berlin. And his face. Gerald Neale. Gerry. Dancing on cloud nine in his arms. His kisses. His touch on her body. Pregnant in no time.

'I'll do right by you,' he'd said. Why? she thought. Later she knew. Because he had done wrong by another many years earlier. Maria Eduarda so young, so beautiful, but it was her old lady's dimpled smile that Hertie saw.

Mutti's grave. Helmut's funeral. Gerry. Skin and bone. Shrunk, nearly disappearing under the sheets.

'I must tell you. I must tell you everything.'

Cruel. Despicable to Thorp. To Maria Eduarda. A thief. A rapist.

'My husband. A criminal. The father of my children a corrupt, immoral man,' she mumbled.

The dream. Always the dream, plaguing her nights. Xaver her beautiful grandson. Skye, the therapist who cured her, who made her understand the dream and the terrors that originated it. A sweet face. Valeria playing the piano. Dachau and the wind whistling through the camp. Arbeit macht frei. The horror. Something beautiful in contrast. Munich. In the auditorium of the Bavarian State Opera, Valeria's face one more time. Enchanted, watching Xaver dance. Falling in love. Always a wonderful time.

And then that blasted basement again. She couldn't get out. The cold. So cold.

'No. No. No. Mutti. Mutti help me.'

Abruptly Hertie opened her eyes wide. Her heart throbbing so fast it felt it would smash her bones and tear her skin apart. She gasped for air, shivering, and recognised her comfortable bedroom in Eduarda's and Ana Maria's home. She'd fallen asleep on the chaise longue and been dreaming. The photographs. The black and white pic of the young Gerald. His and Maria Eduarda's son – Gerry's spitting image but not blonde. She glanced down. It was still on her lap. The corner of the frame snugged in her hand. Luckily it hadn't fallen to the floor and shattered.

Shaking, feeling cold, Hertie stood up and returned the picture to the glass shelf. Trembling she managed to change into her pyjamas, switch off the lights and crawl under the covers. It took a while but lulled by the starlight through the open shutters of her closed windows her eyelids gradually dropped. Her breathing became rhythmical. Peaceful. Hertie fell into a deep sleep only waking early the next morning with the first rays of dawn dancing on her face.

Chapter 4 – Tranquil Revelations

Bright sunshine. After breakfast they walked together to the ocean, excepting Miguel and Ellie who had work to do. Hertie moved slowly, dragging her feet. Not fatigue but a little flustered from her dream the night before. An affectionate voice made her glance up to her left.

'Are you all right, Oma?' Xaver asked, 'you seem to have difficulty walking.'

Hertie patted his hand, replying, 'I'm well mein Schatz. It's just...last night before going to bed I fell asleep on the chaise longue in my room and had the most stupid...well, not stupid but...I guess, disturbing – yes, it's the right word - disturbing dream.'

'What about?'

'Everything. Like I was watching a speeding slide show of moments of my entire life.'

'The recurring nightmare? I thought Skye had cured you of that...I mean explained why it happened. You appeared to be rid of it.'

'Well, the panic featured...and fear. I felt intense fear. And the cold. So cold. Like those glacial nights when Mutti, auntie Jutta, my siblings and I fled East Prussia ahead of the Russian invasion.'

'Come on, stop thinking about it. It was all a long, long time ago. Give me your arm. I'll walk slowly with you. Don't want you stumbling and falling flat on your face now do we, Oma?'

Hertie's lips parted fondly.

'You really are a treasure to me, you know that, my dear?'

He laughed. A pert sparkle in his dark eyes. 'Of course, I know. I'm precious like a ruby or a diamond.'

She slapped his wrist. 'And a shameless little monkey to your grandmother. Show me some respect, young man.'

They laughed together and nearly bumped into Valeria who'd stopped and glanced over her shoulder.

'Everything okay?' she asked.

'Yes, all's fine,' Hertie said, 'my legs don't move as fast as they used to so Xavy waited for me to help me walk safely.'

Valeria nodded. Hertie noticed the affection in their eyes as they looked briefly at each other. And suddenly a strange, distressing notion crept into her mind. Xaver would be all right when she died. Valeria would see to it with her love. Shocked at her own thoughts Hertie nearly tripped, having to hold on to Xaver.

'Steady, Oma,' he placed an arm around her waist to balance her, 'okay?'

'Yes. I wasn't paying attention and the ground's irregular,' she told him.

In that area, the cliffs were not high or steep, with a gentle incline. An easy path followed the rocky walks to the sandy beach below, allowing them to reach it without difficulty. The sea was rough. Noisy. Waves, foamy white manes soaring in the air, thundered at enormous speed toward the coastline, smashing the rocks, assaulting the sand. Heart-stopping. Magnificent. Hertie inhaled the salty air deeply. Breathtakingly beautiful.

They lingered on the beach walking slowly along. Valeria and Xaver took their shoes off, rolled up their trousers and stepped into the water, jumping and shouting it was cold, wetting each other like young children. Hertie's chest swelled. Bliss to watch them playing and see their love blossom. She felt contented. After a couple of hours they walked back to the house to get ready for lunch.

During the meal Hertie asked about the round structure with a dome that she could see from her bedroom window. Visibly pleased at the question Maria Eduarda explained it was her telescope. A relatively large one. The dome opened and the device could be controlled from the computer to focus on objects and areas of the sky that either she or visitors would like to look at. Sometimes local schools visited and Maria Eduarda would explain to the children about the sky.

'I've had telescopes from the moment I began studying astronomy,' she told Hertie, 'portable, movable ones of different sizes – I still do of course – but have always dreamt of having a real, large one in my garden. Where I lived in Boston it wasn't dark enough but the skies above Alentejo are the clearest and darkest in Portugal. The region is dry and scarcely populated. Villages and towns are far from each other. It was the remoteness of this place and what it offered for observing the stars that made me buy it. It's got everything that I love. Little rain, clear skies, warmth, the nearby ocean and little or no light pollution. So, a few years ago I finally realised my dream and had the telescope built,' she paused, then said, 'we can all go there at some stage if you'd like to observe the night sky.'

'Oh, yes please,' they replied in unison and Hertie added, 'I had a look at the sky from my bedroom window last night. Could see the Milky Way and so, so many stars it was impossible to differentiate the constellations. The only one I identified was Orion…not that I know many but it was just like…like a lake, yes, a sea…a sea of stars.'

'The photos in the sitting-room at the back,' Xaver said then, 'are they by the Hubble?'

Hertie noticed the sparkle in Eduarda's eyes at her own words and Xaver's question. She seemed elated at their enthusiasm.

'Yes,' she replied, 'they were both taken by the Hubble. One's the celebrated Pillars of Creation. It shows the three tall monoliths in the Eagle Nebula, circa seven thousand light years away, a region of great activity where stars are formed. The second picture shows the famous Horse Head Nebula, located to the south of the eastern most star in Orion's belt. And the third photo, my personal favourite, it's named the Hubble Deep Field or Hubble North Deep Field. It's an image from a patch of sky which appeared empty from the Earth, in the constellation of Ursa Major. When we turned Hubble and focused it on that little portion of the heavens it took 342 separate exposures with its camera 2 over ten consecutive days in December 1995. The image was assembled from all those different exposures. That's the copy in the back sitting-room. The approximately three thousand objects it depicts are almost all galaxies. So distant that only recently did their light reach us. So, in a manner of speaking, we're able to see galaxies from the past, shortly after they formed. It was the first image that enabled us to study the early universe. Hubble did another set of exposures three years later in a region of sky from the Southern Hemisphere, hence it became known as the Hubble South Deep Field and, of course, in 2004 it took the Hubble Ultra Deep Field and in 2012 the Hubble eXtreme Deep Field. But we'll go one step better than Hubble relatively soon. Scientists are working on a project for a special space telescope – the James Webb Space Telescope, named after James E. Webb, NASA administrator from 1961 to 1968 who played an important role in the Apollo Programme. Some of my former students in the States are involved in this project. This telescope is a joint international collaboration.'

'And will it be better than the Hubble?' Xaver asked. Hertie felt pleased her grandson showed so much interest.

'Yes. It's different,' Maria Eduarda was saying, 'it will be placed much further away from the Earth than Hubble. It'll be able to see in the infrared and have improved sensitivity, meaning longer wavelengths. So, it'll be able to look further back in time and see the first galaxies that formed in the early universe, peer inside dust clouds where stars are forming. It will go further and better than Hubble and complement what we've learned with it, also making new discoveries. Very exciting for all astronomers, cosmologists and astrophysicists, as well as scientists in general I think.'

As she finished speaking Hertie imagined the young Maria Eduarda. The dimples of her smile seemed deeper. Her eyes were like a river of light glittering in the dark. It was gratifying to notice Eduarda hadn't lost her sense of wonder after years and years of studying astronomy and working as an astrophysicist.

As stimulating as the conversation was during lunch, it was all the quieter in the afternoon, Hertie thought. But it wasn't unwelcome. Xaver decided to do some of his ballet exercises on the beach and Valeria went with him. Maria Eduarda sat at her laptop to reply to e-mails. Ellie and Miguel returned to their work of managing the estate. Ana Maria sat outside, facing the ocean to toil on a painting. Hertie picked up a book and joined her. Only mid-March but the temperature so agreeable it would be criminal to remain inside the house.

'Are all the lovely pictures of seascapes around the house yours, Ana Maria?' Hertie asked her host.

'Yes, I love painting, especially the sea and the way light changes it.'

'But they're not all of this site, are they? I went through the house admiring them but didn't recognise most as views from here.'

Ana Maria grinned. 'No, this place inspires me and I look at the effects of the light on the ocean stretching in front of us,' she made a sign with her head, 'but I paint from my imagination. In a way those seascapes are stories I imagine.'

'That's wonderful. Were you a professional painter in America?'

'In a manner of speaking. I studied Art and became an illustrator. I illustrated books, mostly children's books but also created the covers for a wide variety of novels and music albums. The pictures you see around the house are my hobby. Edi loves them and so we hang them in the house.'

'I find them beautiful.'

'Thank you.'

'I truly admire people who're so creative.'

'Thank you again. You really like my pictures?'

Hertie nodded. 'Very much. In fact, I'd like to buy one and take it with me to England to remember my visit and the gorgeous luminosity of Portugal.'

Ana Maria beamed. 'I don't normally sell them. They're my hobby,' she replied, 'but if you really like them you can choose one as a present. I don't want any payment.'

'Oh, but that's very kind. I couldn't possibly—'

Ana Maria dismissed it with a laugh. 'Of course you could and shall accept. It's a gift. I like you and what you've done for Edi deserves no less.'

'I've done nothing.'

'Not true. You came to return the book and the

manuscript that your husband stole all those years ago. Not everyone would've done it. You've made my sister very, very happy. I was only five years old when they were stolen. Didn't really take notice as such. But years later I remember Papa still mourning their loss and Edi's sadness whenever she mentioned them...especially the book, after I'd moved to the States.'

'Thank you. It's important to me to know you and Maria Eduarda appreciate my gesture. I firmly believe it was the right thing to do. It's nice to hear you say it.'

Ana Maria acknowledged her words graciously and returned her attention to the canvas.

For a moment Hertie was silent, then unable to contain her curiosity, she said, 'hope you don't mind me asking but what happened to Ellie? So young and already in a wheelchair. It's sad.'

Ana Maria put down her palette and brush, staring at some distant point ahead.

'It is sad,' she echoed, 'and a stupid accident. Ellie was fifteen. She climbed up a ladder to change a light bulb in the ceiling. Coming down she caught her foot between steps, lost her balance and fell heavily on her back. It was a tall ladder – more than two metres. She damaged her spinal cord just above the waist. Nothing could be done. Since then she's lost the use of her legs. She's very brave and never gave up the things she wanted to do. Three years ago, after ending her languages and accountancy degrees, she travelled alone to Portugal to visit us. On the plane she met Miguel. He helped her. They fell in love. He has a degree in agriculture, which combined with her knowledge as an accountant, are ideal to manage the estate. Edi and I feel very lucky to have them both living and working here. They're happy together.'

'Yes, I can tell. I noticed the love in Miguel's eyes when he so gently carried her outside to take her to their bungalow.'

'He's a lovely young man.'

'Thank you for telling me Ellie's story, Ana Maria. Please return to your painting and forget I'm here. I'll let you work.'

Ana Maria nodded while Hertie began reading her book.

It didn't last long. Dozy from so much sun and fresh air she soon nodded off, abandoning the open book on her lap.

Dinner on that day was a little earlier than usual. Hertie suspected the two sisters had decided to change the time in honour of their guests, not used to eating so late as customary in Portugal. Afterward, Ana Maria suggested they have coffee in the library or music salon. Miguel and Ellie agreed and Maria Eduarda seemed to also think it a good idea.

The room they called library or music salon had impressed Hertie already the night before when she briefly glanced inside during her photo escapade. It was the widest and longest at the front of the house, with three windows, the middle one larger than the other two. It was easy to spot why they called it both things. Shelves full of books from floor to ceiling covered most of the walls. Two pianos – a grand and a mini-grand – faced each other, close to the light that must flood through the glass panes during the day. To the left of the instruments a desk, visibly used often – a little untidy – with a laptop, a black mug with pens and pencils, various papers, books and astronomy magazines scattered all over it. Must be Maria Eduarda's place of work. Miguel and Ellie had their office in the bungalow. A comfortable-looking set of sofas in a claret colour around a low glass coffee table, a settee for two a little aside from the central arrangement and a few chairs that didn't appear to belong there completed the furnishings. And of course Ana Maria's seascapes hung from the few spare spaces left on the walls. The room was friendly. Welcoming. Lived in. People inhabited it all the time for various reasons. Hertie liked it.

Coffee finished Maria Eduarda took her arm, suggesting they sit on the settee, a little apart from the others and talk with a bit more privacy. Hertie agreed. Turning to Valeria Eduarda asked, 'would you play for us, my dear?'

'Of course. What would you like to hear?'

After various requests that ranged from Mozart, Schubert and Beethoven to famous more recent melodies, Valeria sat at the grand piano and began her playing from memory.

'She's good,' Maria Eduarda exclaimed, 'actually very

good.'

'Yes,' Hertie agreed, 'but she doesn't want to make a career out of it though I believe she could. Her dream was to become an opera singer. It didn't materialise due to illness. She plays because she adores music but decided instead for a writing and translating career.'

'Well, she's good at it too. I read some of her articles and interviews. I particularly liked the one with your grandson.'

Pleased Hertie confessed, 'I must say I was over the moon when they became an item.'

'They make a handsome couple, appearing very much in love.'

'I believe they are. Valeria has become my best friend,' Hertie said, 'and Xaver's my favourite grandchild. He's kind, sensitive. I don't know what I'd do if I didn't have him.'

'I understand.'

'Anyway,' Hertie exclaimed, deciding it was time to get to what had brought her over, 'Valeria and Xaver know my own story and all the details of Gerald's deathbed confession. I asked Valeria to write a book about everything once I'm gone.'

'What a great idea.'

'Glad you think so, Eduarda. I worried you might not want it. After what Gerald did to you…you might just wish to let bygones be bygones.'

'No, it's all right. I was very young. Another time. Another life...so to say.'

Thrilled Hertie asserted, 'I'm relieved. However, before we get talking I think I should return what belongs to you.'

Making a sign to Xaver Hertie asked him, 'would you please go to my room and fetch the book and the manuscript, mein Schatz?'

'Of course, Oma.'

Hertie heard his footsteps running up the staircase while listening to Valeria's playing with half an ear. Shortly after Xaver returned. Carrying the two precious items he burst into the room beaming from ear to ear. Carefully placing the objects on Hertie's lap he made a sign to Valeria and the others to join them. They all gathered around the two old ladies. Xaver stepped aside for Ellie to be at the front and pushed a chair for Ana Maria. Hertie lifted her gaze to each of them, noticing the anticipation. Slowly, with great care, she began unbinding the linen wrapped around the items. Cautiously, fearful something might disintegrate, she handed over the two precious objects to Maria Eduarda. First the clear plastic folder containing the manuscript, then the book. Eduarda touched them with the tips of her fingers. Tears in her eyes. She had trouble speaking.

'Thank you.'

It was all she managed to whisper in a voice marred with sadness.

The group remained silent. Ana Maria, her eyes moist, touched her sister's arm. Eduarda held her hand for a moment, smiling briefly at her. A sense of satisfaction, of joy overwhelmed Hertie's chest. Fulfilment. Poetic justice. She had done the right thing. Exhaling she glanced at each person's face, noticing emotions running high. Almost everyone seemed about to cry, including herself. She lifted her eyes to Xaver who caught her gaze and nodded.

'This is a happy moment,' he declared aloud, 'we should celebrate; not sit here like mourners. Valeria, my love, will you play something Mozartian, something joyous, please? I think this calls for a drink of some sort.'

'You're right,' Miguel agreed while Valeria returned to the grand piano, 'I'll get champagne and glasses. Edi loves the stuff. Always has a bottle in the fridge.'

They toasted to everyone's health, to Hertie, to the precious book and manuscript and to Eduarda and Ana Maria. Valeria resumed playing with Mozart's cheerful and beautiful piano sonata in A major, KV 331, the famous *Rondo alla turca*. The others returned to their seats. Hertie watched Maria Eduarda in silence, waiting for her to say something. Clearly her emotions ran deep. Memories must have resurfaced.

Tenderly, as if the objects were made of the most fragile crystal, Maria Eduarda placed the book and the manuscript on the settee between Hertie and herself. Running her fingers over the spine of the book, she looked at Hertie and repeated, 'thank you,' then added, 'I never thought I'd see them again.'

'I felt it my duty,' Hertie replied, 'after Gerald's confession…I was shocked. Not just the theft but also what he…I'm so sorry—'

Maria Eduarda took her hand, saying graciously, 'you needn't be sorry about anything, Hertha. You had nothing to do with it. Gerald was your husband. That's all. You were a child and didn't even know him when it all happened,' she paused and Hertie wondered whether she was going to cry but Eduarda appeared to have herself under control and just continued, 'it all happened a long time ago. I admit I was angry, furious. I felt rage once…not at the theft or at least not directed at Gerald. No-one suspected him of stealing. The police never found any clues. My father gave up searching. It's sad he died without ever knowing what happened to his two favourite, most precious treasures but then he also died without ever meeting his first grandchild, which was his fault. I felt rage once, yes, but didn't allow it to rule my life. I've led a happy life…still do.'

Hertie nodded, a little too emotional to speak. Silence lengthened, lingering between them. Hertie wondered whether to break it but just then Eduarda spoke again.

'You mentioned Valeria had the manuscript authenticated.'

'She did.'

Eduarda had changed the subject. Hertie felt relieved to deal in less emotionally delicate matters.

'And?'

'It's the real thing. Apparently the paper, the ink and whatever else they tested is in line with what was used in the 16th century in India at the time Camões lived there.'

'Wonderful, but could they prove it was written by the hand of the poet?'

'I don't think so. They're certain the extract is from The Lusiads,' Hertie indicated the precious book with her head, 'but not who wrote it. Valeria will be able to explain it better than me. She's got the report and the certificate of authentication from the

British Library to give you later.'

'Marvellous. I'm happy to know as much and, must say ecstatic to have the book back. Thank you one more time, Hertha.'

The music stopped. Valeria had finished the Mozart sonata. The others applauded. Ana Maria requested a Chopin Nocturne. Hertie and Maria Eduarda listened to the music for a moment then returning to the conversation Hertie asked, 'if I may, what did you do after your father expelled you?'

'You may,' Maria Eduarda said, looking through the windows into the darkness outside. To Hertie it appeared as if Eduarda were journeying into the past, recalling a time only she knew. In a quiet, friendly voice she began to speak.

'Papa and I had a talk in his study. He wanted me to tell him the name of the man who'd got me pregnant. I knew if I'd revealed Gerald as the culprit my father would do what fathers did then – force us to marry. But I didn't want to get married to Gerald or anyone else. I would've lost my freedom, my independence. Would never be able to study or enter a profession. So, I refused to tell Papa the man's identity. He shouted, threatened, hit me once across the face but I remained firm in my resolve. To be honest, I thought Papa would eventually see reason and help me but he didn't. Faced with my unshakable decision he ordered me to pack and disappear from his sight,' Eduarda paused, reaching for her champagne flute and sipped a little.

'But you must've been scared,' Hertie commented.

'I was terrified, but also determined I wouldn't submit to any man be it my father or a future husband, least of all to Gerald. Anyway, Papa didn't allow me to say goodbye properly to anyone. Only to our housekeeper, Lucinda, because he didn't notice her actions. She was dedicated to me and my mother before me. I'd known her all my life. My mother died giving birth to me so Lucinda looked after me, carried me as a baby. On the day I told Papa she heard us in the study. Impossible not to. The door was shut but Papa flew into a rage, screaming, shouting and generally pouting. I'm certain most of the domestic staff heard what went on. My stepmother Rosa – Valeria's grandmother – wasn't in the house when the argument ensued. Ana Maria my then very little sister – only five or six – was in Sintra with her nanny. I stormed out of my father's study and rushed upstairs to pack. Lucinda ran after me. She helped me pack a suitcase, asking where would I go. She offered me to stay with her sister in Caxias, a place near Lisbon's Atlantic coast, after Belém where the famous monuments are. I told her I'd go to my mentor, Professor Berta de Almeida, but if she couldn't take me I'd accept Lucinda's and her sister's kind offer. Berta was at the time the only female physicist in Portugal. She'd been mentoring me for years. Papa didn't like her because he believed my so-called progressive ideas,' she laughed, making a sign for inverted commas with her fingers, 'were of her making. I told Berta everything and she helped me. I was too scared to have an abortion. It was illegal. Many horror stories circulated in Lisbon of mutilated girls or others who'd died because of going to these women of dodgy character who did the job for large sums of money but without care and little or no medical knowledge. So, I ruled out abortion. Berta then suggested I ask my godfather – Ricardo Espirito Santo…did Gerald ever mention Ricardo to you?'

Hertie nodded. 'He did. He seemed to have liked and admired him.'

'Yes. Everyone did. Ricardo was a good, intelligent man, much more liberal and understanding than my father but he was also Papa's best friend and I wasn't sure how he'd react if I went to him and asked for his help. So, Berta sent a telegram to my maternal grandmother, Leopoldina, in Cape Verde. She lived on the Island of Fogo where Papa had a coffee plantation that he'd neglected. After my mother died he never went back there. Anyway, the telegram told Grandmama that I was pregnant and Papa had expelled me. Berta also asked my grandmother whether I could go to her. Grandmama quickly replied affirmatively. Berta paid for my passage on a ship to Cape Verde. Never wanted a penny in return. The voyage wasn't without perils because of the war but what other choice did I have? So, I travelled and gave birth to my son in the islands a few months later. But I couldn't stay there. I wanted to study and become an astronomer so had to come back to Portugal. My grandmother very kindly decided to come with me and help me look after the baby. She also provided financial support for the time my little son and I lived with her in Cape Verde. We journeyed to Portugal and I changed my long, aristocratic name – too well known here – and simply became Maria Eduarda do Livramento. My mother's maiden name. With Berta's support I enrolled in the University of Porto to study physics. Grandmama looked after Jorge. I paid for our keep by giving piano lessons and assisting one of my professors at university. Berta visited often to guide me in my studies. I exchanged letters with Lucinda all the way through and it's thanks to her that Ana Maria and I never lost touch. She even managed to travel to Porto a few times, without my father or stepmother finding out about it, to visit me with Ana Maria. Lucinda made my little sister promise that seeing or writing to me was their secret and no-one, not even her Papa could know about it. Ana Maria was as good as it gets and never breathed a word of it,' she heaved her shoulders in a casual gesture, 'that's my life after Papa threw me out. I suppose I disappeared without a trace. Mind you I don't think Papa tried hard to find me if he tried at all. You and Valeria found me easily when you put your minds to it and hired a detective but Papa…well, I suppose I'd stained his honour too much. I'm not bitter. In those days his behaviour was more normal than you may think. But I realise I was lucky. I had people who helped me…Berta, my maternal grandmother, Lucinda. Most girls ended up as prostitutes. I would've probably ended up in the gutter too if it weren't for those three women. I owe it all to them.'

'I understand. But may I ask why did you go to the States? You could've easily carried on your life in Portugal. Things were working out for you.'

'Yes but I wanted to become an astronomer. There were no more advanced studies in Portugal. Women weren't accepted at every superior learning institution. It'd be almost impossible to find work in my field later. I'd graduated with honours from the

Porto University. I looked at European organisations and universities but scientific paths were difficult for females. Berta had contacts in America. In fact, tired of the lack of opportunity for female scientists, she was then in the process of moving to the States for a research position at Cornell University in the state of New York about five and a half hours from Boston, Massachusetts. She had a good contact at Harvard who enabled me to apply for a post-graduate scholarship. I won it. So, Berta, my little boy and I sailed to America in the spring of 1949. Grandmama went back to Cape Verde. I visited every year with Jorge until she died in 1963. Lucinda left my father's employment in 1957 after Ana Maria turned twenty-one and was of age. They travelled to America together. I paid for their passages. Lucinda stayed with us until she died at eighty-four in 1975. Ana Maria studied art in America, became an illustrator and married a teacher, Steve Spencer. Sadly Steve died of cancer after only six years of marriage. Ana Maria didn't marry again. She said Steve was the love of her life. No other man would do. So, she and I stayed together.'

'And you never returned to Portugal?'

'Not then, no. In America I got the chance of a great career and I pursued it. I became an astrophysicist. I've worked with great scientific names. I was involved in famous space projects. I didn't want to return. There was nothing for me here.'

'You never married?'

'No. I failed to see the point. I didn't want to give up my career or to have my life dictated by a man. I had a child more by chance than anything else and I loved him but felt no need for more. Of course I had many lovers throughout the years. I like men and men liked me. They thought me exotic and my choice of profession fascinated them until they realised I wasn't the submissive type. Anyway, I was never serious enough about my relationships to give up my freedom and independence.'

'But eventually you returned to Portugal. When did you decide to come back?'

'After I retired…and age. As one gets older, wrinkles and greys start appearing, memories get clouded and painted in beautiful, harmonious colours. One becomes sentimental and starts desperately missing the places, smells and flavours of childhood. It was no different with me.'

'That was all?'

'It's a lot but...' she paused, visibly reminiscing then added, 'a poem triggered it.'

'A poem?' Hertie couldn't hide her surprise.

Maria Eduarda's lips parted, showing her dimples. There was a slightly mischievous twinkle in her eyes and Hertie had a glimpse of the gorgeous, carefree girl she must have been at the time Gerald met her.

'I might say it's one of my guilty pleasures...poetry I mean.'

'Oh?'

'I've always loved poetry. Indulged in it, diving in all the poetry books in my father's library that no-one else but I ever read. It continued throughout my life. Still does. Anyway, one day in America I stumbled upon a little poem entitled Mar – means sea – by a Portuguese poet I enjoy, Sophia de Mello Breyner Andresen. I read it and deeply felt the longing for the sea, for the ocean. Not just any sea but the sea of Portugal. I missed it. The luminous blue skies during the day, the sunflowers, the bright red poppies, the dark skies of Alentejo at night, the warmth, the general friendliness of its people. And I understood I had to come back and see it all again before dying. I travelled to Portugal for a couple of months. Then I saw this place. It was for sale and had everything my heart desired,' she shrugged, 'so I bought it. I'm happy here. We're happy here. Ana Maria, Ellie, Miguel and me. It's our home, our refuge and our dreams all in one.'

'And what was the poem? I'm curious now. I find it a moving story.'

'Perhaps. Most people would call it sentimental but at my age I'm allowed to be a sentimental old fool.'

She laughed and Hertie joined in.

'I agree. I think we both earned that right.'

'Indeed.'

'What about the poem? Will you tell it to me?'

'I can recite it in Portuguese which you don't understand but I'll give you a good translation afterwards.'

Maria Eduarda got up, went to the desk and searched inside her drawers, returning with a folded light blue sheet of paper. Closing her eyes she recited the lines of the poem in Portuguese.

'I don't understand the words,' Hertie said, 'but it sounds beautiful.'

'It is,' she agreed and leaning forward handed over the blue sheet of paper.

Hertie accepted it and unfolding it saw a brief text printed out from a computer. She read aloud.

'From all corners of the world
I love, with a more powerful, profound devotion
That ecstatic and exposed shore,
Where I merged with the sea, the wind and the moonlight core.'

In a slow motion movement she lowered the paper to her lap. Beautiful. Exquisite. In a rapid flash like lightning she grasped the longing Maria Eduarda had felt for Portugal, the ocean, the luminosity and the night. Lifting her eyes she caught Eduarda's gaze. The two old ladies nodded at each other and Hertie whispered, 'I get it.'

Chapter 5 – Stars Maintain Their Glow

The large grandfather clock in the hall struck half past midnight. Miguel stood up, suggesting time for bed. The others agreed. Meticulously Maria Eduarda wrapped the clear plastic folder with the old manuscript and the first edition of Os Lusíadas in the linen cloth, pressing both against her chest. As the others filed out of the room, wishing each other goodnight, Miguel took Ellie to their bungalow and Maria Eduarda switched off the lights before following her guests and her sister upstairs. Shutting her bedroom door she leaned against it in the dark still embracing the two precious items.

The shutters were up. The waning crescent moon cast a fine strand of light into the room. Once her eyes adjusted she could see enough. Placing the linen parcel on the bed she unwrapped it to reveal the objects in the sparse moonlight. Lovingly she followed the edges of the cover and the spine of the book with her fingertips. Gently she opened it and stared at the pelican, the title and the name of the poet. Her chest swelled. She felt a lump in her throat and wiped a couple of absurd tears with the back of her hand. There was no point in crying. Old age made her foolish. Sappy. It was good to have the items back. The items Gerald – scoundrel – had stolen all those years ago. She had never suspected him. Not even after…well, after he'd done what he did. But then again how could she? One thing had no linkage to the other. Exhaling she abandoned the book and the manuscript on the bed and walked to the balcony. Opening the door she stepped outside to wonder at the sky.

An almost negligible sound to her left made her glance in that direction. Hertie was at her window. Maria Eduarda smiled briefly. Hertie had endured a great deal of suffering and trauma in her childhood and later in her marriage to Gerald, according to what Valeria told her in confidence. More than her fair share. There were plenty of reasons to have become bitter, angry, harsh, disillusioned but, in spite of it all, Hertie was warm-hearted, kind, tolerant, balanced. She liked her. With little more than a whisper Maria Eduarda called out, 'Hertha, would you like to join me here for a night cap?'

'What a lovely idea,' Hertie replied in a similarly quiet voice.

'Wrap up. During the day temperatures are pleasantly warm but nights in March are still chilly.'

Maria Eduarda fetched a bottle of Port and two glasses off a tray on top of the chest of drawers, as well as a couple of blankets from the wardrobe. A little later they sat on the canvas chairs kept on the balcony, blankets over their legs, warm jackets and a glass of Port dancing in their hands.

'I'm not sleepy or tired,' Maria Eduarda said.

'Me neither.'

'When I saw you, I realised I fancied some company and an extra drink.'

'Absolutely,' Hertie said, lifting her glass, 'cheers. How do you toast in Portuguese?'

'À nossa saúde or simply à nossa. It means the same. To our health or, if you like, to us. Sometimes we just say chin-chin which as you may have guessed is the clinking of glasses,' grinning she touched Hertie's glass, 'so à nossa, Hertha. We deserve it.'

'Indeed, we do.'

They giggled like schoolgirls doing something forbidden.

'May I ask you a personal question, Hertha?'

'Of course. I've been doing the same to you.'

'I noticed at dinner you didn't eat the skins of the small potatoes and went through the trouble of peeling each one of them carefully—'

'Oh that,' Hertie interjected, 'there's a simple explanation.'

'Thought it would be.'

'During the war years in Germany there was very little food, especially the last three years. We were lucky to a certain extent because we lived on a small farm and had potatoes. Very little else but we had potatoes. So, my mother would boil the potatoes as the main meal but she never threw away the skins and made soup out of them. We'd eat it all. For years my only meals were boiled potatoes for lunch and potato skin soup for dinner. Sometimes Mutti kept and conserved the skins so she could use them for soup several times. And if there were no more potatoes left she'd roast the skins. I promised myself that one day when I grew up and could eat whatever I wanted I would never ever touch a potato skin again. That's all.'

'Oh, that's terrible. I'm so sorry.'

'Don't be. It wasn't your fault and we were the lucky ones. We survived and weren't thrown into the concentration camps to die like six million Jews, along with the sick, disabled, homosexuals, gypsies and others that Hitler and his supporters murdered.'

'True. You know my father was a personal friend and staunch supporter of Salazar, the Portuguese fascist dictator. While the world was at war, Portugal remained neutral. Salazar's policy. At the time it was a good policy; saved the country from the horrors of war and the collapse of its fragile economy but I only understood how appalling and gruesome Salazar really was years later. In America I learned of all his and the secret police's atrocities. Torture of political prisoners. Censorship. Fake news to suit their needs. Plus the horrific concentration camp in Tarrrafal in the Cape Verdian island of Santiago. Prisoners called it o campo da morte lenta – the camp of slow death – and I was shocked that my father had supported all that.'

'According to Valeria's mother, your half-sister, Maria Helena, Ludovico was a good man and a good father to her and her sisters. She said he was horrified at what had happened in Germany after the war ended. He apparently never spoke about the dictatorship in Portugal after it fell in 1974 but Maria Helena thinks he must have regretted his support of Salazar.'

Maria Eduarda shrugged. 'Perhaps he did. I didn't know my father well, you see, it never crossed my mind he'd throw me out on the streets without a penny but he did just that. I lost all my love and respect for him and sad though it is to admit it, I felt nothing when I found out he'd died in 1989 only a couple of months before his 100th birthday. He had a long happy life and didn't deserve it but life is unfair and cruel for most of the time.'

They remained silent for a long while, reflecting on the past.

'We're turning gloomy,' Eduarda said, 'we should talk about beauty, light, the stars. Lovely life moments.'

'I agree but...we also need the darkness to see the stars. What I mean is without the dark we can't appreciate the light and without bad moments how can we value the good?'

'You're a wise woman, Hertha.'

'Perhaps. Just talking from experience, really.'

Silently Eduarda agreed. Her long life had taught her the same. She glanced at Hertie, quietly gazing up at the sky.

'Do you enjoy the night sky?'

Hertie nodded. 'When I was a child in Germany I used to stare at the heavens from my bedroom window for hours. I often thought whether somewhere up there on one of those planets there would be another little girl like me looking down on Earth and thinking about what mad people we were.'

'I used to think that too.'

Hertie beamed, seeming pleased at their similar thoughts. Then she resumed, 'we learned the planets of the solar system and some constellations at school and I used to try to identify them. Of course, I could only find and name two of them. There were too many and I didn't grasp enough.'

'What could you name then?'

'Possibly the same I do now,' she chuckled, 'the Big Dipper or Ursa Major over there,' she pointed to her right, 'and my favourite—'

'Orion?' Eduarda interjected, indicating the Hunter to the left with her glass.

'How did you—'

'Guess?'

'Yes.'

'It's most people's favourite and the most spectacular group of stars in the night sky. There's Betelgeuse on the top of the left shoulder – a red star, cold, nearing the end of its life and which will explode as a supernova at some stage – and at the bottom on the right that extremely bright star is Rigel – a blue star and therefore very hot.'

'So, in terms of stars, red is cold and blue is hot?'

'Yes, quite the opposite of what we associate the colours with on Earth.'

'I particularly like Orion's Belt and its Sword. One can see them very clearly here. I can even notice a pinkish-red glow around Betelgeuse and a blue shimmer around Rigel. Amazing.'

'The heavens above Alentejo are gorgeous. That's why I wanted a place here and a large telescope in my garden. Tonight is a good night to gaze at the stars. The moon is waning and throws little light so we can see everything else extremely well.'

'Show me other constellations besides Orion and the Big Dipper, please.'

'Tonight you can see the rest of the Big Dipper and why it's called Ursa Major if you look carefully.'

'You're right. I can.'

'And...' Eduarda stood up, 'hang on a second. I'll get my laser pointer.'

She returned a couple of minutes later and sitting down, turned on the pointer. A thin thread of bright red light shot through the sky, seeming to touch a point in the firmament. Rotating the light Eduarda asked, 'can you see a W?'

'Yes. That's Cassiopeia, right?'

'Correct. And there is Andromeda,' she pointed the laser at another patch of sky, 'and right next to it, Pegasus. Can you see them?'

'Oh yes.'

Maria Eduarda pointed out a few more constellations, observing Hertie furtively. She appeared enthralled. Her face transfixed. Eduarda's heart leaped a beat. So wonderful to see someone's thrill at the beauty of the night sky.

'That huge path of light with countless stars, forming an arch across the sky above our heads, it's the Milky Way, isn't it?'

'Yes, part of it,' Eduarda replied.

'So, presumably, we're facing the centre of the galaxy, right?'

'No. Wrong. Our solar system is situated 26,000 light

years away from the centre of the galaxy. We're in the Northern Hemisphere and the North Pole points at the outward universe. So, what we're seeing isn't the centre but a section of one of its outward spiral arms. The view of the Milky Way is better, more spectacular from the Southern Hemisphere, as the South Pole faces its centre,' Eduarda explained, sensing a lump in her throat. Even after so many years each time she admired the breathtaking beauty of the Milky Way emotion took hold of her. She added in a whisper, 'dazzling, isn't it?'

'Beautiful. It...' Hertie appeared bewildered, 'please don't think me foolish but it's so exquisite, so splendid, so...so magnificent, it makes me want to cry.'

'No. It's not silly at all. I feel that way each time I stare at the night sky or observe the universe via my telescope in the garden.'

'As I mentioned, I used to imagine that somewhere up there on one of those stars a similar girl to me was looking down on Earth and wondering about human beings' stupidity. Why they carried out useless, pointless wars and did such horrible things to each other. I always hoped that such a little girl would look at this blue dot and think the same things I did. Absurd, I know.'

Eduarda shook her head. Her chest felt tight. 'No, not absurd,' she declared vehemently, 'never absurd, simply wonderful. It's a true wonder. I believe one should always allow imagination to fly and see the world through the amazed eyes of a child.'

They smiled at each other in silent comprehension, marvelling at the splendour and elegance of the firmament.

'Have you ever regretted the path you took in life?' Hertie broke their silent stargazing after a moment.

'You mean after what happened with Gerald?'

'Yes.'

'I never regretted anything. I was angry. Shocked. After Gerald's act I felt guilty. Dirty. Ashamed. I remember thinking I wanted to die. It took me a while to understand it wasn't my fault and pull myself together. I didn't want to marry Gerald or anyone, least of all for being pregnant. I told Papa because I needed help but he was the wrong person. I don't regret having had my son or cutting all ties with my father.'

'If Gerald hadn't...rap...taken advantage of you, would you have led the same life? Your father must have had other plans for you.'

'You can say rape. I think that's what happened. It was a long time ago. Not a trauma anymore. It was marking and terrible for years but I made peace with it after going to America. I don't know exactly what Gerald confessed to you but what really happened was the following...'

In a steady, quiet voice Maria Eduarda told Hertie everything that had taken place between Gerald and herself, especially on that fateful night in Alentejo. She noticed Hertie's sadness. Her wet gaze. Possibly sympathy for her ordeal and outrage at her dead husband. Gerald was the father of Hertie's children but Maria Eduarda had noticed it pained Hertie what he had done. His confession must be a burden for her. Typical Gerald though. Selfish, thinking only about himself and his needs. Finishing her story, Maria Eduarda refilled their glasses with Port. 'To us, Hertha,' she said lifting the glass.

'To us.'

'You asked earlier whether I'd have led the same life if it weren't for what Gerald did as my father must have had other plans for me?'

Hertie nodded.

'The answer is no. I wouldn't have led a different life. As for Papa...well, my father did have other plans for me but even without the pregnancy I wouldn't have followed them. He wanted me to marry a man with fortune and social position. Didn't want me to study. I always had other ideas. I knew I wanted a degree and to be independent. I might have run away at some stage or other to avoid marrying whoever he might have chosen for me. He didn't allow me to go to university. I couldn't attend lectures until I was of age. After my twenty-first birthday – full age in Portugal at the time instead of eighteen as is now – Papa couldn't stop me anymore. I knew marriage wasn't my thing. Married women in Portugal were under the thumb of their husbands. They couldn't even travel abroad without their authorisation, which only changed after the revolution of April 1974. Being over twenty-one and unmarried gave me a freedom I wouldn't have had otherwise. My father could no longer legally force me to do anything and I needed no special permissions from a husband I didn't have. So, no regrets whatsoever.'

'Didn't you miss your sisters?'

'I missed Ana Maria. I never met the others. But thanks to Lucinda we never lost touch. The others were all born after I'd left. I would've liked to know them but,' she shrugged, 'it's all right. I knew they existed, as well as all my nephews and nieces. Lucinda took care of keeping me informed, as did some of my friends in this country. It was enough. Our lives followed different paths. Papa chose that path when he expelled me from his house and disinherited me.'

'But you're not bitter?'

'Whatever for? Bitterness, just as regret, is a waste of time in my view.'

'True. Life has too much to offer.'

'Yes. It doesn't stop. I've lost many people I loved during the years of my long life but the Earth keeps rotating and the stars maintain their glow. So we must live life to the full and enjoy it during the little time we have on this lovely blue dot.'

Hertie nodded and Eduarda reached out. Their hands intertwined as they finished their Port, continuing to look up and admire the night sky.

Chapter 6 – Rhapsody

Maria Eduarda woke up early. Her head a little sore. The result of a late but agreeable night in the company of Hertie and a bottle of Port. A bit too much Port. She was a little tipsy at the time of going to bed.

Her shutters were up. Still dark outside. The digital clock on her bedside table displayed 5.37 in the morning. Grab a book or try to resume sleeping? That was the question. Stretching she rotated her body sideways. Laying on her left side she faced the glass door and stared at the patch of sky where a section of the Milky Way was still visible. Silence and darkness. Her companions. Always.

Unexpectedly a noise disturbed her peace. Music. Music? Where did it come from? She recognised it. Rachmaninov's Rhapsody on a Theme of Paganini. One of her personal favourites. Was Valeria playing the piano? Before six in the morning? Surely not. But then who? The melody soared from somewhere in the house, floating up the stairs, flooding her room. Maria Eduarda pushed back the covers and floundered in the dark for her dressing-gown. Found it. Without switching on the lights she flung it over her shoulders, opened her bedroom door and stepped barefoot onto the landing. The music was brighter, louder. It came from the ground floor. She stood very still, straining to locate the sound. Locate? How silly. The library. It could only come from the library where she had lodged the pianos and the CD player. With her hand on the banister to assist her steps she walked silently down the stairs. Light escaped under the library door. She opened it wide.

Valeria sat at the grand piano. Miguel at the mini-grand. Miguel could play? Solely with accompanying chords but still a revelation. Ana Maria and Hertha sat on chairs near the instruments. Behind them a small orchestra and people Maria Eduarda didn't know. Who were they? What were they doing in their house? And where was Ellie?

The room appeared different. All furniture pushed aside against the bookshelves or the walls. The rugs rolled up in a corner. And in the middle of the room, moving like the stuff of dreams, Xaver pirouetted millimetre perfect, ending with a beautiful arabesque. Lifting his arms gracefully he then elevated his body in a series of entrechats quatre, followed by four sequential high rotations in the air. The last with one arm thrown up above his head, landing gracefully in near silence. Swiftly changing his position he executed a mind-boggling number of fouettés before finishing with yet another elegant arabesque. Dazzling. Sublime.

Ana Maria and Hertha applauded. Spellbound Maria Eduarda froze. Should she speak? Applaud? No-one had yet noticed her. She didn't wish to spoil the ensemble. The decision to remain silent was taken from her. Valeria began the first chords of variation number 18. The most famous, most beautiful of the twenty-four variations forming Rhapsody on a Theme of Paganini. In that moment, Xaver who had walked to a dark corner of the room returned to its centre gently carrying Ellie in his arms. As the notes gradually left the piano keys under Valeria's agile fingers, Xaver began to dance with Ellie. But how could she? Ellie. Imprisoned for life in a wheelchair. Unable to move. Yet she danced. Xaver held her, an arm around her waist. Her left arm rested on his shoulders. Her legs hung loose alongside his body. Slowly he rotated with her on the spot, then lifting her above his head as if she were weightless he walked around the room, carrying her high up in the air. Ellie appeared to fly, to float, defying gravity. Her face luminous with joy. Her eyes bright. Her smile radiant. She had never looked so lovely. Miguel left the piano and approached Xaver. Featherlike and with infinite care he lowered Ellie into Miguel's waiting arms.

Maria Eduarda pressed a hand to her chest. Her eyes filled with tears. She held her breath, afraid of breaking the magic spell spiralling like smoke in the room.

Valeria returned to the beginning of the same eighteenth variation. The orchestra accompanied her beautifully underlying the piano. The unidentified people standing next to the musicians whose presence Maria Eduarda could not explain moved suddenly forward and stepped to stand next to Xaver in the middle of the room. She gasped for air. Gerald Neale in a white shirt, rolled up sleeves, platinum blonde hair flopping over his forehead, looking exactly as he did in the summer she had met him. Next to him Hertha but not young. Hertha as she was now. And Ana Maria next to her. But little. Five or six years old, brown curls and ready smile just as she'd been as a child. Xaver gestured her to join them. Maria Eduarda hesitated, glancing around. Did Xaver mean herself? He nodded as if he had heard her thoughts. Inhaling deeply she moved forward, realising it was a different Maria Eduarda. As if her younger self had separated from her older one. Bizarre. She felt strong. Youthful. Full of energy. Her life ahead of her. She could see her image as if in a mirror moving toward Xaver. The gorgeous Eduarda she had been as a young woman. Xaver held her hand. She stood on his right side, away from Gerald on the left. And then, as an admirable corps de ballet, they all inexplicably began to dance together. But what was Zuca, her horse, doing there? His large head through the window. He whinnied. Was he trying to come in? Crazy animal. Always fleeing the stables. But there were no stables here. Had he galloped all the way from Sintra? Impossible. Zuca wouldn't know where to go.

Maria Eduarda continued to dance alongside the others. All in perfect sync with Xaver leading, dictating the steps and the movements. She pirouetted but didn't feel dizzy. Incredible. Her body seemed lighter. She could bounce. Jump. As if the world were devoid of gravity. Extraordinary. Suddenly her body took off. She leaped over Zuca's head. Out of the window she went towards the stars. Goose bumps speckled her skin from the chilly air. The silver dots of light punctuating the sky descended on her like gentle snowflakes. Her chest ached. And then…Maria Eduarda opened her eyes wide.

The sun burst into her room, caressing her arms, dancing on her face.

'Dear me,' she exclaimed aloud, uncomprehending for a moment, 'I must have fallen asleep again and dreamed all this. My goodness. What a strange dream.'

Stretching she rolled out of bed, straining to hear the

familiar morning sounds. The house was silent yet she could smell coffee. Maria Eduarda glanced at her clock. Seven fifteen. Someone was up early. The housekeeper wouldn't arrive until nine and looking out of her balcony she noticed all the windows on the first floor as well as in the bungalow next door had their shutters down. Most people appeared to still sleep. She draped her dressing gown around her body, tying it tight at the waist, then gliding into her slippers walked downstairs. The smell of coffee was stronger and led her to the dining room where Xaver sat alone at the table with a pot of coffee and a bowl with yogurt, fresh fruit and cereal. He ate slowly while occasionally glancing at a book opened by his side on the table.

'Good morning. You're up early, young man.'

He turned his head in her direction.

'Good morning, Maria Eduarda,' his voice sounded as fresh water she thought, 'yes, I like to exercise early, have a shower and then eat. Everyone else – except you of course – is still in bed, including my adorable Valeria. I took the liberty of making myself coffee and raiding your kitchen for some food.'

She grinned. 'And so you should,' then added, 'is there still coffee in that pot?'

'Oh yes. Sit down. I'll get you a cup.'

As she began sipping her coffee Maria Eduarda said, 'you know, Xaver, I had a really weird dream about you and the other people in this house…just now before waking up.'

'My grandmother used to have a recurring dream…actually a recurring nightmare. It took me a couple of years to convince her to go to therapy. It helped. She improved and rarely dreams it nowadays.'

'But from what Valeria told me, Hertha's recurring dream was a consequence of the traumatic events she experienced in Germany during and at the end of the war as a child.'

'That's right. I sometimes wonder how Oma turned out to be such a cheerful, kind, balanced person after everything she went through.'

'It isn't easy.'

'No, I don't think it is.'

'Anyway what I meant is different. My dream's nothing of the sort. It isn't recurring. Never dreamt it before and I dare say won't ever again. Simply odd. Weird. Because it was about you and the people who're in this house at the moment.'

'I see. Tell me.'

She narrated the dream, taking care to describe in detail all the dancing. While speaking Maria Eduarda noticed his face changing. His eyes glimmered cheerfully, as if his birthday and Christmas presents had all come at once and unexpectedly.

'I know nothing about ballet but in my dream I knew all the steps you made,' Maria Eduarda finished her tale with a laugh.

'It's an interesting dream,' he said, 'I'm no expert but it seems our presence and the return of items once stolen from your family brought you memories of your youth, I guess. Even the horse...what did you say its name was?'

'Zuca.'

'Funny name.'

'Oh well. He was a Lusitano – died many years ago – and Lusitanos are named in sequence, meaning each year has a different letter and so they receive a name that begins with the letter of the year they were born in.'

'Fascinating. And then? Does it eventually go back to the beginning?'

'Of course.'

Maria Eduarda watched him as he poured more coffee for himself, asking whether she would like another cup.

'I'm fine, thank you,' she replied and after a moment added, 'I was watching your face when I described your dancing in my dream, you seemed...I don't know...happy, thrilled, excited, delighted.'

Grinning he commented, 'yes, all of that and a lot more. You see dancing's my passion. I love ballet with all my heart. I dance from here,' he patted his chest, 'and here,' he touched his head, 'what I mean is that ballet's my life. I dance with my body and soul.'

'What about Valeria?'

He replied without hesitation and what seemed to Maria Eduarda like heartfelt sincerity. His feelings were obviously intense. He impressed her.

'Valeria's my partner,' he declared, 'the woman I want to share my life with and an inspiration. I became a better dancer after I'd met her. Often, I dedicate my performances to her…silently. I don't advertise it…' he paused and smiled, 'not even to her but, in my mind, most times I'm on stage I dance for her.'

'That's beautiful.'

'It's the truth,' he said simply, 'can you understand?'

She nodded. 'I felt that passion but not for a person, I mean like your feelings for ballet, I felt it…I feel it still but for the stars.'

He finished his bowl of yogurt, fresh fruit and cereal. Swallowing the rest of his coffee he stated, 'in your dream you said I danced to the 18th variation from Rachmaninov's Rhapsody on a Theme of Paganini. Valeria was playing it on the piano.'

'Uh-huh,' she acknowledged, 'it's one of my all-time piano favourites.'

'A peculiar coincidence.'

'How so?'

'I'm going to debut in Frederick Ashton's one act ballet to the music of the rhapsody. The ballet is called Rhapsody.'

'Frederick Ashton? A ballet called Rhapsody?' Maria Eduarda echoed, 'I don't think I've ever heard about any of it.'

'Frederick Ashton was a British ballet dancer and choreographer who lived from 1904 to 1988. He created the ballet Rhapsody to the music of Rachmaninov's variations on a Paganini's theme in 1980 for Mikhail Baryshnikov— you know of Baryshnikov?'

'Oh yes. I've seen him dance many times in the States after he defected to the West.'

'Exactly, so Ashton created the ballet for him to perform at his guest appearance with the Royal Ballet during the Queen Mother's birthday celebrations.'

'I see.'

'The lead male's role is in the style of virtuosic Russian ballet, which had its origins in Imperial Russia. The female's role is more in the British ballet style, according to the methods of the Royal Ballet and the Royal Academy of Dance. I guess that's one reason why I was cast to dance the principal male role.'

'What do you mean? You aren't Russian.'

'No, not Russian but I partially trained in Russia, after winning a scholarship for the Mariinsky in St. Petersburg.'

'Fabulous. It must've been fantastic.'

'It was. Hard, very hard work and strict discipline but it made me the dancer I am today for which I'll be forever grateful.'

'And you are debuting in this role?'

'Yes, after we get back. I've been rehearsing it before travelling and will dance it first in London with the Royal Ballet and later in Munich with the Bavarian State Ballet.'

Maria Eduarda raised an eyebrow. 'You're right, it's a peculiar coincidence, actually outright astonishing…not to say spooky since you've never mentioned it to me.'

'You don't believe in such things, do you?'

'Spooky? No. Too much the scientist. Anyway, since you're rehearsing that particular ballet may I dare ask a favour?'

'Of course. You've been a wonderful, thoughtful hostess so ask away.'

'Would you do a demonstration of the ballet Rhapsody tonight for us?'

'Sure. I can do one of my solos if you like.'

'Is it to the tune of the 18th variation?'

'No. That's the pas de deux but I can improvise. It'll be fun.'

'And lovely. Thank you, Xaver.'

'Don't thank me. Meeting you and Ana Maria, returning the precious items and enjoying a few days of bliss around here have meant the world to my grandmother and she means the world to me. So, I'm more than happy to oblige.'

Her heart stirred. There was no hint of irony in his words. Absolutely sincere. Honest. Maria Eduarda touched his arm, acknowledging his gracious speech. She watched him. He stood up, placed the book under his arm and declared it time to wake Valeria.

Xaver opened the door to their bedroom quietly. It was dark. He let his eyes adjust. Valeria was still asleep on her side. Her back to him just as he'd left her earlier. Grinning he jumped on the bed, bouncing her.

'What? There a fire?' she said, visibly confused, turning her head and staring at him.

'Come on, sleeping beauty. Time to get up.'

She slapped his wrist, as he kissed her, saying, 'you are an idiot, Xaver Duverger!'

'Yes but a good idiot. I've lots of good ideas.'

Visibly trying hard not to laugh she exclaimed, 'my heart's racing. You could've given me a heart attack.'

He said nothing. Just jammed her mouth with a passionate kiss. They rolled together in bed for a moment. His breathing changed. He kissed her again, whispering in her ear, 'I want you, my love.'

'You're dressed,' she stated.

'That's easily corrected.'

In a rush he got rid of his clothes and jumped into bed. They made love slowly. Quietly. Enjoying each other's touch. When they finished Xaver put his arms around her. They stayed silent in the warmth of their embrace. The covers tucked around their bodies. Valeria spoke first.

'How long have you been up?'

'Since five.'

'But we're on holiday.'

He shrugged. 'I know but I still have to exercise. I like to do it early. I've already showered and had breakfast.'

'That explains your burst of energy.'

'Didn't you like it, my love?'

As answer she kissed him.

'Maria Eduarda,' he said, 'kept me company while I breakfasted. She had a cup of coffee with me.'

'So she likes to get up early too?'

'No idea. Today she woke up early and came down. Whether it usually happens, I don't know. But anyway, we had a nice chat.'

'About what?'

He didn't answer and instead asked, 'can you play Rachmaninov's Rhapsody on Paganini's theme?'

'Where did that come from?'

'Can you?'

'Yes but I need the score. I don't know it by heart.'

'Maria Eduarda told me it's one of her favourite piano pieces. She must have the music. So, I'm sure it'll be fine.'

'For what? What's going on in that crazy little head of yours?'

First Xaver narrated his conversation with Maria Eduarda and the dream she had told him about. Then, beaming ear to ear like the Cheshire cat, he described his idea.

Late afternoon Xaver pulled Miguel aside. They whispered to each other in a corner for a couple of minutes.

'You two are very secretive,' Ellie said, 'what's going on?'

'Nothing,' they replied in unison.

Xaver and Miguel left the sitting room together. Maria Eduarda lifted her head from a book, wondering. Were they preparing something special for tonight? Being a Saturday Miguel and Ellie weren't working. They were all inside. The weather had clouded over and there was a chill in the air, reminding people winter hadn't quite disappeared yet.

'Those two are up to no good,' Ana Maria smirked, 'mark my words.'

'I think you're right,' Maria Eduarda agreed with her sister.

'Let ourselves be surprised,' Ellie commented.

'Do you know anything we don't, Valeria?' Hertie asked

'No. I know as much as all of you,'

'Hmm. You look furtive, Schätzchen.'

They all laughed and Maria Eduarda added, 'I have to

agree with Hertha about you, Valeria, and with Anita about those two.'

They laughed again and then went quiet, listening. Noises were coming from the library. Heavy things appeared to be pushed across the floor.

'Are they moving the furniture?' Maria Eduarda asked incredulously to no-one in particular.

'Maybe,' Valeria said.

Miguel returned half an hour later but refused to say anything. Xaver remained in the library for over an hour.

'What's he doing in there?' Maria Eduarda wondered aloud. Then she remembered what she had asked him earlier.

'Oh,' she exclaimed, then turning to Valeria asked, 'is he preparing the room for a little private performance for us?'

'Yes. Actually by now, he's warming up. He'll call us soon.'

As if on cue Xaver emerged from the library and into the sitting room. He walked straight to Valeria took her hand and made a sign, indicating the others should follow them. Miguel pushed Ellie in her chair, Ana Maria and Hertha walked with them. Maria Eduarda followed a second later. She must admit her excitement, anticipating what Xaver might have in store for them. As she entered the library the others were already sitting and Xaver was leading Valeria to the grand piano. The furniture and the carpets were all pushed aside to give Xaver enough space to dance. Maria Eduarda sat next to her sister. She watched as Valeria arranged a large score on the manuscript holder of the grand. As good as his word, Xaver walked to the centre of the room, bowed to his tiny audience and announced, 'extracts from Frederick Ashton's ballet Rhapsody to the music of Rachmaninov's Rhapsody on a Theme of Paganini.'

He bowed again and signalled Valeria she could start. Spotlessly, with sheer brilliance, he executed his first solo from the ballet. Maria Eduarda gasped. She glanced around her. The others hung from Xaver's every move as if he'd cast a spell on them, except Hertie. She was smiling knowingly. Maria Eduarda caught her gaze briefly and grasped it. Hertie knew Xaver's power when he danced and unlike the others she wasn't surprised.

Minutes later, as he finished the solo, Valeria began with the first chords of the 18th variation. Xaver stopped in front of Ellie and gently lifted her out of the wheelchair. He carried her in his arms as if she were weightless, improvising a pas de deux. She seemed no more than a feather in his hands. Delicate. Graceful. Beautiful. As the music faded away Xaver returned her sweetly to her chair.

Maria Eduarda looked at her great-granddaughter. Ellie's face was transformed. She looked luminous. Her eyes sparkled. Happiness danced on her lips. She had never seen her looking so pretty.

Xaver walked back to the centre of the room and bowed elegantly, thanking them for their applause. Emotion was in the air. Palpable. Powerful. Maria Eduarda removed her spectacles and wiped away a few tears with her fingers. Through a wet, foggy curtain that stubbornly covered her eyes she saw Hertie throwing a kiss to her grandson while he walked to Valeria and lovingly touched her hand with his lips in a gallant, grateful gesture.

Maria Eduarda stood up and walked toward Xaver, still standing next to Valeria and the piano. The moment he'd offered them would stay with her for the rest of her life. She would always remember it for its exquisite beauty until the day she died.

Grabbing both Xaver's hands she said in a voice tightened by emotion, 'thank you, Xaver, and you too, Valeria, for this wonderful gift.'

He acknowledged with his head, saying simply, 'I just thought it'd be nice to make at least part of your dream come true.'

'Thank you,' she repeated.

Not knowing what else to say, Maria Eduarda turned to go back to her chair. She caught Hertie's slightly wet eyes. They nodded at each other. Then, Maria Eduarda looked out of the window. The clouds were gone. The wind had died. High up, against the black velvet of the sky, the stars glowed.

Valeria's Journal, 2021-2022 – The Ending

Hertie and Maria Eduarda connected and became friends during our ten-day visit in March 2017. They decided to try and see each other from then on once or twice a year. Sadly it did not happen. In March 2018 Hertie suffered a terrible stroke and was taken to hospital. She never recovered and after a second, stronger stroke at the end of April she died in hospital on 5th May 2018, just over two months after her 82nd birthday. Her trip to visit Maria Eduarda a second time had been booked for the end of the month but never took place.

    Hertie's death was hard on me and her family but especially tough on Xaver. He adored his grandmother. Her loss bored deep into his heart. He danced Romeo three days after her funeral and all his emotion was poured into the performance. He had never danced the role so well, reducing to tears many people in the audience during the final scene when Romeo believes Juliet is dead. All his grief gushed out of every muscle, every gesture, each step. Pirouettes, arabesques, jumps were irresistibly profound. Powerful. At times almost visceral. The pain was present but also the love. Each move he made, each expression of his face transformed his dance into a gleaming offer of beauty, touching people softly with the gentle feeling of a freshwater cascade on a summer's day or overpowering them like crushing waves during a storm. As the performance ended, he stood centre stage with the ballerina who had danced Juliet. Sitting in the first row of the stalls I could see the tears running down his face. Applause soared. Bravos roared through the auditorium. He bowed then whispered something to the ballerina. She nodded. Xaver stepped forward to the edge of the stage. In a voice distorted by sorrow he asked for a moment's silence. The audience obeyed. He swallowed, then coughed. I thought he was trying to bring his emotions under control. An instant later he spoke. His voice sounded fragile but the words were clear.

    'If you permit me,' his chest heaved as he breathed in, 'I wish to dedicate this performance to a grand, great lady who died recently and therefore can no longer share my life – Hertha

Lohmeyer-Neale, my grandmother, my friend. Always a guiding light in my life. She should have been here, sitting next to my partner, Valeria, there on the first row,' he pointed in my direction, then breathing in and out a couple of times added, 'tonight I danced for her, for my darling Oma. I thank her for all the love she bestowed upon me and I thank you all for coming to this performance.'

Enraptured by his words the audience remained silent. They held their breath. One could hear a pin fall. It lasted two or three seconds. Then, applause erupted. Rolling waves of sound, moving forward to engulf Xaver. People were delighted. Captivated. Sympathetic. Everyone loses a loved one at some stage in their lives. Anyone feels the need to pay tribute in their own personal way to the person who has forever gone. That's what they told Xaver with their intense, emotional clapping. He thanked them. Then, calling the ballerina to his side, he held her hand and together they bowed, acknowledging the public's understanding and enthusiasm.

Once it had all calmed down, I met Xaver in his dressing room. For a moment he broke down, sobbing in my arms. As our own personal tribute to Hertie, we began compiling and organising her recordings on that same evening well into the night. Eventually I would craft the book she had asked me to write. What better way to celebrate her life? Xaver and I agreed there was none.

I finished writing the first draft of the book a few weeks ago. Xaver read it, made some suggestions but overall was pleased. It made me happy. I annotated his ideas, have edited the computer manuscript a few times and believe it is nearly ready to go to the publisher. Xaver spoke with his friend Oliver Sinclair, the one from the British Library, and through him I managed to engage the interest of a small publishing house. Before I start the publishing process, however, there's another person who must read the manuscript. Maria Eduarda. After all she and her story are featured. I sent her an e-mail with an attached copy.

It's astonishing that she is still alive. In 2020 she celebrated her 100th birthday and it looks like she'll observe her

101st. She replied to my message with an invitation for Xaver and me to visit at the end of the summer in September. Xaver wasn't able to make it. He has a tour of Japan with the Bavarian State Ballet, postponed twice due to the pandemic but possible now even with the restrictions. So I travelled alone. At present, I'm here in Alentejo at the lovely Quinta das Estrelas.

Maria Eduarda now lives only with Miguel and her great-granddaughter Ellie. Ana Maria died last year of Covid. Heartbreaking. I've the impression Eduarda hasn't quite recovered from the loss of her sister. Her mind is lucid. Sharp as ever. But her energy, her sparkle seem to have gone. For the first time since I met her she looks her age. Old. Tired. Wasted. She tells me she has lived for too long. When we first visited with Hertie and returned the items Gerald Neale had once stolen, I asked Maria Eduarda whether she would like to meet my side of the family – her five half-sisters she knew existed but had never seen and all the nephews, nieces, great-nephews and great-nieces. She said no. They knew nothing about her except that she had disappeared when young. They hadn't been born at the time her father expelled her. Their lives had never touched hers. She saw no point in it. Meeting me was enough. She was grateful to have met Hertie, Xaver and me. She tells me that connecting with Hertie was very special. To have the book and the manuscript returned an unexpected pleasure she had never hoped to experience.

'I've led a good, rich, happy life,' she says, as we sit outside on the terrace of the big house at Quinta das Estrelas, watching the sunset, 'I achieved my greatest dreams, have a caring family. But I've lived for too long. I'm exhausted. Drained of all the energy to live. I hope my life will end soon. Ana Maria was sixteen years my junior and this horrible virus took her. It would've been more logical if it were me, given my age, but life seldom follows logic.'

'Don't speak like that. You still have much to give.'

She pats my hand. It reminds me of Hertie who often did it to show she cared.

'You're a lovely girl, Valeria. I like you. I think you've got a good, loving partner too. Xaver's not only an interesting man, he's kind, generous and handsome. You'll be happy together, I'm certain.'

'We are happy together,' I reply stressing the tense of the verb, 'enjoying our life in Munich. We bought a little house there.'

She nods. 'You mentioned.' Then goes quiet, appearing lost in her own world.

After a couple of silent minutes she says, 'I've read the draft of the book you wrote based on Hertha's account of what Gerald told her and her memories from her childhood in Germany.'

'What did you think?'

'I think it's good. Fair. You tell everything in a straightforward, impartial manner. It was the right thing to do. My part of the story is particularly truthful but, from what I know, Hertha's also very real, faithful to what she confided in you.'

'Absolutely. It was my main objective. I owed it to Hertie and to you.'

She smiles. For a moment there's a light in her grass-green eyes. Life returns to her cheeks. I have a glimpse of the youthful Maria Eduarda. Then she asks me a question.

'You could've written yours and Xaver's story too but you chose not to. You wrote my story and Hertha's. Yours and Xaver's seems like a by-product.'

'It is.'

'Why?'

'The book is Hertie's. It's what she asked me to write but it's hers. I've only written it because she felt she lacked the ability. It's her account of her story, of your story through Gerald's confession,' I pause for a moment then holding her hands continue, 'there are many stories I could've told – Hertie's German family's, Xaver's, Ana Maria's, Ellie's and Miguel's, your son's, your other descendants', mine. But interesting though they are, it isn't what Hertie asked me to do. As I've already said, this is her book. Other people's stories are only to be touched to provide the links, the fluidity and the elements that hold the narrative together.'

'I see. Perhaps another time, then. Ellie and Miguel's love story is interesting, I think. And Xaver…well, he'd make a fascinating subject in my opinion.'

I smile enigmatically. 'Perhaps.'

She goes silent again. I watch her furtively. It shocks me. She looks so old, so frail. It's as if life were evaporating gradually through her head. The brief impression of the light, the energy of the young Maria Eduarda have vanished. She looks at me. Her eyes are full of tears.

'I'm tired of living, Valeria. Tired of life. It must end soon.'

I didn't understand what she meant then. She didn't explain. I know now. I left Portugal on 20th September, five days after her 101st birthday. She hadn't wanted a party and Ellie and Miguel respected her wishes. The four of us had a lovely dinner, sang happy birthday with a small candle on a little pastel de nata and that was it.

Two weeks after I'd left Portugal, I received an e-mail from Ellie. Maria Eduarda passed away on 28th September. They think she has died by her own hand, given the letter on her lap. Miguel found her in the morning, sitting at her bedroom's balcony, appearing to be asleep. It looked like she had spent the night in her chair, marvelling at her beloved stars. The doctor diagnosed cardiac arrest as the cause of death but seemed surprised. Maria Eduarda had suffered from a minor heart deficiency, caused by age, and required a daily tablet to regulate the defective heart valve and keep it under control. Only a month earlier she'd had her annual medical and her heart seemed fine.

Ellie says Maria Eduarda looked peaceful and beautiful. Her skin smooth, as if death had rejuvenated her. The doctor first thought it possible she had taken a lethal dose of potassium chloride to stop her heart. Perhaps an injection but they were unable to find a syringe or any vestige of the drug. Then he decided to check her heart tablets and realised she hadn't been taking them regularly – none in fact for the last three weeks – but they could only be certain if he ordered an autopsy.

Ellie tells me she and Miguel chose not to. Maria Eduarda had not wanted to live anymore after Ana Maria's death and repeatedly stated she was tired of life. The end would be welcome. Ellie believes her great-grandmother simply decided it was time to go. So she stopped her tablets. Sensing death approaching she sat on her chair, watching the stars' silver glow above her until her eyelids dropped forever.

The sealed envelope Miguel found on her lap was addressed to him and Ellie. In it Maria Eduarda wrote the following lines that, as per her expressed wish, they were kind enough to send me in a scanned copy of her original letter:

28th September 2021

My darlings Ellie and Miguel

I have lived long enough. One hundred and one years is more than anyone's fair share. I'm tired. It is time to go. I sense it in my bones and the pain in my chest. I have a couple of requests.

First, I want you to send a copy of this letter to my son, Jorge. He was always a light in my life.

Second, I don't wish any of you, here or in America, to be sad. I want you all to celebrate my life. It was a life well lived. Remember me through our beautiful moments together, through what we shared.

Third, I would like to be cremated and my ashes scattered on the grounds of the estate one night under the stars. The estate is now yours, Ellie and Miguel, as you shall find out once my solicitor executes my last will and testament.

Time has come. I feel it. I look up at my adored night sky and think about everything wonderful that I had and about what I lost. When Ana Maria died of Covid last year, I wrote the poem below as a tribute to her. My fourth and final request is that you forward it and my words to Valeria. Perhaps she will add it to her book in one form or other, as she sees fit.

Out of my window shines the silver moon

but sadness floods silently my heart.
My chest fills quietly with gloom
and dry, invisible tears pull me apart.

Birds continue to fly,
Rivers don't stop their flow,
Forests still reach for the sky
And stars maintain their glow.

The sea persists in its motion,
Children still play on the sands.
Suitors search for a love potion
with flowers dancing in their hands.

The sun covered its light
And in my chest a red rose bled.
Her future is no longer bright
It was the end. My sister is dead.

Goodbye to all of you my loves scattered around different parts of this blue dot that is our lovely planet. If I were a religious person and believed in God I would write I'll be joining my sister in heaven. But I am a scientist. We are all part of the cosmos, of the universe. Forged in the stars. Made of stardust to use poetic language.

It is my time to return to the stars.

Maria Eduarda

Today, 24th February 2022, I decided to add her letter as the conclusion to the book before it goes to the editor. I understand now what she meant when she told me she was tired of life and it must end soon. A fitting end for an extraordinary woman. She died as she lived – on her own terms. Nothing else would do. If Hertie were still with us she would agree and encourage me to finish her book – because it really is her book – with Maria

Eduarda's poem and farewell letter thus my decision. And just as I write these final words, I hear about the invasion of the Ukraine by Russian troops, ordered by Russia's dictator President Vladimir Putin. The images on television are shocking, harrowing, heart-breaking. It is good that Hertie is no longer among us. It would devastate her. History repeats itself.

THE END
M G da Mota (2022)

Author's Notes and Bibliography

Stars Maintain Their Glow is a work of fiction based at times on historical fact. It means, except for the historical figures – real people who lived at some stage or other, as described below – all characters in this novel are entirely a product of my imagination and (with a small exception stated below) do not bear any similarities to any person or persons alive or dead. Should people believe they can recognise themselves in this novel, I want to assert here that it's purely coincidental.

Portugal did indeed remain neutral during WWII, which doesn't mean it wasn't impacted. Lisbon, Portugal's capital city, in particular became a nest for refugees and secret agents from both sides of the war. The country was ruled at the time by the iron hand of fascist dictator António de Oliveira Salazar (1889-1970). He died in 1970 but the dictatorship only fell on 25th April 1974. While no bullets were fired and no bombs dropped in Portugal during the war years, the country suffered rationing from 1943 onwards and was at times in imminent danger of being invaded by Spain, aided by Germany, hence the importance for Salazar to keep Portugal neutral and astutely convince Spain to do the same. He was a highly intelligent, shrewd man and cleverly managed to play both sides of the war. No mean feat, considering how small the country is. The advantage for Portugal was its strategic geographical location at the western end of Europe, as well as that of its Portuguese islands of the Azores in the middle of the Atlantic Ocean.

The Polícia de Vigilância e Defesa do Estado (PVDE), which later became the much feared PIDE (Polícia Internacional e de Defesa do Estado) was no stranger to torture and became a pillar of Salazar's dictatorial grip on Portugal. It was only abolished after the revolution of 25th April 1974 when finally the dictatorship fell, democracy was restored and the many political prisoners were liberated. What Valeria tells Hertie in the novel about the 25th April 1974 Revolution – Carnation Revolution – is true, including the story about the lady with the red carnations.

The vast majority of the historical information about Lisbon of the war years was taken from the excellent book *War in the Shadows of the City of Light, 1939-45* by historian Neill Lochery.

The most important books and articles I consulted are listed below, after these notes. However, many of the descriptions of the Lisbon Atlantic coast, the city itself, Sintra and Alentejo are based on my own recollections though these are from a much later date, as I was born many years after the war ended. I know the regions well, especially the locations concerned in the novel. I was born in Portugal and lived in the country until I was 24 years old. I now have dual nationality and Portuguese is one of the two.

Portuguese summers are generally hot and dry with average temperatures around 30 to 35 degrees Celsius. There are always a handful of days where thermometers hit 40 degrees centigrade or higher. However, the summer of 1940 was, as described in the novel, one of the hottest ever and at the time the hottest on record. Temperatures were continuously and consistently reaching 40 degrees or higher from approximately mid-June through to and including the end of August. It would have been more pleasant on the coast or on a shady, forested, hilly place such as Sintra but, in a city like Lisbon, a real nightmare. I tried to express the feeling of heat, especially its effect on people who were not used to such summer temperatures.

Ricardo Espirito Santo (1900-1955) was a historical figure. A Portuguese banker, economist, patron of the arts, and international athlete. A good friend of the Portuguese dictator Salazar, he was apparently also a very charming, eloquent, intelligent and knowledgeable man. He turned his bank, the Banco Espírito Santo (BES), into one of the most important financial institutions in Portugal. It is true that his wife, Maria

Cohen, was Jewish and that he helped Jews from France, including some of the Rothchild family.

It is said that Ian Fleming (1908-1964) used his visits to the Casino in Estoril for a scene in his first James Bond novel entitled Casino Royale, where James Bond is gambling in a French town casino to bankrupt a secret member of Soviet state intelligence. Then a young agent, Fleming visited Lisbon and the Estoril Casino in 1941 while devising Operation Golden Eye and assessing the various intelligence organisations in Portugal's capital city to ascertain smooth cooperation for Golden Eye. Its aim was to ensure that Britain could continue to communicate with Gibraltar if Spain joined or was invaded by the Axis powers (the military alliance of Germany, Italy and later Japan in WWII fighting against the Allies) and to carry out limited sabotage.

BOAC - British Overseas Airways Corporation was the British state-owned airline created in 1939. It operated overseas services throughout World War II and only ceased its operations on 31st March 1974 when it merged with three other airlines to form British Airways.

The Duke (1894-1972) and Duchess (1896-1986) of Windsor were indeed guests of Ricardo Espirito Santo, staying in his home in Cascais, in the summer of 1940. Sir Ronald Hugh Campbell (1883-1953) was the British ambassador in Lisbon from November 1940 to July 1945. However, I took the poetic license of placing him in the city from earlier in the year, i.e. since March 1940. In reality, the British ambassador at the time the Duke and Duchess of Windsor stayed in Portugal was Sir Walford Selby who held the post from 1937 to October 1940. He was allegedly replaced by Sir Ronald Campbell (considered more able) because the British were not pleased with his performance regarding the German propaganda and businesses in Lisbon. In fact it had much to do with the German ambassador to Portugal, Baron Oswald von Hoyningen-Huene (1885-1963), who played the game very cleverly. He was a man of the old aristocratic school of the German diplomatic service and had been busy developing closer ties between Berlin and Lisbon during the years leading up to the war. He studied, and understood, Portuguese language, history and culture, knowing how to appeal to the nationalist sentiments of Salazar and other senior Portuguese personalities. He was sharp, clever, diplomatically astute, good at socialising and an obsessive networker. He was a regular guest at the high table of the dinner parties of the Portuguese and international elite in Lisbon during the war and saw his mission as trying to loosen Anglo-Portuguese ties. Hoyningen-Huene was to play a central role in Lisbon as the war developed, and in particular in the negotiations over vitally important wolfram (or tungsten) supplies from Portugal to Germany.

The Duke and Duchess of Windsor stayed in Portugal from 3rd July to 1st August 1940 and, as mentioned above, did indeed live at Ricardo Espirito Santo's and his wife's weekend home at Boca do Inferno in Cascais, on the Lisbon Atlantic Coast. The golf course in Estoril was one of their popular destinations, as was the restaurant Casa da Laura in Cascais, the restaurant of the Hotel Aviz in Lisbon's city centre, Sintra and Quinta da Marinha, as well as the pinewoods around Cascais. We also know the Duke watched a bullfight in Algés (near Lisbon) on 21st July. They left Portugal in the early hours of 2nd August 1940, sailing first to New York, on the Excalibur, and then heading to the Duke's new post as Governor of the Bahamas. Their visit to Sintra, staying at the home of the Duke of Beja is however my invention. The Duke of Beja and all his family are fictional characters but the feared plot by the Germans to kidnap Edward while he and his wife were in Lisbon is actually true. The information is taken from "The Duke of Windsor and Ricardo Espirito Santo – 1940", written by Carlos Alberto Damas.

The words that Sir Ronald said about Ricardo Espirito Santo in the novel "I'll eat my hat if this man is pro-German" are true. The full quote of what Sir Ronald said appears on pages 19-20 of the

29th annual report of the British Historical Society of Portugal, entitled "The Duke of Windsor and Ricardo Espirito Santo – 1940", written by Carlos Alberto Damas who took the information from the Public Record Office references FO371/26804 and FO71/26802. The report was reviewed in 2002.

Luis de Camões (born 1524 or 1525, died 10th June 1580) is considered Portugal's greatest ever poet. He lived an adventurer's life, full of ups and downs, dying poor and destitute. He travelled often sometimes because he was forced to exile due to his actions. It was in India that he wrote most of his epic poem. Legend says that after being caught in a shipwreck off the coast of Cambodia he swam to safety with only one arm, holding the other with the manuscript of the poem high up in the air. While the shipwreck is true and Camões survived it, no-one knows whether the way he saved the manuscript is the truth. Nevertheless it is a great story in line with the poet's personality and so I decided to mention it in the novel. Camões's sonnets are poems of incredible beauty but his most famous work Os Lusíadas (The Lusiads) is indeed an extraordinary epic in verse on a grand scale. Many of his poems, including The Lusiads are translated into various languages but lose much of their beauty in translation and, if possible, should be read in the original Portuguese to be fully appreciated. The first edition of Os Lusíadas of 1572 and "the other first edition" and their features are true facts that can be verified online or through books on the History of Portugal and of its Literature. It is also true that there are still five or six copies of the first edition of 1572 in existence in Portugal. The manuscript however that may or not be in the hand of the poet is purely my invention.

In Camões's epic poem Os Lusíadas (The Lusiads), which is a feature throughout the novel, Gerald Neale when talking with Maria Eduarda at Ricardo Espirito Santo's dinner for the Duke and Duchess of Windsor mentions the episode of Pedro and Inês by reciting a line from the poem *aquela que depois de ser morta foi Rainha* (the one that after death became Queen). This refers to the **true** story of Pedro (then Prince and heir to the throne of Portugal) and the Galician noblewoman Inês de Castro. It is a tragic love story, more romantic and bloodier than Shakespeare's fictional Romeo and Juliet. Inês de Castro was well connected with noble families of Castille (the most powerful kingdom in Spain) and the Prince was married to Constance of Castille. Inês came to Portugal as lady-in-waiting to Constance. Pedro fell passionately in love with Inês and she with him, beginning to neglect his wife much to the anger of her Castilian family. Pedro's father, King Afonso IV, didn't look with favour on the love affair and hoped it would eventually die as had his son's previous infatuations. However, it did not. Their love and passion for each other grew. The king worried about Inês's influence on his son and that the relationship might create problems between Portugal and Castille since Pedro's wife was from Castille. The king exiled Inês to Coimbra to keep her away from her son but to no avail. And so Afonso IV decided she must die. He sent three of his men to execute her in Coimbra where Inês was detained. They killed her in front of her small child. Pedro was devastated. He sought out the killers, managed to capture two of them and executed them publicly by ripping their hearts out, claiming they had none after having pulverised his own heart. When he became king, and after his wife's death, Pedro had Inês's body exhumed and crowned her his Queen. Camões relates the story in The Lusiads. It is one of the most beautiful episodes in this gorgeous epic poem. Historians disagree whether Inês's coronation after death really took place. I suppose one can never know for sure. Everything else is historical fact, narrated by chroniclers of the time. Inês was later buried at the Monastery of Alcobaça (a small town in the centre of Portugal) where her ornamented tomb can still be seen, opposite Pedro's. According to the story the location in front of each other is deliberate so that on the Last Judgment Day Pedro and Inês can look at each other as they rise from their graves. The two marble tombs are exquisitely sculpted with scenes from their lives and a promise by Pedro that they would be together *até ao fim do mundo* (until the end of the world).

Fernando Pessoa (1888-1935) was another extraordinary Portuguese poet. His work is widely translated and totally fascinating. Again it is much better when read in the original Portuguese. The poems: O menino de sua mãe – a moving poem, depicting the stupidity of war, and his little book Mensagem (which are both mentioned in the novel by Maria Eduarda) are real and truly beautiful works.

The situation of women in Portugal before the revolution of 25th April 1974 was not pleasant. Men had all the rights and women had next to none. Before a woman was of age (at the time 21 years old) she was under the thumb of her father or any other male relative if she no longer had a father. Once a woman was of age and if still unmarried then she would have a little more freedom. An unmarried woman, 21 or older, could enrol at university or apply for a job without the father's permission. However, if the woman was married, she was completely dependent on her husband and must submit to him. Before the 1974 revolution married women did not work outside the home. It was expected of them to stay home, looking after their husband and the children once they came. A married woman could not travel abroad without her husband. If she wanted to do so, she needed a written authorisation from her husband or she would be stopped at the border and returned to her husband. Therefore, a strong woman like Maria Eduarda or her mentor Professor Berta de Almeida would almost certainly avoid marriage like the plague. The revolution of 24th April 1974 did more than just depose the 48-year-old fascist dictatorship, liberate political prisoners, restoring freedom and democracy to the country; it finally gave women their rights, making them equal to men before the law, allowed couples to divorce even if married by the church and lowered becoming of age to 18.

In the novel Maria Eduarda and her family own Lusitano horses. The Lusitano is a Portuguese horse breed, closely related to the Spanish. Both are sometimes referred to as Iberian horses. The fame of the Lusitano horses goes back to the Roman Age. At the time they attributed these animals' outstanding speed to the influence of the West wind! When the Moors invaded the Iberian Peninsula in 711 AD, they brought Berber horses and crossed them with the native horses, developing a new breed that became useful for war, dressage and bull fighting. In 1966 the Portuguese and Spanish stud books split. The Portuguese strain of the Iberian horse was named the Lusitano, after **Lusitania** – the ancient Roman name for the region that modern Portugal roughly occupies. Lusitanos can be any solid colour but are generally grey, bay or chestnut. Originally bred for war, dressage and bullfighting, Lusitanos are still used today in the latter two. They have competed in several **Olympics** and **World Equestrian Events** as part of the Portuguese and Spanish dressage teams. As mentioned in the novel, Lusitano horses are named alphabetically by year, excepting the letters K, W and Y, as they do not exist in the original Portuguese alphabet.

Hertha Lohmeyer-Neale is a fictional character. However she and her memoirs are modelled on a very dear friend of mine who died in 2016. She was German and married an Englishman. She lived in Germany until she married and was only seven years old at the time the war ended in 1945. In the novel, this part of the story does not intend to be and is not an historical account of the horrors of the Holocaust and of what happened in Germany during the period Hitler and the Nazis were in power. It is merely an account of some of my friend's own fragmented recollections of her childhood in Germany during WWII. She saw the war through the eyes of the child she was then. I fictionalised the character, added topics and information from my research to give it context and depth, and modified some details for dramatic and narration purposes. However, the scattered episodes my friend remembered and especially how she felt are as close to what she told me as possible. So, in the novel, Hertie's experiences in the final years of the war as well as the recurring dream and the Dachau episode in 2012 are based on the true stories my friend told me but are not a direct account of her life or her memories.

When Hertie goes to Berlin in 1956, as stated in the novel, the Wall had not yet been built. There were already strict controls from the east sector of Berlin into the west sector. Tensions would continue to grow and culminated with the building of the Berlin Wall, basically overnight on 13th August 1961. It cut West Berlin from the rest of West Germany for 28 years. With the fall of communism, the Wall also fell for good and was demolished in 1989.

While Maria Eduarda's Quinta das Estrelas in Alentejo and all her family's properties that I mention in the novel are fictional, Porto Covo, Sintra, Cascais, Boca do Inferno, as well as other towns and cities in Portugal and Germany are real places that I know well.

Finally, there are a few people I would like to acknowledge. Thank you, as ever, to Alana, my editor, for her outstanding work and support. Thank you to my friend Nancy for reading the first draft, giving me valuable comments and suggestions. Thank you also to my friend Alison for reading and providing feedback. As usual, thank you to my family and my best friend in Portugal for always being there for me with a smile and a caring word. And last but not least, thank you to Malcolm for his patience and for allowing me to use his beautiful photographs as the cover images.

For the completion of this novel I consulted a wide variety of books and articles, the most important of which are listed below:

- LOCHERY, Neill – Lisbon: War in the Shadows of the City of Light, 1939-45, Public Affairs, a Member of the Perseus Book Group, United States, 2011
- BENDERSKY, Joseph W. – A Concise History of Nazi Germany, Rowman & Littlefield Publishers, Inc., Third Edition, United States 2007

- SARAIVA, Prof. José Hermano – História Concisa de Portugal, Publicações Europa-América, 8ª edição, Portugal, 1983
- DAMAS, Carlos Alberto – The Duke of Windsor and Ricardo Espírito Santo, 1940, The British Historical Society of Portugal, 29th Annual Report, reviewed 2002
- VAN DER REYDEN, D. – Identifying the Real Thing (information on authentication of manuscripts), National Park Service and Northeast Document Conservation Center, New York City, 1996
- CAMPOS JUNIOR, António – Luiz de Camões, Volumes I e II, Typographia da empreza d'O Século, Lisboa, 1901
- HASKELL, Arnold – Ballet, Penguin Books Ltd, London, 1955 (I used the Portuguese edition translated by José Estevão Sasportes and published by Publicações Europa-América, Lda, Lisboa, 1960)
- CRAINE, Debra & MACKRELL, Judith – Oxford Dictionary of Dance, Oxford University Press, UK, 2004
- Oxford Dictionary of Quotations, Sixth Edition, Oxford University Press, UK, 2004

Additionally and as always the Britannica Online Encyclopaedia and especially the Wikipedia websites in English, German and Portuguese were an outstanding starting point for finding material, articles and books on the subjects I required for this novel.

M G da Mota

(Shoreham-by-Sea, March 2022)